The Best
DOG STORIES

The Best
DOG STORIES

Edited by Paul D. Staudohar

CHICAGO
REVIEW
PRESS

Library of Congress Cataloging-in-Publication Data
Is available from the Library of Congress.

Jacket and interior design: Emily Brackett/Visible Logic
Front jacket photo: Gone Wild/Photonica/Getty Images

Published by Chicago Review Press, Incorporated
814 North Franklin Street
Chicago, Illinois 60610
ISBN-13: 978-1-55652-667-1
ISBN-10: 1-55652-667-9
Printed in the United States of America
5 4 3 2 1

CONTENTS

ACKNOWLEDGMENTS

My long association with Chicago Review Press includes editing eight books of short stories on baseball, golf, football, boxing, fishing, hunting, and two volumes on a variety of sports. Executive editor Cynthia Sherry has always given inspiration and valuable advice, and the idea for this book came from managing editor Gerilee Hundt. We were discussing possible new topics and she mentioned enjoying reading stories about dogs as a youngster. The librarians at California State University–East Bay helped move things along: Dana Edwards suggested the story "Biscuit," and Lynn LeFleur, Judy Clarence, Kristin Ramsdell, Steve Philibosian, and Aline Soules helped locate materials. Kudos also to librarian John Michaud of *The New Yorker*, the Off-Campus Services at Central Michigan University, and Denise Crozier at Cal State–East Bay. Robert Scheffler, research editor at *Esquire*, was helpful as always. Barry Zepel of Cal State–East Bay gave wise counsel, as did Sandie Sorenson, Gwen Stevenson, and Max Lateiner. Thanks also to Robert Moeller and Shawan Zaid at *Atlantic Monthly*, Florence Eichin at the Penguin Group, and Lina Maria Granada at Brandt & Hochman.

Paul D. Staudohar

INTRODUCTION

The dog is probably the oldest domestic animal. It is certainly the most loved. For over 12,000 years, dogs have lived with humans as hunters, guardians, companions, and objects of adoration. Depictions of dogs on caves, scrolls, and tombs date back to the Bronze Age. In ancient Egypt dogs were considered sacred. Even in today's fragmented and often impersonal society, dogs are often treated as part of the family. They are sumptuously fed, finely groomed, and affectionately pampered.

There are over 400 distinct breeds of dogs that belong to the same species (*Canis familiaris*). Some breeds are ancient, while others were developed as recently as the 1800s. Dog breeds came about for specific purposes, so that their size, speed, and keen sense of sight and smell could be utilized to human advantage. The earliest breeds, typically descended from gray wolves, were used for hunting game.

As society changed from hunting to agriculture, terrier breeds were developed, mostly in England, to control rodents in barns and granaries. Toy-pet breeds like the Chihuahua in Mexico and Pekingese in China were created as lapdogs for wealthy families. Various breeds such as bulldogs, mastiffs, and bull terriers were selected for fighting.

Today, purebred dogs are registered with national organizations like the American Kennel Club and the Kennel Club of England. An objective of these clubs is to encourage dog breeding that best represents the ideal qualities of physical and behavioral characteristics. Begun in 1876, the Westminster Kennel Club Dog Show, held annually at Madison Square Garden in New York, is the oldest and most prestigious bowwow powwow in the United States.

Although purebreds and mutts comprise most of America's 73 million dogs, "designer dogs" have become a hot item. For example, a cross between a labrador and a poodle is a labradoodle, a mix of cocker spaniel and poodle is a cockapoo, and a beagle-pug combination is called a puggle. Proponents of these new breeds say they avoid health problems associated with purebreds. Designer dogs are not allowed to compete in the elite shows, but some of them might be granted official status in the future.

Just as many people are mixtures of nationalities and races, the most common type of dog around the world is the mutt. Although these dogs may lack sophistication and pedigree, they often make the most endearing pets. Mutts don't cost much, if anything, and tend to be less high-strung than purebreds. Whatever kind of dog one fancies, there are plenty of choices.

The loyalty, affection, and exploits of dogs have inspired both prose and poetry, and there is a rich body of short fiction about dogs. Short stories generally do not have the randomness and loose ends customarily found in nonfiction, and they come to the point much quicker than novels. The end of a short story is usually its most attractive feature, and the climaxes are sometimes expected by the reader, sometimes not. Many writers like to surprise their readers by providing a punch or unanticipated twist at the conclusion of a story.

This book contains 23 short stories about dogs. Not all varieties of our canine friends are included, but there are stories about bull terriers, collies, poodles, Irish setters, German shepherds, Dobermans, wolf dogs, hounds, springer spaniels, and Kerry blues, plus a generous helping of mutts. There is even a story about a talking dog.

Literary buffs will recognize some famous authors of yesteryear such as Booth Tarkington, P. G. Wodehouse, Jack London, Anatole France, Ivan Turgenev, and Rudyard Kipling, along with some excellent contemporary writers such as Richard Ford, Bobbie Ann Mason, T. Coraghessan Boyle, Madison Smartt Bell, and Richard Russo. There is also an international flavor to the stories. Eric Knight, Wodehouse, and Kipling all hail from England. Stefan Zweig was from Austria (and later lived in England). Anatole France was French, and Turgenev was Russian. They all write with wonderful sensitivity about human relationships with dogs.

Some of the stories, especially the recent ones, have appeared in outstanding sources such as *The New Yorker, Esquire, Atlantic Monthly, Saturday Evening Post, Southern Review*, and *The Best American Short Stories*. It's hard to top the literary reputations of many of the contributors to the book, and the stories are representative of the best of their work.

So let's turn the page to our first yarn, penned by, arguably, the finest writer of dog stories, Albert Payson Terhune.

The Best
DOG STORIES

BISCUIT
(1932)
Albert Payson Terhune

Albert Payson Terhune (1872–1942) is the best-loved author of novels and short stories on dogs. His most famous book, known throughout the world, is *Lad, A Dog* (1919). Among his other novels are *Bruce* (1920), *Buff: A Collie* (1921), *Gray Dawn* (1927), and *Lad of Sunnybank* (1929).

Countless young people have had their first exposure to top-quality literature with Terhune, who acquired his love of writing from his mother and knowledge of dogs from his father. Although he usually wrote about collies, "Biscuit" is a mixed breed who matures from puppy to adult in this classic Terhune story.

"**H**e's a mutt, isn't he?" asked Grear, eyeing with no favor at all the yellowish and all-but-formless giant puppy that sprawled drowsily at Middon's feet on the sunlit scrap of porch. "Hundred per cent mutt, I'd call him."

"No," drawled old Middon. "You'd miscall him wrong if you was to call him that. The blood of some of the finest champions in the whole dog world is in his veins."

Grear looked down less contemptuously at the hulking pup.

"That so?" he queried. "Champions of what breed?"

"*All* breeds," succinctly answered Middon, adding, as he rumpled the big puppy's flap-ears. "That's the advantage of a mongrel—a cross-breed. If you buy a dog of any one pure breed you'll know he's got to be limited mostly to his own breed-types. A pure-bred can't go far beyond those. But a mongrel can combine the traits of a dozen breeds. That's where he has a big advantage over the thoroughbred. Now young Biscuit here—"

At the sound of his name the eight-month puppy got up from his place in the sun and stood at momentary eager attention. Then, finding he was not wanted by his master, he lay down again, this time with both heavy rear legs stretched out straight behind him. Middon pointed to the odd posture.

"Whatever other breeds went into the melting-pot that boiled down into Biscuit," he commented, "it's a safe bet one of his ancestors was a bulldog. You'll never see a mongrel lie down with his hindlegs straight back of him unless he's got a big splash of bulldog blood somewhere in his India-relish pedigree. The deepness of Biscuit's chest proves the same thing. He—"

"Why do you call him by such a crazy name as 'Biscuit'?" demanded the visitor.

"Lots of reasons," said Middon. "Partly his color. Then because he was so easy and quick to raise, and then got so heavy, all of a sudden; and because he didn't turn out anyways as I expected him to. But mostly because I just happened to name him that, I guess. By the way, Mr. Grear, for a man who's got the costliest kennel of chows in this part of the state, you seem uncommon interested in an animal you call a mutt. If—"

"I am," replied Grear. "Especially just now. That's why I stopped in when I saw him lying here on your steps. Want to sell him?"

Old Man Middon blinked in mild-eyed surprise at the abrupt question. Bleasdell Grear had a national repute as a breeder and exhibitor of super-quality chowchow dogs. His kennels were all but regal. It was a shock to find such a man going about the region buying up mongrels. The visitor noted the incredulous stare, and he explained:

"My wife's sister is coming to spend the summer with us. She and her three children. Till I met those three brats of hers I used to think Herod was a blackguard to slaughter all the children in Bethlehem. Now—well, if Herod ever needs my vote to help carry his district, it's his for the asking. Most children are splendid and I love them. But these three are *not*. Every time the three kids come to see us they nag at me to let them have one of my chows to play with. Till now I've been able to stall them off. But if they're coming for all summer—"

"I get you," nodded Middon. "You want to save one of your three-figure chows from being pestered and mauled and teased to death. You want to do it by getting the kids a good husky mongrel pup, to serve 'em as a combination punching-bag and football and tug-of-war rope and unbreakable doll and so forth. Lots of folks with high-class kennels do that. They're wise. A mongrel can stand up under ten times the mauling that a ticklish-nerved thorough-bred can. Only—"

"How much?" interrupted Grear, poking at the sleeping Biscuit with his toe.

"For Biscuit? I'm not selling him."

"That means you want at least ten dollars for a pup that would be dear at two," translated Grear. "Well, I happen to like him. He looks friendly and steady and strong. So—"

He reached into his cash pocket. Old Man Middon shook his head.

"You don't quite catch my meaning, Mr. Grear," said he. "I'm keeping this pup. He's mine. That means there isn't any price on him."

Grear frowned in perplexity. His eye roamed appraisingly over the shabby little house and the hillside patch of North Jersey farmland behind it. Everything was clean. Everything was at its best. But it was a poor enough best. Throughout were marks of none-too-successful struggle against poverty.

It was because of this apparent sparseness of ready money that Grear had not haggled over a price for the cross-bred pup. Ten whole dollars would mean much to a man of Middon's penury.

"Yep," said the old man. "I'm foolish, I know. Just as foolish, likely, as you're thinking I am. Ten dollars is ten dollars. Sometimes it's a heap more. But Biscuit's my chum. If he keeps on like I've started him—well, I couldn't get anything for ten dollars or for ten times ten dollars that'd be worth as much to me as he's likely to be. He's all that keeps me from feeling pretty blue, now that I'm left alone up here. Since my daughter died it's been mighty forlorn. That's why I kept Biscuit, the time a feller down in the village offered me ten cents to take the little cuss and drown him when he was only two months old. I gave back the feller's ten cents and I kept the puppy. I've learned him a lot already, even if he isn't but a little more'n eight months old yet. See?"

He snapped his fingers. At the signal, the seemingly slumbrous puppy was on his splay feet at once, eagerly alert. Slowly Old Man Middon made a succession of gestures, all but imperceptible, yet all very evidently comprehensible to Biscuit.

In response to them the young cross-breed alternately dropped to the creaky porch floor as if dead; sat up and begged; "waltzed" in a solemn shuffling circle; lifted one paw after another off the ground; rose upon his hindlegs, then on his forepaws, with both hindlegs in air; barked twice

4

and yelped three times; rolled over; and closed the clumsy performance by snatching a pipe from Middon's pocket and, with it in his mouth, parading across the porch on his hindlegs.

There could be no shadow of doubt that Biscuit took an egregious pride and vanity in his own repertoire of tricks, and that those tricks had been taught him by patience instead of through cruelty. No temperamentally vain motion-picture star could have postured with greater self-delight than did the shambling mongrel.

Grear nodded, patting the pup on the head and praising him extravagantly. The visitor was enough of a dog man to understand that the lonely oldster had whiled away many an otherwise desolate hour teaching his four-legged pal these simple exploits, and that the clever young cross-breed was a barrier between the old man and utter solitude.

"You win," said Grear, getting to his feet to take his departure. "If I had realized what a gifted youngster he was, I wouldn't have wasted words by asking if you'd sell him. You're a born trainer, Middon. And, Biscuit is a born trick dog. You're both of you lucky to have each other. . . . Well, I'll go somewhere else to find a mongrel safety valve for those three kids. Good-by."

The old man watched his guest climb into a car and jounce down the hill road toward the village below. Middon's gnarled hand had fallen in unconscious caress on the broad yellow head of his dog. There were affection and comradeship in the touch.

Something rufous and furtive trotted around the corner of the cottage, pausing irresolute for an instant as it came out into the open, and peering down the road after the receding car. Then, as if satisfied the coast was clear, the newcomer glided, rather than ran, up the porch's rickety steps and stood in the sunshine at the top.

He was a three-parts-grown red fox; found in a hollow log, months earlier, by Middon as the old fellow was coming home through the forest. His mother had been shot or had abandoned her baby; for the tiny fox was weak with hunger when Middon chanced upon him.

5

Middon had carried the waif home and brought him up by hand, accustoming him from babyhood to his own presence and to Biscuit's. By dint of his natural gift as an animal-trainer, Middon had made the young fox as much a member of his household as any puppy could have been. Only when strangers were near did the fox remember he was not a dog. Then he would hide cunningly from sight, rejoining Middon and Biscuit as soon as the outsider had gone.

Mincingly he advanced toward Biscuit, now, and touched noses with the puppy, his brushy tail waving like that of a dog. Middon looked down at the two—the mongrel with his honest broad head and round brown eyes and gay openness of expression; the exquisitely graceful fox with his toothpick nose and catlike slitted eyes and hint of unkilled wildness.

"Reynard," he said, whimsically, "it's likely enough you think you're a dog, and it's certain Biscuit thinks you are. But *I* know better. And I'm afraid you'll know better, too, one of these days. All wild things do. It's only a matter of time. Look at Biscuit's face, there! Every corner of his soul and his mind is shining out of those big eyes of his. And these slit eyes of yours don't tell a single thing that's going on behind them, except when they get round and have a greenish light in them. That means you're out of temper. It's the only sign any human can go by, with a fox. But I'm going to do my best by you to make you into a decent, self-respecting, God-fearing dog, Reynard. If I lose, it'll be up to *you*. I—"

Disregarding the homily, Reynard had been patting invitingly at Biscuit with flying forepaws, luring the drowsy mongrel into one of the romps they both loved. Now they went tearing off the porch and across the dooryard, in a scampering and snapping and playfully growling mass, the clownish puppy a sorry match in speed and skill for his more elusive playmate.

"Yes," mused Middon, "a dog turns his soul inside out for his master to see. A fox hasn't any soul to show and he wouldn't show it if he had. Foxes are part cat, I guess. . . . I—I wonder how it will all work out?"

The question as to how it would all work out answered itself in due time, as will all such questions concerning the wild-born. But that was not until months had passed.

Meantime, Biscuit grew from a rangily gawky puppy to a massively powerful dog, as large as a Gordon setter. Reynard changed less, outwardly, growing only into a graceful adult red fox, beautiful of coat.

He and Biscuit were still on tolerably comfortable terms, though their early romping chumship had not deepened into such close comradely relations as would have existed between two dogs of like fraternal upbringing.

Then, of a day, came the definite break.

Twice, in a week, a hen had vanished from Middon's well-stocked coops. The old man's chief source of livelihood was gleaned from his big flock of chickens. The loss of even one fowl was a slice from his capital. The two lost hens had been his best layers.

Naturally, his suspicions rested at once on Reynard. Henceforth the fox was fastened to his kennel by a long chain, whence he could not break free. Biscuit was left at large. His massive honesty forbade suspicion.

Yet, next morning, another hen was gone. The morning after that, the largest rooster of the flock had vanished. Middon left Biscuit loose at night, as usual; but sat up, also, on the porch, in full view of the chickenyard, shotgun in hand. Biscuit dozed at his master's feet. At dawn the old man's head began to nod, then to slump on his breast.

As though he realized that the guardianship of the farmstead depended now solely on himself, Biscuit got to his feet and stood glancing about him. Three or four of the earliest-rising chickens came flapping down from their perches. Two of them emerged from the small opening at the bottom of the coop door, foraging for early food.

Out they came into the rear dooryard, roaming and questing. On the ground, some seven feet from Reynard's kennel, lay a scatter of bread crumbs from the fox's supper. Reynard himself was lying in the doorway of his kennel coop, eyes shut, head on paws. Apparently the day had not yet dawned for him.

One of the hens sighted the crumbs and waddled greedily across to where they were scattered.

Crumb after crumb she gobbled up, oblivious of everything but her own hunger. It was her last meal.

There was a rufous flash, a fluttering, and the hen spun headless on the ground.

That was enough for Biscuit. All his unformed recent suspicions and general distrust of his vulpine acquaintance crystallized at the sight. All his instincts as a watchdog and as a guardian of his adored master's property surged into action.

With a growl and a leap he sprang at the fox. Reynard dropped the slain hen, save only the head, which he swallowed. In the same set of motions he bolted back into his kennel, there snarling scared defiance at the avenger.

Biscuit lunged forward. As he reached the spot, seven feet from the fox-kennel, where flapped and spun the headless hen, he stooped and sniffed at the luckless fowl, as if to nose her from the path of further danger. But the splash of blood that was flung across his face by her death struggles seemed to convince him that she was past help.

With lowered head, he gathered himself anew for a charge at her slayer; to drag Reynard bodily out of his kennel and to wreak dire punishment on him.

The charge was not made. A shout from his master made the mongrel spin around obediently at the call.

Middon had been awakened from his involuntary snooze by the growl and the flapping. He opened his eyes just in time to see Biscuit bending over the hen, apparently having pinned her to the ground. On the crossbreed's honest yellow foreface was a spatter of newly shed blood. The sight told its own story.

Biscuit ran over toward his master; at Middon's amazed yell. The man met him, halfway. Clutching the dog by the scruff of the neck, Middon snatched off his own thick belt. Using the buckle-end as a thong, he brought it down in a shower of cruelly heavy blows upon the mongrel. With all his wiry old strength Middon smote. The cutting buckle bit deep into the tender flesh. Never before had he struck the young dog. But this was a case for dire penalty.

Biscuit shuddered all over, as with ague. Yet he uttered no whimper nor cry to attest to the agony caused by the belt-blows. This was his god who was punishing him. True, the penalty was vilely unjust, and Biscuit knew it. But it was not for him to yowl under punishment—his strain of bulldog blood was standing him in good stead—and above all it was not for him to turn on the man he worshiped.

Well did the mongrel know why he was beaten. Well did he know whose was the blame for this crime whose onus he was bearing. Into his clean heart surged a deathless hate for the fox—a raging urge to get even for his own torture—to punish the crafty animal for whose sins he was suffering.

Reynard, meantime, lay in his kennel, his head pillowed on his forepaws, part of his face showing beyond the coop aperture, his slitted eyes fast shut in seemingly dreamless slumber.

Middon smote and smote afresh, with the whizzing and stinging belt, until his old arm was tired. Then, still gripping Biscuit stranglingly by the neck, he stooped and picked up the slaughtered hen.

Even in his fierce indignation, he noted she was decapitated. But he inferred that Biscuit had killed her by snapping off her head and had been swallowing it when he was caught. That his canine chum should have killed in this wild-beast manner made the old man the angrier at him.

Picking up the hen, Middon tied the belt securely about her legs. Then he fastened it around Biscuit's furry throat, testing his knots to make certain they were firm.

There is no universally sure way to cure a dog of chicken-killing. But the most approved and usually the best remedy is to catch him in the act and then, after whipping him, to tie the dead fowl securely around his neck and to leave it there for three days. By the end of that time—especially if the weather be warm—the chances are that he will not care to go within arm's-length of another chicken as long as he lives.

There are exceptions to the cure, but they go to prove a fairly reliable rule.

Old Man Middon was not brutal. But much of his daily bread was derived from the sale of his eggs and broilers at the village butcher shop. To harbor a chronic chicken-killer was to court bankruptcy.

Also, he had grown to love this jolly and clever young mongrel of his, and it jarred the old man to the quick to realize how far wrong he had been in his estimate of Biscuit. Any lively puppy may spring upon a fowl and destroy it, from gay mischief. But—to slay hen after hen in silent stealth and then to secrete the bones and feathers—to use coyote tactics in the destruction of the property he had been trained to guard—all this savored of the craft and unnatural deviltry of a born "killer."

For such dogs a bullet through the brain is often the one solution. But, because he loved the cross-breed, Middon was minded first to try the effect of a pitiless beating and then the shame of carrying the dead hen about for days. Should this fail to break Biscuit of the slaughter habit, there was nothing for it but to shoot him. Middon's heart revolted from such a course.

Biscuit had stood with head and tail undrooped throughout the unmerciful belting which had raised red welts on his skin from shoulder to loin. Only that aguelike shudder of outraged feelings betrayed the anguish of soul and of body that were torturing him.

Moveless, except for the incessant shivering, he stood while Middon fastened the accursed fowl around his throat. Throughout this performance, as during the beating, his honest big eyes had remained fixed on the furious face of his god, with a startled horror that held a tinge of heartbreak. Middon had noted the look and had steeled himself against it.

Now, as the hen was secured in place, Middon stepped back, panting from his own vehement exertions. Biscuit stood looking up into the man's face, apparently oblivious of the five-pound dead-weight that dangled shamefully from his furry neck.

It was this moment which Reynard chose to waken from his artistically posed snooze and to step yawning out of his kennel coop. His advent was almost simultaneous with an odd thought which had just flashed through Middon's brain.

Half-unconsciously, the old man had observed that the fox was lying fast asleep in his coop, and that all the excitement of hen-killing and of dog-beating, just outside, had not wakened him. This, although Reynard's hair-trigger nerves were forever atingle at the first onset of any kind of strife.

But at last the fox appeared to have roused himself from his refreshing sleep. Waving his white-tipped brush, he minced forward to exchange a morning greeting with his master.

Middon was in no mood to pet him, or, indeed, to be civil to anyone. His heart was heavy within him at the pain he had inflicted on Biscuit and at the mute look in the dog's eyes. The man was turning away, when Biscuit created a diversion which brought him back to the scene at a jump.

Stolidly, with true bulldog heroism, Biscuit had endured his own hideously unjust punishment, though well he knew the culprit was Reynard and not himself. But when the fox came forth so smugly to receive a petting from the man he had robbed—this snapped the last vestige of the cross-breed's hard-held self-control.

With a strangled roar, Biscuit flung himself at the complacently advancing fox.

Reynard did not await his former friend's charge. With the speed of light the fox whirled and darted behind his coop, springing to the full length of the thin chain in a single bound, and hurling his eleven pounds of muscular weight against it, in the hope it might snap before the dog should be upon him.

The well-wrought chain withstood the sharp tug. But the half-rotted leather of the fox's narrow collar did not. Though it dug into Reynard's soft neck with anguishing garrote force, yet its decaying fibers parted.

The fox was free. Gasping from his brief semi-strangulation, Reynard fled at dizzy speed up the slope behind the dooryard—the slope which led to the wooded mountain above.

Few are the dogs that can keep close on the trail of a fresh fox. And the powerful young mongrel had a still greater handicap than his unwieldy size.

As he sprang for the fox, Biscuit had sought to shift his own direction. This when he saw Reynard take that aerial sidewise leap behind the kennel. Gauging the change of direction in too great a hurry, Biscuit's plunging sixty-pound weight smote glancingly against the corner of the kennel-coop.

The impact knocked the dog clean off balance. He rolled over, then scrambled to his feet and dashed up the slope in raging pursuit of his escaped foe. But the delay had given Reynard a start of nearly a hundred feet.

Old Man Middon did not call his dog back. The man did not so much as see Biscuit gallop after the fox until some moments later. At that time he caught a fleeting glimpse of pursuer and pursued, against the skyline. They were vanishing over the ridge which divided his farm from the wilderness of mountain above. It was too late then for his aged voice to carry to the dog.

The reason Middon did not see the beginning of the chase was because his eyes were fixed blinkingly on something much nearer. Biscuit had been knocked flat by his collision with the fox's coop. But the same collision had knocked the coop clean over and upside down.

There, in a neatly-gouged hollow, beneath where the kennel had stood, was a mass of feathers and of gnawed chicken bones.

The sight told its own story to the mountaineer farmer as plainly as could a page of print. It cleared every atom of the mystery of the vanished fowls. Incidentally it cleared Biscuit of any possible shadow of guilt. A chicken-killing dog does not bury the evidences of his crime, day after day, under the kennel of another animal.

To make assurance surer, Middon picked up Reynard's dangling chain and measured the distance from the kennel doorway to the spot where Biscuit had been nosing at the hen. Yes, the killing had been done well within the radius of the chain. A fleck or two of fresh blood just within the kennel door proved that Reynard had not had time to swallow the hen's head without leaving a telltale clue to the deed.

It was then that the remorsefully wondering old man raised his eyes in quest of the dog he had flayed and humiliated. It was then he caught that single brief glimpse of Biscuit and Reynard disappearing over the ridge.

"I—I can see now why he looked at me that way, all the time I was a-whaling him, so cruel!" mumbled Middon, thickly, as he winked his eyes clear of an unbidden mist that crept over them. "Gee! but I wish I had a third foot! I'd sure use it for kicking myself from here to Paterson and back. That's how it is with us humans—we punish first and we find out afterward. We lambaste the only critters on earth that's foolish enough to worship us. It's lucky the good Lord didn't give dogs any more sense than He did. If He had, they'd be too wise to love us fool humans and serve us, like they do. They'd see through us. Maybe they do, anyhow. Maybe they got natures big enough to love us, in spite of what we are. . . . I'd give a month's food and cash not to have treated Biscuit like I did."

After the way of most semi-solitary men, Middon had fallen into the habit of talking to Biscuit—though never to Reynard—as to another human. Now in the dog's absence he found with a start of annoyance that he was jabbering aloud to himself. With an impatient shake, and with a worried look toward the ridge, the old fellow pottered slowly indoors to get breakfast.

He was laying out a busy and tiring day. And he knew well he must fortify himself with food, beforehand. His self-imposed labors were to consist in hunting the mountain for his dog. Biscuit would come back home when Reynard should have outstripped him hopelessly, or should have outwitted him into losing the trail. At least, Middon knew the young dog would make every effort to come home. But he was in doubt as to Biscuit's ability to do it.

Not only would the tired mongrel be weighted down by the heavy hen that dangled from his neck, but the loop of the tough belt was more than likely to hook itself into some tougher bush-stem or outjutting sapling stump or low-spreading tree-branch. In that event Biscuit would be as hopeless and helpless a prisoner as if the cleverest of men had tied him there to die of thirst and hunger.

Not a year earlier, on a day's hunting in the lower reaches of the mountain, the old man had come upon the body of a handsome pointer dog whose owner had had the folly to let him go into the field with a collar on. The pointer, nose to ground, had run past a slanting cedar stump which had passed between his collar and his throat, holding him prisoner until he died.

The same fate might well await Biscuit, thanks to the angry skill wherewith Middon had fastened the belt and its loop to his neck.

Meantime the mongrel was straining every nerve and thew of his powerful young body to catch the elusively fleeing fox. Up the slope, then over the ridge and up the steep face of the mountain itself they tore. For the first mile Reynard held his lead and even increased it a little.

Had he been a forest-reared fox he would have fared better in this first life-and-death race of his. For, from babyhood he would have been accustomed to continuous running, to tireless action of every kind—to the dodging of enemies and the wearying quest of food.

But, from the time he was able to crawl, Reynard had lived soft and had exercised little. His meals had come to him unsought. His nights and part of his days had been spent on the chain. Now he was paying the bill for flesh and softness and inexperience.

True, he ran fast and sure-footedly. But, from almost the first, his was not the true fox speed. To attain that incredible swiftness of foot, one's life must have been from the first a ceaseless physical struggle for sustenance and safety.

Biscuit lumbered after; righteous indignation giving an added driving-force to his mighty young body. He was lean and he was in the pink of condition. Moreover, for the first time in all his friendly span of months, he was goaded on by a consuming rage of vengeance.

His bulldog strain kept him steadfastly in the race, despite every obstacle of broken ground; and it gave him the depth of chest needed for such lung power as the run entailed. But it was quite another ancestor—perhaps a greyhound, more likely a collie—which had endowed him with the unflagging speed that was his when his first lumbering gallop settled into a steady and mile-eating stride.

Still another forebear, a hunting dog, no doubt, had supplied the mystic scenting power which let him follow the rank reek of his quarry unerringly, at such moments as the fox was blotted from his actual view by rocks or by foliage.

Upward and onward raged the chase. The fox had swerved to right and to left, more than once, in an effort to shake off his enemy. But ever the heavy yellow head was behind him again. Ever the splay pads pattered in unerring pursuit, despite Reynard's shrewdest effort to dodge or to double.

Biscuit was too close behind to permit of successful doubling, and Biscuit's nose was too accurate to make safe a sidelong leap into the shelter of copse or tangle.

Then, giving up for the time his attempts to escape through wile, Reynard breasted the mountain's steepest slope afresh, gliding easily upward over rubble and shale on which the heavier pursuer's feet slipped or were cut; flashing in and out of thickets or bramble patches whose thorns took painful toll of Biscuit's coat and nostrils.

But always the heaving and panting dog was after him, making up on cleaner footing what he lost when the going was bad.

Reynard came at last to the summit of the mountain. Far behind him stretched the miles he had traveled. Middon's cottage and hillside farm stood out like a mere fret on the distance-smoothed slope far below.

There was no time to pause and look back, nor even to fill with air his laboring lungs. Close behind plunged and panted and lumbered the mongrel; his honest brown eyes bloodshot and glazed, his mighty jaws dripping foam.

The defunct hen around Biscuit's neck whanged bruisingly against his breast and upper forelegs. Her weight grew heavier and heavier to carry. But he kept on, heedless of the impediment.

Into Biscuit's dizzy brain the ghost of some pit-bull ancestor was snarling his stanch race's never-say-die slogan. Into his thudding heart some gaily cavalier-like ancestor collie was laughing:

"Keep it up! This may be death, but it's grand fun!"

Into his achingly worn-out muscles a racing greyhound great-grandsire was pumping the mysterious coursing speed that had won cup after cup against grueling competition. Truly a mongrel may borrow from many rich ancestral treasure-houses.

Down the farther slope of the mountain, through the hush of the warm autumn day, sped the fox, silent and ghostlike as he slipped through coppice and brier-patch or wormed his way in and out of cairnlike strews of bowlder. Down the slope slithered and stumbled in pursuit the dauntless yellow avenger; now panting and snapping at Reynard's very brush, now blundering confusedly, but undaunted, a hundred feet behind.

The fox was snarling like a rabid cat, and was sobbing like a nightmare-harried child. His hair-trigger nerves were raw. Caution and racial craftiness were cast to the winds. All he thought of was to get far enough ahead of his foe to be able to pause and to draw one long breath into his tortured lungs.

Into a scarlet sumac-clump dashed Reynard, almost at the farther base of the half-unscalable mountain. Behind him staggered the mongrel.

Midway in the copse, Reynard whizzed through a low pile of leaves. From out the leaves, a set of rusty steel jaws arose and gripped him. He had set foot on the pan of a cunningly concealed fox-trap.

Forward pitched the flying red body, thrown off balance by the grip on its hindleg. With awful force the fox's skull crashed against a rock-point just in front of the riffle of leaves.

Merciful and devoid of torment was the end of the sinew-wrenching race, for that race's exhausted pacemaker. Before even the fox's numbed nerves could register to the bemused brain the fact that his hindleg was caught in serried jaws of steel, the impact of the sharp rock-jut cracked the delicate skull. Painlessly, Reynard died.

Biscuit lunged into the sumac-clump, almost at the heels of the fox. There he came to a slidingly stumbling halt. On the ground before him lay Reynard, lifeless and prone. At sight of his enemy there at his feet, Biscuit snarled afresh and drove down his dripping teeth for a back-breaking bite that should finish the fox.

Then, with his jaws a bare inch from Reynard's dead body, Biscuit drew instinctively back. Something told him that his foe was no longer a foe. The mongrel was not of the type to tear and rend the helpless. Since there seemed no longer either fight or flight in the fox, Biscuit's vengeance-lust died within him.

For a few seconds the mongrel bent above Reynard, sniffing in sad astonishment at him. Then, exhausted, Biscuit dropped heavily down among the riffled leaves, panting noisily, tongue out, mouth afoam, heart hammering to suffocation. The dead hen flopped into the leafy swirl.

Long Biscuit lay there, within a yard of the dead fox. Then, bit by bit, the dog's panting waxed less stertorous. He could breathe again without torture. His heart no longer threatened to shake his body to pieces.

Slowly, draggingly, Biscuit lumbered to his feet, the hen dangling heavier than ever. Just beyond were the heavenly sound and scent of running water. The dog was parched and racked with thirst. He made his way on uncertain feet to a brooklet a few rods beyond. There, in a rock-pool, he drank until his tongue could scarcely lap. After which he tumbled down among the brook-edge rubble and slept.

It was dusk before Biscuit waked. Again he drank deep of the pool. Then, on legs whose springiness seemed forever gone, and carrying his abhorred five-pound burden of slain fowl, he began his climb of the mountain which lay between himself and home. He made a detour of the sumac-thicket where lay Reynard.

But, an hour later, a trapper passed that way and did not make a detour. The trapper was on his round of his fox-traps. He grunted appreciatively as he noted the smooth density of the man-raised fox's pelt.

Fox pelts, that season, sold for $11.50 each at the Paterson wholesaler's. The wholesaler cured and dressed the skins and lined them. Then he affixed ornamented snappers to them—the entire process costing him less than $8—and sold them at his own retail fur-store for upward of $60 each.

Thus ended Old Man Middon's first and only experiment in turning a prenatally wild thing into a domestic animal. It is an experiment always foredoomed to failure.

Up the steep mountain-side toiled Biscuit, the hen still thumping against him at every stride. But now there was no need for haste. So he plodded slowly, sometimes taking advantage of easier ground or skirting thick copses and boulder-strews.

Up he went, through the heat of the late autumn day, by dint of slowness and of sense and of rare luck avoiding the catching of his leathern belt loop in any outcrop of tree or rock. His was a stolidly determined progress homeward, not a half-blind rush. He had scope to avert possible obstacles.

But at every mile the miserable hen seemed to double in weight. More than once the fagged-out mongrel lay down to rest and to let his wrenched muscles relax their incessant grind. So passed the rest of the Indian Summer afternoon. Early dusk began to slant across the western sky.

Night fell long before Biscuit recrossed the ridge that marked the forest boundary of his master's farm. Down the slope he blundered and slipped. Fatigue and pain were forgotten as he caught the sight and scent of home. On he pressed, eager and gay.

True, here he had been beaten unmercifully, not twelve hours earlier. Here, too, this repulsive and neck-wearying hen had been strung around his throat. Here he had met black injustice and cruelty, as reward for his own utter devotion.

But he had met them all from the man he worshiped. And it was not in the clean white heart of the mongrel to hold grudge or to sulk, just because his god had ordained to punish him.

All was forgotten—the humiliation, the ingratitude, the hot-red weals athwart his tender skin. Biscuit knew only that he was coming back to his adored master and that the parting had been homesickly long. The reunion was well worth a day of heart-racking toil such as he had undergone.

The one flaw in his rapture of anticipation was a fear lest he be not yet forgiven by Middon for the fault he had not committed, and lest his god might scold or even whip him for the day's wretched truancy.

At the thought, Biscuit's newly-wagging tail drooped. The light of happiness in the big round eyes merged into worry. Dumbly he cast about in his canine mind for some way of appeasing the possible wrath of the man he loved.

As he pattered noiselessly up the front steps and toward the half-open front door of the battered little cottage, his sense of smell told him that Middon had left his rank old brier pipe lying on the arm of his porch chair.

Again Biscuit's tail began to wag. More than once he had won a smile and a pat on the head from Middon by the performance of a certain easily-acquired trick with this same pipe. Perhaps it might serve now to soften the man's heart toward the runaway.

Gleefully Biscuit picked up the pipe and made for the door.

Until late dusk, Middon had scoured the mountainside for his dear dog. Remorse, and a fear lest Biscuit be pinned to earth somewhere by the belt loop, kept the old man on the search long after his rheumatic legs were scarce able to carry his weight. He had worn his voice to a thread by futile shouts of Biscuit's name. Then had had limped home, exhausted and heavy of heart.

Lighting a lamp, he had flung himself into a chair. He had neither strength nor desire for supper. So, head on breast, he sat there, slumping far down and with a tired ache of loneliness and of sorrow at his heart.

Two men at the village speak-easy a mile below had been absorbing far more raw corn liquor than their systems could assimilate. As a result, both were very drunk. They were at the stage of intoxication when all things seem possible and most things highly desirable.

One of them chanced to mention to the other that Old Man Middon had stopped him on the mountain road to ask about a lost dog. The talk shifted to Middon's reputation for having a hidden hoard of cash tucked away some-where in his home—a reputation that is borne by three out of five elderly men who live alone on the outskirts of rural communities.

Then one of the drinkers put two and two together in audaciously brilliant fashion. The miser's watch-dog was lost. The miser himself would be help-less against any two husky men who might go to his house that evening and demand to be told the whereabouts of his cache of gold. Should he refuse to

19

divulge, there was always a way of coercing him into frankness. A poker, heated a few minutes in the kitchen stove, had a wondrous power, it was said, to open the lips of the reticent. Three more drinks, and the plan seemed flawless.

Middon lifted his sunken head hopefully at a shuffling sound on his porch. Then, before he could call Biscuit by name, the door swung partly open and two very drunk and very determined men slipped into the room.

One of them told him, thickly but quite intelligibly, that Middon was known to have much wealth hidden thereabouts and that they were poor and could make good use of some of it. The brief oration ended with a request to produce the hoard and not force the treasure-seekers to use sharper persuasives.

Middon knew full well what he was up against. Not a month passes but rural correspondents of metropolitan papers record the torture and occasional death of a supposed miser at the hands of local toughs. Middon was old and he was tired out. He was unarmed. His shotgun was in an inner room. Yet, gallantly the oldster lurched to his feet, determined to fight such a pitifully useless battle as he was able to, before the torture should begin.

Easily and with entire good-humor, the two shoved him back into his chair. One of them glanced toward the stove, and at the poker alongside it. At the same instant a wordlessly gobbling sound from his companion made the poker-seeker whirl about. The other man had dropped Middon's arm and was staring slack-jawed at the doorway, his eyes bulging idiotically.

With gradual motion the half-shut door was swinging wide. There on the threshold, framed against the outer darkness and vividly clear in the lamp-glare, stood a right impossible Thing.

The creature was a dog—bloodsmeared and muddy and thorn-scratched. He was standing grotesquely on his hindlegs. From his neck, like a grisly cannibal ornament, swung a huge and disreputably rumpled and headless hen. Daintily, between a corner of his foam-dripping jaws the dog held a blackened brier pipe, as if he were smoking it.

For an instant the apparition stood thus. Then, still on his hindlegs, Biscuit began to waddle into the room, toward Middon and the others. It was a spectacle to shake the nerve and the credulity of far soberer onlookers than the drunken marauders.

With a dual screech of terror the men bolted through the nearest window, taking the sash with them, the jagged shower of glass cutting avidly into their faces and hands. Unheeding the multiple cuts, they plunged through, and on into the night; shrieking, babbling, bellowing insanely.

Old Man Middon did not so much as follow aurally the fast-diminishing racket of their progress down the road. He had fallen on his knees, his shaking arms around the muddy and bloody dog; half sobbing as he gathered Biscuit to his breast.

"It would have served me good and right if those brutes had killed me for the cash I haven't got, Biscuit!" he was exclaiming as he ripped loose from his dog's throat the odious hen and belt and flung them out through the shattered window. "It wouldn't have been much worse'n what I tried to do to you this morning. And now you're licking my face and wanting to make friends again! . . . When—when the good Lord gave men the gift of speech instead of giving it to dogs, He made up for it by giving dogs a power of forgiveness that's a million times diviner than anything He ever gave us humans, Biscuit! And—and, oh, Biscuit, how *rotten* ashamed I am! I—"

His voice choked. He buried his working face in the dog's ruff.

Biscuit wriggled all over, in a delirium of happiness, striving to lick the hidden face and to shake hands with both paws at once.

For he saw that his trick entrance into the house had made a tremendous hit with his loved master—even if those two silly and noisy and smelly guests of Middon's hadn't had the good taste to appreciate such cleverness and had taken themselves off in a hurry.

Biscuit was at home again—gloriously at home! His god had forgiven him. What else mattered?

BLACK AND TAN
(1990)
Madison Smartt Bell

The following story is about a man who, after experiencing family tragedies, turns to breeding and training Dobermans as a way of forgetting the past and building a future. Madison Smartt Bell is a highly regarded American novelist and short story writer. He was born and raised in Nashville, Tennessee, and currently resides in Baltimore, where he teaches at Goucher College. He is married to poet Elizabeth Spires.

Bell's books include the acclaimed *Zero Db and Other Stories* (1987), *Soldier's Joy* (1989)—which won the Lillian Smith Award—*Anything Goes* (2002), and *The Stone That the Builder Refused* (2004). "Black and Tan" was originally published in the *Atlantic Monthly*.

Up until his family died out from under him, Peter Jackson used to grow tobacco. His place was a long ways out from town, up on the hillside above Keyhole Lake—you had a nice view of the lake from up there. It was forty or fifty acres that he owned, and an easement down to the lake shore. Maybe a third of that land was too rocky to farm and another third was grown up in cedars, fine old trees he never cared to cut down. There was the place his house was set and what was left you could grow tobacco on. He did just about all the work himself, hiring a couple of hands only once in a while, at cutting and drying time, for instance.

"Tobacco," he was known to say, and then he'd pause and spit a splash of it to one side of the courthouse steps. "Tobacco, now, that's eight days a week . . ." Like most farmers he'd come to town on Saturday, visit the Co-op or the Standard Farm Store, maybe get a few things at the supermarket. When he got done his errands he might wander through the courthouse square and talk a while with this one and that one. One Sunday a month, more or less, he'd drive in with his wife and they'd both go to church, and two, three times a year he'd come in by himself and get falling-down drunk. At the end of his evening he'd just go to sleep in the cab of his truck, then in the morning hitch himself straight and drive on out home. Never caused anybody any more trouble than that. Later on, after he'd got the dogs, he cut out the drinking and the church along with it, right about at the same time.

A steady fellow, then, and mostly known as a hard worker. Quiet, never had a whole lot to say, but what he said was reasonable. Whatever he told you he would do would get done if nothing serious kept him from it. That was the kind of thing any of us might have said of him, supposing we'd been asked.

Amy was the name of his wife, who'd been a Puckett before she married. Never raised any objection to living so far out from town. She was fond of the woods and fond of the lake, so maybe that made up for whatever loneliness there may have been to it. They didn't have any neighbors near, though a couple of Nashville people had built summer houses on the far side of the lake. Like Peter Jackson, Amy was a worker; she grew a garden, put up food for the winter. They were both in the garden picking tomatoes on the late September evening when she all of a sudden fell over dead. Heart attack was what did her in, faster than a bullet. Jackson said he spent a minute twirling around to see where the shot might have come from, before he went to her. They had been working opposite ends of the row, and she was already getting cold by the time he got to her, he said. And she not more than fifty, fifty-five.

Jackson wasn't as broke up about it as you could have thought a man might be, losing his wife in her prime that way. Or if he was, he didn't show it much. There was a good turnout at the funeral, for Amy was well liked around the town. The old hens were forever coming up to him and saying how *terrible* they thought it was, and every time he told them, *No. No, it ain't so terrible, not really. If her time had come to go, then better she went quickly, with no pain.* So everybody said how well he was bearing it. And then his children started to die.

They had two children, son and daughter: June and Richard were their names. Both of them looked fair to rise above their raising, both going on past high school, which neither of their parents had. The boy was putting himself through UT Knoxville on an ROTC scholarship, and then one summer he got himself killed in a training accident, some kind of a foolish, avoidable thing. Well, he went quick too, did Richard. It put Peter Jackson back at the graveside just under a year after they buried Amy. He was dry-eyed again, but tight around the mouth, and whatever people spoke to him he didn't have much to say back. June stood with him the whole time through, hanging on to his elbow and sort of fending people off. It might have been she was already sick herself by that time, though nobody knew anything of it yet.

June was the older of the two. She'd gone to nursing school in Nashville and kept living there once she was done, had herself a job at the Baptist Hospital. After she got that cancer she stayed on as a patient a while but there wasn't anything they could do for her, and in the end she came home to Keyhole Lake to die. Peter Jackson nursed her right on through it, never had any other help at all. It wasn't quick or anything like it; it kept on for five or six months and you didn't have to hear a whole lot about it to know there must have been pain and to spare.

It was mid-March or so when they buried her; there'd been a hard winter and there was still some thin snow on the ground. Peter Jackson stood alone this time, grim and silent for the most part. Nobody had a lot to say to him either. He had gone lean under his hardship, but he was still a fine-looking man, and people said he looked well in his funeral suit. Of course, he'd had his share of opportunity to get the hang of wearing it. As a young man he'd had deep red hair, and now it was rust-colored, patched with gray. His eyebrows were thick and bushy, turning out in devilish points at the sides, and underneath, his deep-set eyes surprised you with the brightness of their green. This time he wouldn't turn back from the grave once they had filled it, and after a minute the priest walked over to stand with him. Shoulder to shoulder, they looked like a matched pair, Mr. Chalk in his black cassock and Jackson in the suit.

Mr. Chalk was fairly new to the town; he'd done a lot of work in the prisons and he wasn't known for wasting his words. A few people crept up near to listen for what he'd find to tell a man like Jackson, which was this:

"Well, you're still here," Mr. Chalk was heard to say.

Jackson spat on the snow and said, "What of it?"

"You're surviving," Mr. Chalk said. "Today's today and then there'll be tomorrow."

"That's right, and it's a curse," Peter Jackson said, and turned on the priest with the tunnels of his eyes. "I been cursed with survival," he said then, speaking in a different tone than before, as if, after all, it were a new discovery.

That spring he didn't plant tobacco. Round about the time he should have been, he was driving all around the county looking at dogs, and going clear to Nashville too. He looked at all the good-sized breeds: collies, Great Danes, German shepherds. There was a story that went along with it, which got out and made the rounds. Funny how many people got to hear of it, because it was a personal kind of a thing for a man like Peter Jackson to go telling.

It appeared that when Peter Jackson was born, his parents had a big old dog that they let live in the house and all. Jackson didn't recall himself what breed of a dog it might have been and there wasn't anybody for him to ask, because his parents were long dead and he never had any brothers or sisters. Anyway, they had worried the dog might eat the baby when they brought him home but it turned out the opposite: the dog loved the child. So much so that in the long run they trusted the dog to watch the baby. They might go out and work their land or even leave the place altogether for a short spell, knowing the dog would see everything was all right. This all happened at that same place at Keyhole Lake, and one time, so the story went, little Peter Jackson, only two or three years old, let himself out of the house somehow and went wandering all the way down to the shore. This old dog went right along with him, saw he didn't drown himself or get hurt any other way, and in the end when the child was tired, the dog brought him on back home.

So Peter Jackson spent that spring driving practically all over creation, looking at different kinds of dogs, and when people wondered how he could be so choosy when he didn't even appear to know what it was he wanted, that was the tale he would tell them. Finally he ended up at the place of this woman way out the Lebanon Road who bred Dobermans. He went out and looked at her dogs a while and went home and came back another day and told her, "Let me have two of them."

"What do you mean, two?" she said. "Do you even know if you want one? Which two did you have in mind, anyway?"

"Pick me out two likely ones," Peter Jackson said. "A male and a female. Ones that ain't too close related." And the next thing anybody knew, he was breeding Dobermans himself. Rebuilt his old drying barn into kennels and fenced in some pens out in front of it. Told anybody who cared to know that Dobermans weren't naturally mean like they had the name for, but that they were smart and naturally loyal and would be inclined to protect you and your house and land without any special training. Although he could supply the training too, if that was what you wanted. He started selling a good many as pets and maybe an equal number as guard dogs. That was about the time the K-9 patrols came into style, so he drew business from the police, and in a year or so people were coming good long distances, even from out of state at times, to buy their dogs from Peter Jackson. He was thought to be so good at it that eventually people began to bring him dogs that other trainers couldn't handle. Which may have been what first gave him the notion of taking in those boys.

Marvin Ferguson, the county judge, was the man Jackson had to go see about this idea. In Franklin, the county judge doubles up as juvenile judge too, so Ferguson had the management of whatsoever people under seventeen or eighteen couldn't seem to keep themselves out of trouble. Of which there were always a few that he couldn't quite figure out what to do with. It was kind of left-handed work for him to be doing anyway. Still, he was leery of Jackson's idea at first. Because Jackson wasn't getting any younger, was he? and his place was clear the hell and gone from anywhere else to speak of, and who knew just how bone-mean some of those boys might turn out to be? But after they had talked a while they arrived at an understanding. When Peter Jackson had gone on home, Judge Ferguson pulled his file on a boy named Willard Clement, and pretty soon he was on the phone arranging for a deputy to drive the boy out to Jackson's place.

The highway runs on the near side of the ridge from the lake, and you got to Peter Jackson's by turning off on a little old dirt driveway that came up over the crest of the hill and dipped down on the other side to stop in front of

Jackson's house, an old log house that had been clapboarded over and added on to a couple or three times. A ways below the house were the dog pens, and any time a car turned in, all those dogs would start in barking. Past the kennels a trail went winding down the hill and twisted in amongst the cedars; you couldn't see quite how it got there from above, but way on down it came out near the little dock where Jackson kept a pirogue tied, for when he wanted to paddle out on the lake and fish.

But the first thing a stranger would be apt to notice, coming over that rise, would be the lake itself. It always looked sort of surprising from the ridgetop. It isn't really keyhole-shaped, just narrow at one end and wide at the other. How come they give it that name is that the middle of the wide part is so deep nobody ever found the bottom, and somebody had the idea it was like that part of a keyhole that just goes clear on through the door. From up by Peter Jackson's house you could always see how the color of the water would change as it neared the middle, homing in on that deep dark circle of blue.

Jackson's dogs stayed in the pens, all but two that were his pets; them he let live in the house and have the run of the whole place. Bronwen he called one of them and the other was Caesar. All his dogs had peculiar names like that, which he looked up in books. When the deputy pulled in to deliver Willard Clement, he found Jackson waiting out in the yard, the two dogs on either side of him. The deputy unlocked Willard out of that caged-up back seat and brought him on down to get introduced. Jackson said hello and then made both of the dogs put up their paws to shake—they were that well trained, almost like folks. Then he turned around all of a sudden and pointed back up the hill and called out, "Hit it, Bronwen," and snapped his fingers twice. The dog went bounding up the hill and jumped up in the air and locked her jaws on a piece of two-by-four Jackson had nailed between two cedar trunks about five feet off of the ground, and she just kept right on hanging there, her whole weight on her teeth so to speak, until Jackson said, "All right, leggo, Bronwen," and then she dropped down. Willard Clement was staring googly-eyed, and you could just practically see it, the deputy said, how any thought he might have had of causing Peter Jackson some type of trouble was evaporating clean out of his mind.

Jackson put Willard Clement up in what had been Richard's room, and that's where he put all the others that came along after him. He kept them busy working with the dogs, first just putting the food out and cleaning the pens, and later on taking them for exercise and helping with the training some. The boys mostly stayed out there six weeks to two months, which was long enough to learn a little something about how to train a dog. And the work told on them, gentled them down some. A number kept on working with animals, one way or another, after they were done their stay at Jackson's. Willard Clement, I believe, finally became a vet.

You couldn't miss the difference in those boys, between the time they got dropped off out there and the time they got picked up again. You'd drive one of them out there locked into the back like something that had rabies, maybe, but when you went back to go get him, likely he'd look like somebody you could trust to ride in the front seat alongside of you. He would be saying *Yes sir* and *No sir* and standing up straight and looking you in the eye. Nobody quite knew what Jackson practiced on those boys, but whatever it was it seemed to work. And a good few of them seemed to really be grateful for it too. There were some that tried going back out to visit him, a lot later on once they were grown, but the funny thing was that Jackson himself never seemed to care too much about seeing any of them again.

There must have been eight or ten of those boys between Clement and Don Bantry. Anyway, he'd been having them for near about two years. There hadn't been a one of them he'd failed to turn around, either, else they probably never would have thought of sending Bantry out there, because that boy was a tough nut to crack. He was about sixteen at that time, but already big as a man. What he was most recently in trouble for was beating up a teacher at the high school and breaking his arm, but there was a long string of things leading up to that: liquor and pot, some car stealing, a burglary, suspicion of a rape he never got tried on. They wouldn't have him at the reform school again, just flat-out wouldn't. Ferguson was in a toss-up whether to try and figure some way to get him tried as an adult or send him out to Jackson's a while, and what he decided shows you how he'd come to think that Peter Jackson was magic.

Bantry had sort of short bowlegs, but big shoulders and longish arms. He had a pelt of heavy black hair all over him, and even his eyebrows met in the middle. He looked a good deal like an ape, and he wasn't above acting like one too. Well, the deputy turned him out of the car, and Jackson had Bronwen and Caesar put up their paws, but Bantry wasn't having any of that. "Ain't shaking hands with no goddamn dog," he said. But it wasn't the first time one of them had said it.

Jackson had Caesar run hit that two-by-four and hang by his jaws a half minute or so. You couldn't have told what Bantry thought, his face never showed a thing, but that trick had always worked before, so the deputy left on out of there. And right from the start, it was war.

Jackson went and got a shovel and handed it to Bantry. Explained to him how to go about cleaning out those dog pens, where he'd find the wheelbarrow at, where to go dump all he shoveled up. Bantry didn't reach to take hold of the shovel, so Jackson finally just let it drop and lean against his shoulder.

"Better get a move on," Jackson said, or something about like it, and then he started walking back down toward the house. He was halfway there when he heard some kind of a noise or shout and turned around in time to see Bantry flinging the shovel like a spear, not quite at him but close enough in his general direction that Bronwen and Caesar started growling. Jackson told the dogs to stay. Bantry had turned and started walking up the drive, where the dust of the deputy's car had not yet even settled, like he didn't know it was at least twenty miles to anywhere else, or didn't care, either one.

"Come on back here before I have the dogs bring you," Peter Jackson called after him.

Bantry kept walking, didn't even glance back. He was near the top of the hill when the dogs got to him, and he swung around and tried to get off a kick, but before he could land one, Bronwen had him by the one arm and Caesar by the other. They clamped on to him just short of breaking his skin and started dragging him back down the drive to where the shovel had landed, just like Jackson had said they would. Bantry came along with them, had no choice, as long as he didn't want his arms torn off. His face was fish white, but Peter Jackson thought it was anger more than fear. Bantry was not the kind that scared easy, though he was sharp enough to know a fight he couldn't win. This time when Jackson offered him the shovel he took it, and he went on and cleaned out the dog runs. For the next week, ten days or so, whatever Jackson told him to do he did it, but did it like a slave, not looking at him or speaking either. He never said anything at all unless he was asked a question, not even at the supper table.

Jackson had a dog named Olwen, with seven pups near ready to wean. He had Bantry feeding the puppies their oatmeal and all. One day when Bantry was coming out of Olwen's run, Jackson snapped his fingers to Caesar. The dog hit Bantry square in the chest, knocked him over flat on his back and stood over him with that whole mouthful of teeth showing white and needle sharp. With all that, Bantry kept most of his cool. He turned his head to one side, slowly, and called out to Peter Jackson.

"What I do now?"

"You been doing something to Olwen's puppies," Jackson told him, walking up closer.

"You never seen me," Bantry said.

"But I still know it," Jackson said. "And if you don't stop, I'll know that too." And he let Bantry lay and think on that a minute before he called Caesar to leave him get back up.

Another week or so went by, Bantry doing his work with his head bowed down, not speaking until he was spoken to and then answering short as he could. Till one evening when Jackson was starting to cook supper and felt like he had a headache coming on. Bantry had just fed Bronwen and Caesar on the kitchen floor, so they were busy over their pans. Jackson stepped into his bedroom to get himself an aspirin, and then Bantry was in there right behind him, already shutting and bolting the door.

"You been waiting your chance quite a while, hadn't you, boy?" Jackson said. And straightaway he hit Bantry over the eye, twisting his fist so it would cut. He thought if he surprised him he might win, or anyway get a chance to open the door back up. But Bantry didn't have his reputation for nothing. Jackson got in a couple more shots and thought maybe he was doing all right, when next thing he knew he was lying on the floor not able to get up again. Then it was quiet for a minute or two except for the dogs scrabbling at the outside of the door. Every so often one or the other would back off and get a running start and throw himself up against it.

"You fight okay for an old man," Bantry said, panting. It was about his first volunteer word since he got there. "But you still lost." Jackson didn't answer him. It was hurting him too much to breathe right then. Bantry reached a handkerchief off the dresser and dabbed at the cut above his eye. Then he picked up the keys of Jackson's truck and twirled the ring around his finger.

"You won't never make it," Jackson said. They were both still again for a minute, listening to the dogs trying to come through the door.

"I could always kill you," Bantry said.

"You'll still come out behind," Jackson said. "I already lived a lot longer than you."

Bantry sat down on the edge of Jackson's bed, looking down at the floor. He still had to hold the handkerchief over his cut to keep the blood from running in his eye.

"What say we just call it a draw?" Jackson said. "We could just go on in the kitchen and eat supper and forget the whole thing."

Bantry looked over at him. "How I know you're telling the truth?" he said.

"Hell, you don't," Peter Jackson said. "But there's always a chance of it. And some chance is better than no chance at all."

Bantry sat and thought a while longer. Then he reached over and unlatched the door. The dogs came in fast, spinning around, slipping a little on the slick board floor. They were in such a hurry to find Bantry and eat him alive they were just about falling over themselves.

"Let him alone," Jackson called out, and both dogs simmered down right away. Then to Bantry: "You come on here and help me up. And let me have that aspirin bottle. That's what I was after in here in the first place."

Another week or so went by. Bantry's cut was healing up; it was not so bad as it looked at first. Jackson had thought his ribs were cracked but it turned out they were only bruised and soon enough they started feeling better. Bantry went on about the same as before, doing what he was told and not saying much, yet Jackson didn't think he was quite so sullen and angry as he had been. Then one afternoon Bantry came up to him and said, "I'm done with the dog runs. All right I go down by the lake a while?"

"Go ahead on," Jackson said. He was right pleased because it was the first time Bantry had asked him for anything, and for that matter it was the first time he'd acted like he knew the lake was even there.

So Bantry went on down the trail and Jackson went and turned out a dog named Theodore he was training for K-9. He had on all the pads he wore whenever he was going to let a dog have at him. After twenty minutes or so he took a break and walked around the low side of the kennels where he could see out to the lake, and that was when he saw Bantry out paddling in the pirogue.

Later on, Jackson couldn't tell just why the sight of it hit him so hard. He hadn't told Bantry he could use the boat, but then he hadn't told him he couldn't either. He might have been trying to run off again; there were people in the houses on the far side of the lake and Bantry might have thought he could get over there and steal one of their cars. But even from that far distance Jackson could see that Bantry didn't know much at all about how to handle a boat: he couldn't keep it headed straight, and he kept heeling it way over to one side or the other.

Whatever his reason was, Jackson decided he wanted to get down there quick. He took out running down the trail, shedding his pads as he went along. Bronwen and Caesar came along with him, and Theodore, who was still out loose, was frisking along after all of them, not taking it too seriously, just having a good time. The trail takes a zig and a zag through the cedar grove, and for the last leg or two Jackson couldn't see the lake at all. When he finally came out at the foot of the path, he saw Bantry had turned the boat over somehow and was thrashing around a good way from it. You could tell by one quick look he didn't know how to swim a stroke. And what kind of a fool would overset a flat-bottomed boat, anyway? He wasn't over the deep part of the lake; if he had been, the way things fell out, he would probably be there yet.

Jackson took off his knee pads, which he hadn't been able to get rid of while he was running. He took off his shoes and some more of his clothes and waded out into the lake. The dogs ran up and down the shoreline barking like crazy, and now and then one of them would put a paw in the water, but they were not dogs that liked to swim. Without thinking, Jackson swam straight out to where Bantry was at and laid a hold to him, only Bantry got a better hold on him first, and dragged him right on under. It was not anything he meant to be doing, exactly, just how any drowning man behaves. He was trying to climb out of the lake over Jackson's back, but Jackson was going down underneath him, getting lightheaded, for no matter what he tried he couldn't raise his head clear for a breath. Then it came to him he had better swim for the bottom. When he dove down he felt Bantry come loose from him and he kept going down till he was free, then out a ways, swimming as far as he could under water before he came back up.

He was tired then, and his banged ribs had started to hurt from that long time he'd been down and holding his breath. For a minute or two he had to lie in a dead-man's float to rest, and then he raised his head and started treading water, slow. It was a cloudy day, no sun at all, and he could feel the cold cutting through to his bones. The surface of the lake was black as oil. Bantry was still struggling about twenty feet from him, but he was near done in by that time. He stared at Jackson, his eyes rolling white. Jackson trod water and looked right back at him until Bantry gave it up and slid down under the lake.

Ripples were widening out from the place where Bantry's head went down, and Peter Jackson kept on treading water. He counted up to twenty-five before he dove. It was ten feet deep, maybe twelve, at the point where they were at, colder yet along the bottom and dark with silt. He didn't find Bantry the first dive he made, though he stayed down until his head was pounding. It took him a count of thirty to get the breath back for another try, and he was starting to think he might have miscalculated. But on the second time he found him and hauled him back up. Bantry was not putting up any fight now; he was not any more than a dead weight. Jackson got him in a cross-chest carry and swam him into the shore.

The dogs were going wild there on the bank, yapping and jumping up and down. Jackson dumped Bantry face down on the gravel and swatted the dogs away. He knelt down and started mashing Bantry's shoulders. There was plenty of water coming out of him, but he was cold and not moving a twitch, and Jackson was thinking he had miscalculated sure enough when Bantry shuddered and coughed and puked a little and then raised up on his elbows. Jackson got off of him and watched him start to breathe. After a little bit, Bantry's eyes came clear.

"You'da let me drown," Bantry said. "You'da just let me . . ."

"You never left me much of a choice," Jackson said.

"You was just setting there watching me drown," Bantry said. He sat up one joint at a time and then let his head drop down and hang over his folded knees. The cut about his eye had opened back up and was bleeding some. In a minute, he started to cry.

Peter Jackson never had seen anybody carrying on the way Bantry was, not some pretty near grown man, at least. He didn't feel any too sorry for Bantry, but it was unpleasant watching him cry like that. It was like watching a baby cry when it can't tell you what's the matter, and there ain't no way for you to tell it to quit. He thought of one thing or another he might say. That he'd had to take a gambler's chance. That a poor risk was better than no hope at all. But he was worn out from swimming and struggling, too tired to feel like talking much. Bantry kept on crying, not letting up, and Peter Jackson got himself on his feet and went limping up to the house with the dogs.

That was what did it for Bantry, though, or so it seemed. Anyway, he was a lot different after that. He acted nicer with the dogs, feeding them treats, stroking them and loving them up, when he never as much as touched one before, if he had a way around it. He began to volunteer to do extra things, helping more around the house and garden, when his chores in the kennel were done. He put on pads and learned to help Jackson train dogs for K-9. He followed Jackson around trying to strike up conversation, like, for a change, he was hungry for company. He was especially nice with Bronwen and Caesar, and Caesar seemed to take a shine to him right back. Bantry had turned the corner, what it looked like. In about two more weeks, Peter Jackson called the courthouse and said they could send somebody out to pick him up.

As it turned out, it was me they sent. I was still a part-time deputy then, and the call came on a Saturday when I was on duty. Bantry was packed and all ready to go when I got there. Soon as I had parked the car he came walking over, carrying his grip. Caesar was walking alongside of him, and every couple of steps they took, Bantry would reach down and give him a pat on the head.

"Hello, Mr. Trimble," he said. He put out his hand and we shook.

"You look bright-eyed and bushy-tailed," I said. "I'd scarce have known you, Bantry."

"You can call me Don," he said, and smiled.

I told him to go on and get in the front while I went down to take a message to Jackson. It surprised me just a touch he hadn't already come out himself. He was sitting on his back stoop when I found him, staring out across the lake. Bronwen was sitting there next to him. Every so often she'd slap her paw up on his knee, like she was begging him for something. Jackson didn't appear to be paying her much mind.

"Well sir, you're a miracle worker," I said. "I wouldn't have believed it if I'd just been told, but it looks like you done it again."

"Hello, Trimble," Jackson said, flicking his eyes over me and then back away. He'd known I was there right along, just hadn't shown it. Bronwen slapped her paw back up on his knee.

"Marvin said tell you he'll have another one ready to send out here shortly," I said. Jackson looked off across the lake.

"I ain't going to have no more of 'm," he said.

"Why not?" I said. Bronwen pawed at him another time, and Jackson reached over and started rubbing her ears.

"Well, I figured something out," Jackson said, still staring down there at the water. "It ain't any different than breaking an animal, what I been doing to them boys."

I stepped up beside him and looked where he was looking, curious to see what might be so interesting down there on the lake. There wasn't so much as a fish jumping. Nothing there but that blue, blue water, cold looking and still like it was ice.

"What if you're right?" I said. "More'n likely it's the very thing they need."

"Yes, but a man is not an animal," he said. He waited a minute, and clicked his tongue. "Anyhow, I'm getting too old," he said.

"You?" I said. "Ain't nobody would call *you* old." It was a true fact I never had thought of him that way myself, though he might have been near seventy by that time. He'd been a right smart older than his wife.

Jackson raised up his left hand and shook it under my nose. I could see how his fingers were getting skinny the way an old man's will, and how loose his wedding band was rattling. Then he laid his hand back down on Bronwen's head.

"I'm old," he said. "I can feel it now sure enough. The days run right by me and I can't get a hold on them. And you want to know what?"

"What?" I said. Walked right into it like the sharp edge of a door.

"It's a relief," Peter Jackson told me. "That's what."

BLUE MILK
(1934)
Booth Tarkington

This story, originally published in the *Saturday Evening Post*, will warm the reader's heart as it tells of a boy's longing to have a puppy and what he does to make that desire a reality. Booth Tarkington (1869–1946), a celebrated figure in American literature, is principally known for his novels and plays. Among his books are *Penrod: His Complete Story* (1913), *The Turmoil* (1915), *Seventeen* (1916), and *The Magnificent Ambersons* (1918), which Orson Welles adapted into the Academy Award–nominated movie of the same name.

Mr. and Mrs. Stone, little Orvie's parents, should not be blamed for a special prejudice they had. After all, they were only a young couple, took pride in the neatness of their house, didn't wish to incur bills for reupholstering furniture, and both were fond of Kitty, Mrs. Stone's cat. They loved their child more than they did Kitty or their furniture, no question; nevertheless, their steadfast refusal to add a pup to the family is comprehensible.

Orvie had more than a longing for a pup, he had a determination to possess one, gave his father and mother little rest from the topic and did all he could to impose his will upon theirs. Their great question had thus become whether it would be worse to have a pup or to have Orvie go on everlastingly asking for one. Then suddenly, without warning, he stopped.

Overnight he ceased to entreat, eschewed the subject completely, and yet was cheerful. This change in him was welcomed by his father; but his mother, who, of course, saw more of Orvie, could not feel it to be natural. She perceived a strangeness in the matter, something morbid, especially as the alteration was accompanied by peculiar manifestations. Disturbed, she spoke to her husband apprehensively.

"Nonsense!" he said. "Let's be grateful for a little peace and thank heaven he's got pups out of his head at last—at least for a little while! Home seems like a different place to me; I'd almost forgotten it could be restful. Two whole days—and he hasn't once asked for a pup! I suppose it's too soon to hope; but maybe—maybe—maybe—oh, maybe he's forgotten pups altogether!"

"No." She shook her head. "You haven't watched him. Really it's very queer. Haven't you even noticed these peculiar noises he's making?"

"What peculiar noises?" Mr. Stone, preparing to leave the breakfast table, moved back his chair, but remained seated. "When does he make 'em?"

"Why, almost any time. He was making some just a few minutes ago before he finished his breakfast, and he made some more in the hall after he left the table. Didn't you notice?"

"Notice? I thought he was trying to hum some terrible kind of whining tune and not succeeding. Usually when children try to sing, they do make peculiar—"

"No," Mrs. Stone interrupted seriously. "He wasn't singing; he was making noises like a pup's whining and barking—at least he was trying to. He does it all the time. I haven't told you what happened last night when I put him to bed, because you didn't get home till so late, how could I? I don't even know what time you finally did get home, and really I think when you feel you have to go to these stag card parties all the time—"

"The first!" her husband said sternly. "The first since 'way last Easter—the only one in five months! Listen. You were talking about what happened when you put Orvie to bed last night. Can't you stick to the subject? Did he ask for a pup again?"

"No. He did the strangest thing I ever knew him to do. Right in the middle of his prayers, kneeling by the bed, he began to bark."

"What?"

"He did," Mrs. Stone insisted. "He'd just said, 'Bless Mamma and Papa' and then he made a noise like this: 'Muff! Muff! Muff!'" Untalented in mimicry, she gave a squeaky imitation of the sounds her son had made. "Yes, he seemed to be barking, or trying to, the way a very young pup does. Then he got into bed and did it some more."

Mr. Stone laughed. "I don't see anything very—"

"Don't you? Wait. I haven't told you the rest of it. After I'd put out the light and gone to my own room, I heard him doing it again; and then a little while later he began whining like a pup. He kept it up so long that I went back to his room and asked him what was the matter. He just said, 'Nothing, Mamma' and then made the whining sound again. I told him to stop doing that and go to sleep, and the minute I was out of the room he began again; and not until I opened the door and said 'Orvie!' did he stop. What's more, I'd heard him making sounds like that every now and then all yesterday. What do you think of it?"

"Nothing. Children often imitate animals; it's kind of an instinct. You hear 'em miaowing or barking or—"

"No," Mrs. Stone said. "Not the way Orvie's doing it. There are times when he sounds almost exactly like a real pup. He—" She paused, lifted a warning hand, and nodded her head toward the open window. "Listen!"

Her husband listened, and then, rising, went to the window and looked out. Upon the cement path just below, his son was passing round the house on his way to the back yard and apparently amusing himself as he went by barking and whining realistically in a small but accurately puplike voice. At the same time he seemed to be scratching himself intimately upon the body; for his right hand and forearm were thrust within the breast of his polka-dotted shirt waist, so that bulk and motion were visible in that locality. Disregarding this scratching, which, though it seemed vigorous, appeared to have no significance, Mr. Stone laughed again.

"Nonsense!" he said. "Orvie's just playing at something or other in his own imagination. Likely enough he's seen or heard some ventriloquist at a movie theater and maybe he's trying to learn to be one himself. Children imitate frogs and cows and dogs and cats and ventriloquists and—"

"No." Mrs. Stone remained serious. "There's something different about this and I'm afraid it might be getting deep-seated—something very peculiar."

Evidently she had a theory, or the beginnings of one; but her husband did not press her to explain it, and more amused than disquieted, went out to the small garage in the rear of the yard, got into his car and set forth for his morning's work in good spirits. Little Orvie immediately came from the vicinity of the alley gate, where he had been lurking, entered the garage, closed the sliding door, smiled happily and began to stroke the front of his polka-dotted waist, which still bulked and moved, though he had withdrawn his hand and forearm from within it.

"Good ole Ralph," he said affectionately. "Good ole Ralphie!"

One button of the polka-dotted waist was already unbuttoned, so to speak; Orvie unbuttoned two more and there promptly emerged upon his front the small black bright-eyed head and immature whiskers of a somewhat Scottish-seeming very young pup.

"Good ole Ralphie!" Orvie said, and fondly placed the pup upon the floor.

Then he went to the garage window and looked forth toward the house. Corbena, the colored cook, had just put a pan upon the top step of the rear veranda, Kitty's morning milk, though Kitty himself had not yet arrived from a night's excursion out amongst 'em, a too-frequent habit of his. Corbena retired within the kitchen, leaving the milk exposed, and little Orvie, opening a closet in the garage, brought therefrom two empty tomato cans.

One of these he half filled with fair water at a spigot, and the other he left empty; then he tenderly placed Ralph in a smallish wooden box inside the closet. This box was comfortable for the occupant, having been made soft and warm with rags and straw, and, though Orvie closed down its hinged lid securely, there were holes bored through the wood, here and there, so that the interior air remained, if not precisely fresh, at least breathable. For greater security, Orvie closed the closet door upon that precious box; then, with his two cans, he went forth, and, keeping an eye upon the screen door of the kitchen, made a chemical alteration of Kitty's morning milk.

When he returned to the garage, the tomato can that had held water was empty; but the other contained milk, and Ralph, released from box and closet, enjoyed it. Afterwards he was replaced in the open box, and little Orvie sat beside it upon the floor of the closet and stroked Ralph from nose to tail repeatedly, shook hands with Ralph gently, opened Ralph's mouth, looked long within, and then delicately examined the interiors of both Ralph's ears.

During this orgy of ineffable possession, little Orvie should have been painted by Sir Joshua Reynolds or even by Sir Thomas Lawrence, who carried further than did Sir Joshua the tradition that children at times glow with an unearthly sweetness surpassing the loveliness of flowers. Little Orvie, intrinsically, was anything but a beautiful child; but if Sir Joshua or Sir Thomas had painted him as he was at this moment, modernists would have execrated the portrait for its prettiness.

The intricate insides of Ralph's ears added an element to little Orvie's expression, the element of pride; and he shone with that radiance of young motherhood in discovery that the first-born is not only alive but consists of incredible structural miracles. Into little Orvie there entered the conviction that Ralph, gloriously his own, was incomparably the most magnificently constructed as well as the strongest, handsomest, best-blooded and most unconquerable dog in the whole world.

Such convictions take little account of facts; Orvie was of course not affected by the circumstance that Ralph was a dubious stray, an outcast wandering loosely upon the very streets a few days earlier. In regard to another fact or circumstance, moreover, little Orvie's conviction was likewise obtuse. Ralph, in reality, was a girl; but Orvie had no more doubt that Ralph was a boy than he had that he himself was a boy. His mind couldn't have entertained for one moment a question upon the matter, and, to avoid unnecessary confusion, it seems best for the rest of us to adopt Orvie's view, to regard Ralph in that light and think of her as "he"—at least whenever that is not impossible.

Suddenly the beauteousness of Orvie's expression vanished; he became alert, and his hand, pausing, permitted Ralph's left ear to become less inside out and return to its customary posture. Two voices were heard from without, a little distant; one was Kitty's and the other Corbena's. Kitty miaowed clearly and persistently, and Corbena responded with sympathetic inquiries, such as are addressed to one in trouble. Orvie closed the lid upon little Ralph, stepped out of the closet, closed it, too, went to the door of the garage, opened it slightly and looked toward the house. His mother had just joined Corbena and Kitty upon the back veranda.

"Yes'm," Corbena was saying. "Kitty ack thataway right along lately, mew and miaow breakfast and supper, too, and don' look right to me—Kitty kind o' gaunt-lookin'. Then look at that milk, gone and done the same thing. Look to me like the minute I pour it in the pan it up and turn bluish on me, so Kitty won't take more'n just a li'l some of it and commence miaowin' and mewin'. I thought maybe somep'n in the pan do it, so I changed pans; but no, ma'am, there that milk bluish again as ever!"

"Poor Kitty!" Mrs. Stone said. "She does seem to look rather thin. Corbena, are you sure the milk you put in the pan was—" She paused, and, instead of continuing her thought about the milk, stared in troubled fascination at her son, who was approaching from the garage.

Little Orvie, walking slowly, had the air of an absent-minded stroller concerned with the far-away. He did not look toward his mother, or Corbena or Kitty, seemed unaware of them and in a muse. At the same time, however, he allowed his lips to move slightly in the production of a dreamy sort of barking and whining: "Muff! Muff! Muff! Um-oo-ee! Um-oo-ee! Um-oo-ee!"

Kitty continued to miaow. Mrs. Stone and Corbena, saying nothing, stared at little Orvie.

"Muff! Muff! Muff!" he said dreamily. "Um-oo-ee! Um-oo-ee! Um-oo-ee!"

Then, continuing his apparently absent-minded barking and whining, and paying no attention to the three upon the veranda, he passed round the corner of the house and from their sight. "Dear me!" Mrs. Stone murmured. "What in the world's the matter with him?"

"Yes'm," Corbena agreed. "That child is somep'n more whut turn queer lately. The way he all time bark and whine like li'l pup look to me, Miz Stone, like maybe you better git doctor come and 'tend to him. Child can git out of his right mind same as grown people can."

"Nonsense!" Mrs. Stone said. "Don't be silly, Corbena, It's just one of those habits children get sometimes."

She spoke with some sharpness; nevertheless, her uneasiness about Orvie was increased by this additional barking and whining; for thus not infrequently do the most promising cerebrations of childhood fail to obtain recognition from adults. Little Orvie, if she had but know the truth, was for the first time in his life really using his mind.

Not forward in school, not quotable for bright saying, Orvie in his own field was accomplishing more than either of his parents would have dared to attempt in theirs. They were both more than four times his age; yet he had completely hoodwinked them, had introduced the forbidden stranger into their very house, not a large one, and undetected, had repeatedly provided Ralph with food from their very table and from their Kitty's very pan. More, he had made Ralph his bedfellow, and the technic he here employed, though it necessarily involved risk, could not have been improved upon.

In the evenings while Orvie was at dinner, Ralph occupied a drawer in Orvie's bureau upstairs. Later, when Mrs. Stone had heard Orvie's prayers and seen him in bed, Orvie rose, took Ralph from the drawer, gave him more of Kitty's milk and then slept with him.

In the morning Orvie returned Ralph to the drawer, descended to breakfast, came up afterward and again removed Ralph from the drawer. Ralph then was borne outdoors in the concealment of little Orvie's shirt waist and thus carried to the box in the garage, whence, during the day, all manner of excursions became feasible. Thus the periods of greater danger—when Ralph occupied the bureau drawer—were reduced to a minimum; the only really crucial moments were those during which Mrs. Stone was putting Orvie to bed, and Orvie and Ralph had twice survived them encouragingly.

Here then was ingenuity, true thinking; Mr. and Mrs. Stone could not possibly have concealed a dog from him as he did from them. But, as if this were not enough, little Orvie's mind soared higher still. There were matters in which Ralph could not be made to understand the requisites for his own safety. As valet, so to say, Orvie did the best he could; but, in the detail of barking and whining, proved himself open to those inspirations sometimes called streaks of genius.

By barking and whining frequently himself, he accustomed his parents and Corbena to hear such sounds in and about the house, and thus planned to provide Ralph—if Ralph's own voice should sometimes be heard—with an alibi.

Such was little Orvie's single-hearted purpose, and such had been his skill in carrying it out that Ralph was now well into his third day of residence with

Mr. and Mrs. Stone without their even dreaming they were that hospitable. Mentally, little Orvie was growing.

Intellectual progress, however, was anything but his mother's interpretation of what was the matter with him, and Mr. Stone also began to take a gloomy view of him at lunch that day. He sent an annoyed side glance in his son's direction. "Orvie, don't sing at the table."

"No, Papa," Orvie said, and barked reticently, as if to himself, "Muff!"

"Don't imitate animals either."

"Animals?" Orvie asked. "No, Papa. Muff! Um-oo-ee!"

"Orvard, did you hear me?"

"Yes, Papa." Orvie was silent; but, after a moment or two, ventured to bark again softly.

"Orvard!" Mr. Stone, staring imperiously at his son, became aware of the odd appearance of Orvie's plate. "Well, I declare!"

Mrs. Stone, preoccupied, looked up. "What's the matter?"

"His plate," her husband said. "Look at it! I just gave him a chop and French-fried potatoes and now there's nothing there. Not a thing! Why, he must eat like an anaconda!"

"Oh, no!" Mrs. Stone protested gently; but she added, "You must learn not to gulp down your food, Orvie; it'll give you indigestion."

"Indigestion!" Orvie's father exclaimed, and he stared harder at the empty plate. "Why, even the bone's gone! Where is it? Orvie, did you drop that chop bone on the floor? Where is it?"

"Where's what, Papa?"

"That chop!" Mr. Stone got up and looked at the rug upon which the table stood. "No, there's nothing there. Where'd it go?"

"Where'd what go, Papa?"

"That chop!" Mr. Stone sat down at his place again. "That chop, or at least the bone! You could eat the chop; but you certainly couldn't eat the bone. Nobody could. What became of it? Did you see it fall?"

"Fall?" Orvie asked. "Fall, Papa?"

"Yes, fall! Fall, fall, fall! If it didn't fall off your plate, where did it go?"

"You mean my chop, Papa?"

"Yes, I do! What became of it?"

Orvie was thoughtful; then seemed to brighten a little. "Maybe it fell out the window, Papa."

"The window?" Mr. Stone breathed heavily. "Ten feet away and with a wire screen in it? Fell out of it?"

Orvie looked absent-minded. "Muff! Muff! Muff!" he said. "Um-oo-ee!"

"Oh, dear!" his father exclaimed, depressed. "Oh, dear me!"

"What, Papa?"

"Nothing!" Mr. Stone simply gave up thinking about the chop bone. Fathers and mothers, confronted frequently by the inexplicable, acquire this rather helpless habit of allowing mysteries to pass unsolved. Orvie applied himself to bread and milk, having just proved that for the sake of Ralph he was glad to deprive himself as well as Kitty. Unobserved legerdemain had removed the chop, with only one small bite out of it, to the interior of his shirt waist, where also were a handful of French-fried potatoes and a few of Ralph's hairs. Beneath Orvie's polka-dotted surface and about his upper middle, that is to say, little Orvie for two days had been far from neat. Bacon, toast, buttered bread, bits of steak and broiled chicken and even cereal had lain against him there during and after recent meals; he was no dietitian and fondly offered Ralph as wide a choice as he could.

"Muff!" he said, finishing his milk. "Um-oo-ee! I'm all through. Can I go out in the yard now, Mamma?"

She nodded gravely, not speaking; whereupon, uttering a few petty barks as he went, he ran outdoors. Mr. Stone, who had arrived after his wife and son had sat down to lunch, glanced across the table inquiringly. "Well, what's on your mind?" he asked, alluding to the preoccupation that had made her unusually silent.

"I'm really getting worried," she informed him. "Really, I mean. Something else happened this morning."

"Something else? Something else than what?"

"Than his barking," she said. "Listen, please. This summer I've been trying to have Orvie begin to cultivate self-reliance, so I've been having him look
after his clothes, to a certain extent, himself. That is, he's supposed to hang
them up when he takes them off, put what's soiled in the clothes basket and
when he puts on fresh ones, get them out of his bureau drawer himself. This
morning about eleven the laundry came and Corbena took Orvie's to his
room to put in his bureau. I wish you'd seen what she found in the middle
drawer! One of his best little white cambric waists with ruffled collars absolutely mangled—almost torn to pieces. She knew when she put it there last
week it was in perfect condition. What's your explanation? What do you think
made him do such a thing?"

"Who?" Mr. Stone asked. "Orvie? You don't mean he did it himself?"

She nodded solemnly. "He admitted it."

"What?"

"He did," Mrs. Stone said. "I called him in and he came in barking. I
showed him the waist and asked him what had happened to it. First he said
he thought Kitty must have done it; but when I showed him how absurd that
was, he admitted he did it himself. I asked him how, and he said he 'guessed he
must have gnawed it'! Those were his very words! What do you say to that?"

"I don't know, I'm sure. It seems odd, but—"

"Odd!" she exclaimed. "Don't you think maybe it's a case for one of
these psychopathic doctors or whatever they call them? Corbena thinks it is.
Corbena said herself we ought to get—"

"Never mind," Mr. Stone said. "I don't care what Corbena thinks we ought
to do. Why did Orvie gnaw it? How did he explain doing such a thing?"

"He didn't explain it. When I asked him why he did it, he'd just say, 'What,
Mamma?' and then make those noises, and that's what upset me the worst.
Do you suppose it could be possible that a child could want something so
long and talk about it so much and brood upon it so intensely that in time
he'd—well, that in time he'd almost begin to have the delusion that he'd
turned into the thing he'd wanted so much?"

"What?" Mr. Stone stared at his wife incredulously, and then, in despair over the elasticities of her imagination, laughed aloud. "Your theory is that Orvie's wanted a dog so long that now he's begun to believe he's a dog himself? So you want a psychoanalyst to prove to him that he's really a boy? Is that your idea?"

"No," she said, annoyed; but nevertheless added, "Still, it's certainly very strange. It's easy for you to make fun of me; but will you kindly tell me why he does all this barking and whining and why he gnawed his little cambric waist like that?"

"Good heavens! There's nothing very strange about a boy's playing to himself that he's a pup. You've heard him playing he's a whole railroad engine, haven't you?" This was spoken confidently; nevertheless, a meeting he had with his son, a few minutes later in the front yard, brought curious doubts into Mr. Stone's mind. As was his custom at noon, he had left his car before the house at the curbstone, and he was on his way to it when Orvie came from the back yard, barking indistinctly.

"Orvie! Where are you going?"

Until thus questioned, Orvie had not observed his father; he betrayed hesitation and embarrassment. Walking slowly, he again had his right hand inside his shirt waist and seemed to be scratching himself strongly. "What, Papa?" He paused at a distance from his father and turned partly away.

"Where are you going?"

"Only across the street to Freddie and Babe's house, Papa," Orvie said, and added quickly and with some emphasis, "Muff! Muff! Um-oo-ee! Um-oo-ee! Muff! Muff!"

"Come here," Mr. Stone said, "What do you want to bark all the time for like that? Come here!"

Orvie moved a few sidelong steps and paused, still keeping his shoulder and back toward his father as much as seemed plausible. The situation, indeed, appeared critical; for Ralph, whom he was carrying inside his shirt waist to show confidentially to the little cousins, Babe and Freddie, had all at once begun to feel lively. Ralph, in fact, was not only squirming in an almost unbearably tickling manner but was also chewing at his young master's fragile undergarment, rending it and at the same time abrading actual surfaces of the young master. To have so much going on sub rosa yet directly under Mr. Stone's eye, and simultaneously to maintain an air of aplomb, was difficult.

For more than two days Ralph had been accustomed to seclusions and inclosures; his adaptation of himself to these environments had hitherto been such a marvel of meekness, or inanity, that Orvie had been encouraged to believe the routine might be carried on permanently, or at least during his own lifetime. Now, however, Ralph, it seemed, desired to frolic, and did frolic—wished, too, a broader field and to gambol in the open air, though apparently he thought that his route thither lay not through the shirt waist but through Orvie. No doubt the legend of the Spartan boy who permitted the fox to gnaw his vitals arose from some such affair and was later poetically garbled; probably the Spartan boy's parents wouldn't let him have a fox.

"Stop scratching yourself!" Mr. Stone said. "Have you got chiggers? What's the matter with you?"

"Nothing, Papa. I——" Orvie interrupted himself, for to his horror Ralph, though briefly, became vocal in a light bark, which had to be covered. Orvie turned his back upon his father and began to walk toward the street, barking loudly.

"Stop that!" Mr. Stone said. "Stop that silly barking, stand still and listen to me!"

"Yes, Papa." Orvie halted tentatively and looked back over his shoulder. "What you want, Papa? Muff! Muff! Um-oo-ee! Um-oo-ee! I got to go over to Babe and Freddie's now, Papa. Muff!"

"Listen to me!" Mr. Stone said, advancing. "Stop all this barking. At your age if you get a habit like that——"

"Yes, Papa. I——Muff!" Orvie said hurriedly, and moved on toward the sidewalk. "Muff! Muff! Ouch! I got to go now, Papa. Honest, I— Um-oo-ee! Papa, I——Muff! Muff!"

Mr. Stone let him go, and, frowning, watched him as he ran barking across the street and into the yard opposite. It could not be denied that little Orvie's behavior was peculiar, at least tinged with something suggestive of a kind of lunacy; and his father, stepping into the waiting automobile, nervously recalled the mystery of the chop bone at lunch. Could it be that Orvie had hidden that bone about his person, intending to bury it later and then dig it up, perhaps? A canine impersonation that would go to such lengths did seem almost unnaturally realistic, and Mr. Stone, as he drove down town, was in fact a little disturbed about his son.

That son, meanwhile, in Freddie's and Babe's yard, had stopped barking, and, after employing his voice for some time in an attempt at yodeling meant to let those within know that he waited for them without, was joined upon the lawn by his two little cousins. He had kept his happy secret to himself about as long as he could; his constantly swelling pride in Ralph, and in himself as owner, now restlessly pressed him to excite the envy of pupless contemporaries.

"What you want, Orvie?" Babe inquired, and she added, "You look awful dirty. Little Cousin M'ree from Kansas City and Cousin Sadie and Cousin Josie are comin' to play with me this afternoon pretty soon. You and Freddie better go somewheres and play by yourselfs because the rest of us'll be all girls and clean."

"Listen," Orvie said. "Freddie, if I show you and Babe a secret will you promise you'll never tell anybody?"

Interested, both Babe and Freddie promised.

"I mean you haf to promise you'll never tell anybody in the whole world or you rather die," Orvie said; and, when they agreed to this, he led them behind a clump of lilac bushes, opened his shirt waist and displayed his treasure.

"Look there," he said. "Its name's Ralph."

Both Freddie and Babe were immediately ecstatic, though Babe interrupted herself to tell Orvie he looked terrible inside the shirt waist and ought to be ashamed to keep Ralph in such an awful place; then shouting, she had something like a little fight with Freddie, as both claimed the privilege simultaneously of holding Ralph against their cheeks to feel how soft he was.

Orvie became nervous. "For good heavens goodnesses sakes hush up!" he said, glancing toward the house. "Here! You give me back my dog!" Decisively he took Ralph from them and restored him into the interior of his shirt waist. "I guess I got enough trouble having Papa and Mama not find out Ralph's my dog without your making all this fuss!"

Babe resented the sequestration of Ralph; she wanted to play with him, made efforts to obtain possession of him, and, when forcible repulsed, became threatening. "You just wait, Orvie Stone! Wait till your papa and mamma find out you got a dog!"

Orvie had to remind her of the consequences of broken honor. "You promised you'd never tell and you'll be a dirty ole story-teller if you do and I'll tell everybody you are one too!"

"I won't tell, Orvie," Babe said coaxingly. "Orvie, please give me that dear little puppy."

"No!"

"I mean just to play with," Babe said. "Orvie, please let me play with that dear little puppy just half an hour. Please, Orvie—"

"No!"

"Of course he won't," Freddie said to Babe. "Orvie's going to let me have Ralph to play with now because I and Orvie are boys and—"

"No!" Orvie said, and buttoned up his shirt waist, inclosing Ralph from view.

At this, naturally, both Freddie and Babe were antagonized, and, as it happened that a sedan just then deposited three speckless little girls upon the sidewalk before the gate, the brother and sister ran to greet the newcomers and to speak at once unfavorably of Orvie, who remained behind the clump of lilacs.

" 'Lo, M'ree, 'lo, Josie, 'lo, Sadie," Babe said. "Dirty ole Orvie's here. He's over behind those bushes because he's got a secret."

"It's in his clo'es," Freddie explained. "It's a secret and I and Babe promised not to tell; but he's got it in his clo'es. Come on look at him and see if you can guess what it is; it's alive."

Little Marie from Kansas City, little Josie and little Sadie shouted with cruel pleasure. "Dirty ole Orvie!" they cried. "Come on! Come on! Come on!"

Thus Orvie, rushed upon, found himself driven from the shelter of the lilac bushes, and decided to leave for home. His five little cousins, however, made his departure difficult; they surrounded him, screaming merrily and spitefully, jostled him, poked him; and in this process the right forefinger of little Marie from Kansas City was electrified by the sensation of encountering a protuberance that squirmed.

She shrieked sincerely in horror. "Oh, oh, oh! He's got a rat in there! It's a rat or a cat or maybe a snake! Oh, you bad dirty little Orvie!"

"I am not!" Orvie cried. "It is not!" Infuriated, both on his own account and Ralph's, and, too, because he never did get on well with little Marie from Kansas City, he became indiscreet. "I have not got any ole rat or ole dirty cat or any snake in here! It's something I wouldn't let you touch even its tail if you cried your ole eyes out begging me!"

"Tail! Tail! Tail!" shouted little Josie and little Sadie, prodding insanely at Orvie. "It's got a tail! It's got a tail! It's got a tail!"

"Its name is Ralph!" Babe cried. "I didn't promise I wouldn't tell what its name was, Orvie. I'm not a story-teller for only tellin' what its name is."

Upon this, little Josie, little Sadie and little Marie from Kansas City were inspired to guess the rest. "It's a dog!" they cried simultaneously. "It's a dog!"

"Yes," Freddie said. "And his papa and mamma won't let him have one either. I didn't promise I wouldn't tell that, because everybody knows it anyways, Orvie."

"Story-tellers!" Orvie shouted at the top of his voice. "Babe and Freddie are dirty ole story-tellers and so's everybody else! You're all every one dirty ole story-tellers!"

"We are not! You're one yourself!" they all assured him, and then, as he bitterly hustled his way out from among them and ran to the street, they ran after him.

Little Marie made her voice piercing. "Orvie's got! Orvie's got! Orvie's got!" she cried, leaving what Orvie had to the imagination of dangerous adult listeners and terrifying him with this imminent menace to his secret. "Orvie's got! Orvie's got! Orvie's got!"

The others took it up. "Orvie's got! Orvie's got! Orvie's got!" they chanted delightedly, pursued him across the street and into his own yard. There he knew not where to turn. With the pack upon him, and the windows of the house open, so that at any moment his mother might hear, comprehend and look forth, he did not dare go to the garage to hide Ralph, nor to enter the house, nor to remain in the yard—nor to run away, when Freddie, Babe, Josie, Sadie and little Marie from Kansas City would certainly run whooping after him. All resources failed him.

"You go home!" he shouted, knowing helplessly how futile this assertion of his rights. "This is my yard and you got to everyone go home, you ole dirty story-tellers you! Go home!"

They enlarged their threat by a monosyllable. "Orvie's got a!" they chanted. "Orvie's got a! Orvie's got a! Orvie's got a!"

Corbena appeared at a kitchen window, obviously interested. Orvie, perceiving her and in terror lest the chanters should complete their chorus with the fatal word "dog," bawled incoherences at the top of his voice to drown them out. "Baw! Waw! Waw! Boo! Yoo! Yoo!"

Tauntingly little Marie chanted the first sound of the word "dog." "Orvie's got a duh!"

The rest took this up immediately. "Orvie's got a duh! Orvie's got a duh! Orvie's got a duh!"

"Baw! Waw! Waw! I have not! You're all story-tellers! Baw! Waw! Waw! Yoo! Yoo!"

They danced about him, encircling him. "Orvie's got a duh!" And then little Josie, the youngest of the group, piercingly added, "awg!" So that Orvie, though he bawled his loudest, feared Corbena might have heard the ruinous completion, "Orvie's got a duh—awg!"

Corbena had, in fact, heard just that. Her interest increased as she looked from the window and listened to the screeching. Then, returning to a polishing of the stove, she engaged herself in thought; but presently, looking forth again, saw that the five little cousins, following some new caprice, were racing back to the yard across the street.

Orvie, brooding, was walking toward the garage, and Corbena decided upon a line of conduct she would follow. No doubt she was influenced by an ill-founded partiality she had always felt for Kitty.

Kitty, as a matter of fact, was usually no bad hand at looking out for himself. True, he was subject to the seemingly haphazard misfortunes of life, as are we all, and the long arm of disastrous coincidence could at any time reach him; but he lived with a bold craftiness solely for himself and seldom failed to take care of Number 1. Orvie, entering the garage with Ralph in his bosom, or a little below, heard a sinisterly eloquent sound as he approached the door of the closet, which he had carelessly left open as he had the lid of the box also.

Ralph, rather overfed, had been indifferent to the chop and French-fried potatoes brought him from the lunch table, had allowed them to remain in the box almost untouched, and now, later, when he might have taken pleasure in them, another was doing that for him.

Kitty, though not aware to whom he owed the blueness of his daily milk, was getting even and didn't intend to be balked. Kitty, that is to say, was in Ralph's box eating Ralph's chop, and the eloquent sound Orvie heard as he came near was the police siren inside of Kitty turned on in nasty warning.

"Get out o' there!" Orvie cried indignantly, and accompanied his words with furious gestures. "Get out o' my dog's own box, you bad ole cat you!"

Kitty rose up out of the box in a tall, dangerous manner, sirening and with his teeth fixed in the chop and the bone projecting like a deformity ever to be part of him; anesthetics and surgeons might remove this chop from him, he made clear, but nothing less should do it. Stepping testily, and with head and chop and rigid tail held high, he went forth with no undue haste, daring all hell to intercept him. He disappeared proudly into the golden light of outdoors.

"You bad ole cat you!" Intimidated, Orvie spoke feebly, though none the less bitterly, for this was the second time Kitty had been caught—so to speak—robbing Ralph's box. "You'll see, you ole cat you! I'll show you!"

Orvie didn't know how or what he was going to show Kitty, but later in the afternoon seized upon an opportunity to show him at least a little something. Having made a sketchy leash and collar out of a length of discarded clothesline, he gave Ralph some too-early lessons in "heeling" in the alley, and, returning, found Kitty again in the box. This time, however, Orvie neither bellowed nor made threatening gestures, but quietly closed the lid on Kitty. Kitty made a few objections; and then, after trifling with cold French-fried potatoes in the dark, philosophically took a nap until Orvie came back from another excursion, raised the lid and said severely, "There! That'll teach you, I guess, you ole cat you!"

Kitty yawned, left the box and walked languidly away; showed so much indifference, indeed, that Orvie was galled.

"You listen, you ole Kitty you!" he called fiercely. "Next time I catch you in my dog's box I'm goin' to slam the lid down and fasten it and keep you in there all day! You better look out!"

Kitty paid not the slightest attention and even had the hardihood to return within the hour, seat himself in Orvie's presence, look at the box and miaow inquiringly.

"You—" Orvie began; but a summons into the house prevented him from further expressing his emotion. Corbena called loudly from the kitchen door.

"Li'l Orvie! You out'n 'at garage? You come in here. You' mamma want you ri' now."

Orvie put Ralph in the box, fastened the lid down, closed the door of the closet and noisily gave himself the pleasure of seeing Kitty precede him into the house.

"Shame!" Corbena said, holding open the screen door of the kitchen for Kitty, but closing it before Orvie arrived. "Shame on you to holler and chase Kitty thataway! No, you ain' go' come in my kitchen and holler and chase Kitty some more. You go round and go in front door and walk upstairs to you' mamma. Go on now! I got somep'n else to do 'cept argue!"

Her words held a meaning hidden from little Orvie, a meaning that would have chilled his blood had he understood it; and, while he was following the route she had insisted upon, and being kept upstairs for a sufficient time by his mother, Corbena completed a brief but thorough investigation. Mrs. Stone, who made a pretext to have little Orvie change his clothes under her own eye, also learned much; and, when Mr. Stone arrived at the house after his day's work, she met him at the front door, drew him into the living room and told him all.

"Two days!" she said, approaching the conclusion of her narrative. "Three days really by this time, and two nights! In the daytime he keeps it in that box in the garage whenever he hasn't got it out playing with it; though when he slips it into the house and up to his room he must carry it inside his waist—I wish you'd seen conditions there!—and Corbena found a rope collar and leash that he leads it by, probably in the alley. Then, when he comes in and goes upstairs to wash his hands and face before dinner, he hides it in his bureau drawer—that's what happened to his cambric ruffled waist—then, after I put him in bed, he gets up and takes it out of the drawer and sleeps with it. Oh, there's no doubt about it! Corbena and I worked it all out. What makes us sure he's had this dog for two whole days without our knowing it, Corbena remembered it was day before yesterday he brought down that box from the attic and carried it out to the garage. What on earth do you think?"

"I don't know." Mr. Stone sighed; then blew out an audible breath suggesting a faint kind of laughter. "In a way it's almost a relief—I mean, to know that he hasn't been getting woozy in the head on account of this dog mania of his. Of course that's why he's been barking—in the hope we mightn't notice if the dog himself barked. Not so dumb, you know! Really seems to show he has ideas—peculiar ones, but at least ideas. What have you done about it? What have you said to Orvie?"

"Nothing. He doesn't dream we even suspect. I waited to see what you'd say, so we could decide together."

"I see." Mr. Stone pondered. "What sort of dog is he?"

"He?" Mrs. Stone uttered a half-hushed outcry. "It isn't! Corbena says it's very small but terribly mongrel, and the worst of it is it's a she!"

"Well, that settles it," Mr. Stone said. "Of course that settles it."

"Yes, of course; but how am I to—"

"Wait," he said. "Let me handle this. I see just what to do."

"Do you?" Mrs. Stone was doubtful. "If you simply mean to call Orvie in and take that dog away from him and tell him he can't have it, I won't answer for the shock to his nervous system. I don't think it should be managed that way."

"Neither do I!" her husband protested. "Don't you think I have any regard for the child's feelings? Don't you suppose I know it's one thing to tell him he can't have a dog and quite another thing to take a dog away from him after he's actually got one? Naturally, I intend to use some diplomacy."

"What kind of diplomacy? I don't see—"

"Listen," he interrupted. "We don't want to get Orvie all harrowed up, or to be harrowed up ourselves. We'll simply let him believe the pup's got out of the box, wandered away and got lost. If we do that, why, of course Orvie'll think maybe he'll find it again some day, so he won't feel too badly about it. For a while he'll poke around looking for it and whistling, of course; then he'll forget all about it."

"I hope so."

"Of course he will," Mr. Stone said. "We won't say a thing to Orvie, and you mustn't let Corbena speak of it to him, either. What's more, he can have the pup sleep with him tonight and we'll let him have another morning and most of the afternoon, too, for that matter, playing with it—pretty near a whole day—and then, toward evening, it'll simply be missing and he won't have so very long to worry about it before bedtime comes and he goes to sleep. Next morning when he wakes up, he'll hardly think of it at all."

"I hope so," she said again. "I do hope so!"

"Why, certainly!" Mr. Stone reassured her. "Tomorrow after lunch I'll have Elmore Jones come down to my office and I'll give him a couple of dollars to drive up here later in his car and take the pup quietly away."

"Elmore Jones? You mean that awful old colored man who used to be a sort of gardener at your father's and stole the lawn mower?"

"That was when Elmore was drinking," Mr. Stone explained, and laughed, though he was little nettled by the criticism of his judgment she seemed to imply. "Father was rather hard on him about that and the rest of us give Elmore little jobs when we can, to help him out. He's got an old car now that he uses as a sort of a truck, and he's perfectly reliable."

"But if he comes in here and walks out to the garage and takes the pup out of that box, and Orvie sees him—"

"Oh, dear me!" Mr. Stone sighed. "Orvie won't be here to see him—not unless you let him. I'll instruct Elmore Jones to come and get the pup tomorrow afternoon at five o'clock exactly; and you can arrange for Orvie to be across the street at Babe's and Freddie's, playing with them, from half-past four to half-past five, can't you?"

"Yes," she said thoughtfully, then looked more cheerful. "Why, yes, I believe that would work out all right. I'll tell Winnie about it this evening and ask her to make sort of a little party of it. I'll get her to ask some of the other children and I'll take Orvie over there myself, between four and half past, and tell him he can stay till almost six o'clock. I'll ask Winnie to have cookies and lemonade and little games, so he'll have a nice happy time; and that way, it seems to me, with a long happy day and a little party to remember—and of course just thinking his pup's lost and may come back some time—why, probably, he won't be much upset."

"Of course he won't," her husband agreed. "Besides that, it isn't as if we were doing anything rather cruel to this pup, because Elmore Jones'll simply take it out in the country twenty-five or thirty miles and leave it near some farmhouse or other, where people usually are glad to have a dog and—"

"Yes," Mrs. Stone said, almost with enthusiasm. "People who live 'way out in the country like that are kind to dogs. They're nearly always glad to find one and give it a good home; so of course we're really not—"

"No, of course we're not. It isn't like telling Elmore Jones to take Orvie's pup out and drown it. No; we're doing the best we can under the circumstances, and I really don't think Orvie'll mind at all."

"No," Mrs. Stone agreed. "I don't think he will, either—not to speak of."

Then, though both parents were thoughtful and perhaps slightly apprehensive, not to say remorseful, they ended by stimulating themselves with something like an exchange of congratulations upon having discovered a plan that would depress their little son's spirits in the least possible degree. On the following afternoon, however, at about ten minutes before six, when Mr. Stone came into the house, he found his wife in a pathetic mood. She was looking out of one of the living-room windows and didn't turn when he approached her.

"How—how did it go?" he asked somewhat hesitantly. "How did Orvie take it?"

"I don't know." She sniffled abruptly, turned and allowed him to see that her eyes were moist and not free from reproachfulness. "Oh, your plan was carried out—carried out quite perfectly! Your old Elmore Jones was here at five. I heard him in the kitchen and Corbena telling him what to do; so it's gone. Orvie's just come back from Winnie's. He's upstairs."

"What did he say?"

"Nothing," Mrs. Stone replied huskily. "Of course he knows, because this is the time he always takes it upstairs and puts it in the bureau drawer, so of course he's been out there—to the empty box. I kept out of his way—just listened to him running upstairs—I felt I simply couldn't face him. I do wonder if you've been really right in doing this to him. I do wonder."

"I!" her husband exclaimed. "Wonder if I'm really right? Me? Didn't you tell me—" He paused. Corbena stood in the doorway.

"Dinner serve'," she said, glanced about the room questioningly and added in a solemn voice, addressing herself to Mrs. Stone, "Milk in 'at pan I set on back porch fer Kitty done gone blue on me again."

"Blue?" Mr. Stone said. "Blue milk? What do you mean, Corbena?"

Corbena's solemnity increased. "Blue," she said. "Milk blue again. Elmore Jones come five o'clock like Miz Stone tell me he goin' to; but he ain't no right bright nice-actin' colored man, Elmore Jones ain't. He come in my kitchen, say he goin' be rich man soon. I say, 'Don' blow all 'at gin in my face, Elmore Jones! Go on open the closet in the garage, git that pup out that box in the closet and go on away from here.' He say, yes'm that box whut he come fer, not me, and shambled on out. I tooken a look in my oven, then I heard him shut the garage door and I went and looked out and he was goin' out the alley gate wif 'at box under his arm. 'I got him!' Elmore Jones holler at me. 'He in here all right,' Elmore Jones holler. Then I heard Elmore Jones's ole clatterbox automobile buzz-chuggin' away. How fur you tell Elmore to go, Mr. Stone?"

"Why, I told him to go twenty-five or thirty—"

Corbena, though interrupting, seemed merely to meditate aloud. "Li'l Orvie come back from his aunt's house 'cross the street li'l while after you tooken him over there this afternoon, Miz Stone. Then he gone back again. I see him pass my kitchen window; and, come to 'member, I didn' tooken no notice then, but seem to me now like he was actin' like he scratchin' hisself under his li'l shirt." Corbena paused and again looked about the room questioningly. "Kitty nowhere in here, Miz Stone?"

"Kitty? No."

"No, Kitty certainly ain't here," Corbena said. "Elmore Jones tell me Mr. Stone done hand him fi'-dolluh bill; tell me he ain't spen' more'n half of it. Miz Stone, you see poor Kitty anywheres at all since about four o'clock?"

"No!" Mrs. Stone gasped. "Oh, my goodness!"

Mr. Stone, staring haggardly, strode out into the hall and halfway up the stairs, but there he paused.

His ascending footsteps must have been heard overhead, for, as he halted, little Orvie's voice promptly became audible.

"Muff! Muff! Muff!" The barking grew louder as Orvie approached the head of the stairway to descend for dinner. "Muff! Um-oo-ee! Um-oo-ee! Um-oo-ee!"

Artistically, the imitated whining was of course plaintive; yet the voice that produced it had never sounded more contented. "Muff! Muff!" said little Orvie: "Um-oo-ee!"

Mr. Stone returned down the stairs he had just impetuously ascended and made a pitiable effort to seem unconscious of how his wife and Corbena were looking at him.

LASSIE COME-HOME
(1938)
Eric Knight

No dog story ever written has been more influential than "Lassie Come-Home." The original story was expanded into a novel in 1940 and later evolved into a long-running American television series. It has been made into several different movies, most recently in 2006 with Peter O'Toole playing the part of the Duke of Rudling, who buys Lassie from a struggling Yorkshire coal-mining family and takes the collie away to Scotland.

Author Eric Knight (1897–1943) was born in England, but immigrated to America at age fifteen. During World War II he served as a major in a U.S. army film unit. Knight continued to write during the war, but his career ended prematurely when he was killed in a military transport plane crash. In addition to "Lassie," Knight also wrote *The Flying Yorkshireman* (1938), *The Happy Land* (1940), and *This Above All* (1941).

The dog had met the boy by the school gate for five years. Now she couldn't understand that times were changed and she wasn't supposed to be there any more. But the boy knew.

So when he opened the door of the cottage, he spoke before he entered.

"Mother," he said, "Lassie's come home again."

He waited a moment, as if in hope of something. But the man and woman inside the cottage did not speak.

"Come in, Lassie," the boy said.

He held open the door, and the tricolor collie walked in obediently. Going head down, as a collie when it knows something is wrong, it went to the rug and lay down before the hearth, a black-white-and-gold aristocrat. The man, sitting on a low stool by the fireside, kept his eyes turned away. The woman went to the sink and busied herself there.

"She were waiting at school for me, just like always," the boy went on. He spoke fast, as if racing against time. "She must ha' got away again. I thought, happen this time, we might just——"

"No!" the woman exploded.

The boy's carelessness dropped. His voice rose in pleading.

"But this time, mother! Just this time. We could hide her. They wouldn't ever know."

"Dogs, dogs, dogs!" the woman cried. The words poured from her as if the boy's pleading had been a signal gun for her own anger. "I'm sick o' hearing about tykes round this house. Well, she's sold and gone and done with, so the quicker she's taken back the better. Now get her back quick, or first thing ye know we'll have Hynes round here again. Mr. Hynes!"

Her voice sharpened in imitation of the Cockney accent of the south. "Hi know you Yorkshiremen and yer come-'ome dogs. Training yer dogs to come 'ome so's yer can sell 'em hover and hover again."

"Well, she's sold, so ye can take her out o' my house and home to them as bought her!"

The boy's bottom lip crept out stubbornly, and there was silence in the cottage. Then the dog lifted its head and nudged the man's hand, as a dog will when asking for patting. But the man drew away and stared, silently, into the fire.

The boy tried again, with the ceaseless guile of a child, his voice coaxing.

"Look, feyther, she wants thee to bid her welcome. Aye, she's that glad to be home. Happen they don't tak' good care on her up there? Look, her coat's a bit poorly, don't ye think? A bit o' linseed strained through her drinking water—that's what I'd gi' her."

Still looking in the fire, the man nodded. But the woman, as if perceiving the boy's new attack, sniffed.

"Aye, tha wouldn't be a Carraclough if tha didn't know more about tykes nor breaking eggs wi' a stick. Nor a Yorkshireman. My goodness, it seems to me sometimes that chaps in this village thinks more on their tykes nor they do o' their own flesh and blood. They'll sit by their firesides and let their own bairns starve so long a t' dog gets fed."

The man stirred, suddenly, but the boy cut in quickly.

"But she does look thin. Look, truly—they're not feeding her right. Just look!"

"Aye," the woman chattered. "I wouldn't put it past Hynes to steal t' best part o' t' dog meat for himself. And Lassie always was a strong eater."

"She's fair thin now," the boy said.

Almost unwillingly the man and woman looked at the dog for the first time.

"My gum, she is off a bit," the woman said. Then she caught herself. "Ma goodness, I suppose I'll have to fix her a bit o' summat. She can do wi' it. But soon as she's fed, back she goes. And never another dog I'll have in my house.

Never another. Cooking and nursing for 'em, and as much trouble to bring up as a bairn!"

So, grumbling and chatting as a village woman will, she moved about, warming a pan of food for the dog. The man and boy watched the collie eat. When it was done, the boy took from the mantelpiece a folded cloth and a brush, and began prettying the collie's coat. The man watched for several minutes, and then could stand it no longer.

"Here," he said.

He took the cloth and brush from the boy and began working expertly on the dog, rubbing the rich, deep coat, then brushing the snowy whiteness of the full ruff and the apron, bringing out the heavy leggings on the forelegs. He lost himself in his work, and the boy sat on the rug, watching contentedly. The woman stood it as long as she could.

"Now will ye please tak' that tyke out o' here?"

The man flared in anger.

"Well, ye wouldn't have me tak' her back looking like a mucky Monday wash, wouldta?"

He bent again, and began fluffing out the collie's petticoats.

"Joe!" the woman pleaded. "Will ye tak' her out o' here? Hynes'll be nosing round afore ye know it. And I won't have that man in my house. Wearing his hat inside, and going on like he's the duke himself—him and his leggings!"

"All right, lass."

"And this time, Joe, tak' young Joe wi' ye."

"What for?"

"Well, let's get the business done and over with. It's him that Lassie runs away for. She comes for young Joe. So if he went wi' thee, and told her to stay, happen she'd be content and not run away no more, and then we'd have a little peace and quiet in the home—though heaven knows there's not much hope o' that these days, things being like they are." The woman's voice trailed away, as if she would soon cry in weariness.

The man rose. "Come, Joe," he said. " Get thy cap."

The Duke of Rudling walked along the gravel paths of his place with his granddaughter, Philippa. Philippa was a bright and knowing young woman, allegedly the only member of the duke's family he could address in unspotted language. For it was also alleged that the duke was the most irascible, vile-tempered old man in the three Ridings of Yorkshire.

"Country going to pot!" the duke roared, stabbing at the walk with his great blackthorn stick. "When I was a young man! Hah! Women today not as pretty. Horses today not as fast. As for dogs—ye don't see dogs today like——"

Just then the duke and Philippa came round a clump of rhododendrons and saw a man, a boy and a dog.

"Ah," said the duke, in admiration. Then his brow knotted. "Damme, Carraclough! What're ye doing with my dog?"

He shouted it quite as if the others were in the next county, for it was also the opinion of the Duke of Rudling that people were not nearly so keen of hearing as they used to be when he was a young man.

"It's Lassie," Carraclough said. "She runned away again and I brought her back."

Carraclough lifted his cap, and poked the boy to do the same, not in any servile gesture, but to show that they were as well brought up as the next.

"Damme, ran away again!" the duke roared. "And I told that utter nin-compoop Hynes to—where is he? Hynes! Hynes! Damme, Hynes, what're ye hiding for?"

"Coming, your lordship!" sounded a voice, far away behind the shrub-beries. And, soon Hynes appeared, a sharp-faced man in check coat, riding breeches, and the cloth leggings that grooms wear.

"Take this dog," roared the duke, "and pen her up! And damme, if she breaks out again, I'll—I'll——"

The duke waved his great stick threateningly, and then, without so much as a thank you or kiss the back of my hand to Joe Carraclough, he went stamping and muttering away.

"I'll pen 'er up," Hynes muttered, when the duke was gone. "And if she ever gets awye agyne, I'll——"

He made as if to grab the dog, but Joe Carraclough's hob-nailed boot trod heavily on Hynes' foot.

"I brought my lad wi' me to bid her stay, so we'll pen her up this time. Eigh—sorry! I didn't see I were on thy foot. Come, Joe, lad."

They walked down the crunching gravel path, along by the neat kennel buildings. When Lassie was behind the closed door, she raced into the high wire run where she could see them as they went. She pressed close against the wire, waiting.

The boy stood close, too, his fingers through the meshes touching the dog's nose.

"Go on, lad," his father ordered "Bid her stay!"

The boy looked around, as if for help that he did not find. He swallowed, and then spoke, low and quickly.

"Stay here, Lassie, and don't come home no more," he said. "And don't come to school for me no more. Because I don't want to see ye no more. 'Cause tha's a bad dog, and we don't love thee no more, and we don't want thee. So stay there forever and leave us be, and don't never come home no more."

Then he turned, and because it was hard to see the path plainly, he stumbled. But his father, who was holding his head very high as they walked away from Hynes, shook him savagely, and snapped roughly: "Look where tha's going!"

Then the boy trotted beside his father. He was thinking that he'd never be able to understand why grownups sometimes were so bad-tempered with you, just when you needed them most.

After that, there were days and days that passed, and the dog did not come to the school gate any more. So then it was not like old times. There were so many things that were not like old times.

The boy was thinking that as he came wearily up the path and opened the cottage door and heard his father's voice, tense with anger: ". . . walk my feet off. If tha thinks I like—"

Then they heard his opening of the door and the voice stopped and the cottage was silent.

That's how it was now, the boy thought. They stopped talking in front of you. And this, somehow, was too much for him to bear.

He closed the door, ran out into the night, and onto the moor, that great flat expanse of land where all the people of that village walked in lonesomeness when life and its troubles seemed past bearing.

A long while later, his father's voice cut through the darkness.

"What's tha doing out here, Joe lad?"

"Walking."

"Aye."

They went on together, aimlessly, each following his own thoughts. And they both thought about the dog that had been sold.

"Tha maun't think we're hard on thee, Joe," the man said at last. "It's just that a chap's got to be honest. There's that to it. Sometimes, when a chap doesn't have much, he clings right hard to what he's got. And honest is honest, and there's no two ways about it."

"Why, look, Joe. Seventeen year I worked in that Clarabelle Pit till she shut down, and a good collier too. Seventeen year! And butties I've had by the dozen, and never a man of 'em can ever say that Joe Carraclough kept what wasn't his, nor spoke what wasn't true. Not a man in his Riding can ever call a Carraclough mishonest."

"And when ye've sold a man summat, and ye've taken his brass, and ye've spent it—well, then done's done. That's all. And ye've got to stand by that."

"But Lassie was—"

"Now, Joe! Ye can't alter it, ever. It's done—and happen it's for t' best. No two ways, Joe, she were getting hard to feed. Why, ye wouldn't want Lassie to be going around getting peaked and pined, like some chaps round here keep their tykes. And if ye're fond of her, then just think on it that now she's got lots to eat, and a private kennel, and a good run to herself, and living like a varritable princess, she is. Ain't that best for her?"

"We wouldn't pine her. We've always got lots to eat."

The man blew out his breath, angrily. "Eigh, Joe, nowt pleases thee. Well then, tha might as well have it. Tha'll never see Lassie no more. She run home once too often, so the duke's taken her wi' him up to his place in Scotland, and there she'll stay. So it's good-by and good luck to her, and she'll never come home no more, she won't. Now, I weren't off to tell thee, but there it is, so put it in thy pipe and smoke it, and let's never say a word about it no more—especially in front of thy mother."

The boy stumbled on in the darkness. Then the man halted.

"We ought to be getting back, lad. We left thy mother alone."

He turned the boy about, and then went on, but as if he were talking to himself.

"Tha sees, Joe, women's not like men. They have to stay home and manage best they can, and just spend the time in wishing. And when things don't go right, well, they have to take it out in talk and give a man hell. But it don't mean nowt, really, so tha shouldn't mind when thy mother talks hard.

"Ye just got to learn to be patient and let 'em talk, and just let it go up t' chimney wi' th' smoke."

Then they were quiet, until, over the rise, they saw the lights of the village. Then the boy spoke: "How far away is Scotland, feyther?"

"Nay, lad, it's a long, long road."

"But how far, feyther?"

"I don't know—but it's a longer road than thee or me'll ever walk. Now, lad. Don't fret no more, and try to be a man—and don't plague thy mother no more, wilta?"

Joe Carraclough was right. It is a long road, as they say in the North, from Yorkshire to Scotland. Much too far for a man to walk—or a boy. And though the boy often thought of it, he remembered his father's words on the moor, and he put the thought behind him.

But there is another way of looking at it; and that's the distance from Scotland to Yorkshire. And that is just as far as from Yorkshire to Scotland. A matter of about four hundred miles it would be, from the Duke of Rudling's place far up in the Highlands, to the village of Holdersby. That would be for a man, who could go fairly straight.

To an animal, how much farther would it be? For a dog can study no maps, read no signposts, ask no directions. It could only go blindly, by instinct, knowing that it must keep on to the south, to the south. It would wander and err, quest and quarter, run into firths and lochs that would send it side-tracking and back-tracking before it could go again on its way—south.

A thousand miles, it would be, going that way—a thousand miles over strange terrain.

There would be moors to cross, and burns to swim. And then those great, long lochs that stretch almost from one side of that dour land to another would bar the way and send a dog questing a hundred miles before it could find a crossing that would allow it to go south.

And, too, there would be rivers to cross, wide rivers like the Forth and the Clyde, the Tweed and the Tyne, where one must go miles to find bridges. And the bridges would be in towns. And in the towns there would be officials—

like the one in Lanarkshire. In all his life he had never let a captured dog get away—except one. That one was a gaunt, snarling collie that whirled on him right in the pound itself, and fought and twisted loose to race away down the city street—going south.

But there are also kind people, too; ones knowing and understanding in the ways of dogs. There was an old couple in Durham who found a dog lying exhausted in a ditch one night—lying there with its head to the south. They took that dog into their cottage and warmed it and fed it and nursed it. And because it seemed an understanding, wise dog, they kept it in their home, hoping it would learn to be content. But, as it grew stronger, every afternoon toward four o'clock it would go to the door and whine, and then begin pacing back and forth between the door and the window, back and forth as the animals do in their cages at the zoo.

They tried every wile and every kindness to make it bide with them, but finally, when the dog began to refuse food, the old people knew what they must do. Because they understood dogs, they opened the door one afternoon and they watched a collie go, not down the road to the right, or to the left, but straight across a field toward the south; going steadily at a trot, as if he knew it still had a long, long road to travel.

Ah, a thousand miles of tor and brae, of shire and moor, of path and road and plowland, of river and stream and burn and brook and beck, of snow and rain and fog and sun, is a long way, even for a human being. But it would seem too far—much, much too far—for any dog to travel blindly and win through.

And yet—and yet—who shall say why, when so many weeks had passed that hope against hope was dying, a boy coming out of school, out of the cloakroom that always smelled of damp wool drying, across the concrete play yard with the black, waxed slides, should turn his eyes to a spot by the school gate from force of five years of habit, and see there a dog? Not a dog, this one, that lifted glad ears above a proud, slim head with its black-and-gold mask; but a dog that lay weakly, trying to lift a head that would no longer lift, trying to wag a tail that was torn and blotched and matted with dirt and burs, and managing to do nothing much except to whine in a weak, happy, crying way as a boy on his knees threw arms about it, and hands touched it that had not touched it for many a day.

Then who shall picture the urgency of a boy, running, awkwardly, with a great dog in his arms running through the village, past the empty mill, past the Labor Exchange, where the men looked up from their deep ponderings on life and the dole? Or who shall describe the high tones of a voice—a boy's voice, calling as he runs up a path: "Mother! Oh, mother! Lassie's come home! Lassie's come home!"

Nor does anyone who ever owned a dog need to be told the sound a man makes as he bends over a dog that has been his for many years; nor how a woman moves quickly, preparing food—which might be the family's condensed milk stirred into warm water; nor how the jowl of a dog is lifted so that raw egg and brandy, bought with precious pence, should be spooned in; nor how bleeding pads are bandaged, tenderly.

That was one day. There was another day when the woman in the cottage sighed with pleasure, for a dog lifted itself to its feet for the first time to stand over a bowl of oatmeal, putting its head down and lapping again and again while its pinched flanks quivered.

And there was another day when the boy realized that, even now, the dog was not to be his again. So the cottage rang again with protests and cries, and a woman shrilling: "Is there never to be no more peace in my house and home?" Long after he was in bed that night the boy heard the rise and fall of the woman's voice, and the steady, reiterative tone of the man's. It went on long after he was asleep.

In the morning the man spoke, not looking at the boy, saying the words as if he had long rehearsed them.

"Thy mother and me have decided upon it that Lassie shall stay here till she's better. Anyhow, nobody could nurse her better than us. But the day that t' duke comes back, then back she goes, too. For she belongs to him, and that's honest, too. Now tha has her for a while, so be content."

In childhood, "for a while" is such a great stretch of days when seen from one end. It is a terrible short time seen from the other.

The boy knew how short it was that morning as he went to school and saw a motorcar driven by a young woman. And in the car was a gray-thatched, terrible old man, who waved a cane and shouted: "Hi! Hi, there! Damme, lad! You there! Hi!"

Then it was no use running, for the car could go faster than you, and soon it was beside you and the man was saying: "Damme, Philippa, will you make this smelly thing stand still a moment? Hi, lad!"

"Yes, sir."

"You're What's-'is-Name's lad, aren't you?"

"Ma feyther's Joe Carraclough."

"I know. I know. Is he home now?"

"No, sir. He's away to Allerby. A mate spoke for him at the pit and he's gone to see if there's a chance."

"When'll he be back?"

"I don't know. I think about tea."

"Eh, yes. Well, yes. I'll drop round about fivish to see that father of yours. Something important."

It was hard to pretend to listen to lessons. There was only waiting for noon. Then the boy ran home.

"Mother! T'duke is back and he's coming to take Lassie away."

"Eigh, drat my buttons. Never no peace in this house. Is tha sure?"

"Aye. He stopped me. He said tell feyther he'll be round at five. Can't we hide her? Oh, mother."

"Nay, thy feyther—"

"Won't you beg him? Please, please. Beg feyther to—"

"Young Joe, now it's no use. So stop thy teasing! Thy feyther'll not lie. That much I'll give him. Come good, come bad, he'll not lie."

"But just this once, mother. Please beg him, just this once. Just one lie wouldn't hurt him. I'll make it up to him. I will. When I'm growed up, I'll get a job. I'll make money. I'll buy him things—and you, too. I'll buy you both anything you want if you'll only—"

For the first time in his trouble the boy became a child, and the mother, looking over, saw the tears that ran openly down his contorted face. She turned her face to the fire, and there was a pause. Then she spoke.

"Joe, tha mustn't," she said softly. "Tha must learn never to want nothing in life like that. It don't do, lad. Tha mustn't want things bad, like tha wants Lassie."

The boy shook his clenched fists in impatience.

"It ain't that, mother. Ye don't understand. Don't yet see—it ain't me that wants her. It's her that wants us! Tha's wha made her come all them miles. It's her that wants us, so terrible bad!"

The woman turned and stared. It was as if, in that moment, she were seeing this child, this boy, this son of her own, for the first time in many years. She turned her head down toward the table. It was surrender.

"Come and eat, then," she said. "I'll talk to him. I will that, all right. I feel sure he won't lie. But I'll talk to him, all right. I'll talk to Mr. Joe Carraclough. I will indeed."

At five that afternoon, the Duke of Rudling, fuming and muttering, got out of a car at a cottage gate to find a boy barring his way. This boy was a boy who stood, stubbornly, saying fiercely: "Away wi' thee! Thy tyke's net here!"

"Damme, Philippa, th' lad's touched," the duke said. "He is. He's touched."

Scowling and thumping his stick, the old duke advanced until the boy gave way, backing down the path out of the reach of the waving blackthorn stick.

"Thy tyke's net here," the boy protested.

"What's he saying?" the girl asked.

"Says my dog isn't here. Damme, you going deaf? I'm supposed to be deaf, and I hear him plainly enough. Now, ma lad, what tyke o' mine's not here?"

As he turned to the boy, the duke spoke in broadest Yorkshire, as he did always to the people of the cottages—a habit which the Duchess of Rudling, and many more members of the duke's family, deplored.

"Coom, coom, ma lad. Whet tyke's net here?"

"No tyke o' thine. Us hasn't got it." The words began running faster and faster as the boy backed away from the fearful old man who advanced. "No tyke could have done it. No tyke can come all them miles. It isn't Lassie. It's another one that looks like her. It isn't Lassie!"

"Why, bless ma heart and sowl," the duke puffed. "Where's thy father, ma lad?"

The door behind the boy opened, and a woman's voice spoke.

"If it's Joe Carraclough ye want, he's out in the shed—and been there shut up half the afternoon."

"What's this lad talking about—a dog of mine being here?"

"Nay," the woman snapped quickly. "He didn't say a tyke o' thine was here. He said it wasn't here."

"Well, what dog o' mine isn't here, then?"

The woman swallowed, and looked about as if for help. The duke stood, peering from under his jutting eyebrows. Her answer, truth or lie, was never spoken, for then they heard the rattle of a door opening, and a man making a pursing sound with his lips, as he will when he wants a dog to follow, and then Joe Carraclough's voice said: "This is t' only tyke us has here. Does it look like any dog that belongs to thee?"

With his mouth opening to cry one last protest, the boy turned. And his mouth stayed open. For there he saw his father, Joe Carraclough, the collie fancier, standing with a dog at his heels—a dog that sat at his left heel patiently, as any well-trained dog should do—as Lassie used to do. But this dog was not Lassie. In fact, it was ridiculous to think of it at the same moment as you thought of Lassie.

For where Lassie's skull was aristocratic and slim, this dog's head was clumsy and rough. Where Lassie's ears stood in twin-lapped symmetry, this dog had one ear draggling and the other standing up Alsatian fashion in a way to give any collie breeder the cold shivers. Where Lassie's coat was rich tawny gold, this dog's coat had ugly patches of black; and where Lassie's apron was a billowing stretch of snow-white, this dog had puddles of off-color blue-merle mixture. Besides, Lassie had four white paws, and this one had one paw white, two dirty-brown, and one almost black.

That is the dog they all looked at as Joe Carraclough stood there, having told no lie, having only asked a question. They all stood, waiting the duke's verdict.

But the duke said nothing. He only walked forward, slowly, as if he were seeing a dream. He bent beside the collie, looking with eyes that were as knowing about dogs as any Yorkshireman alive. And those eyes did not waste themselves upon twisted ears, or blotched marking, or rough head. Instead they were looking at a paw that the duke lifted, looking at the underside of the paw, staring intently at five black pads, crossed and recrossed with the scars where thorns had lacerated, and stones had torn.

For a long time the duke stared, and when he got up he did not speak in Yorkshire accents any more. He spoke as a gentleman should, and he said: "Joe Carraclough, I never owned this dog. 'Pon my soul, she's never belonged to me. Never!"

Then he turned and went stumping down the path, thumping his cane and saying: "Bless my soul. Four hundred miles! Damme, wouldn't ha' believed it. Damme—five hundred miles!"

He was at the gate when his granddaughter whispered to him fiercely.

"Of course," he cried. "Mind your own business. Exactly what I came for. Talking about dogs made me forget. Carraclough! Carraclough! What're ye hiding for?"

"I'm still here, sir."

"Ah, there you are. You working?"

"Eigh, now. Working," Joe said. That's the best he could manage.

"Yes, working, working!" The duke fumed.

"Well, now—" Joe began.

Then Mrs. Carraclough came to his rescue, as a good housewife in Yorkshire will.

"Why, Joe's got three or four things that he's been considering," she said, with proper display of pride. "But he hasn't quite said yes or no to any of them yet."

"Then say no, quick," the old man puffed. "Had to sack Hynes. Didn't know a dog from a drunken filly. Should ha' known all along no damn Londoner could handle dogs fit for Yorkshire taste. How much, Carraclough?"

"Well, now," Joe began.

"Seven pounds a week, and worth every penny," Mrs. Carraclough chipped in. "One o' them other offers may come up to eight," she lied, expertly. For there's always a certain amount of lying to be done in life, and when a woman's married to a man who has made a lifelong cult of being honest, then she's got to learn to do the lying for two.

"Five," roared the duke—who, after all, was a Yorkshireman, and couldn't help being a bit sharp about things that pertained to money.

"Six," said Mrs. Carraclough.

"Five pound ten," bargained the duke, cannily.

"Done," said Mrs. Carraclough, who would have been willing to settle for three pounds in the first place. "But, o' course, us gets the cottage too."

"All right," puffed the duke. "Five pounds ten and the cottage. Begin Monday. But—on one condition. Carraclough, you can live on my land, but I won't have that thick-skulled, screw-lugged, gay-tailed eyesore of a misshapen mongrel on my property. Now never let me see her again. You'll get rid of her?"

He waited, and Joe fumbled for words. But it was the boy who answered, happily, gaily: "Oh, no, sir. She'll be waiting at school for me most o' the time.

And, anyway, in a day or so we'll have her fixed up and coped up so's ye'd never, never recognize her."

"I don't doubt that," puffed the duke, as he went to the car. "I don't doubt ye could do just exactly that."

It was a long time afterward, in the car, that the girl said: "Don't sit there like a lion on the Nelson column. And I thought you were supposed to be a hard man."

"Fiddlesticks, m' dear. I'm a ruthless realist. For five years I've sworn I'd have that dog by hook or crook, and now, egad, at last I've got her."

"Pooh! You had to buy the man before you could get his dog."

"Well, perhaps that's not the worst part of the bargain."

BULLDOG
(2001)
Arthur Miller

In this story a thirteen-year-old boy acquires a puppy and gets more than he expected from the dog's previous owner. "Bulldog" originally appeared in *The New Yorker* and was also included in *The Best American Short Stories 2002*.

Author Arthur Miller (1915–2005) is best known for writing *Death of a Salesman* (1949), one of the most celebrated plays in the history of the American theater. His other popular plays include *The Crucible* (1953) and *After the Fall* (1964). Miller was also an accomplished short story writer.

He saw this tiny ad in the paper: "Black Brindle Bull puppies, $3.00 each." He had something like ten dollars from his housepainting job, which he hadn't deposited yet, but they had never had a dog in the house. His father was taking a long nap when the idea crested in his mind, and his mother, in the middle of a bridge game when he asked her if it would be all right, shrugged absently and threw a card. He walked around the house trying to decide, and the feeling spread through him that he'd better hurry, before somebody else got the puppy first. In his mind, there was already one particular puppy that belonged to him—it was his puppy and the puppy knew it. He had no idea what a brindle bull looked like, but it sounded tough and wonderful. And he had the three dollars, though it soured him to think of spending it when they had such bad money worries, with his father gone bankrupt again. The tiny ad hadn't mentioned how many puppies there were. Maybe there were only two or three, which might be bought by this time.

The address was on Schermerhorn Street, which he had never heard of. He called, and a woman with a husky voice explained how to get there and on which line. He was coming from the Midwood section, and the elevated Culver line, so he would have to change at Church Avenue. He wrote everything down and read it all back to her. She still had the puppies, thank God. It took more than an hour, but the train was almost empty, this being Sunday, and with a breeze from its open wood-framed windows it was cooler than down in the street. Below in empty lots he could see old Italian women, their heads covered with red bandannas, bent over and loading their aprons with dandelions. His Italian school friends said they were for wine and salads. He remembered trying to eat one once when he was playing left field in the lot near his house, but it was bitter and salty as tears. The old wooden train, practically unloaded, rocked and clattered lightly through the hot afternoon. He passed above a block where men were standing in driveways watering their cars as though they were hot elephants. Dust floated pleasantly through the air.

The Schermerhorn Street neighborhood was a surprise, totally different from his own, in Midwood. The houses here were made of brownstone, and were not at all like the clapboard ones on his block, which had been put up only a few years before or, in the earliest cases, in the twenties. Even the sidewalks looked old, with big squares of stone instead of cement, and bits of grass growing in the cracks between them. He could tell that Jews didn't live here, maybe because it was so quiet and unenergetic and not a soul was sitting outside to enjoy the sun. Lots of windows were wide open, with expressionless people leaning on their elbows and staring out, and cats stretched out on some of the sills, many of the women in their bras and the men in underwear trying to catch a breeze. Trickles of sweat were creeping down his back, not only from the heat but also because he realized now that he was the only one who wanted the dog, since his parents hadn't really had an opinion and his brother, who was older, had said, "What are you, crazy, spending your few dollars on a puppy? Who knows if it will be any good? And what are you going to feed it?" He thought bones, and his brother, who always knew what was right or wrong, yelled, "Bones! They have no teeth yet!" Well, maybe soup, he had mumbled. "Soup! You going to feed a puppy *soup*?" Suddenly he saw that he had arrived at the address. Standing there, he felt the bottom falling out, and he knew it was all a mistake, like one of his dreams or a lie that he had stupidly tried to defend as being real. His heart sped up and he felt he was blushing and walked on for half a block or so. He was the only one out, and people in a few of the windows were watching him on the empty street. But how could he go home after he had come so far? It seemed he'd been traveling for weeks or a year. And now to get back on the subway with nothing? Maybe he ought at least to get a look at the puppy, if the woman would let him. He had looked it up in the Book of Knowledge, where they had two full pages of dog pictures, and there had been a white English bulldog with bent front legs and teeth that stuck out from its lower jaw, and a little black-and-white Boston bull, and a long-nosed pit bull, but they had no picture of a brindle bull. When you came down to it, all he really knew about brindle bulls was that they would cost three dollars. But he had to at least get a look at him, his puppy, so he went back down the block and rang the basement doorbell, as the woman had told him to do. The sound was so loud it startled him, but he felt if he ran away and she came out in time to see him it would be even more embarrassing, so he stood there with sweat running down over his lip.

An inner door under the stoop opened, and a woman came out and looked at him through the dusty iron bars of the gate. She wore some kind of gown, light-pink silk, which she held together with one hand, and she had long black hair down to her shoulders. He didn't dare look directly into her face, so he couldn't tell exactly what she looked like, but he could feel her tension as she stood there behind her closed gate. He felt she could not imagine what he was doing ringing her bell and he quickly asked if she was the one who'd put the ad in. Oh! Her manner changed right away, and she unlatched the gate and pulled it open. She was shorter than he and had a peculiar smell, like a mixture of milk and stale air. He followed her into the apartment, which was so dark he could hardly make out anything, but he could hear the high yapping of puppies. She had to yell to ask him where he lived and how old he was, and when he told her thirteen she clapped a hand over her mouth and said that he was very tall for his age, but he couldn't understand why this seemed to embarrass her, except that she may have thought he was fifteen, which people sometimes did. But even so. He followed her into the kitchen, at the back of the apartment, where finally he could see around him, now that he'd been out of the sun for a few minutes. In a large cardboard box that had been unevenly cut down to make it shallower he saw three puppies and their mother, who sat looking up at him with her tail moving slowly back and forth. He didn't think she looked like a bulldog, but he didn't dare say so. She was just a brown dog with flecks of black and a few stripes here and there, and the puppies were the same. He did like the way their little ears drooped, but he said to the woman that he had wanted to see the puppies but hadn't made up his mind yet. He really didn't know what to do next, so, in order not to seem as though he didn't appreciate the puppies, he asked if she would mind if he held one. She said that was all right and reached down into the box and lifted out two puppies and set them down on the blue linoleum. They didn't look like any bulldogs he had ever seen, but he was embarrassed to tell her that he didn't really want one. She picked one up and said, "Here," and put it on his lap.

He had never held a dog before and was afraid it would slide off, so he cradled it in his arms. It was hot on his skin and very soft and kind of disgusting in a thrilling way. It had gray eyes like tiny buttons. It troubled him that the Book of Knowledge hadn't had a picture of this kind of dog. A real bulldog was kind of tough and dangerous, but these were just brown dogs. He sat there on the arm of the green upholstered chair with the puppy on his lap, not knowing what to do next. The woman, meanwhile, had put herself next to him, and it felt like she had given his hair a pat, but he wasn't sure because he had very thick hair. The more seconds that ticked away the less sure he was of what to do. Then she asked if he would like some water, and he said he would, and she went to the faucet and ran water, which gave him a chance to stand up and set the puppy back in the box. She came back to him holding the glass and as he took it she let her gown fall open, showing her breasts like half-filled balloons, saying she couldn't believe he was only thirteen. He gulped the water and started to hand her back the glass, and she suddenly drew his head to her and kissed him. In all this time, for some reason, he hadn't been able to look into her face, and when he tried to now he couldn't see anything but a blur and hair. She reached down to him and a shivering started in the backs of his legs. It got sharper, until it was almost like the time he touched the live rim of a light socket while trying to remove a broken bulb. He would never be able to remember getting down on the carpet—he felt like a waterfall was smashing down on top of his head. He remembered getting inside her heat and his head banging and banging against the leg of her couch. He was almost at Church Avenue, where he had to change for the elevated Culver line, before realizing she hadn't taken his three dollars, and he couldn't recall agreeing to it but he had this small cardboard box on his lap with a puppy mewling inside. The scraping of nails on the cardboard sent chills up his back. The woman, as he remembered now, had cut two holes into the top of the box, and the puppy kept sticking his nose through them.

His mother jumped back when he untied the cord and the puppy pushed up and scrambled out, yapping. "What is he doing?" she yelled, with her hands in the air as though she were about to be attacked. By this time, he'd lost his fear of the puppy and held him in his arms and let him lick his face, and seeing this his mother calmed down a bit. "Is he hungry?" she asked, and stood with her mouth slightly open, ready for anything, as he put the puppy on the floor again. He said the puppy might be hungry, but he thought he could eat only soft things, although his little teeth were as sharp as pins. She got out some soft cream cheese and put a little piece of it on the floor, but the puppy only sniffed at it and peed. "My God in Heaven!" she yelled, and quickly got a piece of newspaper to blot it up with. When she bent over that way, he thought of the woman's heat and was ashamed and shook his head. Suddenly her name came to him—Lucille—which she had told him when they were on the floor. Just as he was slipping in, she had opened her eyes and said, "My name is Lucille." His mother brought out a bowl of last night's noodles and set it on the floor. The puppy raised his little paw and tipped the bowl over, spilling some of the chicken soup at the bottom. This he began to lick hungrily off the linoleum. "He likes chicken soup!" his mother yelled happily, and immediately decided he would most likely enjoy an egg and so put water on to boil. Somehow the puppy knew that she was the one to follow and walked behind her, back and forth, from the stove to the refrigerator. "He follows me!" his mother said, laughing happily.

On his way home from school the next day, he stopped at the hardware store and bought a puppy collar for seventy five cents, and Mr. Schweckert threw in a piece of clothesline as a leash. Every night as he fell asleep, he brought out Lucille like something from a secret treasure box and wondered if he could dare phone her and maybe be with her again. The puppy, which he had named Rover, seemed to grow noticeably bigger every day, although he still showed no signs of looking like any bulldog. The boy's father thought Rover should live in the cellar, but it was very lonely down there and he would never stop yapping. "He misses his mother," his mother said, so every night the boy started him off on some rags in an old wash basket down there, and when he'd yapped enough the boy was allowed to bring him up and let him sleep on some rags in the kitchen, and everybody was thankful for the quiet. His mother tried to walk the puppy in the quiet street they lived on, but he kept tangling the rope around her ankles, and because she was afraid to hurt him she exhausted herself following him in all his zigzags. It didn't always happen, but many times when the boy looked at Rover he'd think of Lucille and could almost feel the heat again. He would sit on the porch steps stroking the puppy and think of her, the insides of her thighs. He still couldn't imagine her face, just her long black hair and her strong neck.

One day, his mother baked a chocolate cake and set it to cool on the kitchen table. It was a least eight inches thick, and he knew it would be delicious. He was drawing a lot in those days, pictures of spoons and forks or cigarette packages or, occasionally, his mother's Chinese vase with the dragon on it, anything that had an interesting shape. So he put the cake on a chair next to the table and drew for a while and then got up and went outside for some reason and got involved with the tulips he had planted the previous fall that were just now showing their tips. Then he decided to go look for a practically new baseball he had mislaid the previous summer and which he was sure, or pretty sure, must be down in the cellar in a cardboard box. He had never really got down to the bottom of that box, because he was always distracted by finding something he'd forgotten he had put in there. He had started down into the cellar from the outside entrance, under the back porch, when he noticed that the pear tree, which he had planted two years before, had what looked like a blossom on one of its slender branches. It amazed him, and he felt proud and successful. He had paid thirty-five cents for the tree on Court Street and thirty cents for an apple tree, which he planted about seven feet away, so as to be able to hang a hammock between them someday. They were still too thin and young, but maybe next year. He always loved to stare at the two trees, because he had planted them, and he felt they somehow knew he was looking at them, and even that they were looking back at him. The back yard ended at a ten-foot-high wooden fence that surrounded Erasmus Field, where the semi-pro and sandlot teams played on weekends, teams like the House of David and the Black Yankees and the one with Satchel Paige, who was famous as one of the country's greatest pitchers except he was a Negro and couldn't play in the big leagues, obviously. The House of Davids all had long beards—he'd never understood why, but maybe they were Orthodox Jews, although they didn't look it. An extremely long foul shot over right field could drop a ball into the yard, and that was the ball it had occurred to him to search for, now that spring had come and the weather was warming up. In the basement, he found the box and was immediately surprised at how sharp his ice skates were, and recalled that he had once had a vise to clamp the skates side by side so that a stone could be rubbed on the blades. He pushed aside a torn fielder's glove, a hockey goalie's glove whose mate he knew had been lost, some pencil stubs and a package of crayons, and a little wooden man whose arms flapped up and down when you pulled a string. Then he heard the puppy yapping over his head, but it was not his usual sound—it was continuous and very sharp and loud. He ran upstairs and saw his mother coming down into the living room from the second floor, her dressing gown flying out behind her, a look of fear on her face. He could hear the scraping of the puppy's nails on the linoleum, and he rushed into the kitchen. The puppy was running around and around in a circle and sort of screaming, and the boy could see at once that his belly was swollen. The cake was on the floor, and most of it was gone. "My cake!" his mother screamed, and picked up the dish with the remains on it and held it up high as though to save it from the puppy, even though practically nothing was left. The boy tried to catch Rover, but he slipped away into the living room. His mother was behind him yelling "The carpet!" Rover kept running, in wider circles now that he had more space, and foam was forming on his muzzle. "Call the police!" his mother yelled. Suddenly, the puppy fell and lay on his side, gasping and making little squeaks with each breath. Since they had never had a dog and knew nothing about veterinarians, he looked in the phone book and found the A.S.P.C.A. number and called them. Now he was afraid to touch Rover, because the puppy snapped at his hand when it got close and he had this foam on his mouth. When the van drew up in front of the house, the boy went outside and saw a young guy removing a little cage from the back. He told him that the dog had eaten practically a whole cake, but the man had no interest and came into the house and stood for a moment looking down at Rover, who was making little yips now but was still down on his side. The man dropped some netting over him and when he slipped him into the cage, the puppy tried to get up and run. "What do you think is the matter with him?" his mother asked, her mouth turned down in revulsion, which the boy now felt in himself. "What's the matter with him is he ate a cake," the man said. Then he carried the cage out and slid it through the back door into the darkness of the van. "What will you do with him?" the boy asked. "You want him?" the man snapped. His mother was standing on the stoop now and overheard them. "We can't have him here," she called over, with fright and definiteness in her voice, and approached the young man. "We don't know how to keep a dog. Maybe somebody who knows how to keep him would want him." The young man nodded with no interest either way, got behind the wheel, and drove off.

The boy and his mother watched the van until it disappeared around the corner. Inside, the house was dead quiet again. He didn't have to worry anymore about Rover doing something on the carpets or chewing the furniture, or whether he had water or needed to eat. Rover had been the first thing he'd looked for on returning from school every day and on waking in the morning, and he had always worried that the dog might have done something to displease his mother or father. Now all that anxiety was gone and, with it, the pleasure, and it was silent in the house.

He went back to the kitchen table and tried to think of something he could draw. A newspaper lay on one of the chairs, and he opened it and inside saw a Saks stocking ad showing a woman with a gown pulled aside to display her leg. He started copying it and thought of Lucille again. Could he possibly call her, he wondered, and do what they had done again? Except that she would surely ask about Rover, and he couldn't do anything but lie to her. He remembered how she had cuddled Rover in her arms and even kissed his nose. She had really loved that puppy. How could he tell her he was gone? Just sitting and thinking of her he was hardening up like a broom handle and he suddenly thought what if he called her and said his family were thinking of having a second puppy to keep Rover company? But then he would have to pretend he still had Rover, which would mean two lies, and that was a little frightening. Not the lies so much as trying to remember, first, that he still had Rover, second, that he was serious about a second puppy, and third, the worst thing, that when he got up off Lucille he would have to say that unfortunately he couldn't actually take another puppy because . . . Why? The thought of all that lying exhausted him. Then he visualized being in her heat again and he thought his head would explode, and the idea came that when it was over she might insist on his taking another puppy. Force it on him. After all, she had not accepted his three dollars and Rover had been a sort of gift, he thought. It would be embarrassing to refuse another puppy, especially when he had supposedly come back to her for exactly that reason. He didn't dare go through all that and gave up the whole idea. But then the thought crept back again of her spreading apart on the floor the way she had, and he returned to searching for some reason he could give for not taking another puppy after he had supposedly come all the way across Brooklyn to get one. He could just see the look on her face on his turning down a puppy, the puzzlement or, worse, anger. Yes, she could very possibly get angry and see through him, realizing that all he had come for was to get into her and the rest of it was nonsense, and she might feel insulted. Maybe even slap him. What would he do then? He couldn't fight a grown woman. Then again, it now occurred to him that by this time she might well have sold the other two puppies, which at three dollars were pretty inexpensive. Then what? He began to wonder, suppose he just called her up and said he'd like to come over again and see her, without mentioning any puppies? He would have to tell only one lie, that he still had Rover and that the family all loved him and so on. He could easily remember that much. He went to the piano and played some chords, mostly in the dark bass, to calm himself. He didn't really know how to play, but he loved inventing chords and letting the vibrations shoot up his arms. He played, feeling as though something inside him had sort of shaken loose or collapsed altogether. He was different than he had ever been, not empty and clear anymore but weighted with secrets and his lies, some told and some untold, but all of it disgusting enough to set him slightly outside his family, in a place where he could watch them now, and watch himself with them. He tried to invent a melody with the right hand and find matching chords with the left. By sheer luck, he was hitting some beauties. It was really amazing how his chords were just slightly off, with a discordant edge but still in some way talking to the right-hand melody. His mother came into the room full of surprise and pleasure. "What's happening?" she called out in delight. She could play and sight-read music and had tried and failed to teach him, because, she believed, his ear was too good and he'd rather play what he heard than do the labor of reading notes. She came over to the piano and stood beside him, watching his hands. Amazed, wishing as always that he could be a genius, she laughed. "Are you making this up?" she almost yelled, as though they were side by side on a roller coaster. He could only nod, not daring to speak and maybe lose what he had somehow snatched out of the air, and he laughed with her because he was so completely happy that he had secretly changed, and unsure at the same time that he would ever be able to play like this again.

THE MIXER
(1917)
P. G. Wodehouse

Pelham Grenville Wodehouse (1881–1975)—a master of English style, imagery, and wit—was one of the most prolific writers of all time. In addition to ninety-two books, he also wrote plays and lyrics for Broadway musicals, and his short stories, especially on golf, are legendary. In 1956 Wodehouse obtained dual citizenship in America and Britain. Among his books are *My Man Jeeves* (1919), *Ukridge* (1924), *The Butler Did It* (1957), and *The Golf Omnibus* (1973).

A dog narrates the story below—he's a nice little fellow who unwittingly gets involved in an attempted burglary.

Looking back, I always consider that my career as a dog proper really started when I was bought for the sum of half a crown by the Shy Man. That event marked the end of my puppyhood. The knowledge that I was worth actual cash to somebody filled me with a sense of new responsibilities. It sobered me. Besides, it was only after that half-crown changed hands that I went out into the great world; and, however interesting life may be in an East End public-house, it is only when you go out into the world that you really broaden your mind and begin to see things.

Within its limitations, my life had been singularly full and vivid. I was born, as I say, in a public-house in the East End, and however lacking a public-house may be in refinement and the true culture, it certainly provides plenty of excitement. Before I was six weeks old, I had upset three policemen by getting between their legs when they came round to the sidedoor, thinking they had heard suspicious noises; and I can still recall the interesting sensation of being chased seventeen times round the yard with a broom-handle after a well-planned and completely successful raid on the larder. These and other happenings of a like nature soothed for the moment but could not cure the restlessness which has always been so marked a trait in my character. I have always been restless, unable to settle down in one place and anxious to get on to the next thing. This may be due to a gipsy strain in my ancestry—one of my uncles traveled with a circus—or it may be the Artistic Temperament, acquired from a grandfather who, before dying of a surfeit of paste in the property-room of the Bristol Coliseum, which he was visiting in the course of a professional tour, had an established reputation on the music-hall stage as one of Professor Pond's Performing Poodles.

I owe the fullness and variety of my life to this restlessness of mine, for I have repeatedly left comfortable homes in order to follow some perfect stranger who looked as if he were on his way to somewhere interesting. Sometimes I think I must have cat blood in me.

The Shy Man came into our yard one afternoon in April, while I was sleeping with Mother in the sun on an old sweater which we had borrowed from Fred, one of the barmen. I heard Mother growl, but I didn't take any notice. Mother is what they call a good watch-dog, and she growls at everybody except Master. At first when she used to do it, I would get up and bark my head off, but not now. Life's too short to bark at everybody who comes into our yard. It is behind the public-house, and they keep empty bottles and things there, so people are always coming and going.

Besides, I was tired. I had had a very busy morning, helping the men bring in a lot of cases of beer and running into the saloon to talk to Fred and generally looking after things. So I was just dozing off again when I heard a voice say, "Well, he's ugly enough." Then I knew that they were talking about me.

I have never disguised it from myself, and nobody has ever disguised it from me, that I am not a handsome dog. Even Mother never thought me beautiful. She was no Gladys Cooper herself, but she never hesitated to criticize my appearance. In fact, I have yet to meet anyone who did. The first thing strangers say about me is "What an ugly dog!"

I don't know what I am. I have a bull-dog kind of a face, but the rest of me is terrier. I have a long tail which sticks straight up in the air. My hair is wiry. My eyes are brown. I am jet black with a white chest. I once overheard Fred saying that I was a Gorgonzola cheese-hound, and I have generally found Fred reliable in his statements.

When I found that I was under discussion, I opened my eyes. Master was standing there, looking down at me, and by his side the man who had just said I was ugly enough. The man was a thin man, about the age of a barman and smaller than a policeman. He had patched brown shoes and black trousers.

"But he's got a sweet nature," said Master.

This was true, luckily for me. Mother always said, "A dog without influence or private means, if he is to make his way in the world, must have either good looks or amiability." But, according to her, I overdid it. "A dog," she used to say, "can have a good heart without chumming with every Tom, Dick, and Harry he meets. Your behavior is sometimes quite un-dog-like." Mother prided herself on being a one-man dog. She kept herself to herself, and wouldn't kiss anybody except Master—not even Fred.

Now, I'm a mixer. I can't help it. It's my nature. I like men. I like the taste of their boots, the smell of their legs, and the sound of their voices. It may be weak of me, but a man has only to speak to me, and a sort of thrill goes right down my spine and sets my tail wagging.

I wagged it now. The man looked at me rather distantly. He didn't pat me. I suspected—what I afterwards found to be the case—that he was shy, so I jumped up at him to put him at his ease. Mother growled again. I felt that she did not approve.

"Why, he's took quite a fancy to you already," said Master.

The man didn't say a word. He seemed to be brooding on something. He was one of those silent men. He reminded me of Joe, the old dog down the street at the grocer's shop, who lies at the door all day, blinking and not speaking to anybody.

Master began to talk about me. It surprised me, the way he praised me. I hadn't a suspicion he admired me so much. From what he said you would have thought I had won prizes and ribbons at the Crystal Palace. But the man didn't seem to be impressed. He kept on saying nothing.

When Master had finished telling him what a wonderful dog I was till I blushed, the man spoke.

"Less of it," he said. "Half a crown is my bid, and if he was an angel from on high you couldn't get another ha'penny out of me. What about it?"

A thrill went down my spine and out at my tail, for of course I saw now what was happening. The man wanted to buy me and take me away. I looked at Master hopefully.

"He's more like a son to me than a dog," said Master, sort of wistful.

"It's his face that makes you feel that way," said the man, unsympathetically. "If you had a son that's just how he would look. Half a crown is my offer, and I'm in a hurry."

"All right," said Master, with a sigh, "though it's giving him away, a valuable dog like that. Where's your half-crown?"

The man got a bit of rope and tied it round my neck.

I could hear Mother barking advice and telling me to be a credit to the family, but I was too excited to listen.

"Good-bye, Mother," I said. "Good-bye, Master. Good-bye, Fred. Good-bye, everybody. I'm off to see life. The Shy Man has bought me for half a crown. Wow!"

I kept running round in circles and shouting, till the man gave me a kick and told me to stop it.

So I did.

I don't know where we went, but it was a long way. I had never been off our street before in my life and didn't know the whole world was half as big as that. We walked on and on, and the man jerking at my rope whenever I wanted to stop and look at anything. He wouldn't even let me pass the time of the day with dogs we met.

When we had gone about a hundred miles and were just going to turn in at a dark doorway, a policeman suddenly stopped the man. I could feel by the way the man pulled at my rope and tried to hurry on that he didn't want to speak to the policeman. The more I saw of the man, the more I saw how shy he was.

"Hi!" said the policeman, and we had to stop.

"I've got a message for you, old pal," said the policeman. "It's from the Board of Health. They told me to tell you you needed a change of air. See?"

"All right!" said the man.

"And take it as soon as you like. Else you'll find you'll get it given you. See?"

I looked at the man with a good deal of respect. He was evidently someone very important, if they worried so about his health.

"I'm going down to the country tonight," said the man.

The policeman seemed pleased.

"That's a bit of luck for the country," he said. "Don't go changing your mind."

And we walked on, and went in at the dark doorway, and climbed about a million stairs, and went into a room that smelt of rats. The man sat down and swore a little, and I sat and looked at him.

Presently I couldn't keep it in any longer.

"Do we live here?" I said. "Is it true we're going to the country? Wasn't that policeman a good sort? Don't you like policemen? I knew lots of policemen at the public-house. Are there any other dogs here? What is there for dinner? What's in that cupboard? When are you going to take me out for another run? May I go out and see if I can find a cat?"

"Stop that yelping," he said.

"When we go to the country, where shall we live? Are you going to be a caretaker at a house? Fred's father is a caretaker at a big house in Kent. I've heard Fred talk about it. You didn't meet Fred when you came to the public-house, did you? You would like Fred. I like Fred. Mother likes Fred. We all like Fred."

I was going on to tell him a lot more about Fred, who had always been one of my warmest friends, when he suddenly got hold of a stick and walloped me with it.

"You keep quiet when you're told," he said.

He really was the shyest man I had ever met. It seemed to hurt him to be spoken to. However, he was the boss, and I had to humor him, so I didn't say any more.

We went down to the country that night, just as the man had told the policeman we would. I was all worked up, for I had heard so much about the country from Fred that I had always wanted to go there. Fred used to go off on a motor-bicycle sometimes to spend the night with his father in Kent, and once he brought back a squirrel with him, which I thought was for me to eat, but Mother said no. "The first thing a dog has to learn," Mother used often to say, "is that the whole world wasn't created for him to eat."

It was quite dark when we got to the country, but the man seemed to know where to go. He pulled at my rope, and we began to walk along a road with no people in it at all. We walked on and on, but it was all so new to me that I forgot how tired I was. I could feel my mind broadening with every step I took.

Every now and then we would pass a very big house which looked as if it was empty, but I knew that there was a caretaker inside, because of Fred's father. These big houses belong to very rich people, but they don't want to live in them till the summer so they put in caretakers, and the caretakers have a dog to keep off burglars. I wondered if that was what I had been brought here for.

"Are you going to be a caretaker?" I asked the man.

"Shut up," he said.

So I shut up.

After we had been walking a long time, we came to a cottage. A man came out. My man seemed to know him, for he called him Bill. I was quite surprised to see the man was not at all shy with Bill. They seemed very friendly.

"Is that him?" said Bill, looking at me.

"Bought him this afternoon," said the man.

"Well," said Bill, "he's ugly enough. He looks fierce. If you want a dog, he's the sort of dog you want. But what do you want one for? It seems to me it's a lot of trouble to take, when there's no need of any trouble at all. Why not do what I've always wanted to do? What's wrong with just fixing the dog, same as it's always done, and walking in and helping yourself?"

"I'll tell you what's wrong," said the man. "To start with, you can't get at the dog to fix him except by day, when they let him out. At night he's shut up inside the house. And suppose you do fix him during the day, what happens then? Either the bloke gets another before night, or else he sits up all night with a gun. It isn't like as if these blokes was ordinary blokes. They're down here to look after the house. That's their job, and they don't take any chances."

It was the longest speech I had ever heard the man make, and it seemed to impress Bill. He was quite humble.

"I didn't think of that," he said. "We'd best start in to train this tyke at once."

Mother often used to say, when I went on about wanting to go out into the world and see life, "You'll be sorry when you do. The world isn't all bones and liver." And I hadn't been living with the man and Bill in their cottage long before I found out how right she was.

It was the man's shyness that made all the trouble. It seemed as if he hated to be taken notice of.

It started on my very first night at the cottage. I had fallen asleep in the kitchen, tired out after all the excitement of the day and the long walks I had had, when something woke me with a start. It was somebody scratching at the window, trying to get in.

Well, I ask you, I ask any dog, what would you have done in my place? Ever since I was old enough to listen, Mother had told me over and over again what I must do in a case like this. It is the ABC of a dog's education. "If you are in a room and you hear anyone trying to get in," Mother used to say, "bark. It may be some one who has business there, or it may not. Bark first, and inquire afterwards. Dogs were made to be heard and not seen."

I lifted my head and yelled. I have a good, deep voice, due to a hound strain in my pedigree, and at the public-house, when there was a full moon, I have often had people leaning out of the windows and saying things all down the street. I took a deep breath and let it go.

"Man!" I shouted. "Bill! Man! Come quick! Here's a burglar getting in!"

Then somebody struck a light, and it was the man himself. He had come in through the window.

He picked up a stick, and he walloped me. I couldn't understand it. I couldn't see where I had done the wrong thing. But he was the boss, so there was nothing to be said.

If you'll believe me, that same thing happened every night. Every single night! And sometimes twice or three times before morning. And every time I would bark my loudest, and the man would strike a light and wallop me. The thing was baffling. I couldn't possibly have mistaken what Mother had said to me. She said it too often for that. Bark! Bark! Bark! It was the main plank of her whole system of education. And yet, here I was, getting walloped every night for doing it.

I thought it out till my head ached, and finally I got it right. I began to see that Mother's outlook was narrow. No doubt, living with a man like Master at the public-house, a man without a trace of shyness in his composition, barking was all right. But circumstances alter cases. I belonged to a man who was a mass of nerves, who got the jumps if you spoke to him. What I had to do was to forget the training I had had from Mother, sound as it no doubt was as a general thing, and to adapt myself to the needs of the particular man who had happened to buy me. I had tried Mother's way, and all it had brought me was walloping, so now I would think for myself.

So next night, when I heard the window go, I lay there without a word, though it went against all my better feelings. I didn't even growl. Someone came in and moved about in the dark, with a lantern, but, though I smelt that it was the man, I didn't ask him a single question. And presently the man lit a light and came over to me and gave me a pat, which was a thing he had never done before.

"Good dog!" he said. "Now you can have this."

And he let me lick out the saucepan in which the dinner had been cooked.

After that, we got on fine. Whenever I heard anyone at the window I just kept curled up and took no notice, and every time I got a bone or something good. It was easy, once you had got the hang of things.

It was about a week after that the man took me out one morning, and we walked a long way till we turned in at some big gates and went along a very smooth road till we came to a great house, standing all by itself in the middle of a whole lot of country. There was a big lawn in front of it, and all round there were fields and trees, and at the back a great wood.

The man rang a bell, and the door opened, and an old man came out.

"Well?" he said, not very cordially.

"I thought you might want to buy a good watch-dog," said the man.

"Well, that's queer, your saying that," said the caretaker. "It's a coincidence. That's exactly what I do want to buy. I was just thinking of going along and trying to get one. My old dog picked up something this morning that he oughtn't to have, and he's dead, poor feller."

"Poor feller," said the man. "Found an old bone with phosphorus on it, I guess."

"What to you want for this one?"

"Five shillings."

"Is he a good watch-dog?"

"He's a grand watch-dog."

"He looks fierce enough."

"Ah!"

So the caretaker gave the man his five shillings, and the man went off and left me.

At first the newness of everything and the unaccustomed smells and getting to know the caretaker, who was a nice old man, prevented my missing the man, but as the day went on and I began to realize that he had gone and would never come back, I got very depressed. I pattered all over the house, whining. It was a most interesting house, bigger than I thought a house could possibly be, but it couldn't cheer me up. You may think it strange that I should pine for the man, after all the wallopings he had given me, and it is odd, when you come to think of it. But dogs are dogs, and they are built like that. By the time it was evening I was thoroughly miserable. I found a shoe and an old clothes-brush in one of the rooms, but could eat nothing. I just sat and moped.

It's a funny thing, but it seems as if it always happened that just when you are feeling most miserable, something nice happens. As I sat there, there came from outside the sound of a motor-bicycle, and somebody shouted.

It was dear old Fred, my old pal Fred, the best old boy that ever stepped. I recognized his voice in a second, and I was scratching at the door before the old man had time to get up out of his chair.

Well, well, well! That was a pleasant surprise! I ran five times round the lawn without stopping, and then I came back and jumped up at him.

"What are you doing down here, Fred?" I said, "Is this caretaker your father? Have you seen the rabbits in the wood? How long are you going to stop? How's Mother? I like the country. Have you come all the way from the public-house? I'm living here now. Your father gave five shillings for me. That's twice as much as I was worth when I saw you last."

"Why, it's young Blackie!" That was what they called me at the saloon. "What are you doing here? Where did you get this dog, Father?"

"A man sold him to me this morning. Poor old Bob got poisoned. This one ought to be just as good a watch-dog. He barks loud enough."

"He should be. His mother is the best watch-dog in London. This cheese-hound used to belong to the boss. Funny him getting down here."

We went into the house and had supper. And after supper we sat and talked. Fred was only down for the night, he said, because the boss wanted him back next day.

"And I'd sooner have my job than yours, Dad," he said. "Of all the lonely places! I wonder you aren't scared of burglars."

"I've got my shot-gun, and there's the dog. I might be scared if it wasn't for him, but he kind of gives me confidence. Old Bob was the same. Dogs are a comfort in the country."

"Get many tramps here?"

"I've only seen one in two months, and that's the feller who sold me the dog here."

As they were talking about the man, I asked Fred if he knew him. They might have met at the public-house, when the man was buying me from the boss.

"You would like him," I said. "I wish you could have met."

They both looked at me.

"What's he growling at?" asked Fred. "Think he heard something?"

The old man laughed.

"He wasn't growling. He was talking in his sleep. You're nervous, Fred. It comes from living in the city."

"Well, I am. I like this place in the daytime, but it gives me the pip at night. It's so quiet. How you can stand it here all the time, I can't understand. Two nights of it would have me seeing things."

His father laughed.

"If you feel like that, Fred, you had better take the gun to bed with you. I shall be quite happy without it."

"I will," said Fred. "I'll take six if you've got them."

And after that they went upstairs. I had a basket in the hall, which had belonged to Bob, the dog who had got poisoned. It was a comfortable basket, but I was so excited at having met Fred again that I couldn't sleep. Besides, there was a smell of mice somewhere, and I had to move around, trying to place it.

I was just sniffing at a place in the wall when I heard a scratching noise. At first I thought it was the mice working in a different place, but, when I listened, I found that the sound came from the window. Somebody was doing something to it from outside.

If it had been Mother, she would have lifted the roof off right there, and so should I, if it hadn't been for what the man had taught me. I didn't think it possible that this could be the man come back, for he had gone away and said nothing about ever seeing me again. But I didn't bark. I stopped where I was and listened. And presently the window came open, and somebody began to climb in.

I gave a good sniff, and I knew it was the man.

I was so delighted that for a moment I nearly forgot myself and shouted with joy, but I remembered in time how shy he was, and stopped myself. But I ran to him and jumped up quite quietly, and he told me to lie down. I was disappointed that he didn't seem more pleased to see me. I lay down.

It was very dark, but he had brought a lantern with him, and I could see him moving about the room, picking things up and putting them in a bag which he had brought with him. Every now and then he would stop and listen, and then he would start moving round again. He was very quick about it, but very quiet. It was plain that he didn't want Fred or his father to come down and find him.

I kept thinking about this peculiarity of his while I watched him. I suppose, being chummy myself, I find it hard to understand that everybody else in the world isn't chummy too. Of course, my experience at the public-house had taught me that men are just as different from each other as dogs. If I chewed Master's shoe, for instance, he used to kick me, but if I chewed Fred's, Fred would tickle me under the ear. And, similarly, some men are shy and some men are mixers. I quite appreciated that, but I couldn't help feeling that the man carried shyness to a point where it became morbid. And he didn't give himself a chance to cure himself of it. That was the point. Imagine a man hating to meet people so much that he never visited their houses till the middle of the night, when they were in bed and asleep. It was silly. Shyness had always been something so outside my nature that I suppose I have never really been able to look at it sympathetically. I have always held the view that you can get over it if you make an effort. The trouble with the man was that he wouldn't make an effort. He went out of his way to avoid meeting people.

I was fond of the man. He was the sort of person you never get to know very well, but we had been together for quite a while, and I wouldn't have been a dog if I hadn't got attached to him.

As I sat and watched him creep about the room, it suddenly came to me that here was a chance of doing him a real good turn in spite of himself. Fred was upstairs, and Fred, as I knew by experience, was the easiest man to get along with in the world. Nobody could be shy with Fred. I felt that if only I could bring him and the man together, they would get along splendidly, and it would teach the man not to be silly and avoid people. It would help to give him the confidence which he needed. I had seen him with Bill, and I knew that he could be perfectly natural and easy when he liked.

It was true that the man might object at first, but after a while he would see that I had acted simply for his good, and would be grateful.

The difficulty was, how to get Fred down without scaring the man. I knew that if I shouted he wouldn't wait, but would be out of the window and away before Fred could get there. What I had to do was to go to Fred's room, explain the whole situation quietly to him, and ask him to come down and make himself pleasant.

The man was far too busy to pay any attention to me. He was kneeling in a corner with his back to me, putting something in his bag. I seized the opportunity to steal softly from the room.

Fred's door was shut, and I could hear him snoring. I scratched gently, and then harder, till I heard the snores stop. He got out of bed and opened the door.

"Don't make a noise," I whispered. "Come on downstairs. I want you to meet a friend of mine."

At first he was quite peevish.

"What's the idea," he said, "coming and spoiling a man's beauty-sleep? Get out."

He actually started to go back into the room.

"No, honestly, Fred," I said, "I'm not fooling you. There *is* a man downstairs. He got in through the window. I want you to meet him. He's very shy, and I think it will do him good to have a chat with you."

"What are you whining about?" Fred began, and then he broke off suddenly and listened. We could both hear the man's footsteps as he moved about.

Fred jumped back into the room. He came out, carrying something. He didn't say any more but started to go downstairs, very quiet, and I went after him.

There was the man, still putting things in his bag. I was just going to introduce Fred, when Fred, the silly ass, gave a great yell.

I could have bitten him.

"What did you want to do that for, you chump?" I said. "I told you he was shy. Now you've scared him."

He certainly had. The man was out of the window quicker than you would have believed possible. He just flew out. I called after him that it was only Fred and me, but at that moment a gun went off with a tremendous bang, so he couldn't have heard me.

I was pretty sick about it. The whole thing had gone wrong. Fred seemed to have lost his head entirely. He was behaving like a perfect ass. Naturally the man had been frightened with him carrying on in that way. I jumped out of the window to see if I could find the man and explain, but he was gone. Fred jumped out after me, and nearly squashed me.

It was pitch dark out there. I couldn't see a thing. But I knew the man could not have gone far, or I should have heard him. I started to sniff round on the chance of picking up his trail. It wasn't long before I struck it.

Fred's father had come down now, and they were running about. The old man had a light. I followed the trail, and it ended at a large cedar tree, not far from the house. I stood underneath it and looked up, but of course I could not see anything.

"Are you up there?" I shouted. "There's nothing to be scared at. It was only Fred. He's an old pal of mine. He works at the place where you bought me. His gun went off by accident. He won't hurt you."

There wasn't a sound. I began to think I must have made a mistake.

"He's got away," I heard Fred say to his father, and just as he said it I caught a faint sound of someone moving in the branches above me.

"No he hasn't!" I shouted. "He's up this tree."

"I believe the dog's found him, Dad!"

"Yes, he's up here. Come along and meet him."

Fred came to the foot of the tree.

"You up there," he said, "come along down."

Not a sound from the tree.

"It's all right," I explained, "he *is* up there, but he's very shy. Ask him again."

111

"All right," said Fred, "stay there if you want to. But I'm going to shoot off this gun into the branches just for fun."

And then the man started to come down. As soon as he touched the ground I jumped up at him.

"This is fine!" I said. "Here's my friend Fred. You'll like him."

But it wasn't any good. They didn't get along together at all. They hardly spoke. The man went into the house, and Fred went after him, carrying his gun. And when they got into the house it was just the same. The man sat in one chair, and Fred sat in another, and after a long time some men came in a motor-car, and the man went away with them. He didn't say good-bye to me.

When he had gone, Fred and his father made a great fuss of me. I couldn't understand it. Men are so odd. The man wasn't a bit pleased that I had brought him and Fred together, but Fred seemed as if he couldn't do enough for me having introduced him to the man. However, Fred's father produced some cold ham—my favorite dish—and gave me quite a lot of it, so I stopped worrying over the thing. As Mother used to say, "Don't bother your head about what doesn't concern you. The only thing a dog need concern himself with is the bill of fare. Eat your bun, and don't make yourself busy about other people's affairs." Mother's was in some ways a narrow outlook, but she had a great fund of sterling common sense.

DOG PEOPLE
(1988)
E. S. Goldman

Not everyone likes dogs. The aging landowner and jogger in this story comes to resent dogs and their owners, and the results of his antipathy make for a riveting tale. E. S. Goldman's story first appeared in the *Atlantic Monthly*, where he has published more stories than any contemporary writer. Goldman didn't start writing until 1987—and turned ninety-three years old in 2006. Several of his stories are collected in *The Palmer Method: Stories* (1995) and *Earthly Justice* (1990), which won the *TriQuarterly's* William Goyen Prize for Fiction. Goldman also wrote a comic novel called *Big Chocolate Cookies* (1988).

Sometimes when Allan Stonnier drove out and the dogs were there, he revved up and aimed. He had an agreement with them that no matter how disdainfully they stood their ground, they would at the last moment lurch out of range if he went no more than a certain speed. The time he brushed McCoors's brown dog he felt bad about it, but the dog hadn't cooperated. The dog was too cocky. Stonnier had nothing against it. How could a man have anything against a dog? After that, when he revved up he was ready to brake, fast.

McCoors was coming through his woodlot and saw Stonnier drive at the dogs. He said, "If you ever hit one of my dogs, I'll break your fucking head."

"I wouldn't hit your dogs. I just want to scare them. Keep your dogs off my property. You have land."

"I'll break your fucking head."

"I'll be where you can find me."

That was a long time ago, when you could still talk to people about their dogs.

This morning Stonnier was out early, and running. It was a typical Cape Cod spring, more evident on calendars from the hardware store than on the land. A dry northeaster thrashed the roadside picket of unleafed oak, cherry, and locust. A patch of melting snow, sprawled like a dirty old sheep dog on the lee side of a downed pine, drained toward the dozer cut that had made Stonnier's lane forty years ago. Stonnier's running shoes threw wet sand from the runnels. He took in all the air his chest would hold; he had been a runner since making the mile relay team at Nauset Regional, and had known ever since that even when the air was foul you had to fill up.

The air held the thaw of dog shit banked over the winter by neighbor dogs on his paths and driveway lane, in his mown field and kitchen garden—butts and drools and knobs, clumped grains and hamburgers, indistinguishable except in shape from their previous incarnation in bags and cans. Stonnier couldn't see how a dog took any nourishment from such food. It looked the same coming as going. No wonder they used so much. From time to time deposits were withdrawn on Stonnier's rakes and shoes, were wheeled into the garage on the tires of his Ford hatchback. Verna's gloves gathered the stuff in the seagrass mulch on the asparagus. He would have been better off to have set out a little later, when the sun was high enough to define the footing better.

He looked as if he had seventy or so disciplined years on him; he was a man of medium height, bony, with a cleaving profile—a fisherman before he had the stake to buy The Fish & Chips. He loped along the lane evasively, like a football player training on a course of automobile tires.

When it still was possible to speak to people about their dogs, Verna had said, "You could talk to him. He probably doesn't realize what his dogs do when he isn't looking."

But why not? He knew the dogs ran all day while he and his wife were away in their store. What did he think the dogs did with what had been put in them when they were turned out in the morning?

McCoors said, "I don't think my dogs did it." He said he would keep an eye on them. He tied them. They barked. They barked from eight o'clock, when he left, to six, when he came home and let them run until dark. Stonnier skipped a stone at them a couple of times, to let them know he didn't want them near his house. They stayed beyond the turn in the driveway so he wouldn't see them.

Stonnier encountered McCoors one day when they both were looking for their property bounds. Stonnier mentioned that the dogs barked all day and McCoors might not know it because he was away.

McCoors said, "If you tie up dogs, they bark." He tied them up to please Stonnier. Now Stonnier was complaining again. McCoors broke off the conversation and walked away. McCoors had a tough body, and eyes that quickly turned mean.

Stonnier told Verna that the man reminded him of a prison guard. "I guess there are all-kinds-of-looking prison guards, but McCoors is what I think of. That's nothing against prison guards." Stonnier always tried to be fair.

Deakler, another two-dog man, bought the place on the other side of the hill. His dogs came over to find out about McCoors's dogs at the same time McCoors's dogs came over to investigate the new neighbors. They met on Stonnier's driveway where it joined the Association lane, smelled each other, peed on the young azaleas Stonnier had raised from cuttings in tin cans, and agreed to meet there each day when their food was sufficiently digested. Wahlerson's half chow and Paul's black Newfie heard about the club and came up the Association lane to join.

Stonnier spoke to Deakler.

Deakler was an affable man who had been the sales vice-president of a generator-reconditioning company and knew how to get along while not giving in. "Well, you know how it is with dogs. You don't want to keep a dog tied up all the time. That's why we moved out here."

"I shouldn't have to take care of other people's dog dirt."

"Shoo them off if they bother you. Do them good."

"They scare my granddaughter when she visits. They charge."

"They never bit anybody. People have dogs. She should get used to them."

"That's up to her, if she wants to get used to dogs charging and growling at her. I had dogs. I like dogs. I have nothing against your dogs. They should stay on their own property. Is that a communist idea?"

Deakler looked at him speculatively, as if it might be.

"I don't like to quarrel with neighbors," Stonnier said. "We'll have to see. There's a leash law. I don't like to be talking law."

Stonnier already knew from the small-animal officer that if you couldn't keep a dog off your property, you had to catch it before you called for somebody to take it away.

"You don't have to catch your own bank robbers," Stonnier had said.

The SAO had cut him down. "That's how the town wants it—don't talk to me."

"Laws are one thing," Deakler said. "This is all Association property. Private property. You don't have to leash your dog if it's on private property."

Deakler told him something he hadn't thought about. The leash law didn't even apply to members of the Association, because the Association was made up of private properties, including the beach and the roads that all the private-property owners owned in common.

"That's why I came out here," Deakler said. "It isn't all closed in, like it is in town."

Stonnier brought it up at the Association meeting in July. Oh, that was twenty-four years ago—how time flies. He remembered getting up to speak to the others on Giusti's patio. He had not in his lifetime before—or later—often spoken in meetings of that size. He thought he could remember every time. Three times at town meeting—about the algae on the pond and the proposed parking ordinance and the newspaper not printing what the Otter River Bank was doing on mortgages—and at the Board of Trade, about extending town water to the new subdivisions. Subjects that affected him. His house. His business. That's how the world worked. You spoke for yourself, and if you made sense, others voted with you even when that went a little against their own interests. That's how he always voted. He didn't sign petitions for things like the new children's park, but he voted for the park. The Taxpayers' Association said the park would put points on the tax bill. That was all right—it still made sense that the kids have a place with a fence around it, where dogs couldn't get in. That was what he would want for his own grandchildren if they lived in town. A few years back he would have asked, "Why don't they fence in the dogs, and let the kids run?" but you couldn't ask anything like that anymore.

Mostly he jogged these days. He paced an easy 120, waiting for his body to tell him how hard he could run. It wasn't his heart, it was his back: were the tendons and nerves lined up so that the jolt passed through like smoke and went off into the air, or would it jam somewhere on his hip or fourth vertebra? He told Verna, "He says it's in the vertebra, but that's not where I feel it." They knew all about hearts, but they didn't know anything about backs except to rest them. They told his father and his grandfather the same thing. He felt secure, and let out to 130.

He had thought his statement—that he had nothing against dogs but that the town leash law ought to prevail in the Association—would appeal to reasonable people. The dogs tramped down the lettuce, shat so that you couldn't trust where to walk after dark, chased cars, growled at strangers. He didn't say "shat," he said "did their business." Somebody said, "They doo-doo on your Brooks Brothers shoes," a reference to a man who at the time was running for President of the USA, and everybody laughed except Morrison and Dannels, who were large contributors to the candidate's committee. Halfway along into the laughter Stonnier caught on and joined to show his fellowship, although he sensed that the joke took the edge off the seriousness of his argument.

He had expected David Haseley would say something. Haseley had several times mentioned to him—or agreed with him—that the dogs were out of hand. As a retired high officer of a very large business in Cleveland, Haseley was usually taken seriously, but he chose not to speak to the motion. Only Larry Henry's widow, Marcia, spoke for it. Verna had been good to Marcia, shopped for her, looked in on her when she was laid up.

Sensing the anger of their neighbors, who spoke of liberties being taken from people everywhere, and now this, the summer people kept quiet or voted with the dog people. The ayes lacked the assertive spine of the nays. Stonnier thought that most members hadn't voted and that a written ballot might have turned out better. But that didn't seem to be the way to press an issue among neighbors.

In a spirit of good will members unanimously supported a resolution that people were responsible for their own dogs. It did not specify how the responsibility should be manifested.

After the meeting Stonnier said to Haseley that he had thought more people would support the leash law. Haseley nodded in the meditative, prudential manner that had earned him his good name and said, "Yes, that's so." He might have meant "I agree with you, that's what you thought." People didn't use words like they used to. "Speak up and say as best you can what you mean, so people know what's in your mind," Stonnier's mother had said to him. Now you had to be sure you asked the right question, or you might not find out what they really thought.

Stonnier hadn't pressed Haseley, toward whom he felt diffident not only because of his bearing but also because the older man was of the management class—as were all the others in the Association but himself. They were vice-presidents, deans, professors, accountants, lawyers; immigrants from Providence, Amherst, Ohio, Pennsylvania; taxed, many of them, in Florida, which the Stonniers had visited in their camper but had not been taken by sufficiently to give it six months and a day every year. The others had all gone beyond high school.

"I still don't know how he voted," he said to Verna.

Allan and Verna Stonnier were second-generation Cape Cod, the only native-born in the West Bay Association, the first to raise children there and see them bused to school in Orleans and then go out on their own. Allan had done well with The Fish & Chips—better than such a modest-looking enterprise had implied—but he remained somewhat apart from the others. His three-acre parcel on the waterfront had cost under three thousand dollars, but that was when you had to bounce a half mile in a rut to get out there.

After the fire at The Fish & Chips, ten years ago, a real-estate woman who called about buying the lot asked about the house, too. She had a customer she thought would pay more than a million dollars for it if Allan would consider selling. They thought he would sell his house and get out, but nothing could make him move after the fire. He was so set that Verna had to make it half a joke when she said that with a million dollars and the insurance from the fire they could live anywhere they wanted. By now the house might be worth two million, the way prices were. He knew it as well as she did, and if he wanted to talk about it, he would say so. "It's the whole country," he said. "Everywhere. You might as well deal with it where you are." A million dollars after tax wasn't all that much anymore anyhow.

McCoors's two dogs came out to yap at him. He said, "*Yah*," and raised his elbow, and they shut up and backed off while he padded on toward the wider, graveled lane that looped through the fifty-three properties in the West Bay Association and carried their owners' cars to the blacktop and town.

Shoeman's black-and-white sort-of spitz bitch met him there and trotted with him companionably. Stonnier considered her a friend. Some mornings she stayed with him past three or four properties, but this morning the collie next door came out and growled and she stopped at the line. "*Yah*," Stonnier growled back at the collie; he raised his elbow and jogged on.

After one spring thaw Stonnier dug a pit near the line close to McCoors's driveway. McCoors was quick to defend the integrity of his property. He had taken his neighbor on the other side to court in a right-of-way dispute. McCoors asked Stonnier what he was doing. He was going to bury dog shit.

"You don't have to do that here," McCoors said.

"It's your dogs," Stonnier said.

That afternoon a man from the Board of Health drove up to the house. Allan was down at The Fish & Chips, watching some workmen shingle a new roof. The man told Verna that burying garbage was against the law. He told her about the hazard to the groundwater supply. He said the fine could be fifty dollars a day as long as the nuisance continued unabated. He left a red notice. This unsettled Verna, because she had always thought ways could be found to work things out.

Allan went to the board and said they were off base. A human being had to get a porcelain bowl and running water and an expensive piping system to get rid of his waste, but a dog could leave it anywhere. Their ruling was off base. The health officer said he didn't write the laws, he enforced them, and Allan better close the pit and not open another one. The newspaper carried a story under the headline "PRIVATE DUMP OWNER THREATENED WITH FINE." Stonnier thought it gave the idea he was trying to get away with something.

He wrote a letter to the editor. Melvin Brate didn't print it. Stonnier thought that Brate was still peeved about a letter he had written earlier, saying that the Otter River Bank was using small type to sneak foreclosures over on people, trying to get out of old, low interest rates into the new crazy rates. Stonnier knew about that because they had done it to his cousin. In his letter to the editor Stonnier gave the names of the man who ran the bank and the men who were on its investment committee and said that was no way for neighbors to act when they had signed their names to a contract. The bank was the biggest advertiser in the paper, so naturally Melvin Brate didn't print the letter. Allan got up at town meeting in non-agenda time and read his bank letter to the voters to let them know what was going on. This was the first time he had ever gotten to his feet to talk to more than a thousand people, and it was no harder than holding your hand in a fire.

Melvin Brate sat with his arms folded and looked hard at the floor while Allan spoke about his newspaper's not saying anything about what the bank was doing. Just that day Brate had published an editorial titled "Your Free

Press: Bastion of Liberty," which he counted on for an award from the League of Weekly Publishers, and here was this fried-clam peddler carrying on. It wasn't surprising that Brate didn't print the dog-shit letter either, even though Stonnier called the stuff "scat."

Verna was secretly glad that the letter wasn't published. She thought a way could be found to deal with the problem so that dog owners wouldn't get upset and people wouldn't look at her sideways and stop going to The Fish & Chips. She knew that speaking to Allan was useless unless she could say it in another way, and she couldn't think of any. He had been such a usual man when she married him, and people were getting the idea he was an oddball. She couldn't clearly see why that was, because he had a right to complain about the dogs; nevertheless, he ought to do it a different way for his own sake, and not write to the paper or take it up at town meeting. It irritated people.

One day Stonnier counted eighteen dogs at the juncture of his land and the Association lane.

The Association lane went into the blacktop that wound and rolled toward the town. The houses on either side were on the required acreage and fully suited to their purposes. Once home to cranberry farmers, fuel dealers, printers, boat builders, lobstermen—Stonnier knew the names that went with the oldest properties—they had been bid away in the sixties and seventies by retirement and stock-market bankrolls at stiff prices. The new owners had the means to dormer up and lay on wings and garages. On some properties two and three houses stood where before there had been a single low shingle house, a big garden, and woods. The newcomers followed the traditional styles of the Chatham Road, rendered for art shows on the high school green—saltboxes, houses-and-a-half, Greek revival, all well shrubbed and fenced. One ghost of gnawed and mossy shingles had withstood all tenders to purchase and a siege of trumpet vines, rampant lilacs, and fattening cedars intent on taking it down.

Only the jolly French house looked as though it ought to have been in the old town, along with other houses of the style built by managers of the company that had laid the telephone cable to France; indeed, it had been trucked from town in the deal with the architectural commission that had licensed the Cable Station Motel to be built. To Stonnier, the French house's journey down the Chatham Road at two miles an hour, with outriders from the telephone company and the electric company and the police, was the most memorable event since the passage of the great glacier, which he had not witnessed. Had he not come into money so late, this would have been the house Stonnier built for his family. The French house sat square on the ground and knew how to shed water off its hat. It looked like a toby jug; it was gold and blue, its cornice was striped with purple, and the door was gunpowder red.

"It's different," he said to Verna, who thought it was a rather queer house that would fit in better if it were white. "You just like things one way or another," he said. He liked the moment of coming out on the blacktop around the corner from West Bay and finding himself two weeks further into spring, jogging by the French house with the long hedge of breaking forsythia skirted with daffodils and crocuses. The air here stank too. Some of it was spring rot coming out of ground. Most of it was dog.

Ahead on the long straight stretch Gordon's basset (that dog must be a hundred years old), carrying his skin like a soaked blanket, turned and turned in the middle of the road, trying to find a way to let his rear end down and create the right precedent for the rest of him. He slept there every morning for an hour or two, unless the snow was a foot deep. Regular drivers knew to watch for him, and the Lord protected Sam the basset against everybody else. That dog was going to get it one day. The driver who did it better have a good head start and not ask around whose dog it was so that he could tell them he was sorry but he had passed another car and there the dog was, in the middle of the road, and he had done his best to avoid him, he was sorry, he knew what it was to lose a dog, he had two himself, don't shoot, please don't shoot. You couldn't know anymore what to expect if there was a dog in it. Juries looked at those dog people out there. If you ran for sheriff, you took questions at public meetings and the dog people heard your answers. Senators wanted some of that dog-PAC money, especially because the dog-PAC people said that what they were really interested in wasn't dogs but good government. If a dog question was coming up at town meeting, you saw people voting you never saw anywhere else. They went home after voting on dogs, and left the rest to find a quorum for the payroll and potholes.

Allan Stonnier was the only human being afoot on the Chatham Road. His red sweatshirt was well known at this hour. Most of the sparse traffic was pickups, with elbows crooked out the windows, wheels crunching and kicking up cans, wrappers, cups, laid down by the pickups that had gone that way earlier, tools and dogs riding behind. He saw Dexter Reddick's green pickup, with the sunburst on the radiator. Without being too obvious, Stonnier adjusted course to the edge of the road. He couldn't be absolutely sure Reddick wouldn't take a swerve at him for the hell of it. He prepared to break from the shoulder for the grass slope. Reddick went by with angry eyes, threw up a finger. Reflexively, Stonnier gave it back. He heard the pickup brake hard behind him and push hard in reverse as it came back. He kept going. Reddick passed, got twenty feet beyond, and put his head out the window.

"What did I see you do?"

"The same as you." By then he was past the truck, and Reddick had to grind back again to talk to him.

"Let me see you do that again, you fuckhead. You old fart. You can't get it up. You firebug. I'll burn your ass." Stonnier kept going. Barricaded behind shovels, rakes, and lawnmowers, Reddick's Labs yammered and spittled at him. Reddick jack-started a groove in the blacktop and went on his way. Stonnier decided to take the side road that went toward the dump.

Pilliard's pack of huskies, brought back from Alaska last year, saw him coming and started their manic racket. Pilliard had one-upped everybody at the Landing Bar with that one. Jesus, twelve huskies, did you ever see such dogs? You could hide your arm in the fur. The strut and drive of those legs. They had Chinese faces as if they were people. Those people fucked their dogs. Pilliard had them in the cyclone-fenced stockade he had put up to hold his cords when he was in the stovewood business. Ten feet high, and ground area about as big as any factory you would find in a place like Cape Cod—lots of room even for twelve huskies.

Pilliard's idea was to take them to fairs and show them, for a good price, pulling a sled he'd fitted with siliconed nylon runners that slipped over turf. Take your picture with a real team of Eskimo huskies. Children's birthday parties. Beats ponies all hollow. Fourth of July parades. He brought Santa Claus to the Mall. Altogether, the bookings amounted to only a dozen brief outings all year. The dogs were used to doing miles of work in cold weather. In the stockade they hung around. At night they could be heard barking for hours for their own reasons, and the sound carried to West Bay.

Verna thought Allan must be running on the dump road, because he would be there about now, and there went Pilliard's huskies. They didn't often see people go by on foot. They acknowledged pedestrians and slow drivers by lunging at the fence, climbing, piling on, snarling, yelping powerfully. Allan had driven her by, and slowed the car so she could hear it up close. It scared her. It was more like mad screaming than barking, all of them exciting each other. Some things Verna wished Allan wouldn't do, and one of them was to run past Pilliard's huskies.

"Run someplace else," Pilliard said. "You don't like dogs and they know it, and they don't like you, so why don't you run someplace else."

What was the use explaining to a man who already knew it that Stonnier was running on a public road, and he was there before the dogs anyhow. And even if he wasn't . . .

Stonnier left them yelping, went over the crest of the rise and around the next corner, running, feeling good, well sweated as he went toward halfway. It was the dumb part of the route, the mall and the file of flat-roofed taxpayers and show-windowed front porches of old downtown; service stations, eating places, clothes shops, music stores, cleaners, laundries, drugstores elbowing to be seen along the old bypassed highway number.

He could have gone around by the marsh road and avoided town, but one thing could be said for Main Street. It smelled better than anywhere else. Better than West Bay behind the dunes, where the ocean lost its innocence; better than the Chatham Road and all the lived-on lanes and roads from the bridge to Province Lands. He had never thought he'd live to see the day when downtown smelled better than the countryside. If a stray wandered into the mall, the small-animal officer showed up fast and snared him into the cage mounted on his police wagon. The merchants saw to it. You couldn't let a leashed dog step onto one of those neat rectangles of shrubbery if you didn't want a ticket. If a dog hunched to empty out, you had to drag him to the library lawn. Even the dog people understood the deal. You left the merchants alone, they left you alone.

Soon after dawn old downtown could have been a movie set in storage. The cars and service trucks of early risers were parked in front of Annie O, who opened first, for the fishermen. The overnight lights in the stores and the streetlights watched him go by. Stanchions of sulfur light guarded the plaza of Canine City, with its eleven veterinarians, four cosmetologists, several outfitters; the portrait studio featured the work of fifteen internationally known dog artists; an architect displayed model residences: cape, half-cape, Federal, Victorian, Bauwowhaus, duplex, ranch.

The stoplight turned irrationally against him, as if programmed to recognize a man of ordinary size in a red sweatshirt running in from the west. The wind batted through the open cross street and went back again behind the solid buffer of storefronts until it came to the empty lot on the cove where The Fish & Chips had been. He faced into it, running in place, when he got there.

The real-estate people never stopped bringing him offers. He was going to leave that up to his daughter to decide. The land was money in the bank. "That's what everybody needs, Verna—something in back of him so no matter how hard he's pushed he doesn't have to give in to others. That's what it's all about. More people could be like that if they didn't want too much."

The Conservation Commission asked, If he wasn't going to use it, would he consider deeding it to them for the honor of his name in Melvin Brate's paper and the tax deduction? They thought a price might be worked out if he met them halfway. He thought about it. He got as far as thinking about what kind of sign he would require them to put up if he sold them the land, but he could never get the wording right. He knew if he got it right they wouldn't do it. He neatened up the section of burned-out foundation the building inspector allowed, and let the lot sit there with the sign.

SITE OF THE FISH & CHIPS RESTAURANT.
BURNED DOWN BY VANDALS A.D. 2002 IN HONOR
OF THEIR DOGS.

Someone stole the sign the first night. He wasn't going to fool with them; he went right to a concrete monument, anchored with bent iron rods into a six-foot-square concrete pad. They tried to jump it out with a chain but they would have needed a dozer and they never got that far. They hit it with a hammer now and then. They painted out the inscription. He used to go back a few times a year to put it in shape, but he hadn't had to touch it for two years now. The old generations had lost interest, and not even the young Reddicks cared much unless something happened to stir them up.

Coming on their first glimpse of salt water in twenty miles, visitors swung onto the apron and reached for their cameras. Alert to station their wives at the photo opportunity where George Washington watered his horse and the salt water beckoned, they walked over to read the legend about the restaurant and the vandals and the dogs. They would throw up their hands. What's that all about? Stonnier himself wasn't satisfied with the statement, but after so many years the story was boring to anybody but himself anyhow.

He had kept a dozen clipped mallards for his own table in a chicken-wire pen half in and half out of the water, the way you penned ducks if you had a waterfront. He had heard a terrible squawking, and when he looked out from the kitchen door the two dogs that patroled Reddick's garage at night were running wild in the pen, breaking wings and necks, tossing every duck they could get their jaws on. He hollered at them, but you couldn't call a dog off anything like that. He got his shotgun and drove a charge into the side of one; the other ran off, and Reddick came over from his garage, goddamning him.

The paper said that Reddick was there to get his dogs, and Stonnier threatened him with the gun to keep him off, and he shot the dog.

A week later a southerly breeze pulled an early-morning fire out of the rubbish trailer onto the shingle. Flame was all through The Fish & Chips by the time the pumper got there. His was the fourth restaurant that went up that fall, and the arson investigator from the state asked him how his business had been. They went over his records at the bank. The insurance company took two years to pay up.

He ran where he stood while he looked around and checked out the site. It was as usual. The fresh northeaster gusted at him out of a mist that lay up to the land at the water's edge. A gull stalked the tidal drain looking for garbage. Another, unseen, cried as if lost. On the scrim of fog his memory raised the shed of The Fish & Chips, with the huge lobster standing guard, and then the new Fish & Chips with the Cape Cod roof and the kitchen wing. He was looking out the back window and saw Reddick's dogs in the pen and went after them. A charred beam leaned on a course of cement block that had been the foundation. Ravined and grainy, the blacktop was being worked by frost and roots. Spindly cedars had found footing. He remembered when they had poured the blacktop: four inches, and four of gravel under it, and then sand, and the cedars had found enough to grow on down there. He felt himself already cooling out, and took off at a 120 jog back through town, wiping sweat from his forehead with the flat of his hand.

The last thing he discussed with himself as he went up the rise at the mall and turned again toward Pilliard's was how his daughter and her children could be made to keep their minds on being positioned not to give in to others. All he could do was leave them the land; they had to understand what it was for. If they sold it, they would have the money, and if you had money, you had all kinds of duties to it. You had to see that you didn't lose any of it, and you had to get the best interest for it, and you bought things you didn't need that brought you new duties, like a place in Florida. The land would stay there to back you up. He didn't stop thinking about that until he got into range of Pilliard's huskies and they started in on him again. Pilliard was carrying an armful of pipe, fence posts maybe, and spat a word he couldn't hear. He kept going.

The wind off the bay blew some of the sound away, but Verna heard the pack distinctly again. She threw a last handful of cracked corn for the quail and jays and listened. She wore untied walking shoes for slippers and a nubby white robe over her nightgown. She had brushed her hair but not in detail, and its style was a simple black-speckled gray flare cut off at her earlobe. She took her wristwatch out of the robe pocket but couldn't read it. Her glasses were still inside, on the table. If that was Allan, he would be nine or ten minutes. Then he would shower and she would be dressed and have breakfast on. It wasn't an egg day. He might want tuna on toast.

The dogs went on. She wasn't dressed to stay out, but the dogs kept barking. She picked up a dead branch, carefully positioned it, and flicked a dog divot into the rough. All the deposits over which oak leaves had settled stirred and gave off a tribal odor, as if they were a single living thing giving warning. She threw another handful of corn without noticing exactly what she was doing. Pilliard's dogs sounded louder, but that couldn't be. They were where they were. In the tops of the scratch pines the wind had not changed. Individual voices could be distinguished rising out of the wild yammer of the pack.

Were Pilliard's dogs out? He leashed and ran them sometimes in the back of the dump, but that was farther, not nearer, and never this early. She felt nervous and wished to know something. She started toward the house to look up Pilliard's name and telephone him but knew immediately that was not the thing to do. The thing to do was to get in the car and drive over there.

She was not constrained now by any civilized notion that she should not be seen, even by herself, to overreact. She suddenly wished to act as quickly and as arbitrarily as she knew how and to get over to the dump road. The Ford spurted back out of the garage, skidded while she pulled on the wheel to get it around, and went out the lane faster than McCoors's dogs had ever seen it come at them. They couldn't believe it was going that fast until it kicked the big kind-of airedale into the ditch. She had no time for regret or succor and pushed the gas harder. The wheels jumped out of potholes and ruts, clawing air, and jolted down. She was frightened by her speed. She held on as if she were a passenger. Coming to the fork at the blacktop she judged—willed, rather—that she could beat the blue car, and cut it off. Its horn lectured her past Sam the basset, sitting on the stripe with his back to her, knowing she wouldn't dare, until she lost the sound at the turn beyond the straightaway.

A quarter mile up toward Pilliard's she saw them on the road. She looked for a human figure but could see only the pack and whatever it was they were larking around on the road. She kept her hand on the horn and drove at them, not thinking any longer that he could possibly have gone another way, or got up a tree, or even gone into Pilliard's house. She put the pedal on the floor. She was angry at Allan for getting himself into anything like this. He could have lived his life like other people. But he hadn't, and that's how it was, and, enraged, she owed him as many of them as she could get her wheels into.

FOR THE LOVE OF A MAN
(1903)
Jack London

Jack London (1876–1916) was born in Oakland, California, and in the early part of the twentieth century he was probably the most widely read author in the world. His classic books, *The Call of the Wild* (1903), *The Sea Wolf* (1904), and *White Fang* (1906), have all been made into movies and are still often read. The following story, set in Alaska, is an excerpt from *The Call of the Wild* and is about the powerful bonds between man and dog.

When John Thornton froze his feet in the previous December, his partners had made him comfortable and left him to get well, going on themselves up the river to get out a raft of saw-logs for Dawson. He was still limping slightly at the time he rescued Buck, but with the continued warm weather even the slight limp left him. And here, lying by the river bank through the long spring days, watching the running water, listening lazily to the songs of birds and the hum of nature, Buck slowly won back his strength.

A rest comes very good after one has traveled three thousand miles, and it must be confessed that Buck waxed lazy as his wounds healed, his muscles swelled out, and the flesh came back to cover his bones. For that matter, they were all loafing, —Buck, John Thornton, and Skeet and Nig, —waiting for the raft to come that was to carry them down to Dawson. Skeet was a little Irish setter who early made friends with Buck, who, in a dying condition, was unable to resent her first advances. She had the doctor trait which some dogs possess; and as a mother cat washes her kittens, so she washed and cleansed Buck's wounds. Regularly, each morning after he had finished his breakfast, she performed her self-appointed task, till he came to look for her ministrations as much as he did for Thornton's. Nig, equally friendly, though less demonstrative, was a huge black dog, half bloodhound and half deerhound, with eyes that laughed and a boundless good nature.

To Buck's surprise these dogs manifested no jealousy toward him. They seemed to share the kindliness and largeness of John Thornton. As Buck grew stronger they enticed him into all sorts of ridiculous games, in which Thornton himself could not forbear to join; and in this fashion Buck romped through his convalescence and into a new existence. Love, genuine passionate love, was his for the first time. This he had never experienced at Judge Miller's down in the sun-kissed Santa Clara Valley. With the Judge's sons, hunting and tramping, it had been a working partnership; with the Judge's grandsons, a sort of pompous guardianship; and with the Judge himself, a stately and dignified friendship. But love that was feverish and burning, that was adoration, that was madness, it had taken John Thornton to arouse.

This man had saved his life, which was something; but, further, he was the ideal master. Other men saw to the welfare of their dogs from a sense of duty and business expediency; he saw to the welfare of his as if they were his own children, because he could not help it. And he saw further. He never forgot a kindly greeting or a cheering word, and to sit down for a long talk with them ("gas" he called it) was as much his delight as theirs. He had a way of taking Buck's head roughly between his hands, and resting his own head upon Buck's, of shaking him back and forth, the while calling him ill names that to Buck were love names. Buck knew no greater joy than that rough embrace and the sound of murmured oaths, and at each jerk back and forth it seemed that his heart would be shaken out of his body so great was its ecstasy. And when, released, he sprang to his feet, his mouth laughing, his eyes eloquent, his throat vibrant with unuttered sound, and in that fashion remained without movement, John Thornton would reverently exclaim, "God! you can all but speak!"

Buck had a trick of love expression that was akin to hurt. He would often seize Thornton's hand in his mouth and close so fiercely that the flesh bore the impress of his teeth for some time afterward. And as Buck understood the oaths to be love words, so the man understood this feigned bite for a caress.

For the most part, however, Buck's love was expressed in adoration. While he went wild with happiness when Thornton touched him or spoke to him, he did not seek these tokens. Unlike Skeet, who was wont to shove her nose under Thornton's hand and nudge and nudge till petted, or Nig, who would stalk up and rest his great head on Thornton's knee, Buck was content to adore at a distance. He would lie by the hour, eager, alert, at Thornton's feet, looking up into his face, dwelling upon it, studying it, following with keenest interest each fleeting expression, every movement or change of feature. Or, as chance might have it, he would lie farther away, to the side or rear, watching the outlines of the man and the occasional movements of his body. And often, such was the communion in which they lived, the strength of Buck's gaze, would draw John Thornton's head around, and he would return the gaze, without speech, his heart shining out of his eyes as Buck's heart shone out.

For a long time after his rescue, Buck did not like Thornton to get out of his sight. From the moment he left the tent to when he entered it again, Buck would follow at his heels. His transient masters since he had come into the Northland had bred in him a fear that no master could be permanent. He was afraid that Thornton would pass out of his life as Perrault and Francois and the Scotch half-breed had passed out. Even in the night, in his dreams, he was haunted by this fear. At such times he would shake off sleep and creep through the chill to the flap of the tent, where he would stand and listen to the sound of his master's breathing.

But in spite of this great love he bore John Thornton, which seemed to bespeak the soft civilizing influence, the strain of the primitive, which the Northland had aroused in him, remained alive and active. Faithfulness and devotion, things born of fire and roof, were his; yet he retained his wildness and wiliness. He was a thing of the wild, come in from the wild to sit by John Thornton's fire, rather than a dog of the soft Southland stamped with the marks of generations of civilization. Because of his very great love, he could not steal from this man, but from any other man, in any other camp, he did not hesitate an instant; while the cunning with which he stole enabled him to escape detection.

His face and body were scored by the teeth of many dogs, and he fought as fiercely as ever and more shrewdly. Skeet and Nig were too good-natured for quarrelling, —besides, they belonged to John Thornton; but the strange dog, no matter what the breed or valor, swiftly acknowledged Buck's supremacy or found himself struggling for life with a terrible antagonist. And Buck was merciless. He had learned well the law of club and fang, and he never forewent an advantage or drew back from a foe he had started on the way to Death. He had lessoned from Spitz, and from the chief fighting dogs of the police and mail, and knew there was no middle course. He must master or be mastered; while to show mercy was a weakness. Mercy did not exist in the primordial life. It was misunderstood for fear, and such misunderstandings made for death. Kill or be killed, eat or be eaten, was the law; and this mandate, down out of the depths of Time, he obeyed.

He was older than the days he had seen and the breaths he had drawn. He linked the past with the present, and the eternity behind him throbbed through him in a mighty rhythm to which he swayed as the tides and seasons swayed. He sat by John Thornton's fire, a broad-breasted dog, white-fanged and long-furred; but behind him were the shades of all manner of dogs, half-wolves and wild wolves, urgent and prompting, tasting the savor of the meat he ate, thirsting for the water he drank, scenting the wind with him, listening with him and telling him the sounds made by the wild life in the forest, dictating his moods, directing his actions, lying down to sleep with him when he lay down, and dreaming with him and beyond him and becoming themselves the stuff of his dreams.

So peremptorily did these shades beckon him, that each day mankind and the claims of mankind slipped farther from him. Deep in the forest a call was sounding, and as often as he heard this call, mysteriously thrilling and luring, he felt compelled to turn his back upon the fire and the beaten earth around it, and to plunge into the forest, and on and on, he knew not where or why; nor did he wonder where or why, the call sounding imperiously, deep in the forest. But as often as he gained the soft unbroken earth and the green shade, the love for John Thornton drew him back to the fire again.

Thornton alone held him. The rest of mankind was as nothing. Chance travelers might praise or pet him; but he was cold under it all, and from a too demonstrative man he would get up and walk away. When Thornton's partners, Hans and Pete, arrived on the long-expected raft, Buck refused to notice them till he learned they were close to Thornton; after that he tolerated them in a passive sort of way, accepting favors from them as though he favored them by accepting. They were of the same large type as Thornton, living close to the earth, thinking simply and seeing clearly; and ere they swung the raft into the big eddy by the saw-mill at Dawson, they understood Buck and his ways, and did not insist upon an intimacy such as obtained with Skeet and Nig.

For Thornton, however, his love seemed to grow and grow. He, alone among men, could put a pack upon Buck's back in the summer travelling. Nothing was too great for Buck to do, when Thornton commanded. One day (they had grub-staked themselves from the proceeds of the raft and left Dawson for the head-waters of the Tanana) the men and dogs were sitting on the crest of a cliff which fell away, straight down, to naked bed-rock three hundred feet below. John Thornton was sitting near the edge, Buck at his shoulder. A thoughtless whim seized Thornton, and he drew the attention of Hans and Pee to the experiment he had in mind. "Jump, Buck!" he commanded, sweeping his arm out and over the chasm. The next instant he was grappling with Buck on the extreme edge, while Hans and Pete were dragging them back into safety.

"It's uncanny," Pete said, after it was over and they had caught their speech.

Thornton shook his head. "No, it is splendid, and it is terrible, too. Do you know, it sometimes makes me afraid."

"I'm not hankering to be the man that lays hands on you while he's around," Pete announced conclusively, nodding his head toward Buck.

"Py Jingo!" was Hans's contribution. "Not mineself either."

It was at Circle City, ere the year was out, that Pete's apprehensions were realized. "Black" Burton, a man evil-tempered and malicious, and been picking a quarrel with a tenderfoot at the bar, when Thornton stepped good-naturedly between. Buck, as was his custom, was lying in a corner, head on paws, watching his master's every action. Burton struck out, without warning, straight from the shoulder. Thornton was sent spinning, and saved himself from falling only by clutching the rail of the bar.

Those who were looking on heard what was neither bark nor yelp, but a something which is best described as a roar, and they saw Buck's body rise up in the air as he left the floor for Burton's throat. The man saved his life by instinctively throwing out his arm, but was hurled backward to the floor with Buck on top of him. Buck loosed his teeth from the flesh of the arm and drove in again for the throat. This time the man succeeded only in partly blocking, and his throat was torn open. Then the crowd was upon Buck, and he was driven off; but while a surgeon checked the bleeding, he prowled up and down, growling furiously, attempting to rush in, and being forced back by an array of hostile clubs. A "miners' meeting," called on the spot, decided that the dog had sufficient provocation, and Buck was discharged. But his reputation was made, and from that day his name spread through every camp in Alaska.

Later on, in the fall of the year, he saved John Thorton's life in quite another fashion. The three partners were lining a long and narrow poling-boat down a bad stretch of rapids on the Forty-Mile Creek. Hans and Pete moved along the bank, snubbing with a thin Manila rope from tree to tree, while Thornton remained in the boat, helping its descent by means of a pole, and shouting directions to the shore. Buck, on the bank, worried and anxious, kept abreast of the boat, his eyes never off his master.

At a particularly bad spot, where a ledge of barely submerged rocks jutted out into the river, Hans cast off the rope, and, while Thornton poled the boat out into the stream, ran down the bank with the end in his hand to snub the boat when it had cleared the ledge. This it did, and was flying down-stream in a current as swift as a mill-race, when Hans checked it with the rope and checked too suddenly. The boat flirted over and snubbed in to the bank bottom up, while Thornton, flung sheer out of it, was carried down-stream toward the worst part of the rapids, a stretch of wild water in which no swimmer could live.

Buck had sprung in on the instant; and at the end of three hundred yards, amid a mad swirl of water, he overhauled Thornton. When he felt him grasp his tail, Buck headed for the bank, swimming with all his splendid strength. But the progress shoreward was slow; the progress down-stream amazingly rapid. From below came the fatal roaring where the wild current went wilder and was rent in shreds and spray by the rocks which thrust through like the teeth of an enormous comb. The suck of the water as it took the beginning of the last steep pitch was frightful, and Thornton knew that the shore was impossible. He scraped furiously over a rock, bruised across a second, and struck a third with crushing force. He clutched its slippery top with both hands, releasing Buck, and above the roar of the churning water shouted: "Go, Buck! Go!"

Buck could not hold his own, and swept on down-stream, struggling desperately, but unable to win back. When he heard Thornton's command repeated, he partly reared out of the water, throwing his head high, as though for a last look, then turned obediently toward the bank. He swam powerfully and was dragged ashore by Pete and Hans at the very point where swimming ceased to be possible and destruction began.

They knew that the time a man could cling to a slippery rock in the face of that driving current was a matter of minutes, and they ran as fast as they could up the bank to a point far above where Thornton was hanging on. They attached the line with which they had been snubbing the boat to Buck's neck and shoulders, being careful that it should neither strangle him nor impede his swimming, and launched him into the stream. He struck out boldly, but not straight enough into the stream. He discovered the mistake too late, when Thornton was abreast of him and a bare half-dozen strokes away while he was being carried helplessly past.

Hans promptly snubbed with the rope, as though Buck were a boat. The rope thus tightening on him in the sweep of the current, he was jerked under the surface, and under the surface he remained till his body struck against the bank and he was hauled out. He was half drowned, and Hans and Pete threw themselves upon him, pounding the breath into him and the water out of him. He staggered to his feet and fell down. The faint sound of Thornton's voice came to them, and though they could not make out the words of it, they knew that he was in his extremity. His master's voice acted on Buck like an electric shock. He sprang to his feet and ran up the bank ahead of the men to the point of his previous departure.

Again the rope was attached and he was launched, and again he struck out, but this time straight into the stream. He had miscalculated once, but he would not be guilty of it a second time. Hans paid out the rope, permitting no slack, while Pete kept it clear of coils. Buck held on till he was on a line straight above Thornton; then he turned, and with the speed of an express train headed down upon him. Thornton saw him coming, and, as Buck struck him like a battering ram, with the whole force of the current behind him, he reached up and closed with both arms around the shaggy neck. Hans snubbed the rope around the tree, and Buck and Thornton were jerked under the water. Strangling, suffocating, sometimes one uppermost and sometimes the other, dragging over the jagged bottom, smashing against rocks and snags, they veered in to the bank.

Thornton came to, belly downward and being violently propelled back and forth across a drift log by Hans and Pete. His first glance was for Buck, over whose limp and apparently lifeless body Nig was setting up a howl, while Skeet was licking the wet face and closed eyes. Thornton was himself bruised and battered, and he went carefully over Buck's body, when he had been brought around, finding three broken ribs.

"That settles it," he announced. "We camp right here." And camp they did, till Buck's ribs knitted and he was able to travel.

That winter, at Dawson, Buck performed another exploit, not so heroic, perhaps, but one that put his name many notches higher on the totem-pole of Alaskan fame. This exploit was particularly gratifying to the three men; for they stood in need of the outfit which it furnished, and were enabled to make a long-desired trip into the virgin East, where miners had not yet appeared. It was brought about by a conversation in the Eldorado Saloon, in which men waxed boastful of their favorite dogs. Buck, because of his record, was the target for these men, and Thornton was driven stoutly to defend him. At the end of half an hour one man stated that his dog could start a sled with five hundred pounds and walk off with it; a second bragged six hundred for his dog; and a third, seven hundred.

"Pooh! pooh!" said John Thornton; "Buck can start a thousand pounds."

"And break it out? and walk off with it for a hundred yards?" demanded Matthewson, a Bonanza King, he of the seven hundred vaunt.

"And break it out, and walk off with it for a hundred yards," John Thornton said coolly.

"Well," Matthewson said, slowly and deliberately, so that all could hear, "I've got a thousand dollars that says he can't. And there it is." So saying, he slammed a sack of gold dust the size of a bologna sausage down upon the bar.

Nobody spoke. Thornton's bluff, if bluff it was, had been called. He could feel a flush of warm blood creeping up his face. His tongue had tricked him. He did not know whether Buck could start a thousand pounds. Half a ton! The enormousness of it appalled him. He had great faith in Buck's strength and had often thought him capable of starting such a load; but never, as now, had he faced the possibility of it, the eyes of a dozen men fixed upon him, silent and waiting. Further, he had no thousand dollars; nor had Hans or Pete.

"I've got a sled standing outside now, with twenty fifty-pound sacks of flour on it," Matthewson went on with brutal directness; "so don't let that hinder you."

Thornton did not reply. He did not know what to say. He glanced from face to face in the absent way of a man who has lost the power of thought and is seeking somewhere to find the thing that will start it going again. The face of Jim O'Brien, a Mastodon King and old-time comrade, caught his eyes. It was a cue to him, seeming to rouse him to do what he would never have dreamed of doing.

"Can you lend me a thousand?" he asked, almost in a whisper.

"Sure," answered O'Brien, thumping down a plethoric sack by the side of Matthewson's. "Though it's little faith I'm having, John, that the beast can do the trick."

The Eldorado emptied its occupants into the street to see the test. The tables were deserted, and the dealers and gamekeepers came forth to see the outcome of the wager and to lay odds. Several hundred men, furred and mittened, banked around the sled within easy distance. Matthewson's sled, loaded with a thousand pounds of flour, had been standing for a couple of hours, and in the intense cold (it was sixty below zero) the runners had frozen fast to the hard-packed snow. Men offered odds of two to one that Buck could not budge the sled. A quibble arose concerning the phrase "break out." O'Brien contended it was Thornton's privilege to knock the runners loose, leaving Buck to "break it out" from a dead standstill. Matthewson insisted that the phrase included breaking the runners from the frozen grip of the snow. A majority of the men who had witnessed the making of the bet decided in his favor, whereat the odds went up to three to one against Buck.

There were no takers. Not a man believed him capable of the feat. Thornton had been hurried into the wager, heavy with doubt; and now that he looked at the sled itself, the concrete fact, with the regular team of ten dogs curled up in the snow before it, the more impossible the task appeared. Matthewson waxed jubilant.

"Three to one!" he proclaimed. "I'll lay you another thousand at that figure, Thornton. What d'ye say?"

Thornton's doubt was strong in his face, but his fighting spirit was aroused— the fighting spirit that soars above odds, fails to recognize the impossible, and is deaf to all save the clamor for battle. He called Hans and Pete to him. Their sacks were slim, and with his own the three partners could rake together only two hundred dollars. In the ebb of their fortunes, this sum was their total capital; yet they laid it unhesitatingly against Matthewson's six hundred.

The team of ten dogs was unhitched, and Buck, with his own harness, was put into the sled. He had caught the contagion of the excitement, and he felt that in some way he must do a great thing for John Thornton. Murmurs of admiration at his splendid appearance went up. He was in perfect condition, without an ounce of superfluous flesh, and the one hundred and fifty pounds that he weighed were so many pounds of grit and virility. His furry coat shone with the sheen of silk. Down the neck and across the shoulders, his mane, in repose as it was, half bristled and seemed to lift with every movement, as though excess of vigor made each particular hair alive and active. The great breast and heavy fore legs were no more than in proportion with the rest of the body, where the muscles showed in tight rolls underneath the skin. Men felt these muscles and proclaimed them hard as iron, and the odds went down to two to one.

"Gad, sir! Gad, sir!" stuttered a member of the latest dynasty, a king of the Skookum Benches. "I offer you eight hundred for him, sir, before the test, sir; eight hundred just as he stands."

Thornton shook his head and stepped to Buck's side.

"You must stand off from him," Matthewson protested. "Free play and plenty of room."

The crowd fell silent; only could be heard the voices of the gamblers vainly offering two to one. Everybody acknowledged Buck a magnificent animal, but twenty fifty-pound sacks of flour bulked too large in their eyes for them to loosen their pouch-strings.

Thornton knelt down by Buck's side. He took his head in his two hands and rested cheek on cheek. He did not playfully shake him, as was his wont, or murmur soft love curses; but he whispered in his ear. "As you love me, Buck. As you love me," was what he whispered. Buck whined with suppressed eagerness.

The crowd was watching curiously. The affair was growing mysterious. It seemed like a conjuration. As Thornton got to his feet, Buck seized his mittened hand between his jaws, pressing in with his teeth and releasing slowly, half-reluctantly. It was the answer, in terms, not of speech, but of love. Thornton stepped well back.

"Now, Buck," he said.

Buck tightened the traces, then slacked them for a matter of several inches. It was the way he had learned.

"Gee!" Thornton's voice rang out, sharp in the tense silence.

Buck swung to the right, ending the movement in a plunge that took up the slack and with a sudden jerk arrested his one hundred and fifty pounds. The load quivered, and from under the runners arose a crisp crackling.

"Haw!" Thornton commanded.

Buck duplicated the manoeuvre, this time to the left. The crackling turned into a snapping, the sled pivoting and the runners slipping and grating several inches to the side. The sled was broken out. Men were holding their breaths, intensely unconscious of the fact.

"Now, MUSH!"

Thornton's command cracked out like a pistol-shot. Buck threw himself forward, tightening the traces with a jarring lunge. His whole body was gathered compactly together in the tremendous effort, the muscles writhing and knotting like live things under the silky fur. His great chest was low to the ground, his head forward and down, while his feet were flying like mad, the claws scarring the hard-packed snow in parallel grooves. The sled swayed and trembled, half-started forward. One of his feet slipped, and one man groaned aloud. Then the sled lurched ahead in what appeared a rapid succession of jerks, though it never really came to a dead stop again . . . half an inch . . . an inch . . . two inches. . . . The jerks perceptibly diminished; as the sled gained momentum, he caught them up, till it was moving steadily along.

Men gasped and began to breathe again, unaware that for a moment they had ceased to breathe. Thornton was running behind, encouraging Buck with short, cheery words. The distance had been measured off, and as he neared the pile of firewood which marked the end of the hundred yards, a cheer began to grow and grow, which burst into a roar as he passed the firewood and halted at command. Every man was tearing himself loose, even Matthewson. Hats and mittens were flying in the air. Men were shaking hands, it did not matter with whom, and bubbling over in a general incoherent babel.

But Thornton fell on his knees beside Buck. Head was against head, and he was shaking him back and forth. Those who hurried up heard him cursing Buck, and he cursed him long and fervently, and softly and lovingly.

"Gad, sir! Gad, sir!" spluttered the Skookum Bench king. "I'll give you a thousand for him, sir, a thousand, sir—twelve hundred, sir."

Thornton rose to his feet. His eyes were wet. The tears were streaming frankly down his cheeks. "Sir," he said to the Skookum Bench king, "no, sir. You can go to hell, sir. It's the best I can do for you, sir."

Buck seized Thornton's hand in his teeth. Thornton shook him back and forth. As though animated by a common impulse, the onlookers drew back a respectful distance; nor were they again indiscreet enough to interrupt.

LYING DOGGO
(1982)
Bobbie Ann Mason

In this story, an aging dog, wobbling on his last legs, is nursed along by his affectionate owners, who are willing him to stay alive. It is a superlative example of the high quality writing that Bobbie Ann Mason is known for. Her novels, short stories, and nonfiction books rank her as one of today's finest authors. In 1986 she won the O. Henry Anthology Award. Mason's recent works include *Zigzagging Down a Wild Trail: Stories* (2001), *Elvis Presley* (2003), and *An Atomic Romance* (2005). She is a writer in residence at the University of Kentucky in Lexington.

Grover Cleveland is growing feeble. His eyes are cloudy, and his muzzle is specked with white hairs. When he scoots along on the hardwood floors, he makes a sound like brushes on drums. He sleeps in front of the woodstove, and when he gets too hot he creeps across the floor.

When Nancy Culpepper married Jack Cleveland, she felt, in a way, that she was marrying a divorced man with a child. Grover was a young dog then. Jack had gotten him at the humane society shelter. He had picked the shyest, most endearing puppy in a boisterous litter. Later, he told Nancy that someone said he should have chosen an energetic one, because quiet puppies often have something wrong with them. That chance remark bothered Nancy; it could have applied to her as well. But that was years ago. Nancy and Jack are still married, and Grover has lived to be old. Now his arthritis stiffens his legs so that on some days he cannot get up. Jack has been talking of having Grover put to sleep.

"Why do you say 'put to sleep'?" their son, Robert, asks. "I know what you mean." Robert is nine. He is a serious boy, quiet, like Nancy.

"No reason. It's just the way people say it."

"They don't say they put *people* to sleep."

"It doesn't usually happen to people," Jack says.

"Don't you dare take him to the vet unless you let me go along. I don't want any funny stuff behind my back."

"Don't worry, Robert," Nancy says.

Later, in Jack's studio, while developing photographs of broken snow fences on hillsides, Jack says to Nancy, "There's a first time for everything, I guess."

"What?"

"Death. I never really knew anybody who died."

"You're forgetting my grandmother."

"I didn't really know your grandmother." Jack looks down at Grover's face in the developing fluid. Grover looks like a wolf in the snow on the hill. Jack says, "The only people I ever cared about who died were rock heroes."

Jack has been buying special foods for the dog—pork chops and liver, vitamin supplements. All the arthritis literature he has been able to find concerns people, but he says the same rules must apply to all mammals. Until Grover's hind legs gave way, Jack and Robert took Grover out for long, slow walks through the woods. Recently, a neighbor who keeps Alaskan malamutes stopped Nancy in the Super Duper and inquired about Grover. The neighbor wanted to know which kind of arthritis Grover had—osteo- or rheumatoid? The neighbor said he had rheumatoid and held out knobbed fingers. The doctor told him to avoid zucchini and to drink lots of water. Grover doesn't like zucchini, Nancy said.

Jack and Nancy and Robert all deal with Grover outside. It doesn't help that the temperature is dropping below twenty degrees. It feels even colder because they are conscious of the dog's difficulty. Nancy holds his head and shoulders while Jack supports his hind legs. Robert holds up Grover's tail.

Robert says, "I have an idea."

"What, sweetheart?" asks Nancy. In her arms, Grover lurches. Nancy squeezes against him and he whimpers.

"We could put a diaper on him."

"How would we clean him up?"

"They do that with chimpanzees," says Jack, "but it must be messy."

"You mean I didn't have an original idea?" Robert cries. "Curses, foiled again!" Robert has been reading comic books about masked villains.

"There aren't many original ideas," Jack says, letting go of Grover. "They just look original when you're young." Jack lifts Grover's hind legs again and grasps him under the stomach. "Let's try one more time, boy."

Grover looks at Nancy, pleading.

Nancy has been feeling that the dying of Grover marks a milestone in her marriage to Jack, a marriage that has somehow lasted almost fifteen years. She is seized with an irrational dread—that when the dog is gone, Jack will be gone too. Whenever Nancy and Jack are apart—during Nancy's frequent trips to see her family in Kentucky, or when Jack has gone away "to think"—Grover remains with Jack. Actually, Nancy knew Grover before she knew Jack. When Jack and Nancy were students, in Massachusetts, the dog was a familiar figure around campus. Nancy was drawn to the dog long before she noticed the shaggy-haired student in the sheepskin-lined corduroy jacket who was usually with him. Once, in a seminar on the Federalist period that Nancy was auditing, Grover had walked in, circled the room, and then walked out, as if performing some routine investigation, like the man who sprayed Nancy's apartment building for silverfish. Grover was a beautiful dog, a German shepherd, gray, dusted with a sooty topcoat. After the seminar, Nancy followed the dog out of the building, and she met Jack then. Eventually, when Nancy and Jack made love in his apartment in Amherst, Grover lay sprawled by the bed, both protective and quietly participatory. Later, they moved into a house in the country, and Nancy felt that she had an instant family. Once, for almost three months, Jack and Grover were gone. Jack left Nancy in California, pregnant and terrified, and went to stay at an Indian reservation in New Mexico. Nancy lived in a room on a street with palm trees. It was winter. It felt like a Kentucky October. She went to a park every day and watched people with their dogs, their children, and tried to comprehend that she was there, alone, a mile from the San Andreas fault, reluctant to return to Kentucky. "We need to decide where we stand with each other," Jack had said when he left. "Just when I start to think I know where you're at, you seem to disappear." Jack always seemed to stand back and watch her, as though he expected her to do something excitingly original. He expected her to be herself, not someone she thought people wanted her to be. That was a twist: he expected the unexpected. While Jack was away, Nancy indulged in crafts projects. At the Free University, she learned batik and macramé. On her own, she learned to crochet. She had never done anything like that before. She threw away her file folders of history notes for the article she had wanted to write. Suddenly, making things with her hands was the only endeavor that made sense. She crocheted a bulky, shapeless sweater in a shell stitch for Jack. She made baby things, using large hooks. She did not realize that such heavy blankets were unsuitable for a baby until she saw Robert—a tiny, warped-looking creature, like one of her clumsily made crafts. When Jack returned, she was in a sprawling adobe hospital, nursing a baby the color of scalded skin. The old song "In My Adobe Hacienda" was going through her head. Jack stood over her behind an unfamiliar beard, grinning in disbelief, stroking the baby as though he were a new pet. Nancy felt she had fooled Jack into thinking she had done something original at last.

"Grover's dying to see you," he said to her. 'They wouldn't let him in here."

"I'll be glad to see Grover," said Nancy. "I missed him."

She had missed, she realized then, his various expressions: the staccato barks of joy, the forceful, menacing barks at strangers, the eerie howls when he heard cat fights at night.

Those early years together were confused and dislocated. After leaving graduate school, at the beginning of the seventies, they lived in a number of places—sometimes on the road, with Grover, in a van—but after Robert was born they settled in Pennsylvania. Their life is orderly. Jack is a free-lance photographer, with his own studio at home. Nancy, unable to find a use for her degree in history, returned to school, taking education and administration courses. Now she is assistant principal of a small private elementary school, which Robert attends. Now and then Jack frets about becoming too middle-class. He has become semipolitical about energy, sometimes attending anti–nuclear power rallies. He has been building a sun space for his studio and has been insulating the house. "Retrofitting" is the term he uses for making the house energy-efficient.

"Insulation is his hobby," Nancy told an old friend from graduate school, Tom Green, who telephoned unexpectedly one day recently. "He insulates on weekends."

"Maybe he'll turn into a butterfly—he could insulate himself into a cocoon," said Tom, who Nancy always thought was funny. She had not seen him in ten years. He called to say he was sending a novel he had written—"about all the crazy stuff we did back then."

The dog is forcing Nancy to think of how Jack has changed in the years since then. He is losing his hair, but he doesn't seem concerned. Jack was always fanatical about being honest. He used to be insensitive about his directness. "I'm just being honest," he would say pleasantly, boyishly, when he hurt people's feelings. He told Nancy she was uptight, that no one ever knew what she thought, that she should be more expressive. He said she "played games" with people, hiding her feelings behind her coy Southern smile. He is more tolerant now, less judgmental. He used to criticize her for drinking Cokes and eating pastries. He didn't like her lipstick, and she stopped wearing it. But Nancy changed too. She is too sophisticated now to eat fried foods and rich pies and cakes, indulging in them only when she goes to Kentucky. She uses makeup now—so sparingly that Jack does not notice. Her cool reserve, her shyness, has changed to cool assurance, with only the slightest shift. Inwardly, she has reorganized. "It's like retrofitting," she said to Jack once, but he didn't notice any irony.

It wasn't until two years ago that Nancy learned that he had lied to her when he told her he had been at the Beatles' Shea Stadium concert in 1966, just as she had, only two months before they met. When he confessed his lie, he claimed he had wanted to identify with her and impress her because he thought of her as someone so mysterious and aloof that he could not hold her attention. Nancy, who had in fact been intimidated by Jack's directness, was troubled to learn about his peculiar deception. It was out of character. She felt a part of her past had been ripped away. More recently, when John Lennon died, Nancy and Jack watched the silent vigil from Central Park on TV and cried in each other's arms. Everybody that week was saying that they had lost their youth.

Jack was right. That was the only sort of death they had known.

Grover lies on his side, stretched out near the fire, his head flat on one ear. His eyes are open, expressionless, and when Nancy speaks to him he doesn't respond.

"Come on, Grover!" cries Robert, tugging the dog's leg. "Are you dead?"

"Don't pull at him," Nancy says.

"He's lying doggo," says Jack.

"That's funny," says Robert. "What does that mean?"

"Dogs do that in the heat," Jack explains. "They save energy that way."

"But it's winter," says Robert. "I'm freezing." He is wearing a wool pullover and a goose-down vest. Jack has the thermostat set on fifty-five, relying mainly on the woodstove to warm the house.

"I'm cold too," says Nancy. "I've been freezing since 1965, when I came North."

Jack crouches down beside the dog. "Grover, old boy. Please. Just give a little sign."

"If you don't get up, I won't give you your treat tonight," says Robert, wagging his finger at Grover.

"Let him rest," says Jack, who is twiddling some of Grover's fur between his fingers.

"Are you sure he's not dead?" Robert asks. He runs the zipper of his vest up and down.

"He's just pretending," says Nancy.

The tip of Grover's tail twitches, and Jack catches it, the way he might grab at a fluff of milkweed in the air.

Later, in the kitchen, Jack and Nancy are preparing for a dinner party. Jack is sipping whiskey. The woodstove has been burning all day, and the house is comfortably warm now. In the next room, Robert is lying on the rug in front of the stove with Grover. He is playing with a computer football game and watching *Mork and Mindy* at the same time. Robert likes to do several things at once, and lately he has included Grover in his multiple activities.

Jack says, "I think the only thing to do is just feed Grover pork chops and steaks and pet him a lot, and then when we can stand it, take him to the vet and get it over with."

"When we can stand it?"

"If I were in Grover's shape, I'd just want to be put out of my misery."

"Even if you were still conscious and could use your mind?"

"I guess so."

"I couldn't pull the plug on you," says Nancy, pointing a carrot at Jack. "You'd have to be screaming in agony."

"Would you want me to do it to you?"

"No. I can see right now that I'd be the type to hang on. I'd be just like my Granny. I think she just clung to life, long after her body was ready to die."

"Would you really be like that?"

"You said once I was just like her—repressed, uptight."

"I didn't mean that."

"You've been right about me before," Nancy says, reaching across Jack for a paring knife. "Look, all I mean is that it shouldn't be a matter of *our* convenience. If Grover needs assistance, then it's our problem. We're responsible."

"I'd want to be put out of my misery," Jack says.

During that evening, Nancy has the impression that Jack is talking more than usual. He does not notice the food. She has made chicken Marengo and is startled to realize how much it resembles chicken cacciatore, which she served the last time she had the same people over. The recipes are side by side in the cookbook, gradations on a theme. The dinner is for Stewart and Jan, who are going to Italy on a teaching exchange.

"Maybe I shouldn't even have made Italian," Nancy tells them apologetically. "You'll get enough of that in Italy. And it will be real."

Both Stewart and Jan say the chicken Marengo is wonderful. The olives are the right touch, Jan says. Ted and Laurie nod agreement. Jack pours more wine. The sound of a log falling in the woodstove reminds Nancy of the dog in the other room by the stove, and in her mind she stages a scene: finding the dog dead in the middle of the dinner party.

Afterward, they sit in the living room, with Grover lying there like a log too large for the stove. The guests talk idly. Ted has been sandblasting old paint off a brick fireplace, and Laurie complains about the gritty dust. Jack stokes the fire. The stove, hooked up through the fireplace, looks like a robot from an old science fiction movie. Nancy and Jack used to sit by the fireplace in Massachusetts, stoned, watching the blue frills of the flames, imagining that they were musical notes, visual textures of sounds on the stereo. Nobody they know smokes grass anymore. Now people sit around and talk about investments and proper flue linings. When Jack passes around the Grand Marnier, Nancy says, "In my grandparents' house years ago, we used to sit by their fireplace. They burned coal. They didn't call it a fireplace, though. They called it a grate."

"Coal burns more efficiently than wood," Jack says.

"Coal's a lot cheaper in this area," says Ted. "I wish I could switch."

"My grandparents had big stone fireplaces in their country house," says Jan, who comes from Connecticut. "They were so pleasant. I always looked forward to going there. Sometimes in the summer the evenings were cool and we'd have a fire. It was lovely."

"I remember being cold," says Nancy. "It was always very cold, even in the South."

"The heat just goes up the chimney in a fireplace," says Jack.

Nancy stares at Jack. She says, "I would stand in front of the fire until I was roasted. Then I would turn and roast the other side. In the evenings, my grandparents sat on the hearth and read the Bible. There wasn't anything *lovely* about it. They were trying to keep warm. Of course, nobody had heard of insulation."

"There goes Nancy, talking about her deprived childhood," Jack says with a laugh.

Nancy says, "Jack is so concerned about wasting energy. But when he goes out he never wears a hat." She looks at Jack. "Don't you know your body heat just flies out the top of your head? It's a chimney."

Surprised by her tone, she almost breaks into tears.

It is the following evening, and Jack is flipping through some contact sheets of a series on solar hot-water heaters he is doing for a magazine. Robert sheds his goose-down vest, and he and Grover, on the floor, simultaneously inch away from the fire. Nancy is trying to read the novel written by the friend from Amherst, but the book is boring. She would not have recognized her witty friend from the past in the turgid prose she is reading.

"It's a dump on the sixties," she tells Jack when he asks. "A really cynical look. All the characters are types."

"Are we in it?"

"No. I hope not. I think it's based on that Phil Baxter who cracked up at that party."

Grover raises his head, his eyes alert, and Robert jumps up, saying, "It's time for Grover's treat."

He shakes a Pet-Tab from a plastic bottle and holds it before Grover's nose. Grover bangs his tail against the rug as he crunches the pill.

Jack turns on the porch light and steps outside for a moment, returning with a shroud of cold air. "It's starting to snow," he says. "Come on out, Grover."

Grover struggles to stand, and Jack heaves the dog's hind legs over the threshold.

Later, in bed, Jack turns on his side and watches Nancy, reading her book, until she looks up at him.

"You read so much," he says. "You're always reading."

"Hmm."

"We used to have more fun. We used to be silly together."

"What do you want to do?"

"Just something silly."

"I can't think of anything silly." Nancy flips the page back, rereading. "God, this guy can't write. I used to think he was so clever."

In the dark, touching Jack tentatively, she says, "We've changed. We used to lie awake all night, thrilled just to touch each other."

"We've been busy. That's what happens. People get busy."

"That scares me," says Nancy. "Do you want to have another baby?"

"No. I want a dog." Jack rolls away from her, and Nancy can hear him breathing into his pillow. She waits to hear if he will cry. She recalls Jack returning to her in California after Robert was born. He brought a God's-eye, which he hung from the ceiling above Robert's crib, to protect him. Jack never wore the sweater Nancy made for him. Instead, Grover slept on it. Nancy gave the dog her granny-square afghan too, and eventually, when they moved back East, she got rid of the pathetic evidence of her creative period—the crochet hooks, the piles of yarn, some splotchy batik tapestries. Now most of the objects in the house are Jack's. He made the oak counters and the dining room table; he remodeled the studio; he chose the draperies; he photographed the pictures on the wall. If Jack were to leave again, there would be no way to remove his presence, the way the dog can disappear completely, with his sounds. Nancy revises the scene in her mind. The house is still there, but Nancy is not in it.

In the morning, there is a four-inch snow, with a drift blowing up the back-porch steps. From the kitchen window, Nancy watches her son float silently down the hill behind the house. At the end, he tumbles off his sled deliberately, wallowing in the snow, before standing up to wave, trying to catch her attention.

On the back porch, Nancy and Jack hold Grover over newspapers. Grover performs unselfconsciously now. Nancy says, "Maybe he can hang on, as long as we can do this."

"But look at him, Nancy," Jack says. "He's in misery."

Jack holds Grover's collar and helps him slide over the threshold. Grover aims for his place by the fire.

After the snowplow passes, late in the morning, Nancy drives Robert to the school on slushy roads, all the while lecturing him on the absurdity of raising money to buy official Boy Scout equipment, especially on a snowy Saturday. The Boy Scouts are selling water-savers for toilet tanks in order to earn money for camping gear.

"I thought Boy Scouts spent their time earning badges," says Nancy. "I thought you were supposed to learn about nature, instead of spending money on official Boy Scout pots and pans."

"This is nature," Robert says solemnly. "It's ecology. Saving water when you flush is ecology."

Later, Nancy and Jack walk in the woods together. Nancy walks behind Jack, stepping in his boot tracks. He shields her from the wind. Her hair is blowing. They walk briskly up a hill and emerge on a ridge that overlooks a valley. In the distance they can see a housing development, a radio tower, a winding road. House trailers dot the hillsides. A snowplow is going up a road, like a zipper in the landscape.

Jack says, "I'm going to call the vet Monday."

Nancy gasps in cold air. She says, "Robert made us promise you won't do anything without letting him in on it. That goes for me too." When Jack doesn't respond, she says, "I'd want to hang on, even if I was in a coma. There must be some spark, in the deep recesses of the mind, some twitch, a flicker of a dream—"

"A twitch that could make life worth living?" Jack laughs bitterly.

"Yes." She points to the brilliantly colored sparkles the sun is making on the snow. "Those are the sparks I mean," she says. "In the brain somewhere, something like that. That would be beautiful."

"You're weird, Nancy."

"I learned it from you. I never would have noticed anything like that if I hadn't known you, if you hadn't got me stoned and made me look at your photographs." She stomps her feet in the snow. Her toes are cold. "You educated me. I was so out of it when I met you. One day I was listening to Hank Williams and shelling corn for the chickens and the next day I was expected to know what wines went with what. Talk about weird."

"You're exaggerating. That was years ago. You always exaggerate your background." He adds in a teasing tone, "Your humble origins."

"We've been together fifteen years," says Nancy. She stops him, holding his arm. Jack is squinting, looking at something in the distance. She goes on, "You said we didn't do anything silly anymore. What should we do, Jack? Should we make angels in the snow?"

Jack touches his rough glove to her face. "We shouldn't unless we really feel like it."

It was the same as Jack chiding her to be honest, to be expressive. The same old Jack, she thought, relieved.

⌒

"Come and look," Robert cries, bursting in the back door. He and Jack have been outside making a snowman. Nancy is rolling dough for a quiche. Jack will eat a quiche but not a custard pie, although they are virtually the same. She wipes her hands and goes to the door of the porch. She sees Grover swinging from the lower branch of the maple tree. Jack has rigged up a sling, so that the dog is supported in a harness, with the canvas from the back of a deck chair holding his stomach. His legs dangle free.

"Oh, Jack," Nancy calls. "The poor thing."

"I thought this might work," Jack explains. "A support for his hind legs." His arms cradle the dog's head. "I did it for you," he adds, looking at Nancy. "Don't push him, Robert. I don't think he wants to swing."

Grover looks amazingly patient, like a cat in a doll bonnet.

"He hates it," says Jack, unbuckling the harness.

"He can learn to like it," Robert says, his voice rising shrilly.

⌒

On the day that Jack has planned to take Grover to the veterinarian, Nancy runs into a crisis at work. One of the children has been exposed to hepatitis, and it is necessary to vaccinate all of them. Nancy has to arrange the details, which means staying late. She telephones Jack to ask him to pick up Robert after school.

"I don't know when I'll be home," she says. "This is an administrative nightmare. I have to call all the parents, get permissions, make arrangements with family doctors."

"What will we do about Grover?"

"Please postpone it. I want to be with you then."

"I want to get it over with," says Jack impatiently. "I hate to put Robert through another day of this."

"Robert will be glad of the extra time," Nancy insists. "So will I."

"I just want to face things," Jack says. "Don't you understand? I don't want to cling to the past like you're doing."

"Please wait for us," Nancy says, her voice calm and controlled.

On the telephone, Nancy is authoritative, a quick decision-maker. The problem at work is a reprieve. She feels free, on her own. During the afternoon, she works rapidly and efficiently, filing reports, consulting health authorities, notifying parents. She talks with the disease-control center in Atlanta, inquiring about guidelines. She checks on supplies of gamma globulin. She is so preoccupied that in the middle of the afternoon, when Robert suddenly appears in her office, she is startled, for a fleeting instant not recognizing him.

He says, "Kevin has a sore throat. Is that hepatitis?"

"It's probably just a cold. I'll talk to his mother." Nancy is holding Robert's arm, partly to keep him still, partly to steady herself.

"When do I have to get a shot?" Robert asks.

"Tomorrow."

"Do I have to?"

"Yes. It won't hurt, though."

"I guess it's a good thing this happened," Robert says bravely. "Now we get to have Grover another day." Robert spills his books on the floor and bends to pick them up. When he looks up, he says, "Daddy doesn't care about him. He just wants to get rid of him. He wants to kill him."

"Oh, Robert, that's not true," says Nancy. "He just doesn't want Grover to suffer."

"But Grover still has half a bottle of Pet-Tabs," Robert says. "What will we do with them?"

"I don't know," Nancy says. She hands Robert his numbers workbook. Like a tape loop, the face of her child as a stranger replays in her mind. Robert has her plain brown hair, her coloring, but his eyes are Jack's—demanding and eerily penetrating eyes that could pin her to the wall.

After Robert leaves, Nancy lowers the venetian blinds. Her office is brilliantly lighted by the sun, through south-facing windows. The design was accidental, nothing to do with solar energy. It is an old building. Bars of light slant across her desk, like a formidable scene in a forties movie. Nancy's secretary goes home, but Nancy works on, contacting all the parents she couldn't get during working hours. One parent anxiously reports that her child has a swollen lymph node on his neck.

"No," Nancy says firmly. "That is *not* a symptom of hepatitis. But you should ask the doctor about that when you go in for the gamma globulin."

Gamma globulin. The phrase rolls off her tongue. She tries to remember an odd title of a movie about gamma rays. It comes to her as she is dialing the telephone. *The Effect of Gamma Rays on Man-in-the-Moon Marigolds.* She has never known what that title meant.

The office grows dim, and Nancy turns on the lights. The school is quiet, as though the threat of an infectious disease has emptied the corridors, leaving her in charge. She recalls another movie, *The Andromeda Strain.* Her work is like the thrill of watching drama, a threat held safely at a distance. Historians have to be detached, Nancy once said, defensively, to Jack, when he accused her of being unfriendly to shopkeepers and waiters. Where was all that Southern hospitality he had heard so much about? he wanted to know. It hits her now that historians are detached about the past, not the present. Jack has learned some of this detachment: he wants to let Grover go. Nancy thinks of the stark images in his recent photographs—snow, icicles, fences, the long shot of Grover on the hill like a stray wolf. Nancy had always liked Jack's pictures simply for what they were, but Jack didn't see the people or the objects in them. He saw illusions. The vulnerability of the image, he once said, was what he was after. The image was meant to evoke its own death, he told her.

By the time Nancy finishes the scheduling, the night maintenance crew has arrived, and the coffeepot they keep in a closet is perking. Nancy removes her contact lenses and changes into her fleece-lined boots. In the parking lot, she maneuvers cautiously along a path past a mountain of black-stained snow. It is so cold that she makes sparks on the vinyl car seat. The engine is cold, slow to turn over.

At home, Nancy is surprised to see balloons in the living room. The stove is blazing and Robert's face is red from the heat.

"We're having a party," he says. "For Grover."

"There's a surprise for you in the oven," says Jack, handing Nancy a glass of sherry. "Because you worked so hard."

"Grover had ice cream," Robert says. "We got Häagen-Dazs."

"He looks cheerful," Nancy says, sinking onto the couch next to Jack. Her glasses are fogged up. She removes them and wipes them with a Kleenex. When she puts them back on, she sees Grover looking at her, his head on his paws. His tail thumps. For the first time, Nancy feels ready to let the dog die.

When Nancy tells about the gamma globulin, the phrase has stopped rolling off her tongue so trippingly. She laughs. She is so tired she throbs with relief. She drinks the sherry too fast. Suddenly, she sits up straight and announces, "I've got a clue. I'm thinking of a parking lot."

"East or West?" Jack says. This is a game they used to play.

"West."

"Aha, I've got you," says Jack. "You're thinking of the parking lot at the hospital in Tucson."

"Hey, that's not fair going too fast," cries Robert. "I didn't get a chance to play."

"This was before you were born," Nancy says, running her fingers through Robert's hair. He is on the floor, leaning against her knees. "We were lying in the van for a week, thinking we were going to die. Oh, God!" Nancy laughs and covers her mouth with her hands.

"Why were you going to die?" Robert asks.

"We weren't really going to die." Both Nancy and Jack are laughing now at the memory, and Jack is pulling off his sweater. The hospital in Tucson wouldn't accept them because they weren't sick enough to hospitalize, but they were too sick to travel. They had nowhere to go. They had been on a month's trip through the West, then had stopped in Tucson and gotten jobs at a restaurant to make enough money to get home.

"Do you remember that doctor?" Jack says.

"I remember the look he gave us, like he didn't want us to pollute his hospital." Nancy laughs harder. She feels silly and relieved. Her hand, on Jack's knee, feels the fold of the long johns beneath his jeans. She cries, "I'll never forget how we stayed around that parking lot, thinking we were going to die."

"I couldn't have driven a block, I was so weak," Jack gasps.

"You were yellow. *I* didn't get yellow."

"All we could do was pee and drink orange juice."

"And throw the pee out the window."

"Grover was so bored with us!"

Nancy says, "It's a good thing we couldn't eat. We would have spent all our money."

"Then we would have had to work at that filthy restaurant again. And get hepatitis again."

"And on and on, forever. We would still be there, like Charley on the MTA. Oh, Jack, do you *remember* that crazy restaurant? You had to wear a ten-gallon hat—"

Abruptly, Robert jerks away from Nancy and crawls on his knees across the room to examine Grover, who is stretched out on his side, his legs sticking out stiffly. Robert, his straight hair falling, bends his head to the dog's heart.

"He's not dead," Robert says, looking up at Nancy. "He's lying doggo."

"Passed out at his own party," Jack says, raising his glass. "Way to go, Grover!"

THE BAR SINISTER
(1902)
Richard Harding Davis

Although fictional, this story is based on a real-life dog of doubtful pedigree known as Englewood Cold Steel, who was a champion of his breed in Canada. Written over a century ago, it is an account of a fighting pit bull that becomes a show dog. Leaving aside the grisly and shocking nature of dogfighting (long since outlawed in North America), the story has the charm of being told by the dog himself, and he's an endearing critter with loads of character.

Author Richard Harding Davis (1864–1916) was himself quite a character. The prototype of the adventurous journalist, he was renowned for on-the-spot reporting of big news events, especially during the Spanish-American war. Soon after becoming a newspaperman, he wrote short stories on the side that made him enormously popular and wealthy. "The Bar Sinister," considered his best work, was first published in *Scribner's Magazine*.

The Master was walking most unsteady, his legs tripping each other. After the fifth or sixth round, my legs often go the same way.

But even when the Master's legs bend and twist a bit, you mustn't think he can't reach you. Indeed, that is the time he kicks most frequent. So I kept behind him in the shadow, or ran in the middle of the street. He stopped at many public houses with swinging doors, those doors that are cut so high from the sidewalk that you can look in under them, and see if the Master is inside. At night, when I peep beneath them, the man at the counter will see me first and say, "Here's the Kid, Jerry, come to take you home. Get a move on you"; and the Master will stumble out and follow me. It's lucky for us I'm so white, for no matter how dark the night, he can always see me ahead, just out of reach of his boot. At night the Master certainly does see most amazing. Sometimes he sees two or four of me, and walks in a circle, so that I have to take him by the leg of his trousers and lead him into the right road. One night, when he was very nasty-tempered and I was coaxing him along, two men passed us, and one of them says, "Look at that brute!" and the other asks, "Which?" and they both laugh. The Master cursed them good and proper.

But this night, whenever we stopped at a public house, the Master's pals left it and went on with us to the next. They spoke quite civil to me, and when the Master tried a flying kick, they gives him a shove. "Do you want us to lose our money?" says the pals.

I had had nothing to eat for a day and a night, and just before we set out the Master gives me a wash under the hydrant. Whenever I am locked up until all the slop pans in our alley are empty, and made to take a bath, and the Master's pals speak civil and feel my ribs, I know something is going to happen. And that night, when every time they see a policeman under a lamppost, they dodged across the street, and when at the last one of them picked me up and hid me under his jacket, I began to tremble; for I knew what it meant. It meant that I was to fight again for the Master.

I don't fight because I like fighting. I fight because if I didn't the other dog would find my throat, and the Master would lose his stakes, and I would be very sorry for him, and ashamed. Dogs can pass me and I can pass dogs, and I'd never pick a fight with none of them. When I see two dogs standing on their hind legs in the streets, clawing each other's ears, and snapping for each other's windpipes, or howling and swearing and rolling in the mud, I feel sorry they should act so, and pretend not to notice. If he'd let me, I'd like to pass the time of day with every dog I meet. But there's something about me that no nice dog can abide. When I trot up to nice dogs, nodding and grinning, to make friends, they always tell me to be off. "Go to the devil!" they bark at me. "Get out!" And when I walk away they shout "Mongrel!" and "Gutter dog!" and sometimes, after my back is turned, they rush me. I could kill most of them with three shakes, breaking the backbone of the little ones and squeezing the throat of the big ones. But what's the good? They *are* nice dogs; that's why I try to make up to them; and, though it's not for them to say it, I *am* a street dog, and if I try to push into the company of my betters, I suppose it's their right to teach me my place.

Of course they don't know I'm the best fighting bull terrier of my weight in Montreal. That's why it wouldn't be fair for me to take notice of what they shout. They don't know that if I once locked my jaws on them I'd carry away whatever I touched. The night I fought Kelley's White Rat, I wouldn't loosen up until the Master made a noose in my leash and strangled me; and, as for that Ottawa dog, if the handlers hadn't thrown red pepper down my nose I *never* would have let go of him. I don't think the handlers treated me quite right that time, but maybe they didn't know the Ottawa dog was dead. I did.

I learned my fighting from my mother when I was very young. We slept in a lumber yard on the river front, and by day hunted for food along the wharves. When we got it, the other tramp dogs would try to take it off us, and then it was wonderful to see mother fly at them and drive them away. All I know of fighting I learned from mother, watching her picking the ash heaps for me when I was too little to fight for myself. No one ever was so good to me as mother. When it snowed and the ice was in the St. Lawrence, she used to hunt alone, and bring me back new bones, and she'd sit and laugh to see me trying to swallow 'em whole. I was just a puppy then; my teeth was falling out. When I was able to fight we kept the whole river range to ourselves. I had the genuine long "punishing" jaw, so mother said, and there wasn't a man or a dog that dared worry us. Those were happy days, those were; and we lived well, share and share alike, and when we wanted a bit of fun, we chased the fat old wharf rats! My, how they would squeal!

Then the trouble came. It was no trouble to me. I was too young to care then. But mother took it so to heart that she grew ailing, and wouldn't go abroad with me by day. It was the same old scandal that they're always bringing up against me. I was so young then that I didn't know. I couldn't see any difference between mother—and other mothers.

But one day a pack of curs we drove off snarled back some new names at her, and mother dropped her head and ran, just as though they had whipped us. After that she wouldn't go out with me except in the dark, and one day she went away and never came back, and, though I hunted for her in every court and alley and back street of Montreal, I never found her.

One night, a month after mother ran away, I asked Guardian, the old blind mastiff, whose Master is the night watchman on our slip, what it all meant. And he told me.

"Every dog in Montreal knows," he says, "except you; and every Master knows. So I think it's time you knew."

Then he tells me that my father, who had treated mother so bad, was a great and noble gentleman from London. "Your father had twenty-two registered ancestors, had your father," old Guardian says, "And in him was the best bull-terrier blood of England, the most ancientest, the most royal; the winning 'blue-ribbon' blood, that breeds champions. He had sleepy pink eyes and thin pink lips, and he was as white all over as his own white teeth, and under his white skin you could see his muscles, hard and smooth, like the links of a steel chain. When your father stood still, and tipped his nose in the air, it was just as though he was saying, 'Oh, yes, you common dogs and men, you may well stare. It must be a rare treat for you colonials to see real English royalty.' He certainly was pleased with hisself, was your father. He looked just as proud and haughty as one of them stone dogs in Victoria Park—them as is cut out of white marble. And you're like him," says the old mastiff—"by that, of course, meaning you're white, same as him. That's the only likeness. But, you see, the trouble is, Kid—well, you see, Kid, the trouble is—your mother—"

"That will do," I said, for then I understood without his telling me, and I got up and walked away, holding my head and tail high in the air.

But I was, oh, so miserable, and I wanted to see mother that very minute, and tell her that I didn't care.

Mother is what I am, a street dog; there's no royal blood in mother's veins, nor is she like that father of mine, nor—and that's the worst—she's not even like me. For while I, when I'm washed for a fight, am as white as clean snow, she—and this is our trouble—she, my mother, is a black-and-tan.

When mother hid herself from me, I was twelve months old and able to take care of myself, and as, after mother left me, the wharves were never the same, I moved uptown and met the Master. Before he came, lots of other menfolks had tried to make up to me, and to whistle me home. But they either tried patting me or coaxing me with a piece of meat; so I didn't take to 'em. But one day the Master pulled me out of a street fight by the hind legs, and kicked me good.

"You want to fight, do you?" says he. "I'll give you all the *fighting* you want!" he says, and he kicks me again. So I knew he was my Master, and I followed him home. Since that day I've pulled off many fights for him, and they've brought dogs from all over the province to have a go at me; but up to that night none, under thirty pounds, had ever downed me.

But that night, so soon as they carried me into the ring, I saw the dog was overweight, and that I was no match for him. It was asking too much of a puppy. The Master should have known I couldn't do it. Not that I mean to blame the Master, for when sober, which he sometimes was—though not, as you might say, his habit—he was most kind to me, and let me out to find food, if I could get it, and only kicked me when I didn't pick him up at night and lead him home.

But kicks will stiffen the muscles, and starving a dog so as to get him ugly-tempered for a fight may make him nasty, but it's weakening to his insides, and it causes the legs to wobble.

The ring was in a hall back of a public house. There was a red-hot white-washed stove in one corner, and the ring in the other. I lay in the Master's lap, wrapped in my blanket, and, spite of the stove, shivering awful; but I always shiver before a fight: I can't help gettin' excited. While the menfolks were a-flashing their money and taking their last drink at the bar, a little Irish groom in gaiters came up to me and gave me the back of his hand to smell, and scratched me behind the ears.

"You poor little pup," says he; "you haven't no show," he says. "That brute in the taproom he'll eat your heart out."

"That's what *you* think," says the Master, snarling. "I'll lay you a quid that Kid chews him up."

The groom he shook his head, but kept looking at me so sorry-like that I begun to get a bit sad myself. He seemed like he couldn't bear to leave off a-patting of me, and he says, speaking low just like he would to a manfolk, "Well, good luck to you, little pup," which I thought so civil of him that I reached up and licked his hand. I don't do that to many men. And the Master he knew I didn't, and took on dreadful.

"What 'ave you got on the back of your hand?" says he, jumping up.

"Soap!" says the groom, quick as a rat. "That's more than you've got on yours. Do you want to smell of it?" and he sticks his fist under the Master's nose. But the pals pushed in between 'em.

"He tried to poison the Kid!" shouts the Master.

"Oh, one fight at a time," says the referee. "Get into the ring, Jerry. We're waiting." So we went into the ring.

I could never just remember what did happen in that ring. He give me no time to spring. He fell on me like a horse. I couldn't keep my feet against him, and though, as I saw, he could get his hold when he liked, he wanted to chew me over a bit first. I was wondering if they'd be able to pry him off me, when, in the third round, he took his hold; and I begun to drown, just as I did when I fell into the river off the Red C slip. He closed deeper and deeper on my throat, and everything went black and red and bursting; and then, when I were sure I were dead, the handlers pulled him off, and the Master give me a kick that brought me to. But I couldn't move none, or even wink, both eyes being shut with lumps.

"He's a cur," yells the Master, "a sneaking, cowardly cur! He lost the fight for me," says he, "because he's a—cowardly cur." And he kicks me again in the lower ribs, so that I go sliding across the sawdust. "There's gratitude fer yer," yells the Master. "I've fed that dog, and nussed that dog and housed him like a prince; and now he puts his tail between his legs and sells me out, he does. He's a coward! I've done with him, I am. I'd sell him for a pipeful of tobacco." He picked me up by the tail, and swung me for the menfolks to see. "Does any gentleman here want to buy a dog," he says, "to make into sausage meat?" he says. "That's all he's good for."

Then I heard the little Irish groom say, "I'll give you ten bob for the dog."

And another voice says, "Ah, don't you do it; the dog's same as dead— mebbe he is dead."

"Ten shilling!" says the Master, and his voice sobers a bit, "make it two pounds and he's yours."

But the pals rushed in again.

"Don't you be a fool, Jerry," they say. "You'll be sorry for this when you're sober. The Kid's worth a fiver."

One of my eyes was not so swelled up as the other, and as I hung by my tail, I opened it, and saw one of the pals take the groom by the shoulder.

"You ought to give 'im five pounds for that dog, mate," he says, "that's no ordinary dog. That dog's got good blood in him, that dog has. Why, his father—that very dog's father—"

I thought he never would go on. He waited like he wanted to be sure the groom was listening.

"That very dog's father," says the pal, "is Regent Royal, son of Champion Regent Monarch, champion bull terrier of England for four years."

I was sore, and torn, and chewed most awful, but what the pal said sounded so fine that I wanted to wag my tail, only couldn't, owing to my hanging from it.

But the Master calls out: "Yes, his father was Regent Royal; who's saying he wasn't? but the pup's a cowardly cur; that's what this pup is. And why? I'll tell you why: because his mother was a black-and-tan street dog, that's why!"

I don't see how I got the strength, but, some way, I threw myself out of the Master's grip and fell at his feet, and turned over and fastened all my teeth in his ankle, just across the bone.

When I woke, after the pals had kicked me off him, I was in the smoking car of a railroad train, lying in the lap of the little groom, and he was rubbing my open wounds with a greasy yellow stuff, exquisite to the smell and most agreeable to lick off.

II

"Well, what's your name—Nolan? Well, Nolan, these references are satisfactory," said the young gentleman my new Master called "Mr. Wyndham, sir." "I'll take you on as second man. You can begin today."

My new Master shuffled his feet and put his finger to his forehead. "Thank you, sir," says he. Then he choked like he had swallowed a fish bone. "I have a little dawg, sir," says he.

"You can't keep him," says "Mr. Wyndham, sir," very short.

"'E's only a puppy, sir," says my new Master, "'e wouldn't go outside the stables, sir."

"It's not that," says "Mr. Wyndham, sir." "I have a large kennel of very fine dogs; they're the best of their breed in America. I don't allow strange dogs on the premises."

The Master shakes his head, and motions me with his cap, and I crept out from behind the door. "I'm sorry, sir," says the Master. "Then I can't take the place. I can't get along without the dawg, sir."

"Mr. Wyndham, sir," looked at me that fierce that I guessed he was going to whip me, so I turned over on my back and begged with my legs and tail.

"Why, you beat him!" says "Mr. Wyndham, sir," very stern.

"No fear!" the Master says, getting very red. "The party I bought him off taught him that. He never learnt that from me!" He picked me up in his arms, and to show "Mr. Wyndham, sir," how well I loved the Master, I bit his chin and hands.

"Mr. Wyndham, sir," turned over the letters the Master had given him. "Well, these references certainly are very strong," he says. "I guess I'll let the dog stay. Only see you keep him away from the kennels—or you'll both go."

"Thank you, sir," says the Master, grinning like a cat when she's safe behind the area railing.

"He's not a bad bull terrier," says "Mr. Wyndham, sir," feeling my head. "Not that I know much about the smooth-coated breeds. My dogs are St. Bernards." He stopped patting me and held up my nose. "What's the matter with his ears?" he says. "They're chewed to pieces. Is this a fighting dog?" he asks, quick and rough-like.

I could have laughed. If he hadn't been holding my nose, I certainly would have had a good grin at him. Me the best under thirty pounds in the Province of Quebec, and him asking if I was a fighting dog! I ran to the Master and hung down my head modest-like, waiting for him to tell my list of battles; but the Master he coughs in his cap most painful. "Fightin' dawg, sir!" he cries.

"Lor' bless you, sir, the Kid don't know the word. 'E's just a puppy, sir, same as you see; a pet dog, so to speak. 'E's a regular old lady's lapdog, the Kid is."

"Well, you keep him away from my St. Bernards," says "Mr. Wyndham, sir," "or they might make a mouthful of him."

"Yes, sir; that they might," says the Master. But when we gets outside he slaps his knee and laughs hisself, and winks at me most sociable.

The Master's new home was in the country, in a province they called Long Island. There was a high stone wall about his home with big iron gates to it, same as Godfrey's brewery; and there was a house with five red roofs; and the stables, where I lived, was cleaner than the aërated bakery shop. And then there was the kennels; but they was like nothing else in this world that ever I see. For the first days I couldn't sleep of nights for fear someone would catch me lying in such a cleaned-up place, and would chase me out of it; and when I did fall to sleep I'd dream I was back in the old Master's attic, shivering under the rusty stove, which never had no coals in it, with the Master flat on his back on the cold floor, with his clothes on. And I'd wake up scared and whimpering, and find myself on the new Master's cot with his hand on the quilt beside me; and I'd see the glow of the big stove, and hear the high-quality horses below stairs stamping in their straw-lined boxes, and I'd snoop the sweet smell of hay and harness soap and go to sleep again.

The stables was my jail, so the Master said, but I don't ask no better home than that jail.

"Now, Kid," says he, sitting on top of a bucket upside down, "you've got to understand this. When I whistle it means you're not to go out of this 'ere yard. These stables is your jail. If you leave 'em I'll have to leave 'em too, and over the seas, in the County Mayo, and old mother will 'ave to leave her bit of a cottage. For two pounds I must be sending her every month, or she'll have naught to eat, nor no thatch over 'er head. I can't lose my place, Kid, so see you don't lose it for me. You must keep away from the kennels," says he, "they're not for the likes of you. The kennels are for the quality. I wouldn't take a litter of them woolly dogs for one wag of your tail, Kid, but for all that they are your betters, same as the gentry up in the big house are my betters. I know my place and keep away from the gentry, and you keep away from the champions."

So I never goes out of the stables. All day I just lay in the sun on the stone flags, licking my jaws, and watching the grooms wash down the carriages, and the only care I had was to see they didn't get gay and turn the hose on me. There wasn't even a single rat to plague me. Such stables I never did see.

"Nolan," says the head groom, "some day that dog of yours will give you the slip. You can't keep a street dog tied up all his life. It's against his natur'." The head groom is a nice old gentleman, but he doesn't know everything. Just as though I'd been a street dog because I liked it! As if I'd rather poke for my vittels in ash heaps than have 'em handed me in a washbasin, and would sooner bite and fight than be polite and sociable. If I'd had mother there I couldn't have asked for nothing more. But I'd think of her snooping in the gutters, or freezing of nights under the bridges, or, what's worst of all, running through the hot streets with her tongue down, so wild and crazy for a drink that the people would shout "mad dog" at her and stone her. Water's so good that I don't blame the menfolks for locking it up inside their houses; but when the hot days come, I think they might remember that those are the dog days, and leave a little water outside in a trough, like they do for the horses. Then we wouldn't go mad, and the policemen wouldn't shoot us. I had so much of everything I wanted that it made me think a lot of the days when I hadn't nothing, and if I could have given what I had to mother, as she used to share with me, I'd have been the happiest dog in the land. Not that I wasn't happy then, and most grateful to the Master, too, and if I'd only minded him, the trouble wouldn't have come again.

But one day the coachman says that the little lady they called Miss Dorothy had come back from school, and that same morning she runs over to the stables to pat her ponies, and she sees me.

"Oh, what a nice little, white little dog!" said she. "Whose little dog are you?" says she.

"That's my dog, miss," says the Master. " 'Is name is Kid." And I ran up to her most polite, and licks her fingers, for I never see so pretty and kind a lady.

"You must come with me and call on my new puppies," says she, picking me up in her arms and starting off with me.

"Oh, but please, miss," cries Nolan, "Mr. Wyndham give orders that the Kid's not to go to the kennels."

"That'll be all right," says the little lady, "they're my kennels too. And the puppies will like to play with him."

You wouldn't believe me if I was to tell you of the style of them quality dogs. If I hadn't seen it myself I wouldn't have believed it neither. The Viceroy of Canada don't live no better. There was forty of them, but each one had his own house and a yard—most exclusive—and a cot and a drinking basin all to hisself. They had servants standing round waiting to feed 'em when they was hungry, and valets to wash 'em; and they had their hair combed and brushed like the grooms must when they go out on the box. Even the puppies had overcoats with their names on 'em in blue letters, and the name of each of those they called champions was painted up fine over his front door just like it was a public house or a veterinary's. They were the biggest St. Bernards I ever did see. I could have walked under them if they'd have let me. But they were very proud and haughty dogs, and looked only once at me, and then sniffed in the air. The little lady's own dog was an old gentleman bull dog. He'd come along with us, and when he notices how taken aback I was with all I see, 'e turned quite kind and affable and showed me about.

"Jimmy Jocks," Miss Dorothy called him, but, owing to his weight, he walked most dignified and slow, waddling like a duck, as you might say, and looked much too proud and handsome for such a silly name.

"That's the runway, and that's the trophy house," says he to me, "and that over there is the hospital, where you have to go if you get distemper and the vet gives you beastly medicine."

"And which of these is your 'ouse, sir?" asks I, wishing to be respectful. But he looked that hurt and haughty. "I don't live in the kennels," says he, most contemptuous. "I am a house dog. I sleep in Miss Dorothy's room. And at lunch I'm let in with the family, if the visitors don't mind. They 'most always do, but they're too polite to say so. Besides," says he, smiling most condescending, "visitors are always afraid of me. It's because I'm so ugly," says he. "I suppose," says he, screwing up his wrinkles and speaking very slow and impressive, "I suppose I'm the ugliest bull dog in America"; and as he seemed to be so pleased to think hisself so, I said "Yes, sir; you certainly are the ugliest ever I see," at which he nodded his head most approving.

"But I couldn't hurt 'em, as you say," he goes on, though I hadn't said nothing like that, being too polite. "I'm too old," he says; "I haven't any teeth. The last time one of those grizzly bears," said he, glaring at the big St. Bernards, "took a hold of me, he nearly was my death," says he. I thought his eyes would pop out of his head, he seemed so wrought up about it. "He rolled me around in the dirt, he did," says Jimmy Jocks, "an' I couldn't get up. It was low," says Jimmy Jocks, making a face like he had a bad taste in his mouth. "Low, that's what I call it—bad form, you understand, young man, not done in my set—and—and low." He growled way down in his stomach, and puffed hisself out, panting and blowing like he had been on a run.

"I'm not a street fighter," he says, scowling at a St. Bernard marked "Champion." "And when my rheumatism is not troubling me," he says, "I endeavor to be civil to all dogs, so long as they are gentlemen."

"Yes, sir," said I, for even to me he had been most affable.

At this we had come to a little house off by itself, and Jimmy Jocks invites me in. "This is their trophy room," he says, "where they keep their prizes. Mine." he says, rather grand-like, "are on the sideboard." Not knowing what a sideboard might be, I said, "Indeed, sir, that must be very gratifying." But he only wrinkled up his chops as much as to say, "It is my right."

The trophy room was as wonderful as any public house I ever see. On the walls was pictures of nothing but beautiful St. Bernard dogs, and rows and rows of blue and red and yellow ribbons; and when I asked Jimmy Jocks why they was so many more of blue than of the others, he laughs and says,

"Because these kennels always win." And there was many shinning cups on the shelves, which Jimmy Jocks told me were prizes won by champions.

"Now, sir, might I ask you, sir," says I, "wot is a champion?"

At that he panted and breathed so hard I thought he would bust hisself. "My dear young friend!" says he, "wherever you have been educated? A champion is a—champion," he says. "He must win nine blue ribbons in the 'open' class. You follow me—that is—against all comers. Then he has the title before his name, and they put his photograph in the sporting papers. You know, of course that *I* am a champion," says he. "I am Champion Woodstock Wizard III, and the two other Woodstock Wizards, my father and uncle, were both champions."

"But I thought your name was Jimmy Jocks," I said.

He laughs right out at that.

"That's my kennel name, not my registered name," he says. "Why, certainly you know that every dog has two names. Now, for instance, what's your registered name and number?" says he.

"I've got only one name," I says. "Just Kid."

Woodstock Wizard puffs at that and wrinkles up his forehead and pops out his eyes.

"Who are your people?" says he. "Where is your home?"

"At the stable, sir," I said. "My Master is the second groom."

At that Woodstock Wizard III looks at me for quite a bit without winking, and stares all around the room over my head.

"Oh, well," says he at last, "you're a very civil young dog," says he, "and I blame no one for what he can't help," which I thought most fair and liberal. "And I have known many bull terriers that were champions," says he, "though as a rule they mostly run with fire engines and to fighting. For me, I wouldn't care to run through the streets after a hose cart, nor to fight," says he: "but each to his taste."

I could not help thinking that if Woodstock Wizard III tried to follow a fire engine he would die of apoplexy, and seeing he'd lost his teeth, it was lucky he had no taste for fighting; but, after his being so condescending, I didn't say nothing.

"Anyway," says he, "every smooth-coated dog is better than any hairy old camel like those St. Bernards, and if ever you're hungry down at the stables, young man, come up to the house and I'll give you a bone, I can't eat them myself, but I bury them around the garden from force of habit and in case a friend should drop in. Ah, I see my mistress coming," he says, "and I bid you good day. I regret," he says, "that our different social position prevents our meeting frequent, for you're a worthy young dog with a proper respect for your betters, and in this country there's precious few of them have that." Then he waddles off, leaving me alone and very sad, for he was the first dog in many days that had spoke to me. But since he showed, seeing that I was a stable dog, he didn't want my company, I waited for him to get well away. It was not a cheerful place to wait, the trophy house. The pictures of the champions seemed to scowl at me, and ask what right such as I had even to admire them, and the blue and gold ribbons and the silver cups made me very miserable. I had never won no blue ribbons or silver cups, only stakes for the old Master to spend in the publics; and I hadn't won them for being a beautiful high-quality dog, but just for fighting—which, or course, as Woodstock Wizard III says, is low. So I started for the stables, with my head down and my tail between my legs, feeling sorry I had ever left the Master. But I had more reason to be sorry before I got back to him.

The trophy house was quite a bit from the kennels, and as I left it I see Miss Dorothy and Woodstock Wizard III walking back toward them, and, also, that a big St. Bernard, his name was Champion Red Elfberg, had broke his chain and was running their way. When he reaches old Jimmy Jocks he lets out a roar like a grain steamer in a fog, and he makes three leaps for him. Old Jimmy Jocks was about a fourth his size; but he plants his feet and curves his back, and his hair goes up around his neck like a collar. But he never had no show at no time, for the grizzly bear, as Jimmy Jocks had called him, lights on old Jimmy's back and tries to break it, and old Jimmy Jocks snaps his gums and claws the grass, panting and groaning awful. But he can't do nothing, and the grizzly bear just rolls him under him, biting and tearing cruel. The odds was all that Woodstock Wizard III was going to be killed; I had fought enough to see that: but not knowing the rules of the game among champions, I didn't like to interfere between two gentlemen who might be settling a private affair, and, as it were, take it as presuming of me. So I stood by, though I was shaking terrible, and holding myself in like I was on a leash. But at that Woodstock Wizard III, who was underneath, sees me through the dust, and calls very faint, "Help, you!" he says. "Take him in the hind leg," he says. "He's murdering me," he says. And then the little Miss Dorothy, who was crying, and calling to the kennel men, catches at the Red Elfberg's hind legs to pull him off, and the brute, keeping his front pats well in Jimmy's stomach, turns his big head and snaps at her. So that was all I asked for, thank you. I went up under him. It was really nothing. He stood so high that I had only to take off about three feet from him and come in from the side, and my long "punishing jaw," as mother was always talking about, locked on his woolly throat, and my back teeth met. I couldn't shake him, but I shook myself and every time I shook myself there was thirty pounds of weight tore at his windpipes. I couldn't see nothing for his long hair, but I heard Jimmy Jocks puffing and blowing on one side, and munching the brute's leg with his old gums. Jimmy was an old sport that day, was Jimmy, or Woodstock Wizard III, as I should say. When the Red Elfberg was out and down I had to run, or those kennel men would have had my life. They chased me right into the stables; and from under the hay I watched the head groom take down a carriage whip and order them to the right about. Luckily Master and the young grooms were out, or that day there'd have been fighting for everybody.

Well, it nearly did for me and the Master. "Mr. Wyndham, sir," comes raging to the stables. I'd half killed his prize-winner, he says, and had oughter be shot, and he gives the Master his notice. But Miss Dorothy she follows him, and says it was his Red Elfberg what began the fight, and that I'd saved Jimmy's life, and that old Jimmy Jocks was worth more to her than all the St.

Bernards in the Swiss mountains—wherever they may be. And that I was her champion, anyway. Then she cried over me most beautiful, and over Jimmy Jocks, too, who was that tied up in bandages he couldn't even waddle. So when he heard that side of it, "Mr. Wyndham, sir," told us that if Nolan put me on a chain we could stay. So it came out all right for everybody but me. I was glad the Master kept his place, but I'd never worn a chain before, and it disheartened me. But that was the least of it. For the quality dogs couldn't forgive my whipping their champion, and they came to the fence between the kennels and the stables, and laughed through the bars, barking most cruel words at me. I couldn't understand how they found it out, but they knew. After the fight Jimmy Jocks was most condescending to me, and he said the grooms had boasted to the kennel men that I was a son of Regent Royal, and that when the kennel men asked who was my mother they had had to tell them that too. Perhaps that was the way of it, but, however, the scandal got out, and every one of the quality dogs knew that I was a street dog and the son of a black-and-tan.

"These misalliances will occur," said Jimmy Jocks, in his old-fashioned way, "but no well-bred dog," says he, looking most scornful at the St. Bernards, who were howling behind the palings, "would refer to your misfortune before you, certainly not cast it in your face. I myself remember your father's father, when he made his début at the Crystal Palace. He took four blue ribbons and three specials."

But no sooner than Jimmy would leave me the St. Bernards would take to howling again, insulting mother and insulting me. And when I tore at my chain, they, seeing they were safe, would howl the more. It was never the same after that; the laughs and the jeers cut into my heart, and the chain bore heavy on my spirit. I was so sad that sometimes I wished I was back in the gutter again, where no one was better than me, and some nights I wished I was dead. If it hadn't been for the Master being so kind, and that it would have looked like I was blaming mother, I would have twisted my leash and hanged myself.

About a month after my fight, the word was passed through the kennels that the New York show was coming, and such goings on as followed I never did see. If each of them had been matched to fight for a thousand pounds and the gate, they couldn't have trained more conscientious. But perhaps that's just my envy. The kennel men rubbed 'em and scrubbed 'em, and trims their hair and curls and combs it, and some dogs they fatted and some they starved. No one talked of nothing but the Show, and the chances "our kennels" had against the other kennels, and if this one of our champions would win over that one, and whether them as hoped to be champions had better show in the "open" or the "limit" class, and whether this dog would beat his own dad or whether his little puppy sister couldn't beat the two of 'em. Even the grooms had their money up, and day or night you heard nothing but praises of "our" dogs, until I, being so far out of it, couldn't have felt meaner if I had been running the streets with a can to my tail. I knew shows were not for such as me, and so all day I lay stretched at the end of my chain, pretending I was asleep, and only too glad that they had something so important to think of that they could leave me alone.

But one day, before the Show opened, Miss Dorothy came to the stables with "Mr. Wyndham, sir," and, seeing me chained up and so miserable, she takes me in her arms.

"You poor little tyke!" says she. "It's cruel to tie him up so; he's eating his heart out, Nolan," she says. "I don't know nothing about bull terriers," says she, "but I think Kid's got good points," says she, "and you ought to show him. Jimmy Jocks had three legs on the Rensselaer Cup now, and I'm going to show him this time, so that he can get the fourth; and, if you wish, I'll enter your dog too. How would you like that, Kid? Maybe you'd meet a pal or two," says she. "It would cheer you up, wouldn't it, Kid?" says she. "How would you like to see the most beautiful dogs in the world?" says she. But I was so upset I could only wag my tail most violent. "He says it would!" says she, though, being that excited, I hadn't said nothing.

So "Mr. Wyndham, sir," laughs, and takes out a piece of blue paper and sits down at the head groom's table.

"What's the name of the father of your dog, Nolan?" says he. And Nolan says: "The man I got him off told me he was a son of Champion Regent Royal, sir. But it don't seem likely, does it?" says Nolan.

"It does not!" says "Mr. Wyndham, sir," short like.

"Aren't you sure, Nolan?" says Miss Dorothy.

"No, miss," says the Master.

"Sire unknown," says "Mr. Wyndham, sir," and writes it down.

"Date of birth?" asks "Mr. Wyndham, sir."

"I—I—unknown, sir," says Nolan. And "Mr. Wyndham, sir," writes it down.

"Breeder?" says "Mr. Wyndham, sir."

"Unknown," says Nolan, getting very red around the jaws, and I drops my head and tail. And "Mr. Wyndham, sir," writes that down.

"Mother's name?" says "Mr. Wyndham, sir."

"She was a—unknown," says the Master. And I licks his hand.

"Dam unknown," says "Mr. Wyndham, sir," and writes it down. Then he takes the paper and reads out loud: " 'Sire unknown, dam unknown, breeder unknown, date of birth unknown.' You'd better call him the 'Great Unknown,'" says he. "Who's paying his entrance fee?"

"I am," says Miss Dorothy.

Two weeks after we all got on a train for New York, Jimmy Jocks and me following Nolan in the smoking car, and twenty-two of the St. Bernards in boxes and crates and on chains and leashes. Such a barking and howling I never did hear; and when they sees me going, too, they laughs fit to kill.

"Wot is this—a circus?" says the railroad man.

But I had no heart in it. I hated to go. I knew I was no "show" dog, even though Miss Dorothy and the Master did their best to keep me from shaming them. For before we set out Miss Dorothy brings a man from town who scrubbed and rubbed me, and sandpapered my tail, which hurt most awful, and shaved my ears with the Master's razor, so they could 'most see clear through 'em, and sprinkles me over with pipe clay, till I shines like a Tommy's crossbelts.

"Upon my word!" says Jimmy Jocks when he first sees me. "Wot a swell you are! You're the image of your granddad when he made his début at the Crystal Palace. He took four firsts and three specials." But I knew he was only trying to throw heart into me. They might scrub, and they might rub, and they might pipe-clay, but they couldn't pipe-clay the insides of me, and they was black-and-tan.

Then we came to a garden, which it was not, but the biggest hall in the world. Inside there was lines of benches a few miles long, and on them sat every dog in America. If all the dog-snatchers in Montreal had worked night and day for a year, they couldn't have caught so many dogs. And they was all shouting and barking and howling so vicious that my heart stopped beating. For at first I thought they was all enraged at my presuming to intrude. But after I got in my place they kept at it just the same, barking at every dog as he come in: daring him to fight, and ordering him out, and asking him what breed of dog he thought he was, anyway. Jimmy Jocks was chained just behind me, and he said he never see so fine a show. "That's a hot class you're in, my lad," he says, looking over into my street, where there were thirty bull terriers. They was all as white as cream, and each so beautiful that if I could have broke my chain I would have run all the way home and hid myself under the horse trough.

All night long they talked and sang, and passed greetings with old pals, and the homesick puppies howled dismal. Them that couldn't sleep wouldn't let no others sleep, and all the electric lights burned in the roof, and in my eyes. I could hear Jimmy Jocks snoring peaceful, but I could only doze by jerks, and when I dozed I dreamed horrible. All the dogs in the hall seemed coming at me for daring to intrude, with their jaws red and open, and their eyes blazing like the lights in the roof. "You're a street dog! Get out, you street dog!" they yells. And as they drives me out, the pipe clay drops off me, and they laugh and shriek; and when I looks down I see that I have turned into a black-and-tan.

They was the most awful dreams, and next morning, when Miss Dorothy come and gives me water in a pan, I begs and begs her to take me home; but she can't understand. "How well Kid is!" she says. And when I jumps into the Master's arms and pulls to break my chain, he says, "If he knew all he had against him, miss, he wouldn't be so gay." And from a book they reads out the name of the beautiful highbred terriers which I have got to meet. And I can't make 'em understand that I only want to run away and hide myself where no one will see me.

Then suddenly men comes hurrying down our street and begins to brush the beautiful bull terriers; and the Master rubs me with a towel so excited that his hands tremble awful, and Miss Dorothy tweaks my ears between her gloves, so that the blood runs to 'em, and they turn pink and stand up straight and sharp.

"Now, then, Nolan," says she, her voice shaking just like his fingers, "keep his head up—and never let the judge lose sight of him." When I hears that my legs breaks under me, for I knows all about judges. Twice the old Master goes up before the judge for fighting me with other dogs, and the judge promises him if he ever does it again he'll chain him up in jail. I knew he'd find me out. A judge can't be fooled by no pipe clay. He can see right through me, and he reads your insides.

The judging ring, which is where the judge holds out, was so like a fighting pit that when I come in it, and find six other dogs there, I springs into position, so that when they lets us go I can defend myself. But the Master smooths down my hair and whispers, "Hold 'ard, Kid, hold 'ard. This ain't a fight," says he. "Look your prettiest," he whispers. "Please, Kid, look your prettiest"; and he pulls my leash so tight that I can't touch my pats to the sawdust, and my nose goes up in the air. There was millions of people a-watching us from the railings, and three of our kennel men, too, making fun of the Master and me, and Miss Dorothy with her chin just reaching to the rail, and her eyes so big that I thought she was a-going to cry. It was awful to think that when the judge stood up and exposed me, all those people, and Miss Dorothy, would be there to see me driven from the Show.

The judge he was a fierce-looking man with specs on his nose, and a red beard. When I first come in he didn't see me, owing to my being too quick for him and dodging behind the Master. But when the Master drags me round and I pulls at the sawdust to keep back, the judge looks at us careless-like, and then stops and glares through his specs, and I knew it was all up with me.

"Are there any more?" asks the judge to the gentleman at the gate, but never taking his specs from me.

The man at the gate looks in his book. "Seven in the novice class," says he. "They're all here. You can go ahead," and he shuts the gate.

The judge he doesn't hesitate a moment. He just waves his hand toward the corner of the ring. "Take him away," he says to the Master, "over there, and keep him away"; and he turns and looks most solemn at the six beautiful bull terriers. I don't know how I crawled to that corner. I wanted to scratch under the sawdust and dig myself a grave. The kennel men they slapped the rail with their hands and laughed at the Master like they would fall over. They pointed at me in the corner, and their sides just shaked. But little Miss Dorothy she presses her lips tight against the rail, and I see tears rolling from her eyes. The Master he hangs his head like he had been whipped. I felt most sorry for him than all. He was so red, and he was letting on not to see the kennel men, and blinking his eyes. If the judge had ordered me right out it wouldn't have disgraced us so, but it was keeping me there while he was judging the highbred dogs that hurt so hard. With all those people staring, too. And his doing it so quick, without no doubt nor questions. You can't fool the judges. They see inside you.

But he couldn't make up his mind about them highbred dogs. He scowls at 'em, and he glares at 'em, first with his head on the one side and then on the other. And he feels of 'em, and orders 'em to run about. And Nolan leans against the rails, with his head hung down, and pats me. And Miss Dorothy comes over beside him, but don't say nothing, only wipes her eye with her finger. A man on the other side of the rail he says to the Master, "The judge don't like your dog?"

"No," says the Master.

"Have you ever shown him before?" says the man.

"No," says the Master, "and I'll never show him again. He's my dog," says the Master, "and he suits me! And I don't care what no judges think." And when he says them kind words, I licks his hand most grateful.

The judge had two of the six dogs on a little platform in the middle of the ring, and he had chased the four other dogs into the corners, where they was licking their chops, and letting on they didn't care, same as Nolan was.

The two dogs on the platform was so beautiful that the judge hisself couldn't tell which was the best of 'em, even when he stoops down and holds their heads together. But at last he gives a sigh, and brushes the sawdust off his knees, and goes to the table in the ring, where there was a man keeping score, and heaps and heaps of blue and gold and red and yellow ribbons. And the judge picks up a bunch of 'em and walks to the two gentlemen who was holding the beautiful dogs, and he says to each, "What's his number?" and he hands each gentlemen a ribbon. And then he turned sharp and comes straight at the Master.

"What's his number?" says the judge. And Master was so scared that he couldn't make no answer.

But Miss Dorothy claps her hands and cries out like she was laughing, "Three twenty-six," and the judge writes it down and shoves Master the blue ribbon.

I bit the Master, and I jumps and bit Miss Dorothy, and I waggled so hard that the Master couldn't hold me. When I get to the gate Miss Dorothy snatches me up and kisses me between the ears, right before millions of people, and they both hold me so tight that I didn't know which of them was carrying of me. But one thing I knew, for I listened hard, as it was the judge hisself as said it.

"Did you see that puppy I gave first to?" says the judge to the gentleman at the gate.

"I did. He was a bit out of his class," says the gate gentleman.

"He certainly was!" says the judge, and they both laughed.

But I didn't care. They couldn't hurt me then, not with Nolan holding the blue ribbon and Miss Dorothy hugging my ears, and the kennel men sneaking away, each looking like he'd been caught with his nose under the lid of a slop can.

We sat down together, and we all three just talked as fast as we could. They was so pleased that I couldn't help feeling proud of myself, and I barked and leaped about so gay that the bull terriers in our street stretched on their chains and howled at me.

"Just look at him!" says one of those I had beat. "What's he giving hisself airs about?"

"Because he's got one blue ribbon!" says another of 'em. "Why, when I was a puppy I used to eat 'em, and if that judge could ever learn to know a toy from a mastiff, I'd have had this one."

But Jimmy Jocks he leaned over from his bench and says, "Well done, Kid. Didn't I tell you so?" What he 'ad told me was that I might get a "commended," but I didn't remind him.

"Didn't I tell you," says Jimmy Jocks, "that I saw your grandfather make his début at the Crystal—"

"Yes, sir, you did, sir," says I, for I have no love for the men of my family.

A gentleman with a showing leash around his neck comes up just then and looks at me very critical. "Nice dog you've got, Miss Wyndham," says he; "would you care to sell him?"

"He's not my dog," says Miss Dorothy, holding me tight. "I wish he were."

"He's not for sale, sir," says the Master, and I was *that* glad.

"Oh, he's yours, is he?" says the gentleman, looking hard at Nolan. "Well, I'll give you a hundred dollars for him," says he, careless-like.

"Thank you, sir; he's not for sale," says Nolan, but his eyes get very big. The gentleman he walked away; but I watches him, and he talks to a man in a golf cap, and by and by the man comes along our street, looking at all the dogs, and stops in front of me.

"This your dog?" says he to Nolan. "Pity he's so leggy," says he. "If he had a good tail, and a longer stop, and his ears were set higher, he'd be a good dog. As he is, I'll give you fifty dollars for him."

But, before the Master could speak, Miss Dorothy laughs and says: "You're Mr. Polk's kennel man, I believe. Well, you tell Mr. Polk from me that the dog's not for sale now any more than he was five minutes ago, and that when he is, he'll have to bid against me for him."

The man looks foolish at that, but he turns to Nolan quick-like. "I'll give you three hundred for him," he says.

"Oh, indeed!" whispers Miss Dorothy, like she was talking to herself. "That's it, is it?" And she turns and looks at me just as though she had never seen me before. Nolan he was a-gaping, too, with his mouth open. But he holds me tight.

"He's not for sale," he growls, like he was frightened; and the man looks black and walks away.

"Why, Nolan!" cried Miss Dorothy, "Mr. Polk knows more about bull terriers than any amateur in America. What can he mean? Why, Kid is no more than a puppy! Three hundred dollars for a puppy!"

"And he ain't no thoroughbred, neither!" cries the Master. "He's 'Unknown,' ain't he? Kid can't help it, of course, but his mother, miss—"

I dropped my head. I couldn't bear he should tell Miss Dorothy. I couldn't bear she should know I had stolen my blue ribbon.

But the Master never told, for at that a gentleman runs up, calling, "Three twenty-six, three twenty-six!" And Miss Dorothy says, "Here he is; what is it?"

"The Winners' class," says the gentleman. "Hurry, please; the judge is waiting for him."

Nolan tries to get me off the chain onto a showing leash, but he shakes so, he only chokes me. "What is it, miss?" he says. "What is it?"

"The Winners' class," says Miss Dorothy. "The judge wants him with the winners of the other classes—to decide which is the best. It's only a form," says she. "He has the champions against him now."

"Yes," says the gentleman, as he hurries us to the ring. "I'm afraid it's only a form for your dog, but the judge wants all the winners, puppy class even."

We had got to the gate, and the gentleman there was writing down my number.

"Who won the open?" asks Miss Dorothy.

"Oh, who would?" laughs the gentleman. "The old champion, of course. He's won for three years now. There he is. Isn't he wonderful?" says he; and he points to a dog that's standing proud and haughty on the platform in the middle of the ring.

I never see so beautiful a dog—so fine and clean and noble, so white like he had rolled hisself in flour, holding his nose up and his eyes shut, same as though no one was worth looking at. Aside of him we other dogs, even though we had a blue ribbon apiece, seemed like lumps of mud. He was a royal gentleman, a king, he was. His master didn't have to hold his head with no leash. He held it hisself, standing as still as an iron dog on a lawn, like he knew all the people was looking at him. And so they was, and no one around the ring pointed at no other dog but him.

"Oh, what a picture!" cried Miss Dorothy. "He's like a marble figure by a great artist—one who loved dogs. Who is he?" says she, looking in her book. "I don't keep up with terriers."

"Oh, you know him," says the gentleman. "He is the champion of champions, Regent Royal."

The Master's face went red.

"And this is Regent Royal's son," cries he, and he pulls me quick into the ring, and plants me on the platform next my father.

I trembled so that I near fell. My legs twisted like a leash. But my father he never looked at me. He only smiled the same sleepy smile, and he still kept his eyes half shut, like as no one, no, not even his own son, was worth his lookin' at.

The judge he didn't let me stay beside my father, but, one by one, he placed the other dogs next to him and measured and felt and pulled at them. And each one he put down, but he never put my father down. And then he comes over and picks me up and sets me back on the platform, shoulder to shoulder with the Champion Regent Royal, and goes down on his knees, and looks into our eyes.

The gentleman with my father laughs, and says to the judge, "Thinking of keeping us here all day, John?" But the judge he doesn't hear him, and goes behind us and runs his hands down my side, and holds back my ears, and takes my jaws between his fingers. The crowd around the ring is very deep now, and nobody says nothing. The gentleman at the score table, he is leaning forward, with his elbows on his knees and his eyes very wide, and the gentleman at the gate is whispering quick to Miss Dorothy, who has turned white. I stood as stiff as stone. I didn't even breathe. But out of the corner of my eye I could see my father licking his pink chops, and yawning just a little, like he was bored.

The judge he had stopped looking fierce and was looking solemn. Something inside him seemed a-troubling him awful. The more he stares at us now, the more solemn he gets, and when he touches us he does it gentle, like he was patting us. For a long time he kneels in the sawdust, looking at my father and at me, and no one around the ring says nothing to nobody.

Then the judge takes a breath and touches me sudden. "It's his," he says. But he lays his hand just as quick on my father. "I'm sorry," says he.

The gentleman holding my father cries:

"Do you mean to tell me—"

And the judge he answers, "I mean the other is the better dog." He takes my father's head between his hands and looks down at him most sorrowful. "The king is dead," says he. "Long live the king! Good-by, Regent," he says.

The crowd around the railings clapped their hands, and some laughed scornful, and everyone talks fast, and I start for the gate, so dizzy that I can't see my way. But my father pushes in front of me, walking very daintily, and smiling sleepy, same as he had just been waked, with his head high, and his eyes shut, looking at nobody.

So that is how I "came by my inheritance," as Miss Dorothy calls it; and just for that, though I couldn't feel where I was any different, the crowd follows me to my bench, and pats me, and coos at me, like I was a baby in a baby carriage. And the handlers have to hold 'em back so that the gentlemen from the papers can make pictures of me, and Nolan walks me up and down so proud, and the men shake their heads and says, "He certainly is the true type, he is!" And the pretty ladies ask Miss Dorothy, who sits beside me letting me lick her gloves to show the crowd what friends we is, "Aren't you afraid he'll bite you?" And Jimmy Jocks calls to me, "Didn't I tell you so? I always knew you were one of us. Blood will out, Kid; blood will out. I saw your grandfather," says he, "make his début at the Crystal Palace. But he was never the dog you are!"

After that, if I could have asked for it, there was nothing I couldn't get. You might have thought I was a show dog, and they was afeard I'd melt. If I wet my pats, Nolan gave me a hot bath and chained me to the stove; if I couldn't eat my food, being stuffed full by the cook—for I am a house dog now, and let in to lunch, whether there is visitors or not—Nolan would run to bring the vet. It was all tommyrot, as Jimmy says, but meant most kind. I couldn't scratch myself comfortable, without Nolan giving me nasty drinks, and rubbing me outside till it burnt awful; and I wasn't let to eat bones for fear of spoiling my "beautiful" mouth, what mother used to call my "punishing jaw"; and my food was cooked special on a gas stove; and Miss Dorothy gives me an overcoat, cut very stylish like the champions', to wear when we goes out carriage driving.

After the next Show, where I takes three blue ribbons, four silver cups, two medals, and brings home forty-five dollars for Nolan, they gives me a "registered" name, same as Jimmy's. Miss Dorothy wanted to call me "Regent Heir Apparent"; but I was *that* glad when Nolan says, "No; Kid don't owe nothing to his father, only to you and hisself. So, if you please, miss, we'll call him Wyndham Kid." And so they did, and you can see it on my overcoat in blue letters, and painted top of my kennel. It was all too hard to understand. For days I just sat and wondered if I was really me, and how it all come about, and why everybody was so kind. But oh, it was so good they was, for if they hadn't been I'd never have got the thing I most wished after. But, because they was kind, and not liking to deny me nothing, they gave it me, and it was more to me than anything in the world.

It came about one day when we was out driving. We was in the cart they calls the dogcart because it's the one Miss Dorothy keeps to take Jimmy and me for an airing. Nolan was up behind, and me, in my new overcoat, was sitting beside Miss Dorothy. I was admiring the view, and thinking how good it was to have a horse pull you about so that you needn't get yourself splashed and have to be washed, when I hears a dog calling loud for help, and I pricks up my ears and looks over the horse's head. And I sees something that makes me tremble down to my toes. In the road before us three big dogs was chasing a little old lady dog. She had a string to her tail, where some boys had tied a can, and she was dirty with mud and ashes, and torn most awful. She was too far done up to get away, and too old to help herself; but she was making a fight for her life, snapping her old gums savage, and dying game. All this I see in a wink, and then the three dogs pinned her down, and I can't stand it no longer, and clears the wheel and lands in the road on my head. It was my stylish overcoat done that, and I cursed it proper, but I gets my pats again quick, and makes a rush for the fighting. Behind me I hear Miss Dorothy cry: "They'll kill that old dog. Wait, take my whip. Beat them off her! The Kid can take care of himself"; and I hear Nolan fall into the road, and the horse come to a stop. The old lady dog was down, and the three was eating her vicious; but as I come up, scattering the pebbles, she hears, and thinking it's one more of them, she lifts her head, and my heart breaks open like someone had sunk his teeth in it. For, under the ashes and the dirt and the blood, I can see who it is, and I know that my mother has come back to me.

I gives a yell that throws them three dogs off their legs.

"Mother!" I cries. "I'm the Kid," I cries. "I'm coming to you. Mother, I'm coming!"

And I shoots over her at the throat of the big dog, and the other two they sinks their teeth into that stylish overcoat and tears it off me, and that sets me free, and I lets them have it. I never had so fine a fight as that! What with mother being there to see, and not having been let to mix up in no fights since I become a prize-winner, it just naturally did me good, and it wasn't three shakes before I had 'em yelping. Quick as a wink, mother she jumps in to help me, and I just laughed to see her. It was so like old times. And Nolan he made me laugh, too. He was like a hen on a bank, shaking the butt of his whip, but not daring to cut in for fear of hitting me.

"Stop it, Kid," he says, "stop it. Do you want to be all torn up?" says he. "Think of the Boston show," says he. "Think of Chicago. Think of Danbury. Don't you never want to be a champion?" How was I to think of all them places when I had three dogs to cut up at the same time? But in a minute two of 'em begs for mercy, and mother and me lets 'em run away. The big one he ain't able to run away. Then mother and me we dances and jumps, and barks and laughs, and bites each other and rolls each other in the road. There never was two dogs so happy as we. And Nolan he whistles and calls and begs me to come to him; but I just laugh and play larks with mother.

"Now, you come with me," says I, "to my new home, and never try to run away again." And I shows her our house with the five red roofs, set on the top of the hill. But mother trembles awful, and says: "They'd never let me in such a place. Does the Viceroy live there, Kid?" says she. And I laugh at her. "No; I do," I says. "And if they won't let you live there, too, you and me will go back to the streets together, for we must never be parted no more." So we trots up the hill side by side, with Nolan trying to catch me, and Miss Dorothy laughing at him from the cart.

"The Kid's made friends with the poor old dog," says she. "Maybe he knew her long ago when he ran the streets himself. Put her in here beside me, and see if he doesn't follow."

So when I hears that I tells mother to go with Nolan and sit in the cart; but she says no—that she'd soil the pretty lady's frock; but I tells her to do as I say, and so Nolan lifts her, trembling still, into the cart, and I runs alongside, barking joyful.

When we drives into the stables I takes mother to my kennel, and tells her to go inside it and make herself at home. "Oh, but he won't let me!" says she.

"Who won't let you?" says I, keeping my eye on Nolan, and growling a bit nasty, just to show I was meaning to have my way.

"Why, Wyndham Kid," says she, looking up at the name on my kennel.

"But I'm Wyndham Kid!" says I.

"You!" cries mother, "You! Is my little Kid the great Wyndham Kid the dogs all talk about?" And at that, she being very old, and sick, and nervous, as mothers are, just drops down in the straw and weeps bitter.

Well, there ain't much more than that to tell. Miss Dorothy she settled it.

"If the Kid wants the poor old thing in the stables," says she, "let her stay."

"You see," says she, "she's a black-and-tan, and his mother was a black-and-tan, and maybe that's what makes Kid feel so friendly toward her," says she.

"Indeed, for me," says Nolan, "she can have the best there is. I'd never drive out no dog that asks for a crust nor a shelter," he says. "But what will Mr. Wyndham do?"

"He'll do what I say," says Miss Dorothy, "and if I say she's to stay, she will stay, and I say—she's to stay!"

And so mother and Nolan and me found a home. Mother was scared at first—not being used to kind people; but she was so gentle and loving that the grooms got fonder of her than of me, and tried to make me jealous by patting of her and giving her the pick of the vittles. But that was the wrong way to hurt my feelings. That's all, I think. Mother is so happy here that I tell her we ought to call it the Happy Hunting Grounds, because no one hunts you, and there is nothing to hunt; it just all comes to you. And so we live in peace, mother sleeping all day in the sun, or behind the stove in the head groom's office, being fed twice a day regular by Nolan, and all the day by the other grooms most irregular. And as for me, I go hurrying around the country to the bench shows, winning money and cups for Nolan, and taking the blue ribbons away from father.

DAUGHTER OF
DANNY THE RED
(1941)
Roderick Lull

The dog in this story is a springer spaniel sired by one of the finest hunting dogs of his time—hence, a prized animal. But, because the sire's owner has died, a conundrum arises as to which of two dogs is the valuable offspring. The story comes down to the character and ethics of the people vying for the right of possession. The story was first published in *Esquire*. Author Roderick Lull also wrote the novel *Call to Battle* (1943).

It was the first time I had seen my uncle alone for weeks, and I was enjoying myself. There was in it a pleasant sense of guilt, what with knowing of the small opinion the women-folk in our family had of his habits and his morals—an opinion that even my father was beginning to share to an extent. My uncle and I were talking seriously of serious things—primarily the raising and training of hunting spaniels, which to most of the men in our country was the most vital of topics. I was having sarsaparilla and my uncle a shot of rye, when the man came into the bar with the news that a bitch sired by Danny the Red was for sale. That would have been big news on any occasion. And now it was tremendous news indeed, for Danny the Red was dead—dead of an accident in the hunting field, which was a proper way for a dog of his ilk to die—and this bitch was the last of his get.

My uncle kept his voice calm as he asked questions, but I could feel the excitement in it. And no wonder. If you know anything of Springer Spaniels at all you will have heard of Danny the Red. There are those who still say he was the finest of them all when it came to real work in the field. And whether he was or whether he wasn't, today more good Springers go back to him, a long trail, than to any other sire.

It seemed that Danny's owner had died shortly after his dog's death and left his widow with two bitches—the one sired by Danny, the other of different breeding. Like most men whose life was the breeding and training and hunting of sporting dogs, he had died poor. His widow was going away to relatives in the East and was selling her possessions. She was now staying with friends near town and had the dogs with her.

My uncle looked down at me and his eyes were bright and eager. "About through, boy?" he asked. We finished our drinks together. "We'll go take a look," he said then. "Glad to have you along. You'll tell me your opinion of her."

My uncle drove the trotter fast. And suddenly my feeling of joyous association was gone. I felt unsure and nervous. For all the effort I gave to trying not to
think of the hunting trip he and my father had taken me on last year, I thought of
it the harder. It was a sore thing too seldom out of my mind. I had failed them, I
knew, and miserably. I hadn't held up my end in anything—not in the shooting,
the skinning and butchering of the deer, or the making of camp and the handling
of the horses. They had been kind about it, especially my uncle, and their kindness had been like a blow in the face. For in their expression, in an occasional
unguarded word between them, it was evident that I was a disappointment and
might, indeed, lack the stuff of manhood entirely. I remembered how desperately
I had wanted to explain, to say something compelling in extenuation, and there
had been no words for it. You came through or you didn't. And now my uncle was
taking me to see a hunting dog and pretending my opinion would be of value. But
again, his kindness was a bitter, hurting thing.

My uncle's brow was furrowed, his face serious and intent. "A bitch of
Dan's," he said as if talking to himself, "could be worth a man's income for a
year. Of course she may be no good—Lord knows Danny sired some of that
kind too. On the other hand . . . "

Ten minutes later my uncle slapped my knee. "There's Hargan's house,
where she's staying. How'd you like to have a hand in the making of her, Bub?"

"That'd be fine," I said in a half whisper, trying not to choke.

"Well, don't go planning on anything yet. No doubt we're due for a disappointment—just a pure waste of time." But I knew by the note in his voice
that he expected the opposite.

The widow, a pale, ineffectual woman who obviously knew nothing of dogs,
led us out to a small wire-enclosed yard at the back of the house, and there were
the two bitches. They were real beauties for you, with bodies soft as velvet to
your hand, yet flexing with good hard muscles beneath the skin. Great eyes, dark
brown and deep. Feet padded well and too big for them, as they should be. And
chests, even though they were little past the suckling stage, that told of strength
and power. They were both black and white and alike as peas in a pod.

Alike as peas in a pod to me, that is. But not to my uncle. For a few minutes he handled them both, then drew one bitch away. He ran his hands down her flanks and stood up. "That's Danny's girl," he said, and so sure was the note in his voice that it was like a man announcing his name.

"There's tags in their collars my husband put there that tells which is which," the widow said. "I don't know one from the other. Only, my husband said one was much more valuable than the other."

My uncle looked idly at the tag on the collar of the dog he had picked, then dropped it and smiled at me. "I was right," he said softly, and there was no vanity in his voice at all. "No man could fail to pick Danny's girl from the other, could he, Bub?"

"No, Uncle Ned." It was a great lie, for I couldn't have told had my life hung on my decision.

"Of course not," he said. He slowly rubbed his chin with one hand and turned to the widow. "What is your price, ma'am?"

She stared at him, and her voice faltered. "My husband said—he said the best one, whichever it is, should bring a hundred dollars. And the other fifty. He said a hundred dollars would be very cheap."

My uncle stared back at her. He looked away—at me, at the ground, at the dogs, at the sky, then at the dogs again. "Too cheap," he said in a low voice. I knew what he was feeling—it would have been a good game to have made a hard bargain with a man who knew what he was doing. But this was obviously different. "I think—well, I will give you a hundred and fifty for her. Fifty now. The rest when I come for her, in about ten days. I have to be away that time. I suppose the people here will be willing that she stay. I'll pay them."

Mrs. Byrnes was still thanking him, to my uncle's embarrassment, when a man's voice behind us said, "Good afternoon."

We swung around. John Forest stood there, his hat pushed back from his forehead. I heard my uncle draw a quick breath. And my uncle's voice when he said, "Good day, Forest," was polite and level and colder than the Arctic. Forest and my uncle had always been enemies, for no reason I understood.

They had argued, and once they had fought. My uncle had said that John Forest was a no-good and a crook. And John Forest had said the time would come when the words would be returned with interest.

Forest turned to the widow. "I'm told you have a bitch of Danny's here. I came to see her."

My uncle answered for her. "I've bought her," he said. "But she's another good bitch to sell. She should get seventy-five for her and she'll make a mistake if she takes a cent less. And—don't touch my dog, Forest."

My uncle strode away and I followed him. I said something about Forest maybe making trouble—after all he had money and was a power in the county. "He won't be making any trouble," my uncle said. "Not unless he wants it back double, with interest. And now I got to hustle and raise that other hundred. I tell you, Bub, she'll make a dog like you never saw before. I could feel it, looking at her."

My mother sniffed when she heard I'd been with Uncle Ned. She spoke to my father. "If he wasn't a relative, you'd never think of letting Joe near him."

"He's my brother and he's the boy's uncle," my father said. The way he spoke, not looking her in the eye, I knew he half-agreed with her, and it made me sick sorrowful to see it.

I didn't go to sleep right off that night. I kept thinking of how surely my uncle had told Danny's bitch from the other, when they looked to me like a pair from one litter. And I kept thinking along with that of how I'd fallen down last year. It was dark thinking, and just before I went off to sleep I wondered if there would ever be happiness in me again.

I was working in the barn when Mr. Selfridge, our nearest neighbor, came by and asked where my father was. I could tell by the grave look on his fat, kindly face that he had bad news. I told him my father was in the house, then went slowly about my work again, wondering what it was he had come to say. Suddenly I was sure it had to do with my uncle. We had been expecting him for three days and I knew he would stop to see us before going to his own ranch.

In half an hour Mr. Selfridge reappeared on the porch, my father with him. I saw my father shake his head, then shake hands awkwardly with Mr. Selfridge, using his left hand. He had broken his right arm a week before and it was still in a splint.

Mr. Selfridge walked out to the road, got into his buggy and drove away. As soon as he had gone my father called, "Joe!" in a high-pitched angry voice, and I dropped my work like hot lead to leg it for the house.

Both my parents were in the kitchen. My father's thin, leathery face was dark as a winter night, and even my mother had lost her usual optimistic expression. But she was trying to cheer him up. "After all," she was saying, "it isn't as if Ned had committed a murder. And there may be a mistake."

My father turned on her furiously. "It may not be murder, but a man who'd steal a dog in this county—" he broke off and lifted his hand in a tired gesture. Then he swung on me. "We're going to town, now. Hitch up. With this blasted arm of mine I can't even drive. Get going."

I said weakly, "What's wrong—is it about Uncle Ned?"

My father's eyes burned hot. "Move!" he said. I moved.

I was ready with the buggy in record time. I drove to the house and sat waiting, my nerves pumping at white heat. At last my father came out, pulling on his hat, my mother following. She handed up my jacket along with a package.

"Be back as soon as we can," my father said shortly. "This may take a while. Don't worry—not that there's nothing to worry about." He kissed her quickly, in the half-embarrassed way he always did, and climbed into the wagon, cursing his bad arm methodically and in sulphurous terms. He lit his pipe and settled back. "We're off," he said then. "And don't think because I can't drive you're going to do any showing off. I'm here to tell you what to do and when to do it and how, and you're listening and doing it."

I was burning to know the story Mr. Selfridge had brought. But for a long time my father sat still, smoking in silence, staring straight ahead with his eyes half shut. Then at last he began to talk. It was curious talk, the sort of a monologue a man makes to himself in times of mental stress. I listened, still as a mouse. Little by little the situation became clear.

My uncle had returned from his trip and gone to get his dog. According to his story there was a dog there all right, but it wasn't Danny's bitch. It was the other, which he learned had been bought by Forest. He'd had no proof, of course—the tags had disappeared. But he swore over and over again that he'd stake his neck on it. The upshot was that he'd gone to Forest's place, beaten him badly and taken the dog which Forest claimed. And now my uncle was in jail and Forest was prosecuting him for assault and battery, which was a small thing in our county, and for the deliberate theft of a valuable hunting dog, which was a very serious thing indeed.

I listened. Finally I couldn't keep silent any longer. "Uncle Ned wouldn't steal a dog, and he couldn't make a mistake like that!" I cried. "Forest's the man they should have arrested."

My father laughed. It was a mirthless laugh. "Easy said. You prove it, boy. You prove it so a judge will believe you. You've got quite a job cut out for you. Particularly after some of those mistakes Ned's made in the past. A man makes so many mistakes and then—well, you can hardly blame people if they come to thinking that maybe he's just a crook."

My voice was shaking when I spoke again. "But look—Uncle Ned knew that dog. He had his choice. I was right with him. Even if he'd been wrong, there were tags to show which dog was which. If he'd wanted the other dog he could have had her. He'd paid his money down before Mr. Forest ever showed up."

My father looked at me with sad impatience in his eyes. "Proves nothing. People would be prepared to believe Ned might make that kind of a mistake—that he'd picked the wrong one. And that when he'd found it out some way he'd tried to repair it by beating up Forest and taking his dog. As for the tags—hell, they don't prove a thing. Anyway, they're gone, according to Selfridge."

I stared at my father's profile, and it was hard and thin. A little muscle moved nervously in his cheek. And there was only one thing left to say. "He knew that dog soon as he saw her, even if the two of them were almost twins," I said. "All he had to do was run his hands over them and watch them move around a minute and it was all over. He said to me it was something anybody could see."

"He was always a great talker," my father said. "Always a man to blow his own horn. And—did you see it too? What he saw?"

I almost said "yes." But my father was looking at me and I knew I never could make him believe me. So I said weakly, "No, but I don't know about dogs the way Uncle Ned does."

Already, I thought, Ned was half condemned in my father's mind. He didn't believe what I said—and no wonder, after the incompetent I'd proved myself when it had come to the showdown last year. There hadn't been a thing I'd been able to do the way they had wanted it. The worst thing of all was my failure to keep from blubbering when I'd cut myself with the axe and they were pouring iodine into the wound. I could remember yet the look in my father's eyes. And I could hear my uncle's flat voice saying, "After all, Fred, he's only fourteen." And my father's voice, "What's that got to do with it? What's fourteen or forty got to do with it?"

I wanted to press right through to town but my father insisted we stop to eat the lunch my mother had hastily put together for us. He sat with his back to a tree, eating awkwardly because of his stiff, useless arm, and his eyes were dark under a furrowed brow. I had a hunch what he was thinking. This might cost money, and money was a thing of which we had mighty little any more. And worse than that it would make a scandal that would speed like lightning through the county and tar all members of the family.

My father finished his lunch and climbed into the buggy. I took my place in the driving seat. "A man could," my father said slowly, and when I looked at him I saw that his teeth were clenched hard on the pipe stem—"a man could talk to Forest and sort of appeal to his better nature, as they say. A man could do that if he had to."

And I knew my father could perform no more bitter task.

We came into town, a worried and woe-begone pair, and drove sedately down the dirt street. "We'll go to see Judge Tolliver," my father said. "Then we'll see Ned, and figure out what to do."

Judge Tolliver was in his office working over some papers. He stood up and shook hands enthusiastically with my father—a little too enthusiastically, I thought. He spoke cheerfully to me and offered us chairs. He asked us our business, though obviously he knew perfectly well.

"Not that I'm not always glad to see you, business or no business, George," he said, rubbing one side of his big red nose with a forefinger. "But this time I take it, it's a professional call."

My father sat down in one of the old pine chairs. I leaned against the wall. "It's about Ned," my father said.

Judge Tolliver looked at the ceiling. He and my father were old acquaintances and it was obvious that he was uncomfortable. "Yes," he said. "Regrettable. A damned shame. Frankly, I can't understand it. I tried to talk to Ned and all I got was curses and wild statements about what he was going to do to Forest."

"I know," my father said. He stood up and walked the length of the room and back. "What kind of case has Forest got?"

"A good case," Judge Tolliver said quietly. "After all, Ned took the dog from him by force. I understand no one can tell one of these damned bitches apart. And that's hardly the point anyway. The burden of proof is on Ned. And if he can't furnish satisfactory proof—well, you know how people feel about such matters around here."

"Do you feel he's guilty, Judge? That he decided he'd slipped in the first place picking a dog and tried to fix it up that crazy way?"

The judge looked at the ceiling again and my father nodded. "We won't take any more of your time, Judge, thanks. We'll go see Ned now, if there's no objection."

"None at all. You know the jailer."

In the doorway my father paused. "When'll the case come up, Judge?"

"Tomorrow at one. I'll grant a delay if you want."

"Don't know what good that could do. Well, thanks, Judge."

Ned was lying on the jail bunk, smoking cigarettes. He looked at us and gave no sign of recognition.

"Ned," my father said, and his voice was hot and sharp.

"So they called out the reserves," Ned said. "What the hell do you want?"

"Did you steal Forest's dog?"

Uncle Ned laughed loudly and I saw my father clench his fists.

"I asked a question and I expect an answer." My father's voice shook with anger.

"Go ahead and expect," my uncle said.

"I see," my father said softly. "I understand. I might have figured it. The truth is, I did, only I tried not to believe myself, my own reason. Just a damned dog thief."

Ned sat up and his chest swelled beneath his thin shirt. "You're my brother," he said. "But I've a mind to break your damned neck."

My father made a contemptuous sound. He grabbed me hard by the arm, his fingers biting like steel bands into my flesh, and we started for the open cell door. I looked back and saw Ned lying down again, rolling a cigarette.

My father did not speak as we walked down the street toward the hotel, and his manner when he demanded a room said plainer than words that he wanted no conversation from the clerk. I'd seen him in black moods before, but none so black as this.

That night I was a long time going to sleep, and when I finally did I dreamed a dream more vivid than any I had ever known. It was a dream of two bitches, alike as peas in a pod so far as I could see, at work in the field. And I was trying desperately to find the difference that was between them, the difference I could not see, for my uncle's future depended upon it. He was accused of a great crime and no one had faith in him save me. But no matter how hard I tried they still seemed alike as those two peas in a pod. Some times I felt for an instant that I saw something that set one apart from the other. But always, when I tried to pin it down it went away, leaving me lost and discouraged.

The dream was fast in my mind when I wakened. My father was already up and it was then that I made the suggestion. He at once dismissed it as useless and I argued with him as I rarely had before. It could do no harm, I pointed out; it might do good. And when he laughed ironically and asked me just how I expected it to do anything save make us ridiculous and emphasize the pathetic feebleness of our defense, I had to admit it was a cloud of an idea. But still, I said—I wished he would. I wished it tremendously.

"All right," he said finally. "I'll do it." He stood up and threw his cigar savagely away. "You go get your own breakfast—I don't want any. I'll take a little walk and do some thinking and I'll drop in on the Judge to ask him if your idea's all right with him."

My father came back a little before noon and that black look was blacker still. The Judge, he said, had agreed to my request that the hearing be held out of doors, with the dogs on the scene.

Promptly at one my father and I drove the two miles out of town to the Judge's little ranch. The Judge and Forest were already there; Forest was smoking a big cigar at a fast rate and complaining about the idiocy of being dragged out here for an open-and-shut case. Ten minutes later a surrey turned in at the gate. My uncle was in it, sitting next to one of the deputies. Another deputy rode in the rear with the two dogs.

I watched my uncle get slowly down from the seat and walk toward Forest and the Judge. He walked past my father and myself without a sign of recognition. He walked straight up to Forest and stopped a half-dozen feet away. He stood with his hands on hips, smiling a little, and stared at him. For a long time Forest stared back. Then he shrugged his shoulders and swung around to say something to the Judge. And my uncle's laugh, hard and bitter, rang out across the hot, level fields.

The deputy took the dogs from the buggy and put them down, leashed together. I looked at them, and normally it would have been an ecstatic, exciting thing. Now it was anything but that. I looked them over carefully and I'd never seen two dogs more perfectly matched. There were minor differences of marking, but you had to look hard to find them. I went to them and stroked their sleek bodies and they quivered with pleasure. I was hoping for something harder than I'd ever hoped for anything before. Maybe it was hoping against hope, but I told myself that the daughter of Danny the Red wouldn't let us down. I told it to myself over and over again, fiercely.

Then the Judge spoke and I turned about toward the little group of men. "This shouldn't take much time," he said slowly. "We all know what the case is about, so there's no need for me to go into it. Mr. Forest, have you anything to say?"

Forest took his time about lighting a fresh cigar. "Only this," he said, and his voice had a dark, hard note about it. "I bought a dog and paid good cash for her. This man Bristol came to my place and said I had stolen his dog. I told him he was crazy and he attacked me. And he took my dog. He claimed that I had taken the wrong one of the two Mrs. Byrnes had sold us. It's true he bought Danny's bitch, as he says, and that I bought the other. Maybe he decided afterwards the other was the better dog. I don't know, I do know what he did."

"You don't deny that Mr. Bristol bought Danny's bitch?"

"Of course not. Maybe he did not know that the best dogs will produce worthless dogs, sometimes."

The Judge nodded. "You can identify your dog, Mr. Forest? Or shall I say, the dog you believed to be yours, the dog whose ownership Mr. Bristol contests?"

Forest pointed to the dog at the left. "You'll notice she has more black on her chest than the other."

The Judge turned to my uncle. "That is the dog you say is yours?"

"Yes. I know that dog is mine."

"At the time of purchase did you notice the slight difference in chest marking?"

"No, but I know the dog. She's from Danny the Red."

"Can you prove the dog is yours?"

My uncle's jaw hardened to a tight, dark line. "I'm not a lawyer. But I know what I know. I was never fooled on a dog."

The Judge drew a long breath and looked around. "Has anyone else anything to say?"

There was a silence. When I spoke my voice sounded to me like thunder and I flushed. "Judge Tolliver," I said, "if you don't mind—it's an idea I got—would you have those dogs turned loose?"

Forest shouted, "I object to this folderol! It's as open and shut a case as you ever saw. Let's put an end to it."

The Judge faced him quietly. "I'll thank you not to interrupt, Mr. Forest." He turned back to me. "All right, I can't see where that can do any good but then it can do no damage either. The dogs are yours, boy."

We were in fine pheasant cover, and I took the dogs from the deputy and led them away from the men toward some long rows of corn. They bounded against me, tangling in the double leash, obviously pleased at the chance to move about. A few feet from the corn I unsnapped the leash. They tore across country exhausting some of their boundless energy. Then they steadied down.

I walked ahead and they walked with me, following erratic courses of their own. They were completely untrained, guided only by instinct, only by the deep, sure knowledge which was as much a part of them as their coats, and as natural and untaught. Suddenly they both paused and stood with noses lifted, sniffing hard. There was something in the wind, their eyes said—there was something there calling to them, something that went far back into the blackness of time and was filled with mysterious meaning and a great compulsion. What it was they did not know—they only knew that it was there, lovely and thrilling and demanding. It was there ahead somewhere, reaching out to them, touching them almost physically, the strongest thing they had ever known.

They charged in, starting together, a pair of wild puppies, driven by instinct as by the lash to where the pheasants crouched. They both had the quality known as style, that which a dog is born with or goes his whole life without. And for me to say one was better or worse than the other would have been the same as saying that there is a difference between hats of the same make and quality and style ranged in a row in a showcase. I remember that my heart was pounding and that I stared until my eyeballs burned and hurt with strain, looking for something, anything, that might distinguish them. I was very close to admitting that it was not there, for me. Oh, it was there for others, all right, for men like my uncle. But not for me. And if that branded me as a failure, it was not a thing to occasion wonder. It was simply the hard, undeniable fact.

Almost, I think, I turned away, heavy with shame for another failure, sick with myself for having made fools of us all, for having even further prejudiced an impossible case. But it was then that a cock pheasant rose, cackling hysterically, and flew away. One dog broke, going wild, raising her voice. And the other dog—well, the other dog followed the pheasant's course too, going fast and hard. There was a way she did it—a thing above and beyond the fact that she was untrained and a puppy. It was a way that went back a long way to an ancient greatness. There are no precise words to describe it. And still, I knew then, it was a thing that any man who knew dogs could never miss. Suddenly I felt a great deal older, and a great deal wiser.

Two more pheasant rose; the field was rich with them. And out there was a good dog, that after proper training would honor any shoot. And out there was another dog that was the raw stuff of greatness. There was the young, small shadow of Danny the Red out there; a hundred youngsters could have been working with her and knowing eyes would have followed none but her.

Then I turned and the Judge was beside me, not five feet away. His eyes were bright and years had gone from his face. "Look," I said, "look at that dog." She was going on now, through the corn, taking it swiftly but thoroughly, covering it all as surely as a blanket covers a bed. "Look!" and now my voice was high-pitched, almost a scream. "Danny the Red was like that—I only saw him once but I know now. There was a man showed me—a man who was handling him at the trial last year." And I said again at the end, there being nothing else to say, "Look!"

The Judge smiled and breathed deeply. Back a little way Forest's voice said, "What damn foolishness is this?" and the Judge acted as if he had not heard it. The Judge said to me softly, "I remember—it's almost like Danny over again. And which dog of the two is it?"

I said, almost whispering, "I don't know." Then I raised my voice, appalled at my own conviction. "But it has to be the one with the blackest chest!"

"Which one," the Judge muttered to himself and then the dog turned toward us. Her chest was very black.

The Judge nodded to the deputy and he went after the dogs. The Judge and I walked back together to Forest, who stood a little away from my father and uncle. "You saw it, Mr. Forest," the Judge said. "The boy knew. It took him to make me see, even, and I've spent more of my life with Springers than a sane man would. I'm glad I'm not that sane, however, which is beside the point. She's Danny's girl."

Forest's face was flushed. His cigar had gone out. He cleared his throat and made a wide gesture. "And you're a Judge!" he said. "A lawyer, and you call that evidence. I'd like to know what a higher court would say."

"Oh, it would say it wasn't evidence," the Judge said. "If you want an appeal it's your right."

Forest looked away and I knew what he was thinking. He might win a case on appeal where only the cold, unseeing letter of the law would apply, and it would be the emptiest victory any man ever won. For in the county the people would know and they would hate and despise him. They would know him for a dog thief and if the law backed up his theft it could not make him less the criminal in the eyes of those who knew the truth.

The Judge's eyes were on Forest. "Well, Forest, what is your decision?"

Forest looked at the Judge, then turned his eyes for a fleeting moment on my uncle and my father. When he spoke his voice was faltering, an old man's voice. "A man can make a mistake," he said. "An honest mistake. Something happened to those tags—I don't know what, but that was the trouble. And if I'm wrong I'm the first to admit it and say I'm sorry. Anyone can make a mistake." He paused, his voice still on a rising note, and looked again around the little circle. The eyes that met his own were level and impassive. He made a little gesture with his left hand, turned and walked rapidly toward his buggy.

The judge smiled, but there was no laughter in the eyes that followed Forest's progress across the field. "He forgot his dog," he said. "One of the boys can take her to his place. Anybody want a ride back with me? I'm going to town and wind this case up officially."

"I guess Ned will be going with us," my father said, and left.

The deputy brought the lovely bitch over and gave my uncle her lead. The three of us stood in a little circle looking down at her. I knelt and ran my hand gently along her back, and her warm wet tongue touched my cheek.

"You know," my uncle said. "I've been thinking."

"About time," my father said sarcastically. "That'll be news to the whole family."

"Shut up," my uncle said good-humoredly. "I've been thinking about two things. First, I guess I sort of owe the boy here an apology."

"Me?" I said, startled.

"Yes. I sort of had the idea you might turn out to be—well, not up to scratch the way I'd like. Shows how wrong a man can be. I know better now, and so does your father."

Hot blood surged up into my face, and I felt a happiness greater than I'd known in all my life.

"And the second thing I've been thinking. Well—I haven't the time a man should give to a dog like this. I've got an awful lot of work piled up at the place. I'd like to see her belong to a man who'd really bring her up the way she deserves."

I felt suddenly as if I'd been slapped hard. "You mean—you are going to sell her?"

My uncle shook his head. "Couldn't do that. The truth is, I was think-ing—oh, hell—" he thrust the lead toward me. "Take her. And you make her into the best pheasant dog this county ever saw or I'll skin you alive."

I looked at him with unbelieving eyes. I tried to speak and failed, I said feebly, "Gee—thanks—"

"Never mind," he barked. "My return will be what you make of her. And remember what I said I'd do if you let us down, me and her. And never think I don't mean it."

THE DOG OF POMPEII
(1932)
Louis Untermeyer

One of the biggest natural disasters in world history took place in A.D. 79 when Mount Vesuvius erupted in a shower of molten lava. Pompeii, a city near Naples, was completely destroyed, buried under volcanic ash. This story is about the relationship between a dog and a man in the ancient city at that fateful time.

Louis Untermeyer (1885–1977) visited a small museum at Pompeii, where a plaster cast of a dog captured his imagination for the story. Untermeyer was a poet, anthologist, biologist, humorist, and story writer and excelled in each category. He wrote for children as well as adults, and his many books include *Modern American Poetry* (1921), *Emily Dickinson* (1927), *The Second Christmas* (1964), and *Tales from the Ballet* (1968).

Tito and his dog Bimbo lived (if you could call it living) under the wall where it joined the inner gate. They really didn't live there; they just slept there. They lived anywhere. Pompeii was one of the gayest of the old Latin towns, but although Tito was never an unhappy boy, he was not exactly a merry one. The streets were always lively with shining chariots and bright red trappings; the open-air theatres rocked with laughing crowds; sham-battles and athletic sports were free for the asking in the great stadium. Once a year the Caesar visited the pleasure-city and the fire-works lasted for days; the sacrifices in the Forum were better than a show. But Tito saw none of these things. He was blind—had been blind from birth. He was known to every one in the poorer quarters. But no one could say how old he was, no one remembered his parents, no one could tell where he came from. Bimbo was another mystery. As long as people could remember seeing Tito—about twelve or thirteen years—they had seen Bimbo. Bimbo had never left his side. He was not only dog, but nurse, pillow, playmate, mother and father to Tito.

Did I say Bimbo never left his master? (Perhaps I had better say comrade, for if any one was the master, it was Bimbo.) I was wrong. Bimbo did trust Tito alone exactly three times a day. It was a fixed routine, a custom understood between boy and dog since the beginning of their friendship, and the way it worked was this: Early in the morning, shortly after dawn, while Tito was still dreaming, Bimbo would disappear. When Tito awoke, Bimbo would be sitting quietly at his side, his ears cocked, his stump of a tail tapping the ground, and a fresh-baked bread—more like a large round roll—at his feet. Tito would stretch himself; Bimbo would yawn; then they would breakfast. At noon, no matter where they happened to be, Bimbo would put his paw on Tito's knee and the two of them would return to the inner gate. Tito would curl up in the corner (almost like a dog) and go to sleep, while Bimbo, looking quite important (almost like a boy) would disappear again. In half an hour he'd be back with their lunch. Sometimes it would be a piece of fruit or a scrap of meat, often it was nothing but a dry crust. But sometimes there would be one of those flat rich cakes, sprinkled with raisins and sugar, that Tito liked so much. At supper-time the same thing happened, although there was a little less of everything, for things were hard to snatch in the evening with the streets full of people. Besides, Bimbo didn't approve of too much food before going to sleep. A heavy supper made boys too restless and dogs too stodgy—and it was the business of a dog to sleep lightly with one ear open and muscles ready for action.

But, whether there was much or little, hot or cold, fresh or dry, food was always there. Tito never asked where it came from and Bimbo never told him. There was plenty of rain-water in the hollows of soft stones; the old egg-woman at the corner sometimes gave him a cupful of strong goat's milk; in the grape-season the fat wine-maker let him have drippings of the mild juice. So there was no danger of going hungry or thirsty. There was plenty of everything in Pompeii—if you knew where to find it—and if you had a dog like Bimbo.

As I said before, Tito was not the merriest boy in Pompeii. He could not romp with the other youngsters and play Hare-and-Hounds and I-spy and Follow-your-Master and Ball-against-the-Building and Jack-stones and Kings-and-Robbers with them. But that did not make him sorry for himself. If he could not see the sights that delighted the lads of Pompeii he could hear and smell things they never noticed. He could really see more with his ears and nose than they could with their eyes. When he and Bimbo went out walking he knew just where they were going and exactly what was happening.

"Ah," he'd sniff and say, as they passed a handsome villa, "Glaucus Pansa is giving a grand dinner tonight. They're going to have three kinds of bread, and roast pigling, and stuffed goose, and a great stew—I think bear-stew—and a fig-pie." And Bimbo would note that this would be a good place to visit tomorrow.

215

Or, "H'm," Tito would murmur, half through his lips, half through his nostrils. "The wife of Marcus Lucretius is expecting her mother. She's shaking out every piece of goods in the house; she's going to use the best clothes—the ones she's been keeping in pine-needles and camphor—and there's an extra girl in the kitchen. Come, Bimbo, let's get out of the dust!"

Or, as they passed a small but elegant dwelling opposite the public-baths, "Too bad! The tragic poet is ill again. It must be a bad fever this time, for they're trying smoke-fumes instead of medicine. Whew! I'm glad I'm not a tragic poet!"

Or, as they neared the Forum, "Mm-m! What good things they have in the Macellum today!" (It really was a sort of butcher-grocer-market-place, but Tito didn't know any better. He called it the Macellum.) "Dates from Africa, and salt oysters from sea-caves, and cuttlefish, and new honey, and sweet onions, and—ugh!—water-buffalo steaks. Come, let's see what's what in the Forum." And Bimbo, just as curious as his comrade, hurried on. Being a dog, he trusted his ears and nose (like Tito) more than his eyes. And so the two of them entered the center of Pompeii.

The Forum was the part of the town to which everybody came at least once during each day. It was the Central Square and everything happened here. There were no private houses; all was public—the chief temples, the gold and red bazaars, the silk-shops, the town-hall, the booths belonging to the weavers and jewel-merchants, the wealthy woolen market, the shrine of the household gods. Everything glittered here. The buildings looked as if they were new—which, in a sense, they were. The earthquake of twelve years ago had brought down all the old structures and, since the citizens of Pompeii were ambitious to rival Naples and even Rome, they had seized the opportunity to rebuild the whole town. And they had done it all within a dozen years. There was scarcely a building that was older than Tito.

Tito had heard a great deal about the earthquake though, being about a year old at the time, he could scarcely remember it. This particular quake had been a light one—as earthquakes go. The weaker houses had been shaken down, parts of the out-worn wall had been wrecked; but there was little loss of life, and the brilliant new Pompeii had taken the place of the old. No one knew what caused these earthquakes. Records showed they had happened in the neighborhood since the beginning of time. Sailors said that it was to teach the lazy city-folk a lesson and make them appreciate those who risked the dangers of the sea to bring them luxuries and protect their town from invaders. The priests said that the gods took this way of showing their anger to those who refused to worship properly and who failed to bring enough sacrifices to the altars and (though they didn't say it in so many words) presents to the priests. The tradesmen said that the foreign merchants had corrupted the ground and it was no longer safe to traffic in imported goods that came from strange places and carried a curse with them. Every one had a different explanation—and every one's explanation was louder and sillier than his neighbor's.

They were talking about it this afternoon as Tito and Bimbo came out of the side-street into the public square. The Forum was the favorite promenade for rich and poor. What with the priests arguing with the politicians, servants doing the day's shopping, tradesmen crying their wares, women displaying the latest fashions from Greece and Egypt, children playing hide-and-seek among the marble columns, knots of soldiers, sailors, peasants from the provinces—to say nothing of those who merely came to lounge and look on—the square was crowded to its last inch. His ears even more than his nose guided Tito to the place where the talk was loudest. It was in front of the Shrine of the Household Gods that, naturally enough, the householders were arguing.

"I tell you," rumbled a voice which Tito recognized as bath-master Rufus's, "there won't be another earthquake in my lifetime or yours. There may be a tremble or two, but earthquakes, like lightnings, never strike twice in the same place."

"Do they not?" asked a thin voice Tito had never heard. It had a high, sharp ring to it and Tito knew it as the accent of a stranger. "How about the two towns of Sicily that have been ruined three times within fifteen years by

the eruptions of Mount Etna? And were they not warned? And does that column of smoke about Vesuvius mean nothing?"

"That?" Tito could hear the grunt with which one question answered
another. "That's always there. We use it for our weather-guide. When the
smoke stands up straight we know we'll have fair weather; when it flattens out
it's sure to be foggy; when it drifts to the east—"

"Yes, yes," cut in the edged voice. "I've heard about your mountain barom-
eter. But the column of smoke seems hundreds of feet higher than usual and
it's thickening and spreading like a shadowy tree. They say in Naples—"

"Oh, Naples!" Tito knew this voice by the little squeak that went with it.
It was Attilio, the cameo-cutter. "*They* talk while we suffer. Little help we got
from them last time. Naples commits the crimes and Pompeii pays the price.
It's become a proverb with us. Let them mind their own business."

"Yes," grumbled Rufus, "and others, too."

"Very well, my confident friends," responded the thin voice which now
sounded curiously flat. "We also have a proverb—and it is this: Those who
will not listen to men must be taught by the gods. I say no more. But I leave a
last warning. Remember the holy ones. Look to your temples. And when the
smoke-tree above Vesuvius grows to the shape of an umbrella-pine, look to
your lives."

Tito could hear the air whistle as the speaker drew his toga about him and
the quick shuffle of feet told him the stranger had gone.

"Now what," said the cameo-cutter, "did he mean by that?"

"I wonder," grunted Rufus, "I wonder."

Tito wondered, too. And Bimbo, his head at a thoughtful angle, looked
as if he had been doing a heavy piece of pondering. By nightfall the argument had been forgotten. If the smoke had increased no one saw it in the
dark. Besides, it was Caesar's birthday and the town was in holiday mood.
Tito and Bimbo were among the merry-makers, dodging the charioteers who
shouted at them. A dozen times they almost upset baskets of sweets and jars
of Vesuvian wine, said to be as fiery as the streams inside the volcano, and a

dozen times they were cursed and cuffed. But Tito never missed his footing. He was thankful for his keen ears and quick instinct—most thankful of all for Bimbo.

They visited the uncovered theatre and, though Tito could not see the faces of the actors, he could follow the play better than most of the audience, for their attention wandered—they were distracted by the scenery, the costumes, the by-play, even by themselves—while Tito's whole attention was centered in what he heard. Then to the city-walls, where the people of Pompeii watched a mock naval-battle in which the city was attacked by the sea and saved after thousands of flaming arrows had been exchanged and countless colored torches had been burned. Though the thrill of flaring ships and lighted skies was lost to Tito, the shouts and cheers excited him as much as any and he cried out with the loudest of them.

The next morning there were *two* of the beloved raisin and sugar cakes for his breakfast. Bimbo was unusually active and thumped his bit of a tail until Tito was afraid he would wear it out. The boy could not imagine whether Bimbo was urging him to some sort of game or was trying to tell something. After a while, he ceased to notice Bimbo. He felt drowsy. Last night's late hours had tired him. Besides, there was a heavy mist in the air—no, a thick fog rather than a mist—a fog that got into his throat and scraped it and made him cough. He walked as far as the marine gate to get a breath of the sea. But the blanket of haze had spread all over the bay and even the salt air seemed smoky.

He went to bed before dusk and slept. But he did not sleep well. He had too many dreams—dreams of ships lurching in the Forum, of losing his way in a screaming crowd, of armies marching across his chest. Of being pulled over every rough pavement of Pompeii.

He woke early. Or, rather, he was pulled awake. Bimbo was doing the pulling. The dog had dragged Tito to his feet and was urging the boy along. Somewhere. Where, Tito did not know. His feet stumbled uncertainly; he was still half asleep. For a while he noticed nothing except the fact that it was hard to breathe. The air was hot. And heavy. So heavy that he could taste it. The air, it seemed, had turned to powder, a warm powder that stung his nostrils and burned his sightless eyes.

Then he began to hear sounds. Peculiar sounds. Like animals under the earth. Hissings and groanings and muffled cries that a dying creature might make dislodging the stones of his underground cave. There was no doubt of it now. The noises came from underneath. He not only heard them—he could feel them. The earth twitched; the twitching changed to an uneven shrugging of the soil. Then, as Bimbo half-pulled, half-coaxed him across, the ground jerked away from his feet and he was thrown against a stone-fountain.

The water—hot water—splashing in his face revived him. He got to his feet, Bimbo steadying him, helping him on again. The noises grew louder; they came closer. The cries were even more animal-like than before, but now they came from human throats. A few people, quicker of foot and more hurried by fear, began to rush by. A family or two—then a section—then, it seemed, an army broken out of bounds. Tito, bewildered though he was, could recognize Rufus as he bellowed past him, like a water-buffalo gone mad. Time was lost in a nightmare.

It was then the crashing began. First a sharp crackling, like a monstrous snapping of twigs; then a roar like the fall of a whole forest of trees; then an explosion that tore earth and sky. The heavens, though Tito could not see them, were shot through with continual flickerings of fire. Lightnings above were answered by thunders beneath. A house fell. Then another. By a miracle the two companions had escaped the dangerous side-steets and were in a more open space. It was the Forum. They rested here a while—how long he did not know.

Tito had no idea of the time of day. He could *feel* it was black—an unnatural blackness. Something inside—perhaps the lack of breakfast and lunch—told him it was past noon. But it didn't matter. Nothing seemed to matter. He was getting drowsy, too drowsy to walk. But walk he must. He knew it. And Bimbo knew it; the sharp tugs told him so. Nor was it a moment too soon.

The sacred ground of the Forum was safe no longer. It was beginning to rock, then to pitch, then to split. As they stumbled out of the square, the earth wriggled like a caught snake and all the columns of the temple of Jupiter came down. It was the end of the world—or so it seemed. To walk was not enough now. They must run. Tito was too frightened to know what to do or where to go. He had lost all sense of direction. He started to go back to the inner gate; but Bimbo, straining his back to the last inch, almost pulled his clothes from him. What did the creature want? Had the dog gone mad?

Then, suddenly, he understood. Bimbo was telling him the way out—urging him there. The sea-gate of course. The sea-gate—and then the sea. Far from falling buildings, heaving ground. He turned, Bimbo guiding him across open pits and dangerous pools of bubbling mud, away from buildings that had caught fire and were dropping their burning beams. Tito could no longer tell whether the noises were made by the shrieking sky or the agonized people. He and Bimbo ran on—the only silent beings in a howling world.

New dangers threatened. All Pompeii seemed to be thronging toward the marine-gate and, squeezing among the crowds, there was the chance of being trampled to death. But the chance had to be taken. It was growing harder and harder to breathe. What air there was choked him. It was all dust now—dust and pebbles, pebbles as large as beans. They fell on his head, his hands—pumice-stones from the black heart of Vesuvius. The mountain was turning itself inside out. Tito remembered a phrase that the stranger had said in the Forum two days ago: "Those who will not listen to men must be taught by the gods." The people of Pompeii had refused to heed the warnings; they were being taught now—if it was not too late.

Suddenly it seemed too late for Tito. The red hot ashes blistered his skin, the stinging vapors tore his throat. He could not go on. He staggered toward a small tree at the side of the road and fell. In a moment Bimbo was beside him. He coaxed. But there was no answer. He licked Tito's hands, his feet, his face. The boy did not stir. Then Bimbo did the last thing he could—the last thing he wanted to do. He bit his comrade, bit him deep in the arm. With a cry of pain, Tito jumped to his feet, Bimbo after him. Tito was in despair, but Bimbo was determined. He drove the boy on, snapping at his heels, worrying his way through the crowd; barking, baring his teeth, heedless of kicks or falling stones. Sick with hunger, half-dead with fear and sulphur-fumes, Tito pounded on, pursued by Bimbo. How long he never knew. At last he staggered through the marine-gate and felt soft sand under him. Then Tito fainted. . . .

Some one was dashing sea-water over him. Some one was carrying him toward a boat.

"Bimbo," he called. And then louder, "Bimbo!" But Bimbo had disappeared.

Voices jarred against each other. "Hurry—hurry!" "To the boats!" "Can't you see the child's frightened and starving!" "He keeps calling for some one!" "Poor boy, he's out of his mind." "Here, child—take this!"

They tucked him in among them. The oar-locks creaked; the oars splashed; the boat rode over toppling waves. Tito was safe. But he wept continually.

"Bimbo!" he wailed. "Bimbo! Bimbo!"

He could not be comforted.

Eighteen hundred years passed. Scientists were restoring the ancient city; excavators were working their way through the stones and trash that had buried the entire town. Much had already been brought to light—statues, bronze instruments, bright mosaics, household articles; even delicate paintings had been preserved by the fall of ashes that had taken over two thousand lives. Columns were dug up and the Forum was beginning to emerge.

It was at a place where the ruins lay deepest that the Director paused.

"Come here," he called to his assistant. "I think we've discovered the remains of a building in good shape. Here are four huge millstones that were most likely turned by slaves or mules—and here is a whole wall standing with shelves inside it. Why! It must have been a bakery. And here's a curious thing. What do you think I found under this heap where the ashes were thickest? The skeleton of a dog!"

"Amazing!" gasped his assistant. "You'd think a dog would have had sense enough to run away at the time. And what is that flat thing he's holding between his teeth? It can't be a stone."

"No. It must have come from this bakery. You know it looks to me like some sort of cake hardened with the years. And, bless me, if those little black pebbles aren't raisins. A raisin-cake almost two thousand years old! I wonder what made him want it at such a moment?"

"I wonder," murmured the assistant.

THE LASTING BOND
(1914)
James Oliver Curwood

James Oliver Curwood (1878–1927) distinguished himself as a writer of stories on animal life and human adventures in the wild northland of America. The story below is an episode from his book *Kazan*, which features a wolf dog who becomes attached to a human family living in the hinterland but finds his soul mate in a female wild wolf. Among Curwood's other books are *The Bear* (1916), *The Country Beyond: A Romance of the Wilderness* (1922), and *The Hunted Woman* (1926).

Half a mile away, at the summit of a huge mass of rock which the Indians called the Sun Rock, he and Gray Wolf had found a home; and from here they went down to their hunts on the plain, and often the girl's voice reached up to them, calling, "Kazan! Kazan! Kazan!"

Through all the long winter, Kazan hovered thus between the lure of Joan and the cabin—and Gray Wolf.

Then came Spring—and the Great Change.

The rocks, the ridges and the valleys were taking on a warmer glow. The poplar buds were ready to burst. The scent of balsam and of spruce grew heavier in the air each day, and all through the wilderness, in plain and forest, there was the rippling murmur of the spring floods finding their way to Hudson's Bay. In that great bay, there was the rumble and crash of the ice fields thundering down in the early break-up through the Roes Welcome—the doorway to the Arctic, and for that reason there still came with the April wind an occasional sharp breath of winter.

Kazan had sheltered himself against that wind. Not a breath of air stirred in the sunny spot the Wolf-dog had chosen for himself. He was more comfortable than he had been at any time during the six months of terrible winter—and as he slept, he dreamed.

Gray Wolf, his wild mate, lay near him, flat on her belly, her forepaws reaching out, her eyes and nostrils as keen and alert as the smell of man could make them. For there was that smell of man, as well as of balsam and spruce, in the warm spring air. She gazed anxiously and sometimes steadily, at Kazan as he slept. Her own gray spine stiffened when she saw the tawny hair along Kazan's back bristle at some dream vision. She whined softly as his upper lip snarled back, showing his long white fangs. But for the most part Kazan lay quiet, save for the muscular twitchings of legs, shoulders and muzzle, which always tell when a Dog is dreaming; and as he dreamed there came to the door of the cabin out on the plain a blue-eyed girl-woman, with a big brown braid over her shoulder, who called through the cup of her hands, "Kazan, Kazan, Kazan!"

The voice reached faintly to the top of the Sun Rock, and Gray Wolf flattened her ears. Kazan stirred, and in another instant he was awake and on his feet. He leaped to an out-cropping ledge, sniffing the air and looking far out over the plain that lay below them.

Over the plain, the woman's voice came to them again, and Kazan ran to the edge of the rock and whined. Gray Wolf stepped softly to his side and laid her muzzle on his shoulder. She had grown to know what the Voice meant. Day and night she feared it, more than she feared the scent or sound of man.

Since she had given up the pack and her old life for Kazan, the Voice had become Gray Wolf's greatest enemy, and she hated it. It took Kazan from her. And wherever it went, Kazan followed.

Night after night it robbed her of her mate, and left her to wander alone under the stars and the moon, keeping faithfully to her loneliness, and never once responding with her own tongue to the hunt-calls of her wild brothers and sisters in the forests and out on the plains. Usually she would snarl at the Voice, and sometimes nip Kazan lightly to show her displeasure. But to-day, as the Voice came a third time, she slunk back into the darkness of a fissure between two rocks, and Kazan saw only the fiery glow of her eyes.

Kazan ran nervously to the trail their feet had worn up to the top of the Sun Rock, and stood undecided. All day, and yesterday, he had been uneasy and disturbed. Whatever it was that stirred him seemed to be in the air, for he could not see it or hear it or scent it. But he could *feel* it. He went to the fissure and sniffed at Gray Wolf; usually she whined coaxingly. But her response to-day was to draw back her lips until he could see her white fangs.

A fourth time the Voice came to them faintly, and she snapped fiercely at some unseen thing in the darkness between the two rocks. Kazan went again to the trail, still hesitating. Then he began to go down. It was a narrow wind-ing trail, worn only by the pads and claws of animals; for the Sun Rock was a huge crag that rose almost sheer up for a hundred feet above the tops of the spruce and balsam, its bald crest catching the first gleams of the sun in the morning and the last glow of it in the evening. Gray Wolf had first led Kazan to the security of the retreat at the top of the rock.

When he reached the bottom he no longer hesitated, but darted swiftly in the direction of the cabin. Because of that instinct of the wild that was still in him, he always approached the cabin with caution. He never gave warning, and for a moment Joan was startled when she looked up from her baby and saw Kazan's shaggy head and shoulders in the open door. The baby struggled and kicked in her delight, and held out her two hands with cooing cries to Kazan. Joan, too, held out a hand.

"Kazan!" she cried softly. "Come in, Kazan!"

Slowly the wild red light in Kazan's eyes softened. He put a forefoot on the sill, and stood there, while the girl urged him again. Suddenly his legs seemed to sink a little under him, his tail drooped and he slunk in with that doggish air of having committed a crime. The creatures he loved were in the cabin, but the cabin itself he hated. He hated all cabins, for they all breathed of the club and the whip and bondage. Like all Sledge-dogs, he preferred the open snow for a bed, and the spruce-tops for shelter.

Joan dropped her hand to his head, and at its touch there thrilled through him that strange joy that was his reward for leaving Gray Wolf and the wild. Slowly he raised his head until his black muzzle rested on her lap, and he closed his eyes while that wonderful little creature that mystified him so—the baby—prodded him with her tiny feet, and pulled his tawny hair. He loved these baby-maulings even more than the touch of Joan's hand.

Motionless, sphinx-like, undemonstrative in every muscle of his body, Kazan stood, scarcely breathing. More than once this lack of demonstration had urged Joan's husband to warn her. But the Wolf that was in Kazan, his wild aloofness, even his mating with Gray Wolf, had made her love him more. She understood, and had faith in him.

In the days of the last snow, Kazan had proved himself. A neighboring trapper had run over with his team, and the baby Joan had toddled up to one of the big huskies. There was a fierce snap of jaws, a scream of horror from Joan, a shout from the men as they leaped toward the pack. But Kazan was ahead of them all. In a gray streak that traveled with the speed of a bullet, he was at the big husky's throat. When they pulled him off, the husky was dead. Joan thought of that now, as the baby kicked and tousled Kazan's head.

"Good old Kazan," she cried softly, putting her face down close to him. "We're glad you came, Kazan, for we're going to be alone tonight—baby and I. Daddy's gone to the post, and you must care for us while he's away."

She tickled his nose with the end of her long shining braid. This always delighted the baby, for in spite of his stoicism Kazan had to sniff and sometimes to sneeze, and twig his ears. And it pleased him, too. He loved the sweet scent of Joan's hair.

"And you'd fight for us, if you had to, wouldn't you?" she went on. Then she rose quietly. "I must close the door," she said. "I don't want you to go away again to-day, Kazan. You must stay with us."

Kazan went off to his corner, and lay down. Just as there had been some strange thing at the top of the Sun Rock to disturb him that day, so now there was a mystery that disturbed him in the cabin. He sniffed the air, trying to fathom its secret. Whatever it was, it seemed to make his mistress different, too. And she was digging out all sorts of odds and ends of things about the cabin, and doing them up in packages. Late that night, before she went to bed, Joan came and snuggled her hand close down beside him for a few moments.

"We're going away," she whispered, and there was curious tremble that was almost a sob in her voice. "We're going home, Kazan. We're going away down where his people live—where they have churches, and cities, and music, and all the beautiful things in the world. And we're going to take *you*, Kazan!"

Kazan didn't understand. But he was happy at having the woman so near to him, and talking to him. At these times, he forgot Gray Wolf. The Dog that was in him surged over his quarter-strain of wildness, and the woman and the baby alone filled his world. But after Joan had gone to her bed, and all was quiet in the cabin, his old uneasiness returned. He rose to his feet and moved stealthily about the cabin, sniffing at the walls, the door and the things his mistress had done into packages. A low whine rose in his throat. Joan, half asleep, heard it, and murmured:

"Be quiet, Kazan. Go to sleep—go to sleep—"

Long after that, Kazan stood rigid in the center of the room, listening, trembling. And faintly he heard, far away, the wailing cry of Gray Wolf. But to-night it was not the cry of loneliness. It sent a thrill through him. He ran to the door, and whined, but Joan was deep in slumber and did not hear him. Once more he heard the cry, and only once. Then the night grew still. He crouched down near the door.

Joan found him there, still watchful, still listening, when she awoke in the early morning. She came to open the door for him, and in a moment he was gone. His feet seemed scarcely to touch the earth as he sped in the direction of the Sun Rock. Across the plain he could see the cap of it already painted with a golden glow.

He came to the narrow winding trail, and wormed his way up it swiftly.

Gray Wolf was not at the top to greet him. But he could smell her, and the scent of that other thing was strong in the air. His muscles tightened; his legs grew tense. Deep down in his chest there began the low rumble of a growl. He knew now what that strange thing was that had haunted him, and made him uneasy. It was *life*. Something that lived and breathed and invaded the home which he and Gray Wolf had chosen. He bared his long fangs, and a snarl of defiance drew back his lips. Stiff-legged, prepared to spring, his neck and head reaching out, he approached the two rocks between which

Gray Wolf had crept the night before. She was still there. And with her was *something else*. After a moment the tenseness left Kazan's body. His bristling crest drooped until it lay flat. His ears shot forward, and he put his head and shoulders between the two rocks, and whined softly. And Gray Wolf whined. Slowly Kazan backed out, and faced the rising sun. Then he lay down, so that his body shielded the entrance to the chamber between the rocks.

Gray Wolf was a mother.

The Tragedy on Sun Rock

All that day Kazan guarded the top of the Sun Rock. Fate, and the fear and brutality of masters, had heretofore kept him from fatherhood, and he was puzzled. Something told him now that he belonged to the Sun Rock, and not to the cabin. The call that came to him from over the plain was not so strong. At dusk Gray Wolf came out from her retreat, and slunk to his side, whimpering, and nipped gently at his shaggy neck. It was the old instinct of his fathers that made him respond by caressing Gray Wolf's face with his tongue. Then Gray Wolf's jaws opened, and she laughed in short panting breaths, as if she had been hard run. She was happy, and as they heard a little snuffling sound from between the rocks, Kazan wagged his tail, and Gray Wolf darted back to her young.

The babyish cry and its effect upon Gray Wolf taught Kazan his first lesson in fatherhood. Instinct again told him that Gray Wolf could not go down to the hunt with him now—that she must stay at the top of the Sun Rock. So when the moon rose he went down alone, and toward dawn returned with a big white Rabbit between his jaws. It was the wild in him that made him do this, and Gray Wolf ate ravenously. Then he knew that each night hereafter he must hunt for Gray Wolf—and the little whimpering creatures hidden between the two rocks.

The next day, and still the next, he did not go to the cabin, though he heard the voices of both the man and the woman calling him. On the fifth he

231

went down, and Joan and the baby were so glad that the woman hugged him, and the baby kicked and laughed and screamed at him, while the man stood by cautiously, watching their demonstrations with a gleam of disapprobation in his eyes.

"I'm afraid of him," he told Joan for the hundredth time. "That's the Wolf-gleam in his eyes. He's of a treacherous breed. Sometimes I wish we'd never brought him home."

"If we hadn't—where would the baby—have gone!" Joan reminded him, a little catch in her voice.

"I had almost forgotten that," said her husband. "Kazan, you old devil, I guess I love you, too." He laid his hand caressingly on Kazan's head. "Wonder how he'll take to life down there?" he asked. "He has always been used to the forests. It'll seem mighty strange."

"And so—have I—always been used to the forests," whispered Joan. "I guess that's why I love Kazan—next to you and the baby. Kazan—dear old Kazan!"

This time Kazan felt and scented more of the mysterious change in the cabin. Joan and her husband talked incessantly of their plans when they were together; and when the man was away, Joan talked to the baby, and to him. And each time that he came down to the cabin during the week that followed, he grew more and more restless, until at last the man noticed the change in him.

"I believe he knows," he said to Joan one evening. "I believe he knows we're preparing to leave." Then he added: "The river was rising again to-day. It will be another week before we can start, perhaps longer."

That same night the moon flooded the top of the Sun Rock, with a golden light, and out into the glow of it came Gray Wolf, with her three little whelps toddling behind her. There was much about these soft little balls that tumbled about him and snuggled in his tawny coat that reminded Kazan of the baby. At times they made the same queer, soft little sounds, and they staggered about on their four little legs just as helplessly as baby Joan made her way about on two. He did not fondle them, as Gray Wolf did, but the touch of them, and their babyish whimperings, filled him with a kind of pleasure that he had never experienced before.

The moon was straight above them, and the night was almost as bright as day, when he went down again to hunt for Gray Wolf. At the foot of the rock, a big white Rabbit popped up ahead of him, and he gave chase. For a half a mile he pursued, until the Wolf instinct in him rose over the Dog, and he gave up the futile race. A Deer he might have overtaken, but small game the Wolf must hunt as the Fox hunts it; and he began to slip through the thickets slowly and as quietly as a shadow. He was a mile from the Sun Rock when two quick leaps put Gray Wolf's supper between his jaws. He trotted back slowly, dropping the big seven-pound Snow-shoe Hare now and then to rest.

When he came to the narrow trail that led to the top of the Sun Rock, he stopped. In that trail was the warm scent of strange feet. The Rabbit fell from his jaws. Every hair in his body was suddenly electrified into life. What he scented was not the scent of a Rabbit, a Marten or a Porcupine. Fang and claw had climbed the path ahead of him. And then, coming faintly to him from the top of the rock, he heard sounds which sent him up with a terrible whining cry. When he reached the summit he saw in the white moonlight a scene that stopped him for a single moment. Close to the edge of the sheer fall to the rocks, fifty feet below, Gray Wolf was engaged in a death-struggle with a huge gray Lynx. She was down—and under, and from her there came a sudden sharp terrible cry of pain.

Kazan flew across the rock. His attack was the swift assault of the Wolf, combined with the greater courage, the fury and the strategy of the husky. Another husky would have died in that first attack. But the Lynx was not a Dog or a Wolf. It was "Mow-lee, the Swift," as the Sarcees had named it—the quickest creature in the wilderness. Kazan's inch-long fangs should have sunk deep in its jugular. But in a fractional part of a second, the Lynx had thrown itself back like a huge soft ball, and Kazan's teeth buried themselves in the flesh of its neck instead of the jugular. And Kazan was not now fighting the fangs of a Wolf in the pack, or of another husky. He was fighting claws—claws that ripped like twenty razor-edged knives, and which even a jugular hold could not stop.

Once he had fought a Lynx in a trap, and he had not forgotten the lesson the battle had taught him. He fought to pull the Lynx *down*, instead of forcing it on its back, as he could have done with another Dog or a Wolf. He knew that when on its back, the fierce Cat was most dangerous. One rip of its powerful hind-feet could disembowel him. Behind him he heard Gray Wolf sobbing and crying, and he knew that she was terribly hurt. He was filled with the rage and strength of two Dogs, and his teeth met through the flesh and hide of the Cat's throat. But the big Lynx escaped death by half an inch. It would take a fresh grip to reach the jugular, and suddenly Kazan made the deadly lunge. There was an instant's freedom for the Lynx, and in that moment it flung itself back, and Kazan gripped at its throat—*on top*.

The Cat's claws ripped through his flesh, cutting open his side—a little too high to kill. Another stroke and they would have cut to his vitals. But they had struggled close to the edge of the rock wall; and suddenly, without a snarl or a cry, they rolled over. It was fifty or sixty feet to the rocks of the ledge below, and even as they pitched over and over in the fall, Kazan's teeth sank deeper. They struck with terrific force, Kazan uppermost. The shock sent him half a dozen feet from his enemy. He was up like a flash, dizzy, snarling, on the defensive. The Lynx lay limp and motionless where it had fallen. Kazan came nearer, still prepared, and sniffed cautiously. Something told him that the fight was over. He turned and dragged himself slowly along the ledge to the trail, and returned to Gray Wolf.

Gray Wolf was no longer in the moonlight. Close to the two rocks lay the limp and lifeless bodies of the three pups. The Lynx had torn them to pieces. With a whine of grief, Kazan approached the two boulders and thrust his head between them. Gray Wolf was there, crying to herself in that terrible sobbing way. He went in, and began to lick her bleeding shoulders and head. All the rest of that night she whimpered with pain. With dawn she dragged herself out to the lifeless little bodies on the rock.

And then Kazan saw the terrible work of the Lynx. For Gray Wolf was blind—not for a day or a night, but blind for all time. A gloom that no sun could break had become her shroud. And perhaps again it was that instinct of animal creation, which often is more wonderful than man's reason, that told Kazan what had happened. For he knew now that she was helpless—more helpless than the little creatures that had gamboled in the moonlight a few hours before. He remained close beside her all that day.

Vainly that day did Joan call for Kazan. Her voice rose to the Sun Rock, and Gray Wolf's head snuggled closer to Kazan, and Kazan's ears dropped back, and he licked her wounds. Late in the afternoon Kazan left Gray Wolf long enough to run to the bottom of the trail and bring up the Snow-shoe Rabbit. Gray Wolf nuzzled the fur and flesh, but would not eat. Still a little later Kazan urged her to follow him to the trail. He no longer wanted to stay at the top of the Sun Rock, and he no longer wanted Gray Wolf to stay there. Step by step he drew her down the winding path away from her dead puppies. She would move only when he was very near her—so near that she could touch his scarred flank with her nose.

They came at last to the point in the trail where they had to leap down a distance of three or four feet from the edge of a rock, and here Kazan saw how utterly helpless Gray Wolf had become. She whined, and crouched twenty times before she dared make the spring, and then she jumped stiff-legged, and fell in a heap at Kazan's feet. After this Kazan did not have to urge her so hard, for the fall impinged on her the fact that she was safe only when her muzzle touched her mate's flank. She followed him obediently when they reached the plain, trotting with her foreshoulder to his hip.

Kazan was heading for a thicket in the creek bottom half a mile away, and a dozen times in that short distance Gray Wolf stumbled and fell. And each time that she fell Kazan learned a little more of the limitations of blindness. Once he sprang off in pursuit of a Rabbit, but he had not taken twenty leaps when he stopped and looked back. Gray Wolf had not moved an inch. She stood motionless, sniffing the air—waiting for him! For a full minute, Kazan stood, also waiting. Then he returned to her. Ever after this he returned to her.

Ever after this he returned to the point where he had left Gray Wolf, knowing that he would find her there.

All that day they remained in the thicket. In the afternoon, he visited the cabin. Joan and her husband were there, and both saw at once Kazan's torn side and his lacerated head and shoulders.

"Pretty near a finish fight for him," said the man, after he had examined him. "It was either a Lynx or a Bear. Another Wolf could not do that."

For half an hour, Joan worked over him, talking to him all the time, and fondling him with her soft hands. She bathed his wounds in warm water, and then covered them with a healing salve, and Kazan was filled again with that old restful desire to remain with her always, and never to go back into the forests. For an hour she let him lie on the edge of her dress, with his nose touching her foot, while she worked on baby things. Then she rose to prepare supper, and Kazan got up—a little wearily—and went to the door. Gray Wolf and the gloom of the night were calling him, and he answered that call with a slouch of his shoulders and a drooping head. Its old thrill was gone. He watched his chance, and went out through the door. The moon had risen when he rejoined Gray Wolf. She greeted his return with a low whine of joy, and nuzzled him with her blind face. In her helplessness she looked happier than Kazan in all his strength.

From now on, during the days that followed, it was a last great fight between blind and faithful Gray Wolf and the woman. If Joan had known of what lay in the thicket, if she could once have seen the poor creature to whom Kazan was now all life—the sun, the stars, the moon, and food—she would have helped Gray Wolf. But as it was, she tried to lure Kazan more and more to the cabin, and slowly she won.

At last the great day came, eight days after the fight on the Sun Rock. Kazan had taken Gray Wolf to a wooded point on the river two days before, and there he had left her the preceding night when he went to the cabin. This time a stout babiche thong was tied to the collar round his neck, and he was fastened to a staple in the log wall. Joan and her husband were up before it was light next day. The sun was just rising when they all went out, the man carrying the baby, and Joan leading him. Joan turned and locked the cabin door, and Kazan heard a sob in her throat as they followed the man down to the river. The big canoe was packed and waiting. Joan got in first, with the baby. Then, still holding the babiche thong, she drew Kazan up close to her, so that he lay with his weight against her.

The sun fell warmly on Kazan's back as they shoved off, and he closed his eyes, and rested his head on Joan's lap. Her hand fell softly on his shoulder. He heard again that sound which the man could not hear, the broken sob in her throat, as the canoe moved slowly down to the wooded point.

Joan waved her hand back at the cabin, just disappearing behind the trees.

"Good-by!" she cried sadly. "Good-by—" And then she buried her face close down to Kazan and the baby, and sobbed.

The man stopped paddling.

"You're not sorry—Joan?" he asked.

They were drifting past the point now, and the scent of Gray Wolf came to Kazan's nostrils, rousing him, and bringing a low whine from his throat.

"You're not sorry—we're going?" Joan shook her head.

"No," she replied. "Only I've—always lived here—in the forests—and they're home."

The point with its white finger of sand was behind them now. And Kazan was standing rigid, facing it. The man called to him and Joan lifted her head. She, too, saw the point, and suddenly the babiche leash slipped from her fingers, and a strange light leaped into her blue eyes as she saw what stood at the end of that white tip of sand. It was Gray Wolf. Her blind eyes were turned toward Kazan. At last Gray Wolf, the faithful, understood. Scent told her what her eyes could not see. Kazan and the man-smell were together. And they were going—going—going—

"Look!" whispered Joan.

The man turned. Gray Wolf's forefeet were in the water. And now, as the canoe drifted farther and farther away, she settled back on her haunches, raised her head to the sun which she could not see, and gave her last long wailing cry for Kazan.

The canoe lurched. A tawny body shot through the air—and Kazan was gone.

The man reached forward for his rifle. Joan's hand stopped him. Her face was white.

"Let him go back to her! Let him go—let him go!" she cried. "It is his place—with her."

And Kazan reaching the shore, shook the water from his shaggy hair, and looked for the last time toward the woman. The canoe was drifting slowly around the first bend. A moment more and it disappeared.

Gray Wolf had won.

THE TALKING DOG
OF THE WORLD
(1988)
Ethan Mordden

The earlier stories in the book by Wodehouse and Davis are narrated by dogs, but this tale goes a bit further by introducing a clown
dog in an amateur circus that supposedly has the gift of gab. This
delightful spoof originally appeared in *The New Yorker*. Author Ethan
Mordden is best known for five volumes of short fiction called *Buddies*
(1986) and has also written nonfiction books on music and the theater. Among his books are *The American Theater* (1981), *Rogers and
Hammerstein* (1992), and *One More Kiss: The Broadway Musical in
the 1970s* (2003).

In Hanley, West Virginia, close on to Wheeling, where I lived when I was little, there was a poky little circus run by Hopey Paris. Most places don't have their own circus on the premises, not even a little one like Hopey's, which had almost no animals and a busted trapeze and these admission tickets that must have been printed up before the Civil War. You couldn't even read what they said on them anymore. In Hanley we figured it was O.K. to have this circus, though most of us didn't care about it one way or the other. Anyway, you never knew when Hopey was going to put his circus on, because he ran it by whim. Also, he owned the dime store. I expect what he got out of the dime store he plowed back into keeping the circus going, since he didn't own anything else.

It was like this about having the circus: Some night in light weather, mostly at the tip end of summer, when everyone would just sit around and wait for something cool to happen, Hopey would come up from his end of town and find a crowd on the steps of wherever it was they were . . . someone's porch, whoever had beer. He'd wait about three lulls, nodding and shaking along with the gist of things as they got said. Then he'd go, "Guess I'll have to have the circus tonight." And everyone would get everyone else and go on over, because, look, what else is there to do? You go to the circus.

What a funny circus—but how much do you want for free? Hopey handed out the admission tickets in a little booth at the entrance and you would take your seat inside the tent, which stood in Hopey's back yard, hanging on by a thread to these old poles, It wasn't a big tent, of course, but, as it is said, size isn't substance. And then Hopey would come in with a whip and this hat he got somewhere to be a ringmaster in. You'd want to think he would look pathetic, wouldn't you? Hopey Paris trying to hold down a circus all by himself in Hanley? He didn't, though. He didn't look much like anything. But he did have a star attraction, the clown dog.

It's crazy about dogs—how some can do things and some can't. I knew a dog once that caught softballs in the air if you threw them underhand. Then he'd go racing off with the ball in his teeth and you'd have to trap him and pry the ball out with a stick. That was his trick, I guess is how he looked at it. And my father had a dog named Bill who was quite a hero in his day. Bill ran away finally and never came back.

But the clown dog sure was prime. He had this costume—a yellow coat sort of thing with polka dots, which he wore fastened around his middle, and a red cone hat with a little pom-pom at the top. Whether the circus was on or off, and in all weathers, never, never did you see the clown dog out of costume. And his trick was he could talk. That dog could really talk.

This was why we would always come back to see the same old one-man circus, with no animals or clowns except one animal clown, like that was all you needed to call it a circus. The tent was hardly alive at all, the big-top tent itself. But you always had to go back, because you wanted to see how the trick was done. Because no dog, not even a circus trick dog, can talk. But the thing about tricks is whether or not you can figure them out. That's the art of tricks, right there. And the clown dog, though he often roamed around his end of town like any other dog, free in the sun, except he was dressed—the clown dog would never do his talking except in the circus. This was probably the deal he made with Hopey, who was, after all, his master. You'd suppose that they must have come to terms on something that important.

That's what's so funny. Because, speaking of dogs, my father never did come to terms with his dog, Bill, though he would try, hard as stone, to make that dog his. He trained it and trained it. It must have run near on to two years of sessions in Sunshine's field, and Bill just didn't ever submit and be trained. My father was a ferocious trainer by the standards of any region, but he couldn't get Bill to obey even the most essential commands. And he never could teach him not to chase around the davenport, especially late at night, when Bill most felt like a run. "I will have that dog behave," my father said, and I recall how he looked, like behavior was just around the corner. But Bill would not be suppressed. Sometimes he would come when you called, sometimes not. But even when he did come he had this funny look on him, as if he was coming over just to find out why you persisted in calling his name when it had already been established that he wasn't about to respond.

Bill was a mutt, not like the clown dog, who was a poodle—a very distinct breed. You can't miss a poodle, especially in a polka-dot coat and a cone hat with a pom-pom. But Bill was just another dog you might know, kind of slow for his race and disobedient but generally normal, except once when he was The Hero of '62. They called him that because he accidentally bit this management scud who was getting on everybody's nerves at the factory the summer before the strike.

McCosker, I think this guy's name was—one of those mouthy hirelings absolutely corrupted by a little power. He had been tacking up a notice by the front gate—some mouthy, powerful thing about something else you weren't supposed to do. He was just busy as anything tacking away and being hated by the people who were standing around watching. Suddenly Bill bounded over to where McCosker was. I guess maybe Bill thought he saw something to eat near his foot, but McCosker took it for some stunt and he made a sudden move and Bill got thrilled and bit him.

It was a tiny little bite on the ankle, kind of in passing, but McCosker screamed like he was being murdered and all the men cheered and patted Bill. And they all shook my father's hand, and mine, too. So Bill was The Hero of '62.

This is a funny thing. Because all Bill had done was what a dog will do every so often, whereas the clown dog was truly some kind of dog. Everybody said so. You just could not tell in any way that he wasn't talking when Hopey Paris brought him on for his circus turn. Now, that was a trained dog if ever there was one. Yet nobody ever called the clown dog a hero. And the clown dog never ran away, either, which Bill did once. Once is all it takes.

I guess you have to figure that a dog that goes around in circus clothes isn't going to earn the respect of the community. Besides him being a poodle, which is not one of your heroic breeds of dog. But I liked him, because he was the first thing I can remember in all my life. Hunkering back down in my mind as far as I can go, I reach a picture of the clown dog talking in the circus, and the polka dots, and the hat. I wonder if he ever had a name, because he was always known as the clown dog that I ever heard, and I don't recall Hopey ever calling to him. Sometimes Hopey would act like that dog was this big secret, cocking an eyebrow and looking cagey if you asked after him, as if everyone in town hadn't seen the circus a hundred times.

I expect the clown dog must have liked me, because he used to follow me around some days with his coat and his dumb little hat. He looked so sad. I guess he sensed that he was supposed to be a secret, because he tended to hang back a little, like someone who has already been tagged out of a game and is waiting for the next thing to start. I don't recall that he even barked. And he never gave in to us when we tried to get him to talk out of the circus.

Of course we had listened, with all the concentration of adolescents, to the exact words Hopey used in the act, when the clown dog would speak, and we would try these words on the clown dog ourselves—imitating Hopey's voice even, and standing the way he stood, to be an imperial ringmaster. But we couldn't make it happen; never did the clown dog utter a word out of his context, the circus. It was the strangest thing.

I was just thinking that I would have hated to be around Bill someday if someone tried to get him into a hat with pom-poms.

I was at college when Bill ran away, so I only know about it second hand, from stories. I couldn't help thinking it was presumable that in the end Bill would take a walk one day and not come back. It was presumable. But still I was surprised to hear of it. It was Easter, when I was a freshman, and the first sight I got of home when I got off the bus was my father cutting the grass with the Johnsons' lawnmower and Bill nowhere to be seen. I knew something was wrong then, because Bill never missed a chance to play dogfight with the Johnsons' lawnmower, which always enraged my father. Bill would growl at it, for starters, lying way off somewhere, and slowly creep toward it, paw by paw. Then he'd run around it, fussing and barking, and at last he'd get into rushing it, like he was going in for the kill, only to back up snarling at the last second.

So when I saw the lawnmower and no Bill I thought he must be sick, but my father said he had run off, maybe as far back as October sometime. I listened carefully to this, though he didn't talk carefully, not ever in all his life that I knew him. Whatever he was thinking when he spoke, that's what he'd say, as tough as you can take it. He didn't expect Bill back, he said, and he didn't miss him. He said it, and I believe him.

"No," he said lazily, because he is lazy. "I don't miss him. You run away from home and don't come back, nobody misses you at all. That's the rule."

I don't know of any rule saying you don't miss a runaway dog, even if he never comes back. If he's of a mind to run, there's usually a good reason. My father used to say, "There's always a reason for something, and sometimes two."

That was one of his wisdoms. He had wisdoms for most things that came up in life—lawyers, school, elections, working. He had his wisdoms for Bill, too, even when it was really clear that that dog was born to go his own way in a nice wisdom of the animal kingdom.

I can see why that dog took off, anyway, because my father wasn't any too easy to get along with, especially when proclaiming one of his wisdoms. But despite what he said and how he looked saying it, I suppose he really did love that dog. Or he wanted to love it, which would be the way people like my father express affection. It must have threatened to tear him up some when Bill deserted him.

That was a bad time, too, with the strike coming sooner or later but sure as doom. I wasn't around for the strike. I was sixteen when I finished high school, and I could still have been young some more and not done much of anything with myself, but I had more ambition than to work in the factory or pump gas on Route 16. So I went to college on what you might call a soccer scholarship. My father always poked fun at me for playing soccer. "What kind of sport is that for a man, chasing a ball around with your feet? You look like a bunch of giant bugs" was his view of it. But soccer took me to college, on a full scholarship. It's true, I guess; soccer isn't much of a sport, and this wasn't much of a college. But one wisdom might be that college is college. Anyway, I went.

I came home for Easter because I was only two states away—one long bus ride. Besides, they closed the dorms on me—they were painting—and I had to go somewhere. That first night, Thursday, when I came home and saw the lawnmower and learned that Bill had run away, I was standing in the yard with my bag, like a salesman, and I decided to walk around town instead of just being home. Because I already knew about home, but I felt mysterious about Hanley—that it was a place filled with riddles that ought to be solved, even by someone who had lived his whole life of sixteen years so far in it.

I thought maybe I would take a look over to Hopey Paris's circus, in case that should be going on. Or maybe I would talk Hopey into doing his show just for me, because it was extremely rare that the circus would happen this early in the year. I had an idea that Hopey favored me over some others of my generation there in Hanley because I had always been the keenest of all to see the clown dog and figure out how he talked, and Hopey was pleased to be appreciated, even by kids.

He liked to think (I'm guessing at this) that his circus, starring the clown dog, which he celebrated as The Talking Dog of the World—that his circus was what kept the town from feeling too complete. You might suppose that a town with a circus is more complete than most, but instead I sense that it is less complete, and therefore more open and more free. Because a circus is magic. And having its own private circus reminds the town of all the other magic things it doesn't have. It puts the town a little in touch with another town, a secret town that is the ghostly image of itself, a kind of myth in a mirror. Now, so long as the town is aware of its ideal twin, it will wonder about itself, and never think it knows everything there is to know, and not pretend that it is complete. Which I think is all to the good. So no wonder I liked to watch the clown dog's act. And that's why I went over to Hopey Paris's circus on my first night back from college—to watch the ghost dance by me again. Even after all those years, I still didn't understand how the clown dog did his trick.

This was the act. Hopey comes in with his whip and his hat and he stands in the ring. "And now we take great pride and the most highly principled pleasure"—this is exactly what he said every time—"in presenting for your delectation and enlightenment the one and only clown dog—The Talking Dog of the World!"

And out from behind a flap of the tent, in his coat and pom-pom hat, the clown dog would trot in. And he would sit on his hind legs looking expectantly at Hopey. That same old coat and hat. That poor little clown dog. Or I guess maybe he was well off, even if no one called him a hero.

In any case, Hopey would say, "Tell these folks here assembled who you *are*"—like that, with everything on the "are." And—I swear to God—the clown dog would answer, as if he was going to growl first. But no, it was this funny talking—"Clown . . . dog." Like that, broken up into words. It was a high voice, tensely placed, like the sounds puppets make on television. And of course we were looking madly from the clown dog to Hopey and back, to see that trick.

Then Hopey would say, "Who is the *clown dog*?" And the clown dog would answer, "Me." Something screwy would happen in his mouth, as if he were biting a fly or had bubble gum. And his head would tilt. But he talked, all right, and that was some trick. Just these two questions were all the talking, though. Because then Hopey would shout, "Leap, clown dog!" and the poodle just leaped right into Hopey's arms and licked his face. That was the whole act, and that was also the whole circus.

I miss that circus, for it is miles away from me now. All my youth and adventures in Hanley seem remote rare things to savor, like slides of ruins in a stereopticon—though I keep my memories somewhat close to me by writing about them, as you can see. I write to preserve (even to rescue) them. But when I went home that Easter I didn't have the circus in mind as something you ever lose hold of, because I didn't realize about growing old. Now, that is a term for you—"growing old." And it, too, has a trick: it contains the thought that things vanish. They function, and they pass, and you also pass along, and perhaps you come to the big city here (as I have), and you learn a new function, like writing, and think about who you are. And somewhere in there you remember the old things, and the other place, and suddenly you realize how much you miss them. And this tells you how you have your own completion to accomplish.

I didn't reckon on any of this at the time, back in Hanley on my Easter vacation. I was just out for a stroll. I should have stopped and seen everything the way a camera sees, marking it down, so when I grew old everything that was there wouldn't have vanished even in completion. I just wanted a little peace.

The thing was that if I was sixteen the clown dog must have been well on to thirteen or fourteen. He just never acted old, so it was not something to realize. Fourteen is old for a dog, and that's near as long as a dog can last without vanishing, even if he still acts spry and bouncy and leaps into your arms when you tell him. So I just went up to Hopey's door and knocked, thinking he'd be there like always, and maybe Hopey would rustle up the circus just for me in honor of my coming back from college on my first holiday.

The house was lit inside, but no one answered, so I went around to the back, where the tent was. Except there was no tent there now. You could see the tracks in the dirt where it used to be, all the time before, and some of the bleacher seats were still there, a little wrecked, like someone had been trying to take them apart and then suddenly changed his mind. And as I stood there wondering, I heard Hopey's back door open. I turned and saw him in the doorway, so I asked him where the circus had gone to.

"My little clown dog passed away," Hopey said, "so I cut down the tent and dissolved the circus."

It happened in October, he said, which would have been only a few weeks after I left town for school. I didn't know what to tell him without making it seem like I was holding another funeral, and I was worried about words because I got distracted thinking about the clown dog's little hat and how sad he looked in it sometimes. You know how touchy it can be, lurking about a place and looking like a stranger. And what if I asked how did it happen and only made Hopey feel worse? I didn't ask. I must have stood there for a whole minute trying to get my mouth around a sentence.

"He liked you, you know," Hopey said suddenly. "Perhaps you suppose that I was busy in the store, but I knew who his friends were. He was a pickety chooser, but he had exquisite taste in people. Didn't you think so?"

"I think he was a shy little fellow," I said.

"Yes, that he was."

"I'm sorry, Hopey. I came over especially to see him again." Now that I'd found my tongue, I expected he would break down or get very quiet, but he was just so calm. The clown dog used to follow me around, I wanted to say. We tried to make him talk. But we never hurt him.

"Since he liked you," said Hopey, "do you want to plumb the mystery of how he talked?"

I had to smile now. "It was a trick, wasn't it?"

"It was a tip-top trick," Hopey replied, "because nobody knew how it was done. Bet I shouldn't spoil it for you after all this. Should I? Do you want to know?"

"I think I ought to plumb the mystery, if he liked me, after all."

"He didn't like everyone," said Hopey. "But I believe he was exceptionally popular in the town."

"I guess he had to be," I said. "No other circus dog that I heard tell of has ever been the headline attraction."

"Well, he certainly was that. And he led a rich life. He was The Talking Dog of the World."

Hopey asked me about college then, and I told him, and after a while there was this natural space to say goodbye, so I left. Hopey forgot to tell me the trick and I forgot to remind him that I should know it, but I didn't think it was fitting to go back there just then, and before I was halfway home I was glad I didn't find out.

You'd think I would be unhappy to learn that the clown dog had died, but in a way that conversation with Hopey was the only nice thing that happened that whole vacation. My father was in a terrible mood the whole time, spitting out wisdoms like he was on a quota system and falling behind. He kept talking about the strike that everyone knew was going to happen, and finally, a few days before I was due to go back to school, he asked me didn't I think my place was here with the people I'd known all my life instead of at some college?

It seemed to me that the place to be during a strike was as far from it as possible, and college would do for that as well as any. And that's what I told him. So he said if I felt that way about it I might as well get going right now.

"Just like Bill," he said.

I was waiting for that. I didn't have anything prepared to say back to it, but I knew it was coming. I don't care. It was meant to hurt me, but it didn't, though I must admit it began to gnaw on me after a while ... because I hoped it was true.

I really did.

"Just like Bill," he said, but he meant more like "Go vanish."

"Just like Bill"—because I was leaving him, too. Well, there's always a reason for something, and sometimes two. I never went back to Hanley, either;

maybe Bill did, after I left, but I won't. I have heard those words often since in my mind, *Just like Bill*, in just the way he said it, looking so smug that he had doped it out at last, made the simple sum and added another wisdom to his collection. I could accept it if I had to, but the truth is I am no way like Bill, all told. I am not like anyone. Whenever someone asks who I am, I say, "Me," just like the clown dog did, because it cheers me to remember him, and to think back on how I could have heard the trick if I had wanted to, which is as close as anybody ought to get. That was a strange, but fine, animal.

JUPITER
(1925)

Stefan Zweig

Like many breeds, bulldogs can behave unpredictably and may not be suitable for small children. The bulldog in this story is a surly beast, and the story grows with anticipation of what will happen to the dog and how his character will be revealed. Author Stefan Zweig (1881–1942) was born in Austria and later moved to England. He wrote several biographies of famous persons: Honoré Balzac, Erasmus of Rotterdam, Ferdinand Magellan, Marie Antoinette, Mary Queen of Scots, and Leo Tolstoy. Zweig also wrote historical analyses, novels, and many short stories in his brilliant career.

I shall never forget the picture he made as he stood there on the edge of the canal, he, the criminal, the monster, looking on the work he had done. Heaven knows we were none of us rational at that moment, with the horror that gripped us; and yet I can recall thinking that I knew how he felt, that I knew what was passing in that vengeful little brain of his—that extraordinary brain.

But let me try, if only for myself, to reconstruct the whole story.

When I retired some eight years ago, my wife and I decided to look for a quiet home in the country. We found the place we wanted near a little town called Dover in upper New York State. An old canal ran through the section; a century ago it had been busy with the barge traffic of the time; then the railways came, traffic dwindled, the lock caretakers were dismissed, and now its atmosphere of desertion made it romantic and mysterious.

Here, on the crest of a hill a few miles out from town, overlooking the canal, was the home we bought. Sitting on our garden terrace at the water's edge, we could see the house, the trees, the garden and meadows reflected in the smooth surface of the stream. We were not entirely isolated, for there was another house fairly similar to ours a few hundred yards away.

Not long after we moved in, a pretty, slender woman, hardly more than twenty-eight or twenty-nine, came over one morning and introduced herself—Mrs. Sturgis, our neighbor. Her eyes were intelligent and kind, her manner attractive, and we were soon talking as if we had known each other for years. Mr. Sturgis, it seemed, worked in Buffalo, and although it was a journey of an hour and a half for him every morning and night on the train, he did not mind it because of the beauty of the country here.

Her manner of speaking of him struck me as rather strange, I remember thinking—as if she did not miss him and yet as if at the same time she was devoted to him.

A few days later, on a Saturday morning, we were starting out for a walk along the canal when we heard footsteps behind us, and a tall, strongly built man came up and offered his hand. He was Roger Sturgis, he had heard of us from his wife, and seeing us pass just then, he had come down to say hello. Wasn't it a glorious morning! Didn't we think it was the most beautiful spot on earth? Could we imagine anyone living in a city, when there was a place like this?

He talked with such enthusiasm, such fluency, that you had hardly a chance to get a word in edgewise; but this allowed me to have a good look at him. He was perhaps thirty-five, a huge ox of a man, six feet anyway, with great broad shoulders. What good nature! He went on talking and laughing without pause. He gave out so strong a feeling of happiness, of utter content-ment, that one was carried away against one's will. Both of us were stimulated by him and delighted to think that such a jovial fellow was our neighbor.

But this enthusiasm did not last. There was nothing to be said against Roger Sturgis. He was kind, sympathetic, helpful—a decent trustworthy man. And yet—

The truth was, he became intensely difficult to bear because he was so boisterously, overwhelmingly and permanently cheerful. Everything was for the best in this best of all possible worlds. His house was perfect. His wife was perfect. His garden was perfect; and the pipe he smoked was the very best pipe ever made.

Never, before I met Roger Sturgis, could I have dreamt that such good qualities could exhaust you and drive you almost to despair.

I began to understand now the strange contradiction in his wife's man-ner of speaking of him. He loved her passionately, as he loved passionately everything he owned. I have never seen such tenderness as he lavished on her; the pride he took in showing her off bordered on the embarrassing. She felt this, but what could she do about it? You cannot quarrel with such supreme devotion!

As we talked about it, my wife and I began to think that what the Sturgises needed was a child. And it seemed, my wife told me, that Mrs. Sturgis had wanted children, that this was the great disappointment of their married life. They had expected a child in the first year of their marriage, in the second and in the third. After eight years, they had given up hope.

It was at about this time that Betty went to visit an old friend of hers in Rochester. When she returned, she had what she thought was an excellent suggestion. Her friend owned a female bull terrier that had given birth to a litter of adorable puppies. Betty had refused one for us, feeling that we could not take care of it properly, but thought that it might make a wonderful pet for Mrs. Sturgis.

I agreed, and that night I asked them if they would like it.

Mrs. Sturgis was silent—she was always silent when he was there—but he accepted with enthusiasm. Certainly! Why hadn't he thought of it before? What a marvelous idea! He couldn't thank me enough.

Two days later the puppy arrived, a comical, lovable little thing, all loose skin and big paws, pure white, a perfect specimen.

The result was not at all what we expected.

Our intention had been to provide a companion for her, but it was Sturgis who took possession of the dog. It was not long before he was telling me on every occasion that there had never been such a dog, a more intelligent one, a more beautiful one, a bull terrier of terriers, a king of his race.

It seems incredible now, the effect this new passion produced in Roger Sturgis. Sometimes we'd hear a noisy barking in their house. It wasn't Jupiter. It was Sturgis, lying prone on the floor, carrying on as if he were a child, playing with his pet. I swear the dog's diet gave him far more concern than his own. I know that once when a newspaper mentioned typhoid in an adjoining county, Jupiter was given bottled water to drink.

Yet there was an advantage to it, in that Sturgis's preoccupation with the bull terrier spared his wife and us some of his exuberance. He would play with Jupiter for hours, never wearying, taking him off on long walks; and Heaven knows it did not make Mrs. Sturgis jealous. Her husband had found a new shrine at which to worship, and for her it was a blessed relief.

All this time Jupiter was growing, the wrinkles in his coat filling out with hard tough flesh, his chest broadening, his legs thickening, his great long jaws becoming more massive.

I admit that he was a most handsome animal, sleek, groomed, combed. And at first he was a good-natured one. But this began to change. Imperceptibly, then more and more quickly. He was intelligent and observant, and it was not difficult for him to perceive that his master—his slave, rather—adored him, overlooked any misdemeanor. The result was inevitable.

Disobedient? Jupiter was far more than disobedient. He became tyrannical. He would not tolerate anything in the house centering around anyone else. If there were visitors and he was outside, he would hurl himself against the door, shaking it under his great weight, confident that Sturgis would leap up to open it. Then he would enter without so much as a glance at the guests, jump on the sofa, the best piece of furniture, and lie there, aloof, bored, proud.

Whenever he was called, he would make Sturgis wait. He would not feed himself if Sturgis was there; Sturgis had to coax him into it. And although during the days he would behave more or less as any normal dog—running in the meadows, chasing chickens, digging, exploring—as soon as the time came for Sturgis's return from the city his attitude changed completely. He would lie back lazily on the sofa, not glancing at Sturgis as he came in, not responding with so much as a wag of his tail to the man's hearty, "Hello there, Jupe! Good old Jupe!"

He was the despot, more and more confident of his power.

He discovered an amusing and perverse new game. It was the habit of some poor people in a little settlement not far away to bring their clothes in baskets to wash them in the canal. Jupiter knew the days when they came. He would steal down on them and, at the proper moment, charge at the baskets and with a butt of his great head send them flying into the canal; and then off he would go, his jaws open as if in laughter, his little pinkish eyes flashing, defying the washerwomen to catch him—as if, even if they had caught him, they could do anything, for he was a powerful as a horse. In the end they went elsewhere, and Jupiter had one more proof of his omnipotence.

A year went by. Jupiter was in his prime, a huge beast, impudent and overbearing, cunning in his special art—for art it was—of humiliating his slavish master.

Then the new day came.

For the past week or so Mrs. Sturgis had given us the impression that she was avoiding anything worthy of being called a conversation. Betty and I could not help noticing this sudden diffidence, and one afternoon she made up her mind to face it.

"Judith," she said, "I'm much older than you and I haven't any reason to feel shy, so I'm going to break the ice. If we've done anything to offend you, I do wish you'd tell me what it is."

Mrs. Sturgis stammered, hesitated, and then came out with it: After nine years of married life she had thought she would never be a mother, but now—well, she had gone to the doctor and he had confirmed it: yes, she was to have a child. Imagine her joy!—but somehow she couldn't bring herself to tell her husband; she was almost afraid of the violence of his reaction! We knew what he was like. So she had been wondering—would it be possible—would we mind very much if we had a talk with him and prepared the ground?

Of course we were delighted. I left a note for Sturgis asking him to come over the moment he returned from town. And at six-thirty that afternoon there he was, brimful of that extraordinary vitality.

"Roger," I said, "I'm going to ask you a funny question. If you had one wish, for anything in the world, what would you want?"

Half-serious, half-laughing, Sturgis shook his head.

"What would I wish for? Why—"

"Surely there's something!"

"What's the joke?"

"I'm serious. Come on, what do you want above all else?"

He grinned. "Why," he said, "I'm darned if I know what I'd wish for! After all, I've got everything I want—my wife, my house, my job, my—" He was going to say "my dog," but thought better of it; he knew how we felt about that infernal beast.

"Then how about Mrs. Sturgis?" I said. "What do you think she'd want?"

He looked at me in bewilderment. "What could she possibly want?"

"Perhaps something more than a dog."

At last he understood. His eyes opened so wide that we saw the whites. With one bound he was out of his chair, through the door and scrambling over the lawn and the garden fence, and we heard the door of his house slam.

We both laughed. We weren't surprised by his reaction.

But someone else was surprised—someone who, lying lazily on the sofa, with half-closed eyes, was waiting for the evening homage that he had come to think was his due. Someone who was waiting for the man to enter, to kneel beside him, to pat him. Someone who was waiting to ignore that homage.

But what was this? Without a word of greeting, the man rushed past into the bedroom, and Jupiter heard the talking and laughing and crying that went on and on and on, Jupiter, the tyrant, the smug, the proud—ignored!

An hour passed. The maid brought him his food. Contemptuously, he turned aside. He growled at the maid. They would see that he was not going to be snubbed! But this evening no one seemed to realize that he had refused his food. There was Sturgis talking to his wife without interruption, overwhelming her with anxious advice and affection. Jupiter was too proud to force his way to his master's attention. Curled up in a corner, he waited.

He waited in vain.

The next morning Sturgis rushed by him again without a look. And he had the same experience that night, the following morning, the following night. Day after day.

He was intelligent, but this was beyond him. He became nervous and irritable. He would not approach Sturgis; not he. It was Sturgis who must return to his senses, who must come to him.

In the third week Jupiter went lame. In normal circumstances Sturgis would have rushed for the vet, but now neither he nor anyone else noticed the limp, and Jupiter, in exasperation, had to give it up. A few days later he attempted a hunger strike—such was his intelligence, his subtlety. But no one worried. For two full days he refused his meals heroically. For all anyone seemed to care, he might starve himself to death.

Finally, his animal hunger was stronger than his will power—yes, I say his will power, and I mean it, for I knew that dog—and he ate again, but, I am sure, without enjoyment.

He grew thinner. He walked in a different way. Instead of swaggering around insolently, he half crawled. His coat, formerly brushed lovingly every day, lost its silky shine. His pinkish little eyes were puzzled. When you met him he actually lowered his head so that you would not see his eyes and hurried by.

All his tricks, his fasting, his limping, were to no avail. Something was, and remained, changed in this house that he had ruled. What distinguishes the animal mind from the human is that the former is limited to past and present; it cannot imagine the future. And so Jupiter, with all his intelligence, could do no more than sense with agony and despair that something was growing and preparing itself in the house, something invisible, something that was against him—this enemy, this fiend, this thief!

Months later he reached the end—or if not exactly the end, something like it. If he had been a human, I think he would have committed suicide. He vanished. He was gone for three full days. Not until the evening of the third did he turn up once more—dirty, hungry, looking as though he had been in a fight. In his raging, impotent fury he must have attacked every strange dog he had come across. But he came back, as a man would come back after touching the bottom depths. Perhaps, perhaps by now—

But new humiliations awaited him. No one to greet him. No one to welcome him home. The maid would not even let him in the house!

Actually this was more than justified, for Mrs. Sturgis's time had come, and the house was full of busy people. Sturgis had an intense sentimental desire to have the baby born in their home, and since the local hospital was crowded then anyway, the doctor had consented. So the doctor was there, and a nurse, and Mrs. Sturgis's mother, and my wife and I.

And Roger Sturgis. Face flushed, trembling with excitement, getting in everyone's way, he waited.

Outside the front door, Jupiter waited too.

What were they doing in there? He heard voices, the splashing of water, the tinkling of glass and metal. What was happening was beyond his comprehension, but instinctively he felt that it was It—It, the thing that had caused his downfall, his humiliation. It, the invisible, the infamous, cowardly enemy. It was now going to appear, and as soon as that door was opened, It would not escape!

His powerful muscles were tensed. He crouched, waiting.

Of all this, we in the house of course had no idea. Betty and I were delegated by the doctor to keep Sturgis in the living room. Because of his enormous capacity for emotion, it was a harrowing job. But at last the good news came—a girl—and sometime later the bedroom door opened and the nurse appeared with the little bundle.

The doctor followed, smiling.

"Well, Mr. Sturgis!" he said. "Go ahead! Hold her in your arms for a minute and tell us how it feels to be a father!"

Trembling, the big man reached out his arms and the nurse put the baby in them and looked down at her with tears on his cheeks.

The doctor was putting on his gloves. "Everything's all right," he said. "Nothing to worry about, so I'll be getting along."

Bidding us good-by, he opened the front door.

In that split second something shot past between his legs. Jupiter was there in the room.

His eyes were on Sturgis; his little pinkish eyes were on the bundle in his master's arms, and he knew, I know he knew, that this was It. With a raging cry, he charged.

So sudden and fierce was the attack that the great strapping man staggered under the violence of it and fell against the wall. At the last moment he tried instinctively to save the child by raising it above his head. Betty was nearest him. She seized the bundle and thrust it at the nurse, who was in the bedroom door. She pushed the nurse into the bedroom and swung the door shut with all her might.

Now Sturgis had recovered his balance, and with a fury as savage as the dog's he threw himself on Jupiter. Chairs and tables crashed to the floor. The doctor and I at last came to our senses, and picking up anything we could lay our hands on, we battered the animal into unconsciousness. We bound him with rope and dragged him from the room to the lawn outside.

Sturgis was swaying like a drunken man. His coat had been ripped and we noticed now—what he was not even aware of, himself—that blood was dripping down his right arm. The doctor got him into the other bed-room, undressed him and attended to the gash Jupiter's teeth had left. Then, exhausted physically and emotionally, Sturgis fell asleep.

But what was to be done with Jupiter?

"Shoot him," I said, but the doctor objected. The dog must be put under observation; he might be hydrophobic, in which case Sturgis would require treatment. And so Jupiter, tightly bound, still only half conscious, was driven off in the doctor's car.

We heard later that the Pasteur test showed no signs of hydrophobia and that the dog seemed to be quiet and well-behaved. Sturgis, once his adoring master, of course never wished to see him again. The doctor happened to learn that a hardware man in town was looking for a watchdog; he was told about Jupiter and offered to take him.

So he vanished from our horizon. Before long, none of us, even Sturgis, ever thought of him.

For now, needless to say, Sturgis had a new idol, infinitely more precious, on which he lavished all his passion and tenderness. Every day, every hour, every minute, he discovered new delights in his beautiful little baby. He could hardly stand to tear himself away in the morning to go to his office, and half a dozen times each day he would call up to see how she was. Every night when he returned he brought some new toy—a rattle, a teething ring, a thousand and one gadgets. His adoration was complete.

As I have said, none of us thought of Jupiter, a bad dream forgotten— until one night I was forcibly reminded of his existence.

For some reason I could not get to sleep. At last I got up, put on my robe, went into the kitchen and warmed some milk and drank it. Passing through the living room on my way back to bed, I saw through the window how lovely the night was, and for a while I stood there looking out. Behind a veil of thin silvery clouds the moon sailed high, and each time the clouds fell from its face the whole garden shimmered as though beneath a blanket of driven snow. There was not a sound. I felt that if a leaf had dropped from a tree I would have heard it fall . . .

It gave me a start when in this great milky silence I noticed something moving along the hedge that separated our property from the Sturgises'.

It was Jupiter.

He crept forward slowly, his belly almost touching the ground. It was as if he had come to reconnoiter, to spy out the land, very cautiously, very stealthily, moving with none of that brash swaggering self-assurance that had been his. Instinctively I leaned out the window to see him better. My elbow brushed against a flowerpot on the sill and knocked it to the ground. With one noiseless bound the huge dog leaped into the darkness. There was the garden again, empty, shimmering.

I closed and barred the window.

Yet the next morning it seemed silly. He was only a dog, not a rational thing, a thinking being; not a wolf, a tiger, a beast of prey! So I did not mention what I had seen to the Sturgises. But when a few days later I was working in the garden and saw their maid hanging out the baby's clothes on the line, I went over and asked her if she had seen Jupiter lately.

She said she had not told Mrs. Sturgis, not wanting to upset her, but a week ago she had had a strange experience. She had taken the baby out in its carriage when a car had passed them on the road. The moment the car went by, she heard an angry barking. Looking up, she had caught a glimpse of a big white dog sitting beside the driver. It was a commercial car, a delivery truck—"Hardware," it said on the side.

Who else but Jupiter? What other explanation than that he had seen the carriage, the maid, the baby, recognized them and barked his hatred?

Now I did feel afraid. The dog had not forgotten. I had happened to see him one night. How many other nights had he returned and crept spying around the house?

"If you ever see him," I said to the maid, "you must tell Mr. Sturgis at once, or if he isn't home, tell me. The next time I'm in town I'll warn the hardware man that he must keep the dog leashed."

But I asked myself: Is it possible for a dog to remember so bitterly, so vividly? Human rivalry is one thing, but this was a dumb animal, with a new master, new surroundings, and he had been there for months now. Could a dog remember so long?

Perhaps not the ordinary domestic pet, good old Rover or Jack or Sport. But this was not an ordinary dog. This dog had been spoiled. He had been given a ridiculous amount of attention and worship, and suddenly it had all been taken away. This dog was intelligent, with a warped, bitter intelligence. I hated him, but the fact that I thought of him in that way—a way in which I would never expect to think of an animal—showed that I respected his intelligence, that I admitted it.

What should I have done? Told the police my fears? Asked to have the dog put out of the way? Perhaps so; perhaps I was to blame; but at times it did seem absurd, and I could fancy the police laughing at me—"What is this, a dog, or a master criminal?"—and the hardware man saying, "Why, he's a good dog, a fine watchdog; he's valuable; he was given to me and I don't want to give him up."

So I did nothing. I worried about it and thought this way and that way and in the end did nothing, and the days passed, and we came to that Sunday, the final unforgettable day.

We had gone over to the Sturgises' that beautiful Sunday afternoon. We were sitting talking on the lower terrace, from which the slope of the hill descends to the canal. Near by, on this level ground, stood the baby carriage, and, needless to say, Sturgis kept interrupting our conversation to call attention to the baby, to go over and wiggle his fingers at her and smile and talk.

By and by Mrs. Sturgis called to us from the house, a hundred feet or so above the lower terrace. "Come on," she said, "the tea's on the table. Hurry, or the toast will get cold." We went first; Sturgis lingered. We were in the house and sitting down by the time he came in. Mrs. Sturgis poured and we talked of the weather and the roses and so on until, as always, Sturgis returned to his favorite subject.

"The baby's asleep. You know, it's wonderful how well-behaved she is. Never wakes us at night, none of this crying or—"

"Is she in the sun?" Mrs. Sturgis asked.

"Just a little; it's good for her. I would have brought her up here but I thought the movement might wake her."

"You left her on the terrace?" I asked. I had assumed that he had wheeled the carriage up.

"Yes. Why? She's sleeping, you know, and I thought—"

I was uneasy. He sensed it. He half rose, looking at me. It was as if that tremendous all-devoted love of his for the child gave him the power to read the thought that was not even fully formed in my mind.

"Oh, Roger, sit down and finish your tea," Mrs. Sturgis said. "Really, you're worse than an old woman, the way you worry!"

She was smiling. He was not. I was looking at him and he at me, and although I tried to dismiss the thought from my mind, I couldn't. He did not sit down. Something, I do not know what, perhaps some slight sound, even from that far away, drew him to the door. And we heard his awful, anguished exclamation.

It was not loud but it was, I think, the most horrible noise I have ever heard, a choking convulsive sound, the last sound a man might make dying in agony.

"For God's sake, what is it?" I cried.

It was as if, from the horror of what he saw, Sturgis could not move. We shoved back our chairs, rushed to his side. That movement released him from the trance. He tore the door open and leaped across the veranda.

The baby carriage was no longer on the terrace.

Then I saw it. It was in the canal. It had rolled down the slope and into the water. It was still upright and floating, by some miracle, but as we looked— and this happened only in seconds, even as we still tried to comprehend what we saw—it slowly began to turn on its side, to sink.

And Jupiter stood on the bank.

He, Jupiter, the great white beast. He who, in the days when he ruled this house, had amused himself by dashing down to the canal and butting the baskets of laundry into it, pushing them down the slope with his powerful muscles. He stood and watched the carriage sinking, he the victor, he who had triumphed at last.

The carriage turned over. There was a flutter of white sheets, of arms and legs waving, and the child rolled out of the carriage into the water.

Then I saw the dog's great muscles go tense. I saw him throw himself into the canal. It was only a few feet out from the bank. His tremendous jaws opened, and the child lay in his grasp. The jaws were gentle. Jupiter thrust himself back and dragged the baby up on the bank. And now Sturgis reached it. He grabbed the child in his arms and hugged her. He saw that she breathed, that she was safe.

The dog stood looking at them, at the master who had worshipped him and the enemy who had destroyed that worship, the enemy in his master's loving arms, the enemy that he had restored to his one-time master's arms.

Sturgis knelt. I saw his face working. He knelt, hugging the baby, but he looked now not at her but at the dog. I saw him stretch a hand toward the dog. I heard what he said:

"Jupiter."

The hand was reached out to stroke the dog. The dog stood still.

"Come here—old Jupiter."

Jupiter turned and went away, and Roger Sturgis was left alone with his child.

I know now who was the victor.

DOGOLOGY

(2002)

T. Coraghessan Boyle

This is a zany tale about a woman interested in animal behavior who communes with a small army of dogs. Not surprisingly, she becomes the talk of the neighborhood. The story digresses into tales of children raised by wolves in India and then morphs into something of a love story. T. Coraghessan Boyle is one of the most creative, funny, and entertaining writers anywhere. He frequently contributes to *The New Yorker* (where this story is from), *Playboy*, *Esquire*, and *Harper's*. He is the author of eleven novels and eight collections of stories, including *Water Music* (1980), *Without a Hero and Other Stories* (1992), *Riven Rock* (1998), *Tooth and Claw* (2005), and *Talk Talk* (2006). Boyle is the founder and director of the creative writing program in the English Department at the University of Southern California.

Rumors

It was the season of mud, drainpipes drooling, the gutters clogged with debris, a battered and penitential robin fixed like a statue on every lawn. Julian was up early, a Saturday morning, beating eggs with a whisk and gazing idly out the kitchen window and into the colorless hide of the day, expecting nothing, when all at once the scrim of rain parted to reveal a dark, crouching presence in the far corner of the yard. At first glance, he took it to be a dog—a town ordinance that he particularly detested disallowed fences higher than three feet, and so the contiguous lawns and flower beds of the neighborhood had become a sort of open savanna for roaming packs of dogs—but before the wind shifted and the needling rain closed in again he saw that he was wrong. This figure, partially obscured by the resurgent forsythia bush, seemed out of proportion, all limbs, as if a dog had been mated with a monkey. What was it, then? Raccoons had been at the trash lately, and he'd seen an opossum wavering down the street like a pale ghost one night after a dreary, overwrought movie Cara had insisted upon, but this was no opossum. Or raccoon, either. It was dark in color, whatever it was—a bear, maybe, a yearling strayed down from the high ridges along the river, and hadn't Ben Ober told him somebody on F Street had found a bear in their swimming pool? He put down the whisk and went to fetch his glasses.

A sudden eruption of thunder set the dishes rattling on the drainboard, followed by an uncertain flicker of light that illuminated the dark room as if the bulb in the overhead fixture had gone loose in the socket. He wondered how Cara could sleep through all this, but the wonder was short-lived, because he really didn't give a damn one way or the other if she slept all day, all night, all week. Better she should sleep and give him some peace. He was in the living room now, the gloom ladled over everything, shadows leeching into black holes behind the leather couch and matching armchairs, and the rubber plant a dark ladder in the corner. The thunder rolled again, the lightning flashed. His glasses were atop the TV, where he'd left them the night before while watching a sorry documentary about the children purportedly raised by wolves in India back in the nineteen-twenties, two stringy girls in sepia photographs that revealed little and could have been faked, in any case. He put his glasses on and padded back into the kitchen in his stocking feet already having forgotten why he'd gone to get the glasses in the first place. Then he saw the whisk in a puddle of beaten egg on the counter, remembered, and peered out the window again.

The sight of the three dogs there—a pair of clownish chows and what looked to be a shepherd mix—did nothing but irritate him. He recognized this trio; they were the advance guard of the army of dogs that dropped their excrement all over the lawn, dug up his flower beds, and, when he tried to shoo them, looked right through him as if he didn't exist. It wasn't that he had anything against dogs, per se—it was their destructiveness he objected to, their arrogance, as if they owned the whole world and it was their privilege to do as they liked with it. He was about to step to the back door and chase them off, when the figure he'd first seen—the shadow beneath the forsythia bush—emerged. It was no animal, he realized with a shock, but a woman, a young woman dressed all in black, with her black hair hanging wet in her face and the clothes stuck to her like a second skin, down on all fours like a dog herself, sniffing. He was dumbfounded. As stunned and amazed as if someone had just stepped into the kitchen and slapped him till his head rolled back on his shoulders.

He'd been aware of the rumors—there was a new couple in the neighborhood, over on F Street, and the woman was a little strange, dashing through people's yards at any hour of the day or night, baying at the moon, and showing her teeth to anyone who got in her way—but he'd dismissed them as some sort of suburban legend. Now here she was, in his yard, violating his privacy, in the company of a pack of dogs he'd like to see shot—and their owners, too. He didn't know what to do. He was frozen in his own kitchen, the omelette pan sending up a metallic stink of incineration. And then the three dogs lifted their heads as if they'd heard something in the distance, the thunder boomed overhead, and suddenly they leaped the fence in tandem and were gone. The woman rose up out of the mud at this point—she was wearing a sodden turtle-neck, jeans, a watch cap—locked eyes with him across the expanse of the rain-screened yard for just an instant, or maybe he was imagining this part of it, and then she turned and took the fence in a single bound, vanishing into the rain.

Cynomorph

Whatever it was they'd heard, it wasn't available to her, though she'd been trying to train her hearing away from the ceaseless clatter of the mechanical and tune it to the finer things, the wind stirring in the grass, the alarm call of a fallen nestling, the faintest sliver of a whimper from the dog three houses over, begging to be let out. And her nose. She'd made a point of sticking it in anything the dogs did, breathing deeply, rebooting the olfactory receptors of a brain that had been deadened by perfume and underarm deodorant and all the other stifling odors of civilization. Every smell was a discovery, and every dog discovered more of the world in ten minutes running loose than a human being would discover in ten years of sitting behind the wheel of a car or standing at the lunch counter in a deli or even hiking the Alps. What she was doing, or attempting to do, was nothing short of reordering her senses so that she could think like a dog and interpret the whole world—not just the human world—as dogs did.

Why? Because no one had ever done it before. Whole hordes wanted to be primatologists or climb into speedboats and study whales and dolphins or cruise the veldt in a Land Rover to watch the lions suckle their young beneath the baobabs, but none of them gave a second thought to dogs. Dogs were beneath them. Dogs were common, pedestrian, no more exotic than the housefly or the Norway rat. Well, she was going to change all that. Or at least that was what she'd told herself after the graduate committee rejected her thesis, but that was a long time ago now, two years and more—and the door was rapidly closing.

But here she was, moving again, and movement was good, it was her essence: up over the fence and into the next yard, dodging a clothesline, a cooking grill, a plastic trike, a sandbox, reminding herself always to keep her head down and go quadrupedal whenever possible, because how else was she going to hear, smell, and see as the dogs did? Another fence, and there, at the far end of the yard, a shed, and the dense rust-colored tails of the chows wagging. The rain spat in her face, relentless. It had been coming down steadily most of the night, and now it seemed even heavier, as if it meant to drive her back indoors where she belonged. She was shivering—had been shivering for the past hour, shivering so hard she thought her teeth were coming loose—and as she ran, doubled over in a crouch, she pumped her knees and flapped her arms in an attempt to generate some heat.

What were the dogs onto now? She saw the one she called Barely disappear behind the shed and snake back out again, her tail rigid, sniffing now, barking, and suddenly they were all barking—the two chows and the semi-shepherd she'd named Factitious because he was such a sham, pretending he was a rover when he never strayed more than five blocks from his house on E Street. There was a smell of freshly turned earth, of compost and wood ash, of the half-drowned worms that Snout the Afghan loved to gobble up off the pavement. She glanced toward the locked gray vault of the house, concerned that the noise would alert whoever lived there, but it was early yet, no lights on, no sign of activity. The dogs' bodies moiled. The barking went up a notch. She ran, hunched at the waist, hurrying.

And then, out of the corner of her eye, she'd caught a glimpse of A1, the big-shouldered husky who'd earned his name by consuming half a bottle of steak sauce beside an overturned trash can one bright January morning. He was running—but where had he come from? She hadn't seen him all night and assumed he'd been wandering out at the limits of his range, over in Bethel or Georgetown. She watched him streak across the yard, ears pinned back, head low, his path converging with hers until he disappeared behind the shed. Angling round the back of the thing—it was aluminum, one of those prefab articles they sell in the big warehouse stores—she found the compost pile her nose had alerted her to (good, good: she was improving) and a tower of old wicker chairs stacked up six feet high. A1 never hesitated. He surged in at the base of the tower, his jaws snapping, and the second chow, the one she called Decidedly, was right behind him—and then she saw: there was something there, a face with incendiary eyes, and it was growling for its life in a thin continuous whine that might have been the drone of a model airplane buzzing overhead.

What was it? She crouched low, came in close. A straggler appeared suddenly, a fluid sifting from the blind side of the back fence to the yard—it was Snout, gangly, goofy; the fastest dog in the neighborhood and the widest ranger, A1's wife and the mother of his dispersed pups. And then all five dogs went in for the kill.

The thunder rolled again, concentrating the moment, and she got her first clear look: cream-colored fur, naked pink toes, a flash of teeth and burdened gums. It was an opossum, unlucky, doomed, caught out while creeping back to its nest on soft marsupial feet after a night of foraging among the trash cans. There was a roil of dogs, no barking now, just the persistent unravelling growls that were like curses, and the first splintering crunch of bone. The tower of wicker came down with a clatter, chairs upended and scattered, and the dogs hardly noticed. She glanced around her in alarm, but there was nobody to be seen, nothing moving but the million silver drill bits of the rain boring into the ground. Just as the next flash of lightning lit the sky, A1 backed out from under the tumble of chairs with the carcass clenched in his jaws, furiously shaking it to snap a neck that was already two or three times broken, and she was startled to see how big the thing was—

272

twenty pounds of meat, gristle, bone, and hair, twenty pounds at least. He shook it again, then dropped it at his wife's feet as an offering. It lay still, the other dogs extending their snouts to sniff at it dispassionately, scientists themselves, studying and measuring, remembering. And, when the hairless pink young emerged from the pouch, she tried not to feel anything as the dogs snapped them up one by one.

Cara

"You mean you didn't confront her?" Cara was in her royal-purple robe—her "wrapper," as she insisted on calling it, as if they were at a country manor in the Cotswolds entertaining Lord and Lady Muckbright instead of in a tract house in suburban Connecticut—and she'd paused with a forkful of mushroom omelette halfway to her mouth. She was on her third cup of coffee and wearing her combative look.

"Confront her? I barely had time to recognize she was human." He was at the sink, scrubbing the omelette pan, and he paused to look bitterly out into the gray vacancy of the yard. "What did you expect me to do, chase her down? Make a citizen's arrest? What?"

The sound of Cara buttering her toast—she might have been flaying the flesh from a bone—set his teeth on edge. "I don't know," she said, "but we can't just have strangers lurking around anytime they feel like it, can we? I mean, there are *laws*—"

"The way you talk you'd think I invited her. You think I like mental cases peeping in the window so I can't even have a moment's peace in my own house?"

"So do something."

"What? You tell me."

"Call the police, why don't you? That should be obvious, shouldn't it? And that's another thing—"

That was when the telephone rang. It was Ben Ober, his voice scraping through the wires like a set of hard chitinous claws scrabbling against the side of the house. "Julian?" he shouted. "Julian?"

Julian reassured him. "Yeah," he said, "it's me. I'm here."

"Can you hear me?"

"I can hear you."

"Listen, she's out in my yard right now, out behind the shed with a, I don't know, some kind of wolf, it looks like, and that Afghan nobody seems to know who's the owner of—"

"Who?" he said, but even as he said it he knew. "Who're you talking about?"

"The dog woman." There was a pause, and Julian could hear him breathing into the mouthpiece as if he were deep underwater. "She seems to be—I think she's killing something out there."

The Wolf Children of Mayurbhanj

It was high summer, just before the rains set in, and the bush had shrivelled back under the sun till you could see up the skirts of the sal trees, and all that had been hidden was revealed. People began to talk of a disturbing presence in the jungle outside the tiny village of Godamuri in Mayurbhanj district, of a *bhut*, or spirit, sent to punish them for their refusal to honor the authority of the maharaja. This thing had twice been seen in the company of a wolf, a vague pale slash of movement in the incrassating twilight, but it was no wolf itself, of that the eyewitnesses were certain. Then came the rumor that there were two of them, quick, nasty, bloodless things of the night, and that their eyes flamed with an infernal heat that incinerated anyone who looked into them, and panic gripped the countryside. Mothers kept their children close, fires burned in the night. Then, finally, came the news that these things were concrete and actual and no mere figments of the imagination: their den had been found in an abandoned termitarium in the dense jungle seven miles southeast of the village.

The rumors reached the Reverend J. A. L. Singh, of the Anglican mission and orphanage at Midnapore, and in September, after the monsoon clouds had peeled back from the skies and the rivers had receded, he made the long journey to Godamuri by bullock cart. One of his converts, a Kora tribesman by the name of Chunarem, who was prominent in the area, led him to the site. There, the Reverend, an astute and observant man and an amateur hunter acquainted with the habits of beasts, saw evidence of canine occupation of the termite mound—droppings, bones, tunnels of ingress and egress—and instructed that a machan be built in an overspreading tree. Armed with his dependable 20-bore Westley Richards rifle, the Reverend sat breathlessly in the machan and concentrated his field glasses on the main entrance to the den. The Reverend Singh was not one to believe in ghosts, other than the Holy Spirit, perhaps, and he expected nothing more remarkable than an albino wolf or perhaps a sloth bear gone white with age or dietary deficiency.

Dusk filtered up from the forest floor. Shadows pooled in the under-growth, and then an early moon rose up pregnant from the horizon to soften them. Langurs whooped in the near distance, cicadas buzzed, a hundred species of beetles, moths, and biting insects flapped round the Reverend's ears, but he held rigid and silent, his binoculars fixed on the entrance to the mound. And then suddenly a shape emerged, the triangular head of a wolf, then a smaller canine head, and then something else altogether, with a neatly rounded cranium and foreshortened face. The wolf—the dam—stretched herself and slunk off into the undergrowth, followed by a pair of wolf cubs and two other creatures, which were too long-legged and rangy to be canids; that was clear at a glance. Monkeys, the Reverend thought at first, or apes of some sort. But then, even though they were moving swiftly on all fours, the Reverend could see, to his amazement, that these weren't monkeys at all, or wolves or ghosts, either.

Denning

She no longer bothered with a notepad or the pocket tape recorder she'd once used to document the telling yip or strident howl. These were the accoutrements of civilization, and civilization got in the way of the kind of freedom she required if she was ever going to break loose of the constraints that had shackled field biologists from the beginning. Even her clothes seemed to get in the way, but she was sensible enough of the laws of the community to understand that they were necessary, at least for now. Still, she made a point of wearing the same things continuously for weeks on end—sans underwear or socks—in the expectation that her scent would invest them, and the scent of the pack, too. How could she hope to gain their confidence if she smelled like the prize inside a box of detergent?

One afternoon toward the end of March, as she lay stretched out beneath a weak pale disk of a sun, trying to ignore the cold breeze and concentrate on the doings of the pack—they were excavating a den in the vacant quadrangle of former dairy pasture that was soon to become the J and K blocks of the ever-expanding development—she heard a car slow on the street a hundred yards distant and lifted her head lazily, as the dogs did, to investigate. It had been a quiet morning and a quieter afternoon, with A1 and Snout, as the alpha couple, looking on placidly as Decidedly, Barely, and Factitious alternated the digging and a bulldog from B Street she hadn't yet named lay drooling in the dark wet earth that flew from the lip of the burrow. Snout had been chasing cars off and on all morning—to the dogs, automobiles were animate and ungovernable, big unruly ungulates that needed to be curtailed—and she guessed that the fortyish man climbing out of the sedan and working his tentative way across the lot had come to complain, because that was all her neighbors ever did: complain.

And that was a shame. She really didn't feel like getting into all that right now—explaining herself, defending the dogs, justifying, forever justifying—because for once she'd got into the rhythm of dogdom, found her way to that sacred place where to lie flat in the sun and breathe in the scents of fresh earth, dung, sprouting grass was enough of an accomplishment for a day. Children were in school, adults at work. Peace reigned over the neighborhood. For the dogs—and for her, too—this was bliss. Hominids had to keep busy, make a buck, put two sticks together, order and structure and *complain*, but canids could know contentment, and so could she, if she could only penetrate deep enough.

Two shoes had arrived now. Loafers, buffed to brilliance and decorated with matching tassels of stripped hide. They'd come to rest on a trampled mound of fresh earth no more than twenty-four inches from her nose. She tried to ignore them, but there was a bright smear of mud or excrement gleaming on the toe of the left one; it *was* excrement, dog—the merest sniff told her that, and she was intrigued despite herself, though she refused to lift her eyes. And then a man's voice was speaking from somewhere high above the shoes, so high up and resonant with authority it might have been the voice of the alpha dog of all alpha dogs—God himself.

The tone of the voice, but not the sense of it, appealed to the dogs, and the bulldog, who was present and accounted for because Snout was in heat, hence the den, ambled over to gaze up at the trousered legs in lovesick awe. "You know," the voice was saying, "you've really got the neighborhood in an uproar, and I'm sure you have your reasons, and I know these dogs aren't yours—" The voice faltered. "But Ben Ober—you know Ben Ober? Over on C Street? Well, he's claiming you're killing rabbits or something. Or you were. Last Saturday. Out on his lawn?" Another pause. "Remember, it was raining?"

A month back, two weeks ago, even, she would have felt obliged to explain herself, would have soothed and mollified and dredged up a battery of behavioral terms—proximate causation, copulation solicitation, naturalistic fallacy—to cow him, but today, under the pale sun, in the company of the pack, she just couldn't seem to muster the energy. She might have grunted—or maybe that was only the sound of her stomach rumbling. She couldn't remember when she'd eaten last.

The cuffs of the man's trousers were stiffly pressed into jutting cotton prows, perfectly aligned. The bulldog began to lick at first one, then the other. There was the faintest creak of tendon and patella, and two knees presented themselves, and then a fist, pressed to the earth for balance. She saw a crisp white strip of shirt cuff, the gold flash of watch and wedding band.

"Listen," he said, "I don't mean to stick my nose in where it's not wanted, and I'm sure you have your reasons for, for" —the knuckles retrenched to balance the movement of his upper body, a swing of the arm, perhaps, or a jerk of the head—"all this. I'd just say live and let live, but I can't. And you know why not?"

She didn't answer, though she was on the verge—there was something about his voice that was magnetic, as if it could adhere to her and pull her to her feet again—but the bulldog distracted her. He'd gone up on his hind legs with a look of unfocussed joy and begun humping the man's leg, and her flash of epiphany deafened her to what he was saying. The bulldog had revealed his name to her: from now on she would know him as Humper.

"Because you upset my wife. You were out in our yard and I, she—Oh, Christ," he said, "I'm going about this all wrong. Look, let me introduce myself—I'm Julian Fox. We live on B Street, 2236? We never got to meet your husband and you when you moved in. I mean, the development's got so big—and impersonal, I guess—we never had the chance. But if you ever want to stop by, maybe for tea, a drink—the two of you, I mean—that would be, well, that would be great."

A Drink on B Street

She was upright and smiling, though her posture was terrible and she carried her own smell with her into the sterile sanctum of the house. He caught it immediately, unmistakably, and so did Cara, judging from the look on her face as she took the girl's hand. It was as if a breeze had wafted up from the bog they were draining over on G Street to make way for the tennis courts; the door stood open, and here was a raw infusion of the wild. Or the kennel. That was Cara's take on it, delivered in a stage whisper on the far side of the swinging doors to the kitchen as she fussed with the hors d'oeuvres and he poured vodka for the husband and tap water for the girl: *She smells like she's been sleeping in a kennel.* When he handed her the glass, he saw that there was dirt under her nails. Her hair shone with grease and there were bits of fluff or lint or something flecking the coils of it where it lay massed on her shoulders. Cara tried to draw her into small talk, but she wouldn't draw—she just kept nodding and smiling till the smile had nothing of greeting or joy left in it.

Cara had got their number from Bea Chiavone, who knew more about the business of her neighbors than a confessor, and one night last week she'd got through to the husband, who said his wife was out—which came as no surprise—but Cara had kept him on the line for a good ten minutes, digging for all she was worth, until he finally accepted the invitation to their "little cocktail party." Julian was doubtful, but before he'd had a chance to comb his hair or get his jacket on, the bell was ringing and there they were, the two of them, arm in arm on the doormat, half an hour early.

The husband, Don, was acceptable enough. Early thirties, bit of a paunch, his hair gone in a tonsure. He was a computer engineer. Worked for I.B.M. "Really?" Julian said. "Well, you must know Charlie Hsiu, then—he's at the Yorktown office?"

Don gave him a blank look.

"He lives just up the street. I mean, I could give him a call, if, if—" He never finished the thought. Cara had gone to the door to greet Ben and Julie Ober, and the girl, left alone, had migrated to the corner by the rubber plant, where she seemed to be bent over now, sniffing at the potting soil. He tried not to stare—tried to hold the husband's eye and absorb what he was saying about interoffice politics and his own role on the research end of things ("I guess I'm what you'd call the ultimate computer geek, never really get away from the monitor long enough to put a name to a face")—but he couldn't help stealing a glance under cover of the Obers' entrance. Ben was glad-handing, his voice booming, Cara was cooing something to Julie, and the girl (the husband had introduced her as Cynthia, but she'd murmured, "Call me C.f., capital 'C,' lowercase 'f'") had gone down on her knees beside the plant. He saw her wet a finger, dip it into the soil, and bring it to her mouth.

While the La Portes—Cara's friends, dull as woodchips—came smirking through the door, expecting a freak show, Julian tipped back his glass and crossed the room to the girl. She was intent on the plant, rotating the terra-cotta pot to examine the saucer beneath it, on all fours now, her face close to the carpet. He cleared his throat, but she didn't respond. He watched the back of her head a moment, struck by the way her hair curtained her face and spilled down the rigid struts of her arms. She was dressed all in black, in a ribbed turtleneck, grass-stained jeans, and a pair of canvas sneakers that were worn through at the heels. She wasn't wearing socks, or, as far as he could see, a brassiere, either. But she'd clean up nicely, that was what he was thinking—she had a shape to her, anybody could see that, and eyes that could burn holes right through you. "So," he heard himself say, even as Ben's voice rose to a crescendo at the other end of the room, "you, uh, like houseplants?"

She made no effort to hide what she was doing, whatever it may have been—studying the weave of the carpet, looking at the alignment of the baseboard, inspecting for termites, who could say? —but instead turned to gaze up at him for the first time. "I hope you don't mind my asking," she said in her hush of a voice, "but did you ever have a dog here?"

He stood looking down at her, gripping his drink, feeling awkward and foolish in his own house. He was thinking of Seymour (or "See More," because as a pup he was always running off after things in the distance), picturing him now for the first time in how many years? Something passed through him then, a pang of regret carried in his blood, in his neurons: Seymour. He'd almost succeeded in forgetting him. "Yes," he said. "How did you know?"

She smiled. She was leaning back against the wall now, cradling her knees in the net of her interwoven fingers. "I've been training myself. My senses,

I mean." She paused, still smiling up at him. "Did you know that when the Ninemile wolves came down into Montana from Alberta they were following scent trails laid down years before? Think about it. All that weather, the seasons, trees falling and decaying. Can you imagine that?"

"Cara's allergic," he said. "I mean, that's why we had to get rid of him. Seymour. His name was Seymour."

There was a long braying burst of laughter from Ben Ober, who had an arm round Don's shoulder and was painting something in the air with a stiffened forefinger. Cara stood just beyond him, with the La Portes, her face glowing as if it had been basted. Celia La Porte looked from him to the girl and back again, then arched her eyebrows wittily and raised her long-stemmed glass of Viognier, as if toasting him. All three of them burst into laughter. Julian turned his back.

"You didn't take him to the pound—did you?" The girl's eyes went flat. "Because that's a death sentence, I hope you realize that."

"Cara found a home for him."

They both looked to Cara then, her shining face, her anchorwoman's hair. "I'm sure," the girl said.

"No, really. She did."

The girl shrugged, looked away from him. "It doesn't matter," she said with a flare of anger. "Dogs are just slaves, anyway."

Kamala and Amala

The Reverend Singh had wanted to return to the site the following afternoon and excavate the den, convinced that these furtive night creatures were in fact human children, children abducted from their cradles and living under the dominion of beasts—unbaptized and unsaved, their eternal souls at risk— but urgent business called him away to the south. When he returned, late in the evening, ten days later, he sat over a dinner of cooked vegetables, rice and dal, and listened as Chunarem told him of the wolf bitch that had haunted the village two years back, after her pups had been removed from a den in the forest and sold for a few annas apiece at the Khuar market. She could be seen as dusk fell, her dugs swollen and glistening with extruded milk, her eyes shining with an unearthly blue light against the backdrop of the forest. People threw stones, but she never flinched. And she howled all night from the fringes of the village, howled so that it seemed she was inside the walls of every hut simultaneously, crooning her sorrow into the ears of each sleeping villager. The village dogs kept hard by, and those that didn't were found in the morning, their throats torn out. "It was she," the Reverend exclaimed, setting down his plate as the candles guttered and moths beat at the netting. "She was the abductress—it's as plain as morning."

A few days later, he got up a party that included several railway men and returned to the termite mound, bent on rescue. In place of the rifle, he carried a stout cudgel cut from a mahua branch. He brought along a weighted net as well. The sun hung overhead. All was still. And then the hired beaters started in, the noise of them racketing through the trees, coming closer and closer until they converged on the site, driving hares and bandicoot rats and the occasional gaur before them. The railway men tensed in the machan, their rifles trained on the entrance to the burrow, while Reverend Singh stood by with a party of diggers to effect the rescue when the time came. It was unlikely that the wolves would have been abroad in daylight, and so it was no surprise to the Reverend that no large animal was seen to run before the beaters and seek the shelter of the den. "Very well," he said, giving the signal, "I am satisfied. Commence the digging."

As soon as the blades of the first shovels struck the mound, a protracted snarling could be heard emanating from the depths of the burrow. After a few minutes of the tribesmen's digging, the she-wolf sprang out at them, ears flattened to her head, teeth flashing. One of the diggers went for her with his spear just as the railway men opened fire from the machan and turned her, snapping, on her own wounds; a moment later, she lay stretched out dead in the dust of the laterite clay. In a trice the burrow was uncovered, and there they were, the spirits made flesh, huddled in a defensive posture with the two wolf cubs, snarling and panicked, scrabbling at the clay with their broken nails to dig themselves deeper. The tribesmen dropped their shovels and ran, panicked themselves, even as the Reverend Singh eased himself down into the hole and tried to separate child from wolf.

The larger of the children, her hair a feral cap that masked her features, came at him biting and scratching, and finally he had no recourse but to throw his net over the pullulating bodies and restrain each of the creatures separately in one of the long, winding *gelaps* the local tribesmen use for winter wear. On inspection, it was determined that the children were females, aged approximately three and six, of native stock, and apparently, judging from the dissimilarity of their features, unrelated. The she-wolf, it seemed, had abducted the children on separate occasions, perhaps even from separate locales, and over the course of some time. Was this the bereaved bitch that Chunarem had reported? the Reverend wondered. Was she acting out of a desire for revenge? Or merely trying, in her own unknowable way, to replace what had been taken from her and ease the burden of her heart?

In any case, he had the children confined to a pen so that he could observe them, before caging them in the back of the bullock cart for the trip to Midnapore and the orphanage, where he planned to baptize and civilize them. He spent three full days studying them and taking notes. He saw that they persisted in going on all fours, as if they didn't know any other way, and that they fled from sunlight as if it were an instrument of torture. They thrust forward to lap water like the beasts of the forest and took nothing in their mouths but bits of twig and stone. At night they came to life and stalked the enclosure with shining eyes like the *bhuts* that half the villagers still believed them to be. They did not know any of the languages of the human species, but communicated with each other—and with their sibling wolves—in a series of grunts, snarls, and whimpers. When the moon rose, they sat on their haunches and howled.

It was Mrs. Singh who named them, some weeks later. They were pitiful, filthy, soiled with their own urine and excrement, undernourished, and under-sized. They had to be caged to keep them from harming the other children, and Mrs. Singh, though it broke her heart to do it, ordered them put in restraints, so that the filth and the animal smell could be washed from them, even as their heads were shaved to defeat the ticks and fleas they'd inherited from the only mother they'd ever known. "They need delicate names," Mrs. Singh told her husband, "names to reflect the beauty and propriety they will grow into." She named the younger sister Amala, after a bright-yellow flower native to Bengal, and the elder Kamala, after the lotus that blossoms deep in the jungle pools.

Running with the Pack

The sun stroked her like a hand, penetrated and massaged the dark yellowing contusion that had sprouted on the left side of her rib cage. Her bones felt as if they were about to crack open and deliver their marrow and her heart was still pounding, but at least she was here, among the dogs, at rest. It was June, the season of pollen, the air super-charged with the scents of flower-ing, seeding, fruiting, and there were rabbits and squirrels everywhere. She lay prone at the lip of the den and watched the pups—long-muzzled like their mother and brindled Afghan peach and husky silver—as they wor-ried a flap of skin and fur that Snout had peeled off the hot black glistening surface of the road and dropped at their feet. She was trying to focus on the dogs—on A1, curled up nose to tail in the trampled weed after regurgitating a mash of kibble for the pups, on Decidedly, his eyes half closed as currents of air brought him messages from afar, on Humper and Factitious—but she couldn't let go of the pain in her ribs and what the pain foreshadowed from the human side of things.

Don had kicked her. Don had climbed out of the car, crossed the field, and stood over her in his suede computer-engineer's ankle boots with the waffle bottoms and reinforced toes and lectured her while the dogs slunk low and rumbled deep in their throats. And, as his voice had grown louder, so, too, had the dogs' voices, until they were a chorus commenting on the ebb and flow of the action. When was she going to get her ass up out of the dirt and act like a normal human being? That was what he wanted to know. When was she going to cook a meal, run the vacuum, do the wash— his underwear, for Christ's sake? He was wearing dirty underwear, did she know that?

She had been lying stretched out flat on the mound, just as she was now. She glanced up at him as the dogs did, taking in a piece of him at a time, no direct stares, no challenges. "All I want," she said, over the chorus of growls and low, warning barks, "is to be left alone."

"Left alone?" His voice tightened in a little yelp. "Left alone? You need help, that's what you need. You need a shrink, you know that?"

She didn't reply. She let the pack speak for her. The rumble of their response, the flattened ears and stiffened tails, the sharp, savage gleam of their eyes should have been enough, but Don wasn't attuned. The sun seeped into her. A grasshopper she'd been idly watching as it bent a dandelion under its weight suddenly took flight, right past her face, and it seemed the most natural thing in the world to snap at it and break it between her teeth.

Don let out some sort of exclamation—"My God, what are you doing? Get up out of that, get up out of that now!" —and it didn't help matters. The dogs closed in. They were fierce now, barking in savage recusancy, their emotions twisted in a single cord. But this was Don, she kept telling herself, Don from grad school, bright and buoyant Don, her mate, her husband, and what harm was there in that? He wanted her back home, back in the den, and that was his right. The only thing was, she wasn't going.

"This isn't research. This is bullshit. Look at you!"

"No," she said, giving him a lazy, sidelong look, though her heart was racing, "it's dog shit. It's on your shoes, Don. It's in your face. In your precious computer—"

That was when he'd kicked her. Twice, three times, maybe, Kicked her in the ribs as if he were driving a ball over an imaginary set of uprights in the distance, kicked and kicked again—before the dogs went for him. A1 came in first, tearing at a spot just above his right knee, and then Humper, the bulldog who, she now knew, belonged to the feathery old lady up the block, got hold of his pant leg while Barely went for the crotch. Don screamed and thrashed, all right—he was a big animal, two hundred and ten pounds, heavier by far than any of the dogs—and he threatened in his big animal voice and fought back with all the violence of his big animal limbs, but he backed off quickly enough, threatening still, as he made his way across the field and into the car. She heard the door slam, heard the motor scream, and then there was the last thing she heard: Snout barking at the wheels as they revolved and took Don down the street and out of her life.

Survival of the Fittest

"You know he's locked her out, don't you?"

"Who?" Though he knew perfectly well.

"Don. I'm talking about Don and the dog lady?"

There was the table, made of walnut varnished a century before, the crystal vase full of flowers, the speckless china, the meat, the vegetables, the pasta. Softly, so softly he could barely hear it, there was Bach, too, piano pieces—partitas—and the smell of the fresh-cut flowers.

"Nobody knows where she's staying, unless it's out in the trash or the weeds or wherever. She's like a bag lady or something. Bea said Jerrilyn Hunter said she saw her going through the trash one morning. Do you hear me? Are you even listening?"

"I don't know. Yeah. Yeah, I am." He'd been reading lately. About dogs. Half a shelf of books from the library in their plastic covers—behavior, breeds, courting, mating, whelping. He excised a piece of steak and lifted it to his lips. "Did you hear the Leibowitzes' Afghan had puppies?"

"*Puppies*?" What in God's name are you talking about?" Her face was like a burr under the waistband, an irritant, something that needed to be removed and crushed.

"Only the alpha couple gets to breed. You know that, right? And so that would be the husky and the Leibowitzes' Afghan, and I don't know who the husky belongs to—but they're cute, real cute."

"You haven't been—? Don't tell me. Julian, use your sense: she's out of her mind. You want to know what else Bea said?"

"The alpha bitch," he said, and he didn't know why he was telling her this, "she'll actually hunt down and kill the pups of any other female in the pack who might have got pregnant, a survival-of-the-fittest kind of thing—"

"She's crazy, bonkers, out of her *fucking* mind, Julian. They're going to have her committed, you know that? If this keeps up. And it will keep up, won't it, Julian? Won't it?"

The Common Room at Midnapore

At first they would take nothing but raw milk. The wolf pups, from which they'd been separated for reasons both of sanitation and acculturation, eagerly fed on milk-and-rice pap in their kennel in one of the outbuildings, but neither of the girls would touch the pan-warmed milk or rice or the stewed vegetables that Mrs. Singh provided, even at night, when they were most active and their eyes spoke a language of desire all their own. Each morning and each evening before retiring, she would place a bowl on the floor in front of them, trying to tempt them with biscuits, confections, even a bit of boiled meat, though the Singhs were vegetarians themselves and repudiated the slaughter of animals for any purpose. The girls drew back into the recesses of the pen the Reverend had constructed in the orphanage's common room, showing their teeth. Days passed. They grew weaker. He tried to force-feed them balls of rice, but they scratched and tore at him with their nails and their teeth, setting up such a furious caterwauling of hisses, barks, and snarls as to give rise to rumors among the servants that he was torturing them. Finally, in resignation, and though it was a risk to the security of the entire orphanage, he left the door to the pen open in the hope that the girls, on seeing the other small children at play and at dinner, would soften.

In the meantime, though the girls grew increasingly lethargic—or perhaps because of this—the Reverend was able to make a close and telling examination of their physiology and habits. Their means of locomotion had transformed their bodies in a peculiar way. For one thing, they had developed thick pads of callus at their elbows and knees, and toes of abnormal strength and inflexibility—indeed, when their feet were placed flat on the ground, all five toes stood up at a sharp angle. Their waists were narrow and extraordinarily supple, like a dog's, and their necks dense with the muscle that had accrued there as a result of leading with their heads. And they were fast, preternaturally fast, and stronger by far than any other children of their respective ages that the Reverend and his wife had ever seen. In his diary, for the sake of posterity, the Reverend noted it all down.

Still, all the notes in the world wouldn't matter a whit if the wolf children didn't end their hunger strike, if that was what this was, and the Reverend and his wife had begun to lose hope for them, when the larger one—the one who would become known as Kamala—finally asserted herself. It was early in the evening, the day after the Reverend had ordered the door to the pen left open, and the children were eating their evening meal while Mrs. Singh and one of the servants looked on and the Reverend settled in with his pipe on the veranda. The weather was typical for Bengal in that season, the evening heavy and close, every living thing locked in the grip of the heat, and all the mission's doors and windows standing open to receive even the faintest breath of a breeze. Suddenly, without warning, Kamala bolted out of the pen, through the door, and across the courtyard to where the orphanage dogs were being fed scraps of uncooked meat, gristle, and bone left over from the preparation of the servants' meal, and before anyone could stop her she was down among them, slashing with her teeth, fighting off even the biggest and most aggressive of them until she'd bolted the red meat and carried off the long, hoofed shinbone of a gaur to gnaw in the farthest corner of her pen.

And so the Singhs, though it revolted them, fed the girls on raw meat until the crisis had passed, and then they gave them broth, which the girls lapped from their bowls, and finally meat that had been at least partially cooked. As for clothing—clothing for decency's sake—the girls rejected it as unnatural and confining, tearing any garment from their backs and limbs with their teeth, until Mrs. Singh hit on the idea of fashioning each of them a single tight-fitting strip of cloth they wore knotted round the waist and drawn up over their privates, a kind of diaper or loincloth they were forever soiling with their waste. It wasn't an ideal solution, but the Singhs were patient—the girls had suffered a kind of deprivation no other humans had ever suffered—and they understood that the ascent to civilization and light would be steep and long.

When Amala died, shortly after the wolf pups had succumbed to what the Reverend presumed was distemper communicated through the orphanage dogs, her sister wouldn't let anyone approach the body. Looking back on it, the Reverend would see this as Kamala's most human moment—she was grieving, grieving because she had a soul, because she'd been baptized before the Lord and was no wolfling or jungle *bhut* but a human child after all, and here was the proof of it. But poor Amala. Her, they hadn't been able to save. Both girls had been dosed with sulfur powder, which caused them to expel a knot of roundworms up to six inches in length and as thick as the Reverend's little finger, but the treatment was perhaps too harsh for the three-year-old, who was suffering from fever and dysentery at the same time. She'd seemed all right, feverish but calm, and Mrs. Singh had tended her through the afternoon and evening. But when the Reverend's wife came into the pen in the morning Kamala flew at her, raking her arms and legs and driving her back from the straw in which her sister's cold body lay stretched out like a figure carved of wood. They restrained the girl and removed the corpse. Then Mrs. Singh retired to bandage her wounds and the Reverend locked the door of the pen to prevent any further violence. All that day, Kamala lay immobile in the shadows at the back of the pen, wrapped in her own limbs. When night fell, she sat back on her haunches behind the rigid geometry of the bars and began to howl, softly at first, and then with increasing force and plangency until it was the very sound of desolation itself, rising up out of the compound to chase through the streets of the village and into the jungle beyond.

Going to the Dogs

The sky was clear all the way to the top of everything, the sun so thick in the trees that he thought it would catch there and congeal among the motionless leaves. He didn't know what prompted him to do it, exactly, but as he came across the field he balanced first on one leg and then the other, to remove his shoes and socks. The grass—the weeds, wildflowers, puffs of mushroom, clover, swaths of moss—felt clean and cool against the lazy progress of his bare feet. Things rose up to greet him, things and smells he'd forgotten all about, and he took his time among them, moving forward only to be distracted again and again. He found her, finally, in the tall nodding weeds that concealed the entrance of the den, playing with the puppies. He didn't say hello, didn't say anything—just settled in on the mound beside her and let the pups surge into his arms. The pack barely raised its collective head.

Her eyes came to him and went away again. She was smiling, a loose, private smile that curled the corners of her mouth and lifted up into the smooth soft terrain of the silken skin under her eyes. Her clothes barely covered her anymore, the turtleneck torn at the throat and sagging across one clavicle, the black jeans hacked off crudely—or maybe chewed off—at the peaks of her thighs. The sneakers were gone altogether, and he saw that the pale-yellow soles of her feet were hard with callus, and her hair—her hair was struck with sun and shining with the natural oil of her scalp.

He'd come with the vague idea—or, no, the very specific idea—of asking her for one of the pups, but now he didn't know if that would do, exactly. She would tell him that the pups weren't hers to give, that they belonged to the pack, and though each of the pack's members had a bed and a bowl of kibble awaiting it in one of the equitable houses of the alphabetical grid of the development springing up around them, they were free here, and the pups, at least, were slaves to no one. He felt the thrusting wet snouts of the creatures in his lap, the surge of their animacy, the softness of the stroked ears, and the prick of the milk teeth, and he smelled them, too, an authentic smell compounded of dirt, urine, saliva, and something else also: the unalloyed sweetness of life. After a while, he removed his shirt, and so what if the pups carried it off like a prize? The sun blessed him. He loosened his belt, gave himself some breathing room. He looked at her, stretched out beside him, at the lean, tanned, running length of her, and he heard himself say, finally, "Nice day, isn't it?"

"Don't talk," she said. "You'll spoil it."

"Right," he said. "Right. You're right."

And then she rolled over, bare flesh from the worried waistband of her cutoffs to the dimple of her breastbone and her breasts caught somewhere in between, under the yielding fabric. She was warm, warm as a fresh-drawn bath, the touch of her communicating everything to him, and the smell of her, too—he let his hand go up under the flap of material and roam over her breasts, and then he bent closer, sniffing.

Her eyes were fixed on his. She didn't say anything, but a low throaty rumble escaped her throat.

Waiting for the Rains

The Reverend Singh sat there on the veranda, waiting for the rains. He'd set his notebook aside, and now he leaned back in the wicker chair and pulled meditatively at his pipe. The children were at play in the courtyard, an array of flashing limbs and animated faces, attended by their high, bright catcalls and shouts. The heat had loosened its grip ever so perceptibly, and they were, all of them, better for it. Except Kamala. She was indifferent. The chill of winter, the damp of the rains, the full merciless sway of the sun—it was all the same to her. His eyes came to rest on her where she lay across the courtyard in a stripe of sunlight, curled in the dirt with her knees drawn up beneath her and her chin resting atop the cradle of her crossed wrists. He watched her for a long while as she lay motionless there, no more aware of what she was than a dog or an ass, and he felt defeated, defeated and depressed. But then one of the children called out in a voice fluid with joy, a moment of triumph in a game among them, and the Reverend couldn't help but shift his eyes and look.

THE COMING OF RIQUET
(1919)
Anatole France

Along with Balzac, Rabelais, and Maupassant, Anatole France (1844–1924) stands at the pinnacle of French literature. His book *Penguin Island* (1909) is world famous. Other masterpieces include *The Life of Joan of Arc* (1908), *The Red Lily* (1910), and *The Human Tragedy* (1917). In this gem of a short story, a tiny puppy shows up at the home of a philologist and ingratiates itself into the master's heart.

Seated at his table one morning in front of the window, against which the leaves of the plane tree quivered, M. Bergeret, who was trying to discover how the ships of Aeneas had been changed into nymphs, heard a tap at the door, and forthwith his servant entered, carrying in front of her, opossum-like, a tiny creature whose black head peeped out from the folds of her apron, which she had turned up to form a pocket. With a look of anxiety and hope upon her face, she remained motionless for a moment, then she placed the little thing upon the carpet at her master's feet.

"What's that?" asked M. Bergeret.

It was a little dog of doubtful breed, having something of the terrier in him, and a well-set head, a short, smooth coat of a dark tan color, and a tiny little stump of a tail. His body retained its puppy-like softness, and he went sniffling at the carpet.

"Angélique," said M. Bergeret, "take this animal back to its owner."

"It has no owner, Monsieur."

M. Bergeret looked silently at the little creature, who had come to examine his slippers, and was giving little sniffs of approval. M. Bergeret was a philologist, which perhaps explains why at this juncture he asked a vain question.

"What is he called?"

"Monsieur," replied Angélique, "he has no name."

M. Bergeret seemed put out at this answer: he looked at the dog sadly, with a disheartened air.

Then the little animal placed its two front paws on M. Bergeret's slipper, and, holding it thus, began innocently to nibble at it. With a sudden access of compassion M. Bergeret took the tiny nameless creature upon his knee. The dog looked at him intently, and M. Bergeret was pleased at his confiding expression.

"What beautiful eyes!" he cried.

The dog's eyes were indeed beautiful, the pupils of a golden-flecked chest-nut set in warm white. And his gaze spoke of simple, mysterious thoughts, common alike to the thoughtful beasts and simple men of the earth.

Tired, perhaps, with the intellectual effort he had made for the purpose of entering into communication with a human being, he closed his beauti-ful eyes, and, yawning widely, revealed his pink mouth, his curled-up tongue, and his array of dazzling teeth.

M. Bergeret put his hand into the dog's mouth, and allowed him to lick it, at which old Angélique gave a smile of relief.

"A more affectionate little creature doesn't breathe," she said.

"The dog," said M. Bergeret, "is a religious animal. In his savage state he worships the moon and the lights that float upon the waters. These are his gods, to whom he appeals at night with long-drawn howls. In the domes-ticated state he seeks by his caresses to conciliate those powerful genii who dispense the good things of this world—to wit, men. He worships and honors men by the accomplishment of the rites passed down to him by his ances-tors: he licks their hands, jumps against their legs, and when they show signs of anger towards him he approaches them crawling on his belly as a sign of humility, to appease their wrath."

"All dogs are not the friends of man," remarked Angélique. "Some of them bite the hand that feeds them."

"Those are the ungodly, blasphemous dogs," returned M. Bergeret, "insensate creatures like Ajax, the son of Telamon, who wounded the hand of the golden Aphrodite. These sacrilegious creatures die a dreadful death, or lead wandering and miserable lives. They are not to be confounded with those dogs who, espousing the quarrel of their own particular god, wage war upon his enemy, the neighboring god. They are heroes. Such, for example, is the dog of Lafolie, the butcher, who fixed his sharp teeth into the leg of the tramp Pied-d'Alouette. For it is a fact that dogs fight among themselves like men, and Turk, with his snub nose, serves his god Lafolie against the robber dogs, in the same way that Israel helped Jehovah to destroy Chamos and Moloch."

The puppy, however, having decided that M. Bergeret's remarks were the reverse of interesting, curled up his feet and stretched out his head, ready to go to sleep upon the knees that harbored him.

"Where did you find him?" asked M. Bergeret.

"Well, Monsieur, it was M. Dellion's *chef* gave him to me."

"With the result," continued M. Bergeret, "that we now have this soul to care for."

"What soul?" asked Angélique.

"This canine soul. An animal is, properly speaking, a soul; I do not say an immortal soul. And yet, when I come to consider the positions this poor little beast and I myself occupy in the scheme of things, I recognize in both exactly the same right to immortality."

After considerable hesitation, old Angélique, with a painful effort that made her upper lip curl up and reveal her two remaining teeth, said:

"If Monsieur does not want a dog, I will return him to M. Dellion's *chef*; but you may safely keep him, I assure you. You won't see or hear him."

She had hardly finished her sentence when the puppy, hearing a heavy van rolling down the street, sat bolt upright on M. Bergeret's knees, and began to bark both loud and long, so that the window-panes resounded with the noise.

M. Bergeret smiled.

"He's a watch-dog," said Angélique, by way of excuse. "They are by far the most faithful."

"Have you given him anything to eat?" asked M. Bergeret.

"Of course," returned Angélique.

"What does he eat?"

"Monsieur must be aware that dogs eat bread and meat."

Somewhat piqued, M. Bergeret retorted that in her eagerness she might very likely have taken him away from his mother before he was old enough to leave her, upon which he was lifted up again and re-examined, only to make sure of the fact that he was at least six months old.

M. Bergeret put him down on the carpet, and regarded him with interest.

"Isn't he pretty?" said the servant.

"No, he is not pretty," replied M. Bergeret. "But he is engaging, and has beautiful eyes. That is what people used to say about me," added the professor, "when I was three times as old, and not half as intelligent. Since then I have no doubt acquired an outlook upon the universe which he will never attain. But, in comparison with the Absolute, I may say that my knowledge equals his in the smallness of its extent. Like his, it is a geometrical point in the infinite." Then, addressing the little creature who was sniffing the waste-paper basket, he went on: "Smell it out, sniff it well, take from the outside world all the knowledge that can reach your simple brain through the medium of that black truffle-like nose of yours. And what though I at the same time observe, and compare, and study? We shall never know, neither the one nor the other of us, why we have been put into this world, and what we are doing in it. What are we here for, eh?"

As he had spoken rather loudly, the puppy looked at him anxiously, and M. Bergeret, returning to the thought which had first filled his mind, said to the servant:

"We must give him a name."

With her hands folded in front of her she replied laughingly that that would not be a difficult matter.

Upon which M. Bergeret made the private reflection that to the simple all things are simple, but that clear-sighted souls, who look upon things from many and divers aspects, invisible to the vulgar mind, experience the greatest difficulty in coming to a decision about even the most trivial matters. And he cudgelled his brains, trying to hit upon a name for the little living thing that was busily engaged in nibbling the fringe of the carpet.

"All the names of dogs," thought he, "preserved in the ancient treatises of the huntsmen of old, such as Fouilloux, and in the verses of our sylvan poets such as La Fontaine—Finaud, Miraut, Briffaut, Ravaud, and such-like names, are given to sporting dogs, who are the aristocracy of the kennel, the chivalry of the canine race. The dog of Ulysses was called Argos, and he was a hunter too, so Homer tells us. 'In his youth he hunted the little hares of Ithaca, but now he was old and hunted no more.' What we require is something quite different. The names given by old maids to their lap-dogs would be more suitable, were they not usually pretentious and absurd. Azor, for instance, is ridiculous!"

So M. Bergeret ruminated, calling to memory many a dog name, without being able to decide, however, on one that pleased him. He would have like to invent a name, but lacked the imagination.

"What day is it?" he asked at last.

"The ninth," replied Angélique. "Thursday, the ninth."

"Well, then!" said M. Bergeret, "can't we call the dog Thursday, like Robinson Crusoe who called his man Friday, for the same reason?"

"As Monsieur pleases," said Angélique. "But it isn't very pretty."

"Very well," said M. Bergeret, "find a name for the creature yourself, for, after all, you brought him here."

"Oh, no," said the servant. "I couldn't find a name for him; I'm not clever enough. When I saw him lying on the straw in the kitchen, I called him Riquet, and he came up and played about under my skirts."

"You called him Riquet, did you?" cried M. Bergeret. "Why didn't you say so before? Riquet he is and Riquet he shall remain; that's settled. Now be off with you, and take Riquet with you. I want to work."

"Monsieur," returned Angélique, "I'm going to leave the puppy with you; I will come for him when I get back from market."

"You could quite well take him to market with you," retorted M. Bergeret.

"Monsieur, I am going to church as well."

It was quite true that she really was going to church at Saint-Exupère, to ask for a Mass to be said for the repose of her husband's soul. She did that regularly once a year, not that she had even been informed of the decease of Borniche, who had never communicated with her since his desertion, but it was a settled thing in the good woman's mind that Borniche was dead. She had therefore no fear of his coming to rob her of the little she had, and did her best to fix things up to his advantage in the other world, so long as he left her in peace in this one.

"Eh!" ejaculated M. Bergeret. "Shut him up in the kitchen or some other convenient place, and do not wor———"

He did not finish his sentence, for Angélique had vanished, purposely pretending not to hear, that she might leave Riquet with his master. She wanted them to grow used to one another, and she also wanted to give poor, friendless M. Bergeret a companion. Having closed the door behind her, she went along the corridor and down the steps.

M. Bergeret set to work again and plunged head foremost into his *Virgilius nauticus*. He loved the work; it rested his thoughts, and became a kind of game that suited him, for he played it all by himself. On the table beside him were several boxes filled with pegs, which he fixed into little squares of cardboard to represent the fleet of Aeneas. Now while he was thus occupied he felt something like tiny fists tapping at his legs. Riquet, whom he had quite forgotten, was standing on his hind legs patting his master's knees, and wagging his little stump of a tail. When he tired of this, he let his paws slide down the trouser leg, then got up and began his coaxing over again. And M. Bergeret, turning away from the printed lore before him, saw two brown eyes gazing up at him lovingly.

"What gives a human beauty to the gaze of this dog," he thought, "is probably that it varies unceasingly, being by turns bright and vivacious, or serious and sorrowful; because through these eyes his little dumb soul finds expression for thought that lacks nothing in depth nor sequence. My father was very fond of cats, and consequently, I liked them too. He used to declare that cats are the wise man's best companions, for they respect his studious hours. Bajazet, his Persian cat, would sit at night for hours at a stretch, motionless and majestic, perched on a corner of his table. I still remember the agate eyes of Bajazet, but those jewel-like orbs concealed all thought, that owl-like stare was cold, and hard, and wicked. How much do I prefer the melting gaze of the dog!"

Riquet, however, was agitating his paws in frantic fashion, and M. Bergeret, who was anxious to return to his philological amusements, said kindly, but shortly:

"Lie down, Riquet!"

Upon which Riquet went and thrust his nose against the door through which Angélique had passed out. And there he remained, uttering from time to time plaintive, meek little cries. After a while he began to scratch, making a gentle rasping noise on the polished floor with his nails. Then the whining began again followed by more scratching. Disturbed by these sounds, M. Bergeret sternly bade him keep still.

Riquet peered at him sorrowfully with his brown eyes, then, sitting down, he looked at M. Bergeret again, rose, returned to the door, sniffed underneath it, and wailed afresh.

"Do you want to go out?" asked M. Bergeret.

Putting down his pen, he went to the door, which he held a few inches open. After making sure that he was running no risk of hurting himself on the way out, Riquet slipped through the doorway and marched off with a composure that was scarcely polite. On returning to his table, M. Bergeret, sensitive man that he was, pondered over the dog's action. He said to himself:

"I was on the point of reproaching the animal for going without saying either good-bye or thank you, and expecting him to apologize for leaving me. It was the beautiful human expression of his eyes that made me so foolish. I was beginning to look upon him as one of my own kind."

After making this reflection M. Bergeret applied himself anew to the metamorphosis of the ships of Aeneas, a legend both pretty and popular, but perhaps a trifle too simple in itself for expression in such noble language. M. Bergeret, however, saw nothing incongruous in it. He knew that the nursery tales have furnished material for nearly all epics, and that Virgil had carefully collected together in his poem the riddles, the puns, the uncouth stories, and the puerile imaginings of his forefathers; that Homer, his master and the master of all the bards, had done little more than tell over again what the good wives of Ionia and the fishermen of the islands had been narrating for more than a thousand years before him. Besides, for the time being, this was the least of his worries; he had another far more important preoccupation. An expression, met with in the course of the charming story of the metamorphosis, did not appear sufficiently plain to him. That was what was worrying him.

"Bergeret, my friend," he said to himself, "this is where you must open your eyes and show your sense. Remember that Virgil always expresses himself with extreme precision when writing on the technique of the arts; remember that he went yachting at Baïae, that he was an expert in naval construction, and that therefore his language, in this passage, must have a precise and definite signification."

And M. Bergeret carefully consulted a great number of texts, in order to throw a light upon the word which he could not understand, and which he had to explain. He was almost on the point of grasping the solution, or, at any rate, he had caught a glimpse of it, when he heard a noise like the rattling of chains at his door, a noise which, although not alarming, struck him as curious. The disturbance was presently accompanied by a shrill whining, and M. Bergeret, interrupted in his philological investigations, immediately concluded that these importunate wails must emanate from Riquet.

As a matter of fact, after having looked vainly all over the house for Angélique, Riquet had been seized with a desire to see M. Bergeret again. Solitude was as painful to him as human society was dear. In order to put an end to the noise, and also because he had a secret desire to see Riquet again, M. Bergeret got up from his arm-chair and opened the door, and Riquet re-entered the study with the same coolness with which had had quitted it, but as soon as he saw the door close behind him he assumed a melancholy expression, and began to wander up and down the room like a soul in torment.

He had a sudden way of appearing to find something of interest beneath the chairs and tables, and would sniff long and noisily; then he would walk aimlessly about or sit down in a corner with an air of great humility, like the beggars who are to be seen in church porches. Finally he began to bark at a cast of Hermes which stood upon the mantel-shelf, whereupon M. Bergeret addressed him in words full of just reproach.

"Riquet! such vain agitation, such sniffing and barking were better suited to a stable than to the study of a professor, and they lead one to suppose that your ancestors lived with horses whose straw litters they shared. I do not reproach you with that. It is only natural you should have inherited their habits, manners, and tendencies as well as their close-cropped coat, their sausage-like body, and their long, thin nose. I do not speak of your beautiful eyes, for there are few men, few dogs even, who can open such beauties to the light of day. But, leaving all that aside, you are a mongrel, my friend, a mongrel from your short, bandy legs to your head. Again I am far from despising you for that. What I want you to understand is that if you desire to live with me, you will have to drop your mongrel manners and behave like a *scholar*, in other words, to remain silent and quiet, to respect work, after the manner of Bajazet, who of a night would sit for four hours without stirring, and watch my father's pen skimming over the paper. He was a silent and tactful creature. How different is your own character, my friend! Since you came into this chamber of study your hoarse voice, your unseemly snufflings and your whines, that sound like steam whistles, have constantly confused my thoughts and interrupted my reflections. And now you have made me lose the drift of an important passage in Servius, referring to the construction of one of the ships of Aeneas. Know then, Riquet, my friend, that this is the house of silence and the abode of meditation, and that if you are anxious to stay here you must become literary. Be quiet!"

Thus spoke M. Bergeret. Riquet, who had listened to him with mute astonishment, approached his master, and with suppliant gesture placed a timid paw upon the knee, which he seemed to revere in a fashion that savored of long ago. Then a kind thought struck M. Bergeret. He picked him up by the scruff of his neck, and put him upon the cushions of the ample easy chair in which he was sitting. Turning himself round three times, Riquet lay down, and then remained perfectly still and silent. He was quite happy. M. Bergeret was grateful to him, and as he ran through Servius he occasionally stroked the close-cropped coat, which, without being soft, was smooth and very pleasant to the touch. Riquet fell into a gentle doze, and communicated to his master the generous warmth of his body, the subtle, gentle heat of a living, breathing thing. And from that moment M. Bergeret found more pleasure in his *Virgilius naticus*.

From floor to ceiling his study was lined with deal shelves, bearing books arranged in methodical order. One glance, and all that remains to us of Latin thought was ready to his hand. The Greeks lay halfway up. In a quiet corner, easy to access, were Rabelais, the excellent story-tellers of the *Cent nouvelles nouvelles*, Bonaventure des Périers, Guillaume Bouchet, and all the old French "conteurs," whom M. Bergeret considered better adapted to humanity than writings in the more heroic style, and who were the favorite reading of his leisure. He possessed them in cheap modern editions only, but he had discovered a poor bookbinder in the town who covered his volumes with leaves from a book of anthems, and it gave M. Bergeret the keenest pleasure to see these free-spoken gentlemen thus clad in Requiems and Misereres. This was the sole luxury and the only peculiarity of his austere library. The other books were paper-backed or bound in poor and worn-out bindings. The gentle friendly manner in which they were handled by their owner gave them the look of tools set out in a busy man's workshop. The books of archaelogy and art found a resting-place on the highest shelves, not by any means out of contempt, but because they were not so often used.

Now, while M. Bergeret worked at his *Virgilius nauticus* and shared his chair with Riquet, he found, as chance would have it, that it was necessary to consult Ottfried Müller's little *Manual*, which happened to be on one of the topmost shelves.

There was no need of one of these tall ladders on wheels topped by railings and a shelf, to enable him to reach the book; there were ladders of this description in the town library, and they had been used by all the great book-lovers of the eighteenth and nineteenth centuries; indeed, several of the latter had fallen from them, and thus died honorable deaths, in the manner spoken of in the pamphlet entitled: *Des bibliophiles qui moururent en tombant de leur échelle*. No, indeed! M. Bergeret had no need of anything of the sort. A small pair of folding steps would have served his purpose excellently well, and he had once seen some in the shop of Clérambaut, the cabinet-maker, in the Rue de Josde. They folded up, and looked just the thing, with their bevelled uprights each pierced with a trefoil as a grip for the hand. M. Bergeret would have given anything to possess them, but the state of his finances, which were somewhat involved, forced him to abandon the idea. No one knew better than he did that financial ills are not mortal, but, for all that, he had no steps in his study.

In place of such a pair of steps he used an old cane-bottomed chair, the back of which had been broken, leaving only two horns or antennae, which had shown themselves to be more dangerous than useful. So they had been cut to the level of the seat, and the chair had become a stool. There were two reasons why this stool was ill-fitted to the use to which M. Bergeret was wont to put it. In the first place the woven-cane seat had grown slack with long use, and now contained a large hollow, making one's foothold precarious. In the second place the stool was too low, and it was hardly possible when standing upon it to reach the books on the highest shelf, even with the finger-tips. What generally happened was that in the endeavor to grasp one book, several others fell out; and it depended upon their being bound or paper-covered whether they lay with broken corners, or sprawled with leaves spread like a fan or a concertina.

Now, with the intention of getting down the *Manual* of Ottfried Müller, M. Bergeret quitted the chair he was sharing with Riquet, who, rolled into a ball with his head tight pressed to his body, lay in warm comfort, opening one voluptuous eye, which he re-closed as quickly. Then M. Bergeret drew the stool from the dark corner where it was hidden and placed it where it was required, hoisted himself upon it, and managed, by making his arm as long as possible, and straining upon tiptoe, to touch, first with one, then with two fingers, the back of a book which he judged to be the one he was needing. As for the thumb, it remained below the shelf and rendered no assistance whatever. M. Bergeret, who found it therefore exceedingly difficult to draw out the book, made the reflection that the reason why the hand is a precious implement is on account of the position of the thumb, and that no being could rise to be an artist who had four feet and no hands.

"It is to the hand," he reflected, "that men owe their power of becoming engineers, painters, writers, and manipulators of all kinds of things. If they had not a thumb as well as their other fingers, they would be as incapable as I am at this moment, and they could never have changed the face of the earth as they have done. Beyond a doubt it is the shape of the hand that has assured to man the conquest of the world."

Then, almost simultaneously, M. Bergeret remembered that monkeys, who possess four hands, have not, for all that, created the arts, nor disposed that earth to their use, and he erased from his mind the theory upon which he had just embarked. However, he did the best he could with his four fingers. It must be known that Ottfried Müller's *Manual* is composed of three volumes and an atlas. M. Bergeret wanted volume one. He pulled out first the second volume, then the atlas, then volume three, and finally the book that he required. At last he held it in his hands. All that now remained for him to do was to descend, and this he was about to do when the cane seat gave way beneath his foot, which passed through it. He lost his balance and fell to the ground, not as heavily as might have been feared, for he broke his fall by grasping at one the uprights of the bookshelf.

He was on the ground, however, full of astonishment, and wearing on one leg the broken chair; his whole body was permeated and as though constricted by a pain that spread all over it, and that presently settled itself more particularly in the region of the left elbow and hip upon which he had fallen. But, as his anatomy was not seriously damaged, he gathered his wits together;

he had got so far as to realize that he must draw his right leg out of the stool in which it had so unfortunately become entangled, and that he must be careful to raise himself up on his right side, which was unhurt. He was even trying to put this into execution when he felt a warm breath upon his cheek, and turning his eyes, which fright and pain had for the moment fixed, he saw close to his cheek Riquet's little face.

At the sound of the fall Riquet had jumped down from the chair and run to his unfortunate master; he was now standing near him in a state of great excitement; then he commenced to run round him. First he came near out of sympathy, then he retreated out of fear of some mysterious danger. He understood perfectly well that a misfortune had taken place, but he was neither thoughtful nor clever enough to discover what it was; hence his anxiety. His fidelity drew him to his suffering friend, and his prudence stopped him on the very brink of the fatal spot. Encouraged at length by the calm and silence which eventually reigned, he licked M. Bergeret's neck and looked at him with eyes of fear and of love. The fallen master smiled, and the dog licked the end of his nose. It was a great comfort to M. Bergeret, who freed his right leg, stood erect, and limped good-humoredly back to his chair.

Riquet was there before him. All that could be seen of his eyes was a gleam between the narrow slit of the half-closed lids. He seemed to have forgotten all about the adventure that a moment before had so stirred them both. The little creature lived in the present, with no thought of time that had run its course; not that he was wanting in memory, inasmuch as he could remember, not his own past alone, but the faraway past of his ancestors, and his little head was a rich storehouse of useful knowledge; but he took no pleasure in remembrance, and memory was not for him, as it was for M. Bergeret, a divine muse.

Gently stroking the short, smooth coat of his companion, M. Bergeret addressed him in the following affectionate terms:

"Dog! at the price of the repose which is dear to your heart, you came to me when I was dismayed and brought low. You did not laugh, as any young person of my own species would have done. It is true that however joyous or terrible nature may appear to you at times, she never inspires you with a sense of the ridiculous. And it is for that very reason, because of your innocent gravity, that you are the surest friend a man can have. In the first instance I inspired confidence and admiration in you, and now you show me pity.

"Dog! when we first met on the highway of life, we came from the two poles of creation; we belong to different species. I refer to this with no desire to take advantage of it, but rather with a strong sense of universal brotherhood. We have hardly been acquainted two hours, and my hand has never yet fed you. What can be the meaning of the obscure love for me that has sprung up in your little heart? The sympathy you bestow on me is a charming mystery, and I accept it. Sleep, friend, in the place that you have chosen!"

Having thus spoken, M. Bergeret turned over the leaves of Ottfried Müller's *Manual*, which with marvelous instinct he had kept in his hand both during and after his fall. He turned over the pages, and could not find what he sought.

Every moment, however, seemed to increase the pain he was feeling.

"I believe," he thought, "that the whole of my left side is bruised and my hip swollen. I have a suspicion that my right leg is grazed all over and my left elbow aches and burns, but shall I cavil at pain that has led me to the discovery of a friend?"

His reflections were running thus when old Angélique, breathless and perspiring, entered the study. She first opened the door, and then she knocked, for she never permitted herself to enter without knocking. If she had not done so before she opened the door, she did it after, for she had good manners, and knew what was expected of her. She went in therefore, knocked, and said:

"Monsieur, I have come to relieve you of the dog."

M. Bergeret heard these words with decided annoyance. He had not as yet inquired into his claims to Riquet, and now realized that he had none. The thought that Madame Borniche might take the animal away from him filled him with sadness, yet, after all, Riquet did belong to her. Affecting indifference, he replied:

"He's asleep; let him sleep!"

"Where is he? I don't see him," remarked old Angélique.

"Here he is," answered M. Bergeret. "In my chair."

With her two hands clasped over her portly figure, old Angélique smiled, and, in a tone of gentle mockery, ventured:

"I wonder what pleasure the creature can find in sleeping there behind Monsieur!"

"That," retorted M. Bergeret, "is his business."

Then, as he was of inquiring mind, he immediately sought of Riquet his reasons for the selection of his resting-place, and lighting on them, replied with his accustomed candor:

"I keep him warm, and my presence affords a sense of security; my comrade is a chilly and homely little animal." Then he added: "Do you know, Angélique? I will go out presently and buy him a collar."

DOG
(1996)
Richard Russo

Next up is a story about a nine-year-old boy who wants a dog in the worst way. His parents are college professors so, naturally, the matter gets a lot of thought and discussion. Originally from *The New Yorker*, this tale was written by 2002 Pulitzer Prize winner Richard Russo. Among his books are *Nobody's Fool* (1993), *Straight Man* (1997), *Empire Falls* (2001), and *The Whore's Child and Other Stories* (2002).

They're nice to have—a dog.
—*The Great Gatsby*

Truth be told, I'm not an easy man. I can be an entertaining one, though it's been my experience that most people don't want to be entertained. They want to be comforted. And, of course, my idea of entertaining might not be yours. According to those who know me best, I am exasperating. According to my parents, I was an exasperating child as well. They divorced when I was in junior high school, and they agree on little except that I was an impossible child. The story they tell of me, William Henry Devereaux, Jr., and my dog is eerily similar in its facts, its conclusions, even the style of its telling, no matter which of them is telling it. Here's the story they tell:

I was nine, and the house we were living in, which belonged to the university, was my fourth. This was the late fifties. My parents were academic nomads, my father then and now an academic opportunist, always in the vanguard of whatever was trendy and chic in literary criticism. In early middle age he was already a full professor, with several published books, all of them "hot," and the subject of intense debate at English Department cocktail parties. The academic position he favored was the "distinguished visiting professor" variety, usually created for him, duration of visit a year or two at the most, perhaps because it's hard to remain distinguished among people who know you. Usually, his teaching responsibilities were light, a course or two a year. Otherwise, he was expected to read and think and write and publish and acknowledge in the preface of his next book the generosity of the institution that provided him with the academic good life. My mother, also an

English professor, was hired as part of the package deal, to teach a full load and thereby help balance the books.

The houses we lived in were elegant, old, high-ceilinged, drafty, either on or close to campus. They had hardwood floors and smoky fireplaces with fires in them only when my father held court, which he did either on Friday afternoons, our large rooms filling up with obsequious junior faculty and nervous grad students, or Saturday evenings, when my mother gave dinner parties for the chairman of the department, or the dean, or a visiting poet. In all situations I was the only child, and I must have been a lonely one, because what I wanted more than anything in the world was a dog.

Predictably, my parents did not. Probably the terms of living in these university houses were specific regarding pets. By the time I was nine I'd been lobbying hard for a dog for a year or two. My father and mother were hoping I would outgrow this longing, given enough time. I could see this hope in their eyes and it steeled my resolve, intensified my desire. What did I want for Christmas? A dog. What did I want for my birthday? A dog. What did I want on my ham sandwich? A dog. It was a deeply satisfying look of pure exasperation they shared at such moments, and if I couldn't have a dog, this was the next best thing.

Life continued in this fashion until finally my mother made a mistake, a doozy of a blunder born of emotional exhaustion and despair. She, far more than my father, would have preferred a happy child. One spring day after I'd been badgering her pretty relentlessly, she sat me down and said, "You know, a dog is something you earn." My father heard this, got up, and left the room, grim acknowledgment that my mother had just conceded the war. Her idea was to make the dog conditional. The conditions to be imposed would be numerous and severe, and I would be incapable of fulfilling them, and so when I didn't get the dog it would be my own fault. This was her logic, and the fact that she thought such a plan might work illustrates that some people should never be parents and she was one of them.

I immediately put into practice a plan of my own to wear my mother down. Unlike hers, my plan was simple and flawless. Mornings I woke up talking about dogs and nights I fell asleep talking about them. When my mother and father changed the subject, I changed it back. "Speaking of dogs," I would say, a forkful of my mother's roast poised at my lips, and I'd be off again. Maybe no one *had* been speaking of dogs, but, never mind, we were speaking of them now. At the library I checked out half a dozen books on dogs every two weeks and left them lying open around the house. I pointed out dogs we passed on the street, dogs on television, dogs in the magazines my mother subscribed to. I discussed the relative merits of various breeds at every meal. My father seldom listened to anything I said, but I began to see signs that the underpinnings of my mother's personality were beginning to corrode in the salt water of my tidal persistence, and when I judged that she was nigh to complete collapse I took every penny of the allowance money I'd been saving and spent it on a dazzling, bejewelled dog-collar-and-leash set at the overpriced pet store around the corner.

During this period when we were constantly "speaking of dogs," I was not a model boy. I was supposed to be "earning a dog," and I was constantly checking with my mother to see how I was doing, just how much of a dog I'd earned, but I doubt whether my behavior changed a jot. I wasn't really a bad boy. Just a noisy, busy, constantly needy boy. Mr. In-and-Out, my mother called me, because I was in and out of rooms, in and out of doors, in and out of the refrigerator. "Henry," my mother would plead with me, "light somewhere." One of the things I often needed was information, and I constantly interrupted my mother's reading and paper grading to get it. My father, partly to avoid having to answer my questions, spent most of his time in his book-lined office on campus, joining my mother and me only at mealtimes, so that we could speak of dogs as a family. Then he was gone again, blissfully unaware, I thought at the time, that my mother continued to glare homicidally, for long minutes after his departure, at the chair he'd so recently occupied. But he claimed to be close to finishing the book he was working on, and this was a powerful excuse to offer a woman with as much abstract respect for books and learning as my mother possessed.

Gradually, she came to understand that she was fighting a battle she couldn't win, and that she was fighting it alone. I now know that this was part of a larger cluster of bitter marital realizations, but at the time I sniffed nothing in the air but victory. In late August, during what people refer to as the dog days, when she made one last weak condition, final evidence that I had earned a dog, I relented and truly tried to reform my behavior. It was literally the least I could do.

What my mother wanted of me was to stop slamming the screen door. The house we were living in, it must be said, was an acoustic marvel akin to the Whispering Gallery in the dome of St. Paul's, where muted voices travel across a great open space and arrive, clear and intact, at the other side of the great dome. In our house the screen door swung shut on a tight spring, the straight wooden edge of the door encountering the doorframe like a gunshot played through a guitar amplifier set on stun, the crack transmitting perfectly, with equal force and clarity, to every room in the house, upstairs and down. That summer I was in and out that door dozens of times a day, and my mother said it was like living in a shooting gallery. It made her wish the door wasn't shooting blanks. If I could just remember not to slam the door, then she'd see about a dog. Soon.

I did better, remembering about half the time not to let the door slam. When I forgot, I came back in to apologize, though sometimes I forgot then, too. Still, I was trying, and that, combined with the fact that I carried the expensive dog collar and leash with me everywhere I went, apparently moved my mother, because at the end of that first week of diminished door slamming my father went somewhere on Saturday morning, refusing to reveal where, so of course I knew. "What *kind*?" I pleaded with my mother while he was gone. But she claimed not to know. "Your father's doing this," she said, and I thought I saw a trace of misgiving in her expression.

When he returned, I saw why. He'd put it in the back seat, and when he pulled the car in and parked along the side of the house, I saw from the kitchen window its chin resting on the back of the rear seat. I think it saw me,

313

too, but if so it did not react. Neither did it seem to notice that the car had stopped, that my father had got out and was holding the front seat forward. He had to reach in, take the dog by the collar, and pull.

As the animal unfolded its long legs and stepped tentatively, arthritically, out of the car, I saw that I had been both betrayed and outsmarted. In all the time we had been "speaking of dogs," what I'd been seeing in my mind's eye was puppies. Collie puppies, beagle puppies, Lab puppies, shepherd puppies, but none of that had been inked anywhere, I now realized. If not a puppy, a young dog. A rascal, full of spirit and possibility, a dog with new tricks to learn. *This* dog was barely ambulatory. It stood, head down, as if ashamed at something done long ago in its puppydom, and I thought I detected a shiver run through its frame when my father closed the car door behind it.

The animal was, I suppose, what might have been called a handsome dog. A purebred, rust-colored Irish setter, meticulously groomed, wonderfully mannered, the kind of dog you could safely bring into a house owned by the university, the sort of dog that wouldn't really violate the no-pets clause, the kind of dog, I saw clearly, you'd get if you really didn't want a dog or to be bothered with a dog. It had belonged, I later learned, to a professor emeritus of the university who'd been put into a nursing home earlier in the week, leaving the animal an orphan. It was like a painting of a dog, or a dog you'd hire to pose for a portrait, a dog you could be sure wouldn't move.

Both my father and the animal came into the kitchen reluctantly, my father closing the screen door behind them with great care. I like to think that on the way home he'd suffered a misgiving, though I could tell that it was his intention to play the hand out boldly. My mother, who'd taken in my devastation at a glance, studied me for a moment and then my father.

"What?" he said.

My mother just shook her head.

My father looked at me, then back at her. A violent shiver palsied the dog's limbs. The animal seemed to want to lie down on the cool linoleum but to have forgotten how. It offered a deep sigh that seemed to speak for all of us.

"He's a good dog," my father said rather pointedly, to my mother. "A little high-strung, but that's the way with purebred setters. They're all nervous."

This was not the sort of thing my father knew. Clearly he was repeating the explanation he'd been given when he picked up the dog.

"What's his name?" my mother said, apparently for something to say.

My father had neglected to ask. He checked the dog's collar for clues.

"Lord," my mother said. "Lord, Lord."

"It's not like we can't name him ourselves," my father said, irritated now. "I think it's something we can manage, don't you?"

"You could name him after a passé school of literary criticism," my mother suggested.

"It's a she," I said, because it was.

It seemed to cheer my father, at least a little, that I'd allowed myself to be drawn into the conversation. "What do you say, Henry?" he wanted to know. "What'll we name him?"

This second faulty pronoun reference was too much for me. "I want to go out and play now," I said, and I bolted for the screen door before an objection could be registered. It slammed behind me, hard, its gunshot report even louder than normal. As I cleared the steps in a single leap, I thought I heard a thud back in the kitchen, a dull muffled echo of the door, and then I heard my father say, "What the hell?" I went back up the steps, cautiously now, meaning to apologize for the door. Through the screen I could see my mother and father standing together in the middle of the kitchen, looking down at the dog, which seemed to be napping. My father nudged a haunch with the toe of his cordovan loafer.

He dug the grave in the back yard with a shovel borrowed from a neighbor. My father had soft hands and they blistered easily. I offered to help, but he just looked at me. When he was standing, mid-thigh, in the hole he'd dug, he shook his head one last time in disbelief. "Dead," he said. "Before we could even name him."

I knew better than to correct the pronoun again, so I just stood there thinking about what he'd said while he climbed out of the hole and went over to the back porch to collect the dog where it lay under an old sheet. I could tell by the careful way he tucked that sheet under the animal that he didn't want to touch anything dead, even newly dead. He lowered the dog into the hole by means of the sheet, but he had to drop it the last foot or so. When the animal thudded on the earth and lay still, my father looked over at me and shook his head. Then he picked up the shovel and leaned on it before he started filling in the hole. He seemed to be waiting for me to say something, so I said, "Red."

My father's eyes narrowed, as if I'd spoken in a foreign tongue. "What?" he said.

"We'll name her Red," I explained.

In the years after he left us, my father became even more famous. He is sometimes credited, if credit is the word, with being the Father of American Literary Theory. In addition to his many books of scholarship, he has also written a literary memoir that was short-listed for a major award and which offers insight into the personalities of several major literary figures of the twentieth century, now deceased. His photograph often graces the pages of the literary reviews. He went through a phase where he wore crewneck sweaters and gold chains beneath his tweed coat, but now he's photographed mostly in an oxford-cloth button-down shirt, tie, and jacket, in his book-lined office at the university. But to me, his son, William Henry Devereaux, Sr., is most real standing before me in his ruined cordovan loafers, leaning on the handle of a borrowed shovel, examining his dirty, blistered hands and receiving my suggestion of what to name a dead dog. I suspect that digging our dog's grave was one of relatively few experiences in his life (excepting carnal ones) that did not originate on the printed page. And when I suggested that we name the dead dog Red, he looked at me as if I myself had just stepped from the pages of a book he'd started to read years ago and then put down when something else caught his interest. "What?" he said, dropping the shovel, so that its handle hit the earth between my feet. "What?"

It's not an easy time for any parent, this moment when the realization dawns that you've given birth to something that will never see things the way you do, despite the fact that it is your living legacy, that it bears your name.

MUMÚ
(1903)

Ivan Turgenev

Set in Moscow over a century ago, this is the story of a deaf mute, a giant of a man, who befriends a small dog. The great Russian writer Ivan Turgenev's (1818–1883) book *Fathers and Sons* is considered one of the all-time classic novels and was published in translation by the Modern Library in 1917 and 1961. His translated works also include *First Love, and Other Stories* (1904), *Dream Tales and Prose Poems* (1906), *Liza* (1914), and *The Novels of Ivan Turgenev* (1970).

In one of the remote streets of Moscow, in a grey house with white pillars, an entresol, and a crooked balcony, dwelt in former days a well-born lady, a widow, surrounded by numerous domestics. Her sons were in the service in Petersburg, her daughters were married; she rarely went out into society, and was living out the last years of a miserly and tedious old age in solitude. Her day, cheerless and stormy, was long since over; but her evening also was blacker than night.

Among the ranks of her menials, the most remarkable person was the yard porter, Gerásim, a man six feet five inches in height, built like an epic hero, and a deaf-mute from his birth. His mistress had taken him from the village, where he lived alone, in a tiny cottage, apart from his brethren, and was considered the most punctual of the taxable serfs. Endowed with remarkable strength, he did the work of four persons. Matters made progress in his hands, and it was a cheerful sight to watch him when he ploughed and, applying his huge hands to the primitive plough, seemed to be carving open the elastic bosom of the earth alone, without the aid of his little nag; or about St. Peter's Day wielding the scythe so shatteringly that he might even have hewn off a young birchwood from its roots; or threshing briskly and unremittingly with a chain seven feet in length, while the firm, oblong muscles on his shoulders rose and fell like levers. His uninterrupted muteness imparted to his indefatigable labour a grave solemnity. He was a splendid peasant, and had it not been for his infirmity, any maiden would willingly have married him. . . . But Gerásim was brought to Moscow, boots were bought for him, a broom and a shovel were put into his hand, and he was appointed to be the yard porter.

At first he felt a violent dislike for his new life. From his childhood he had been accustomed to field labour, to country life. Set apart by his infirmity from communion with his fellow men, he had grown up dumb and mighty, as a tree grows on fruitful soil. . . . Transported to the town, he did not understand what was happening to him;—he felt bored and puzzled, as a healthy young bull is puzzled when he has just been taken from the pasture, where the grass grew up to his belly,—when he has been taken, and placed in a railway wagon,—and, lo, with his robust body enveloped now with smoke and sparks, again with billows of steam, he is drawn headlong onward, drawn with rumble and squeaking, and whither—God only knows! Gerásim's occupations in his new employment seemed to him a mere farce after his onerous labours as a peasant; in half an hour he had finished everything, and he was again standing in the middle of the courtyard and staring, openmouthed, at all the passers-by, as though desirous of obtaining from them the solution of his enigmatic situation; or he would suddenly go off to some corner and, flinging his broom or his shovel far from him, would throw himself on the ground face downward, and lie motionless on his breast for whole hours at a time, like a captured wild beast.

But man grows accustomed to everything, and Gerásim got used, at last, to town life! He had not much to do; his entire duty consisted in keeping the courtyard clean, fetching a cask of water twice a day, hauling and chopping up wood for the kitchen and house, and in not admitting strangers, and keeping watch at night. And it must be said that he discharged his duty with zeal; not a chip was ever strewn about his courtyard, nor any dirt; if in muddy weather the broken-winded nag for hauling water and the barrel entrusted to his care got stranded anywhere, all he had to do was to apply his shoulder, and not only the cask but the horse also would be pried from the spot. If he undertook to chop wood, his axe would ring like glass, and splinters and billets would fly in every direction; and as for strangers—after he had, one night, caught two thieves and had banged their heads together and mauled them so that there was no necessity for taking them to the police station afterward, everyone in the neighbourhood began to respect him greatly, and even by day passers-by who were not in the least rascals, but simply strangers to him, at the sight of the ominous yard porter would brandish their arms as though in self-defense.

With all the other domestics Gerásim sustained relations which were not exactly friendly—they were afraid of him—but gentle. They expressed their meaning to him by signs, and he understood them, accurately executed all orders but knew his own rights also, and no one dared to take his seat at table. On the whole, Gerásim was of stern and serious disposition, and was fond of orderliness in all things; even the cocks did not venture to fight in his presence—but if they did, woe be to them! If he caught sight of them he would instantly seize them by the legs, whirl them round like a wheel half a dozen times in the air, and hurl them in opposite directions. There were geese also in his mistress's courtyard, but a goose, as everybody knows, is a serious and sensible bird; Gerásim respected them, tended them, and fed them; he himself bore a resemblance to a stately gander.

One evening as he was walking by the river and quietly staring into the water, it suddenly seemed to him as though something were floundering in the ooze close to the bank. He bent down and, behold, a small puppy, white with black spots, which, despite all its endeavours, utterly unable to crawl out of the water, was struggling, slipping, and quivering all over its wet, gaunt little body. Gerásim gazed at the unfortunate puppy, picked it up with one hand, thrust it into his breast, and set out with great strides homeward. He entered his little den, laid the rescued puppy on his bed, covered it with his heavy coat, ran first to the stable for straw, then to the kitchen for a cup of milk. Cautiously throwing back the coat and spreading out the straw, he placed the milk on the bed. The poor little dog was only three weeks old; it had only recently got its eyes open, and one eye even appeared to be a little larger than the other; it did not yet know how to drink out of a cup, and merely trembled and blinked. Gerásim grasped it lightly with two fingers by the head, and bent its muzzle down to the milk. The dog suddenly began to drink greedily, snorting, shaking itself, and lapping. Gerásim gazed and gazed, and then suddenly began to laugh. . . . All night he fussed over it, put it to bed, wiped it off, and at last fell asleep himself beside it in a joyous, tranquil slumber.

No mother tends her infant as Gerásim tended his nursling. (The dog proved to be a bitch.) In the beginning she was very weak, puny, and ill-favoured, but little by little she improved in health and looks, and at the end of eight months, thanks to the indefatigable care of her rescuer, she had turned into a very fair sort of a dog of Spanish breed, with long ears, a feathery tail in the form of a trumpet, and large, expressive eyes. She attached herself passionately to Gerásim, never left him by a pace, and was always following him, wagging her tail. And he had given her a name, too,—the dumb know that their bellowing attracts other people's attention to them:—he called her Mumú. All the people in the house took a liking to her, and also called her dear little Mumú. She was extremely intelligent, fawned upon everyone, but loved Gerásim alone. Gerásim himself loved her madly . . . and it was disagreeable to him when others stroked her: whether he was afraid for her, or jealous of her—God knows! She waked him up in the morning by tugging at his coattails; she led to him by the reins the old water horse, with whom she dwelt in great amity; with importance depicted on her face, she went with him to the river; she stood guard over the brooms and shovels, and allowed no one to enter his room. He cut out an aperture in his door expressly for her, and she seemed to feel that only in Gerásim's little den was she the full mistress, and therefore, on entering it, with a look of satisfaction, she immediately leaped upon the bed. At night she did not sleep at all, but she did not bark without discernment, like a stupid watchdog, which, sitting on its haunches and elevating its muzzle, and shutting its eyes, barks simply out of tedium, at the stars, and usually three times in succession; no! Mumú's shrill voice never resounded without cause! Either a stranger was approaching too close to the fence, or some suspicious noise or rustling had arisen somewhere. . . . In a word, she kept capital watch.

Truth to tell, there was, in addition to her, an old dog in the courtyard, yellow in hue speckled with dark brown, Peg-top by name (*Voltchók*); but that dog was never unchained, even by night, and he himself, owing to his decrepitude, did not demand freedom, but lay there, curled up in his kennel, and only now and then emitted a hoarse, almost soundless bark, which he immediately broke off short, as though himself conscious of its utter futility.

Mumú did not enter the manor house, and when Gerásim carried wood to the rooms she always remained behind and impatiently awaited him, with ears pricked up, and her head turning now to the right, then suddenly to the left, at the slightest noise indoors. . . .

In this manner still another year passed. Gerásim continued to discharge his avocations as yard porter and was very well satisfied with his lot, when suddenly an unexpected incident occurred. . . . Namely, one fine summer day the mistress, with her hangers-on, was walking about the drawing room. She was in good spirits, and was laughing and jesting; the hangers-on were laughing and jesting also, but felt no particular mirth; the people of the household were not very fond of seeing the mistress in merry mood, because, in the first place, at such times she demanded instantaneous and complete sympathy from everyone, and flew into a rage if there was a face which did not beam with satisfaction; and, in the second place, these fits did not last very long, and were generally succeeded by a gloomy and cross-grained frame of mind. On that day, she seemed to have got up happily; at cards, she held four knaves: the fulfillment of desire (she always told fortunes with the cards in the morning),—and her tea struck her as particularly delicious, in consequence whereof the maid received praise in words and ten kopéks in money. With a sweet smile on her wrinkled lips, the lady of the house strolled about her drawing room and approached the window. A flower garden was laid out in front of the window, and in the very middle of the border, under a rosebush, lay Mumú assiduously gnawing a bone. The mistress caught sight of her.

"My God!"—she suddenly exclaimed;—"what dog is that?"

The hanger-on whom the mistress addressed floundered, poor creature, with that painful uneasiness which generally takes possession of a dependent person when he does not quite know how he is to understand his superior's exclamation.

"I . . . d . . . do . . . on't know, ma'am," she stammered; "I think it belongs to the dumb man."

"My God!"—her mistress interrupted her:—"why, it is a very pretty dog! Order it to be brought hither. Has he had it long? How is it that I have not seen it before? . . . Order it to be brought hither."

The hanger-on immediately fluttered out into the anteroom.

"Man, man!"—she screamed,—"bring Mumú here at once! She is in the flower garden."

"And so her name is Mumú,"—said the mistress;—"a very nice name."

"Akh, very nice indeed, ma'am!"—replied the dependent.—"Be quick, Stepán!"

Stepán, a sturdy young fellow, who served as footman, rushed headlong to the garden and tried to seize Mumú; but the latter cleverly slipped out of his fingers and, elevating her tail, set off at full gallop to Gerásim, who was in the kitchen beating out and shaking out the water cask, twirling it about in his hands like a child's drum. Stepán ran after her, and tried to seize her at the very feet of her master; but the agile dog would not surrender herself into the hands of a stranger, and kept leaping and evading him. Gerásim looked on at all this tumult with a grin; at last Stepán rose in wrath, and hastily gave him to understand by signs that the mistress had ordered the dog to be brought to her. Gerásim was somewhat surprised, but he called Mumú, lifted her from the ground, and handed her to Stepán. Stepán carried her into the drawing room, and placed her on the polished wood floor. The mistress began to call the dog to her in a caressing voice. Mumú, who had never in her life been in such magnificent rooms, was extremely frightened, and tried to dart through the door, but, rebuffed by the obsequious Stepán, fell to trembling, and crouched against the wall.

"Mumú, Mumú, come hither to me,"—said the mistress;— "come, thou stupid creature . . . don't be afraid. . . ."

"Come, Mumú, come to the mistress,"—repeated the dependents;—"come!" But Mumú looked anxiously about and did not stir from the spot.

"Bring her something to eat,"—said the mistress.—"What a stupid thing she is! She won't come to the mistress. What is she afraid of?"

"She feels strange still,"—remarked one of the dependents, in a timid and imploring voice.

Stepán brought a saucer of milk and set it in front of Mumú, but Mumú did not even smell of the milk, and kept on trembling and gazing about her, as before.

"Akh, who ever saw such a creature!"—said the mistress, as she approached her, bent down, and was on the point of stroking her; but Mumú turned her head and displayed her teeth in a snarl.—The mistress hastily drew back her hand.

A momentary silence ensued. Mumú whined faintly, as though complaining and excusing herself. . . . The mistress retreated and frowned. The dog's sudden movement had frightened her.

"Akh!"—cried all the dependents with one accord:—"She didn't bite you, did she? God forbid!" (Mumú had never bitten anyone in her life.) "Akh! Akh!"

"Take her away,"—said the old woman, in an altered voice,—"the horrid little dog! What a vicious beast she is!"

And slowly turning, she went toward her boudoir. The dependents exchanged timorous glances and started to follow her, but she paused, looked coldly at them, said: "Why do you do that? for I have not bidden you," and left the room.

The dependents waved their hands in despair at Stepán; the latter picked up Mumú and flung her out into the yard as speedily as possible, straight at Gerásim's feet; and half an hour later a profound stillness reigned in the house, and the old gentlewoman sat on her divan more lowering than a thundercloud.

What trifles, when one comes to think of it, can sometimes put a person out of tune!

The lady was out of sorts until evening, talked with no one, did not play cards, and passed a bad night. She took it into her head that they had not given her the same *eau de cologne* which they usually gave her, that her pillow smelled of soap, and made the keeper of the linen closet smell all the bed linen twice,—in a word, she was upset and extremely incensed. On the following morning she ordered Gavríla to be summoned to her presence an hour earlier than usual.

"Tell me, please,"—she began, as soon as the latter, not without some inward quaking, had crossed the threshold of her boudoir,—"why that dog was barking in our courtyard all night long? It prevented my getting to sleep!"

"A dog, ma'am . . . which one, ma'am? . . . Perhaps it was the dumb man's dog,"—he uttered in a voice that was not altogether firm.

"I don't know whether it belongs to the dumb man or to someone else, only it interfered with my sleep. And I am amazed that there is such a horde of dogs! I want to know about it. We have a watch-dog, have we not?"

"Yes, ma'am, we have, ma'am, Peg-top, ma'am."

"Well, what need have we for any more dogs? They only create disorder. There's no head to the house,—that's what's the matter. And what does the dumb man want of a dog? Who has given him permission to keep a dog in my courtyard? Yesterday I went to the window, and it was lying in the garden; it had brought some nasty thing there, and was gnawing it,—and I have roses planted there . . ."

The lady paused for a while.

"See that it is removed this very day . . . dost hear me?"

"I obey, ma'am."

"This very day. And now, go. I will have thee called for thy report later."

Gavríla left the room.

As he passed through the drawing room, the major-domo transferred a small bell from one table to another, for show, softly blew his duck's-bill nose in the hall, and went out into the anteroom. In the anteroom, on a locker, Stepán was sleeping in the attitude of a slain warrior in a battalion picture, with his bare legs projecting from his coat, which served him in lieu of a coverlet.

The major-domo nudged him, and imparted to him in an undertone some order, to which Stepán replied with a half-yawn, half-laugh. The major-domo withdrew, and Stepán sprang to his feet, drew on his kaftan and his boots, went out and came to a standstill on the porch. Five minutes had not elapsed before Gerásim made his appearance with a huge fagot of firewood on his back, accompanied by his inseparable Mumú. (The mistress had issued orders that her bedroom and boudoir were to be heated even in summer.) Gerásim stood sideways to the door, gave it a push with his shoulder, and precipitated himself into the house with his burden. Mumú, according to her wont, remained behind to wait for him. Then Stepán, seizing a favourable moment, made a sudden dash at her, like a hawk pouncing on a chicken, crushed her to the ground with his breast, gathered her up in his arms, and, without stopping to don so much as his cap, ran out into the street with her, jumped into the first drozhky that came to hand, and galloped off to the Game Market. There he speedily hunted up a purchaser, to whom he sold her for half a ruble, stipulating only that the latter should keep her tied up for at least a week, and immediately returned home; but before he reached the house, he alighted from the drozhky, and making a circuit of the house, he leaped over the fence into the yard from a back alley; he was afraid to enter by the wicket, lest he should encounter Gerásim.

But his anxiety was wasted; Gerásim was no longer in the courtyard. On coming out of the house he had instantly bethought himself of Mumú; he could not remember that she had ever failed to await his return, and he began to run in every direction to hunt for her, to call her after his own fashion . . . he dashed into his little chamber, to the hayloft; he darted into the street,—hither and thither. . . . She was gone! He appealed to the domestics, with the most despairing signs inquired about her; pointing fourteen inches from the ground, he drew her form with his hands. . . . Some of them really did not know what had become of Mumú, and only shook their heads; others did know and grinned at him in reply, but the major-domo assumed a very pompous mien and began to shout at the coachman. Then Gerásim fled far away from the courtyard.

Twilight was already falling when he returned. One was justified in assuming, from his exhausted aspect, from his unsteady gait, from his dusty clothing, that he had wandered over the half of Moscow. He halted in front of the mistress's windows, swept a glance over the porch on which seven house serfs were gathered, turned away, and bellowed once more: "Mumú!"—Mumú did not respond. He went away. All stared after him, but no one smiled, no one uttered a word . . . and the curious postilion, Antípka, narrated on the following morning in the kitchen that the dumb man had moaned all night long.

All the following day Gerásim did not show himself, so that Potáp the coachman was obliged to go for water in his stead, which greatly displeased coachman Potáp. The mistress asked Gavríla whether her command had been executed. Gavríla replied that it had. The next morning Gerásim emerged from his chamber to do his work. He came to dinner, ate, and went off again, without having exchanged greetings with anyone. His face, which was inanimate at the best of times, as is the case with all deaf-and-dumb persons, now seemed to have become absolutely petrified. After dinner he again quitted the courtyard, but not for long, returned, and immediately directed his steps to the hay barn. Night came, a clear, moonlight night. Sighing heavily and incessantly tossing from side to side, Gerásim was lying there, when he suddenly felt as though something were tugging at the skirts of his garments; he trembled all over, but did not raise his head, nevertheless, and even screwed his eyes up tight; but the tugging was repeated, more energetically than before; he sprang to his feet . . . before him, with a fragment of rope about her neck, Mumú was capering about. A prolonged shriek of joy burst from his speechless breast; he seized Mumú and clasped her in a close embrace; in one moment she had licked his nose, his eyes, and his beard. . . . He stood still for a while, pondering, cautiously slipped down from the haymow, cast a glance around him, and having made sure that no one was watching him, he safely regained his little chamber.

Even before this Gerásim had divined that the dog had not disappeared of her own volition; that she must have been carried away by the mistress's command; for the domestics had explained to him by signs how his Mumú had snapped at her—and he decided to take precautions of his own. First he fed Mumú with some bread, caressed her, and put her to bed; then he began to consider how he might best conceal her. At last he hit upon the idea of leaving her all day in his room, and only looking in now and then to see how she was getting along, and taking her out for exercise at night. He closed the opening in his door compactly by stuffing in an old coat of his, and as soon as it was daylight he was in the courtyard, as though nothing had happened, even preserving (innocent guile!) his former dejection of countenance. It could not enter the head of the poor deaf man that Mumú would betray herself by her whining; as a matter of fact, everyone in the house was speedily aware that the dumb man's dog had come back and was locked up in his room; but out of compassion for him and for her, and partly, perhaps, out of fear of him, they did not give him to understand that his secret had been discovered.

The major-domo alone scratched the back of his head and waved his hand in despair, as much as to say: "Well, I wash my hands of the matter! Perhaps the mistress will not get to know of it!" And never had the dumb man worked so zealously as on that day; he swept and scraped out the entire courtyard, he rooted up all the blades of grass to the very last one, with his own hand pulled up all the props in the garden fence, with a view to making sure that they were sufficiently firm, and then hammered them in again,—in a word, he fussed and bustled about so, that even the mistress noticed his zeal.

Twice in the course of the day Gerásim went stealthily to his captive; and when night came, he lay down to sleep in her company, in the little room, not in the hay barn, and only at one o'clock did he go out to take a stroll with her in the fresh air. Having walked quite a long time with her in the courtyard, he was preparing to return, when suddenly a noise resounded outside the fence in the direction of the alley. Mumú pricked up her ears, began to growl, approached the fence, sniffed, and broke forth into a loud and piercing bark.

Some drunken man or other had taken it into his head to nestle down there for the night. At that very moment, the mistress had just got to sleep after a prolonged "nervous excitement"; she always had these excited fits after too hearty a supper. The sudden barking woke her; her heart began to beat violently, and to collapse.

"Maids, maids!"—she moaned.—"Maids!"

The frightened maids flew to her bedroom.

"Okh, okh, I'm dying!"—said she, throwing her hands apart in anguish. —"There's that dog again, again! . . . Okh, send for the doctor! They want to kill me. . . . The dog, the dog again! Okh!"

And she flung back her head, which was intended to denote a swoon.

They ran for the doctor, that is to say, for the household medical man, Kharitón. The whole art of this healer consisted in the fact that he wore boots with soft soles, understood how to feel the pulse delicately, slept fourteen hours out of the twenty-four, spent the rest of the time in sighing, and was incessantly treating the mistress to laurel drops. This healer immediately hastened to her, fumigated with burnt feathers, and, when the mistress opened her eyes, immediately presented to her on a silver tray a wineglass with the inevitable drops.

The mistress took them, but immediately, with tearful eyes, began to complain of the dog, of Gavríla, of her lot, that she, a poor old woman, had been abandoned by everyone, that no one had any pity on her, and that everyone desired her death. In the meantime the unlucky Mumú continued to bark, while Gerásim strove in vain to call her away from the fence.

"There . . . there . . . it goes again! . . ." stammered the mistress, and again rolled up her eyes. The medical man whispered to one of the maids; she rushed into the anteroom, and explained matters to Stepán; the latter ran to awaken Gavríla, and Gavríla, in a passion, gave orders that the whole household should be roused.

Gerásim turned round, beheld the twinkling lights and shadows in the windows, and, foreboding in his heart a catastrophe, he caught up Mumú under his arm, ran into his room, and locked the door. A few moments later, five men were thumping at his door, but, feeling the resistance of the bolt, desisted. Gavríla ran up in a frightful hurry, ordered them all to remain there until morning and stand guard, while he himself burst into the maids' hall and gave orders through the eldest companion, Liubóff Liubímovna,—together with whom he was in the habit of stealing and enjoying tea, sugar, and other groceries,—that the mistress was to be informed that the dog, unfortunately, had run home again from somewhere or other, but that it would not be alive on the morrow, and that the mistress must do them the favour not to be angry, and must calm down. The mistress probably would not have calmed down very speedily had not the medical man, in his haste, poured out forty drops instead of twelve. The strength of the laurel took its effect—in a quarter of an hour the mistress was sleeping soundly and peacefully, and Gerásim was lying, all pale, on his bed, tightly compressing Mumú's mouth.

On the following morning the mistress awoke quite late. Gavríla was waiting for her awakening in order to make a decisive attack upon Gerásim's asylum, and was himself prepared to endure a heavy thunderstorm. But the thunderstorm did not come off. As she lay in bed, the mistress ordered the eldest dependent to be called to her.

"Liubóff Liubímovna,"—she began in a soft, weak voice; she sometimes liked to pretend to be a persecuted and defenceless sufferer; it is needless to state that at such times all the people in the house felt very uncomfortable:— "Liubóff Liubímovna, you see what my condition is; go, my dear, to Gavríla Andréitch, and have a talk with him; it cannot be possible that some nasty little dog or other is more precious to him than the tranquility, the very life of his mistress! I should not like to believe that,"—she added, with an expression of profound emotion:—"Go my dear, be so good, go to Gavríla Andréitch."

Liubóff Liubímovna betook herself to Gavríla's room. What conversation took place between them is not known; but a while later a whole throng of domestics marched through the courtyard in the direction of Gerásim's little den; in front walked Gavríla, holding on his cap with his hand, although there was no wind; around him walked footmen and cooks; Uncle Tail gazed out of the window, and issued orders—that is to say, he merely spread his hands apart; in the rear of all, the small urchins leaped and capered, one half of them being strangers who had run in. On the narrow stairway leading to the den sat one sentry; at the door stood two others with clubs. They began to ascend the staircase, and occupied it to its full length. Gavríla went to the door, knocked on it with his fist, and shouted:

"Open!"

A suppressed bark made itself audible; but there was no reply.

"Open, I say!"—he repeated.

"But, Gavríla Andréitch,"—remarked Stepán from below:—"he's deaf, you know—he doesn't hear."

All burst out laughing.

"What is to be done?"—retorted Gavríla from the top of the stairs.

"Why, he has a hole in his door,"—replied Stepán;—"so do you wiggle a stick around in it a bit."

Gavríla bent down.

"He has stuffed it up with some sort of coat, that hole."

"But do you poke the coat inward."

At this point another dull bark rang out.

"See there, see there, she's giving herself away!"—someone remarked in the crowd, and again there was laughter.

Gavríla scratched behind his ear.

"No, brother,"—he went on at last;—"do thou poke the coat through thyself, if thou wishest."

"Why, certainly!"

And Stepán scrambled up, took a stick, thrust the coat inside, and began to wiggle the stick about in the opening, saying: "Come forth, come forth!" He was still wiggling the stick when the door of the little chamber flew suddenly and swiftly open—and the whole train of menials rolled head over heels down the stairs, Gavríla in the lead. Uncle Tail shut the window.

"Come, come, come, come!"—shouted Gavríla from the courtyard;— "just look out, look out!"

Gerásim stood motionless on the threshold. The crowd assembled at the foot of the staircase. Gerásim stared at all these petty folk in their foreign kaftans from above, with his arms lightly set akimbo; in his scarlet peasant shirt he seemed like a giant in comparison with them. Gavríla advanced a pace.

"See here, brother,"—said he:—"I'll take none of thy impudence."

And he began to explain to him by signs: "The mistress insists upon having thy dog: hand it over instantly, or 'twill be the worse for thee."

Gerásim looked at him, pointed to the dog, made a sign with his hand at his own neck, as though he were drawing up a noose, and cast an inquiring glance at the major-domo.

"Yes, yes,"—replied the latter, nodding his head;—"yes, she insists."

Gerásim dropped his eyes, then suddenly shook himself, again pointed at Mumú, who all this time had been standing by his side, innocently wagging her tail and moving her ears to and fro with curiosity, repeated the sign of strangling over his own neck, and significantly smote himself on the breast, as though declaring that he would take it upon himself to annihilate Mumú.

"But thou wilt deceive,"—waved Gavríla to him in reply.

Gerásim looked at him, laughed disdainfully, smote himself again on the breast, and slammed the door.

All present exchanged glances in silence.

"Well, and what's the meaning of this?"—began Gavríla.—"He has locked himself in."

"Let him alone, Gavríla Andréitch,"—said Stepán;—"he'll do it, if he has promised. That's the sort of fellow he is. . . . If he once promises a thing, it's safe. He isn't like us folks in that respect. What is true is true. Yes."

"Yes,"—repeated all, and wagged their heads.—"That's so. Yes."

Uncle Tail opened the window and said "Yes," also.

"Well, we shall see, I suppose,"—returned Gavríla;—"but the guard is not to be removed, notwithstanding. Hey, there, Eróshka!"—he added, addressing a poor man in a yellow nankeen kazák coat, who was reckoned as the gardener:—"what hast thou to do? Take a stick and sit here, and if anything happens, run for me on the instant."

Eróshka took a stick and sat down on the last step of the staircase. The crowd dispersed, with the exception of a few curious bodies and the small urchins, while Gavríla returned home, and through Liubóff Liubímovna gave orders that the mistress should be informed that everything had been done, and that he himself, in order to make quite sure, had sent the postilion for a policeman. The mistress tied a knot in her handkerchief, poured *eau de cologne* on it, sniffed at it, wipe her temples, sipped her tea and, being still under the influence of the laurel drops, fell asleep again.

An hour after all this commotion, the door of the tiny den opened and Gerásim made his appearance. He wore a new holiday kaftan; he was leading Mumú by a string. Eróshka drew aside and let him pass. Gerásim directed his way toward the gate. All the small boys who were in the court-yard followed him with their eyes in silence. He did not even turn round; he did not put on his cap until he reached the street. Gavríla despatched after him that same Eróshka, in the capacity of observer. Eróshka, perceiving from afar that he had entered an eating house in company with his dog, awaited his reappearance.

In the eating house they knew Gerásim and understood his signs. He ordered cabbage soup with meat, and seated himself, with his arms resting on the table. Mumú stood beside his chair, calmly gazing at him with her intelligent eyes. Her coat was fairly shining with gloss: it was evident that she had recently been brushed. They brought the cabbage soup to Gerásim. He crumbled up bread in it, cut the meat up into small pieces, and set the plate on the floor. Mumú began to eat with her customary politeness, hardly touching her muzzle to the food; Gerásim stared long at her; two heavy tears rolled suddenly from his eyes; one fell on the dog's sloping forehead, the other into the soup. He covered his face with his hand. Mumú ate half a plateful and retired, licking her chops. Gerásim rose, paid for the soup, and set out, accompanied by the somewhat astounded glance of the waiter. Eróshka, on catching sight of Gerásim, sprang round the corner, and, allowing him to pass, again set out on his track.

Gerásim walked on without haste, and did not release Mumú from the cord. On reaching the corner of the street he halted, as though in thought, and suddenly directed his course, with swift strides, straight toward the Crimean Ford. On the way he entered the yard of a house, to which a wing was being built, and brought thence two bricks under his arm. From the Crimean Ford he turned along the bank, advanced to a certain spot, where stood two boats with oars, tied to stakes (he had already noted them previously), and sprang into one of them, in company with Mumú. A lame little old man emerged from behind a hut placed in one corner of a vegetable garden, and shouted at him. But Gerásim only nodded his head, and set to rowing so vigorously, although against the current, that in an instant he had darted off to a distance of a hundred fathoms. The old man stood and stood, scratched his back, first with the left hand then with the right, and returned, limping, to his hut.

But Gerásim rowed on and on. And now he had left Moscow behind him. Now, already, meadows, fields, groves stretched along the shores, and peasant cottages made their appearance. It smacked of the country. He flung aside the oars, bent his head down to Mumú, who was sitting in front of him on a dry thwart,—the bottom was inundated with water,—and remained motionless, with his mighty hands crossed on her back, while the boat drifted a little backward with the current toward the town. At last Gerásim straightened up hastily, with a sort of painful wrath on his face, wound the rope around the bricks he had taken, arranged a noose, put it on Mumú's neck, lifted her over the river, for the last time gazed at her. . . . She gazed back at him confidingly and without alarm, waving her little tail slightly. He turned away, shut his eyes, and opened his hands. . . . Gerásim heard nothing, neither the swift whine of the falling Mumú, nor the loud splash of the water; for him the noisiest day was silent and speechless, as not even the quietest night is to us, and when he opened his eyes again, the little waves were hurrying down the river as before; as before they were plashing about the sides of the boat, and only far astern toward the shore certain broad circles were spreading.

MURDER AT THE DOG SHOW
(1957)
Mignon G. Eberhart

The next story is a whodunit solved by an amateur detective who happens to be a dog enthusiast. Author Mignon G. Eberhart (1899–1996),
one of the great mystery writers, has dozens of books and stories to her
credit. Her novels include *The Dark Garden* (1933), *Five Passengers
from Lisbon* (1946), *Never Look Back* (1951), *RSVP Murder* (1966), and
Three Days for Emeralds (1988).

The P.A. system warbled, Dr. Marrer—Dr. Marrem—Dr. Richard Marrrry, through the hospital corridors; I translated it to Dr. Richard Marly and went to the charge desk where I was referred to a telephone. It was Jean calling. "Richard—I was shot at just now in the park."

"That's funny. It sounded as if you said somebody shot at you."

"I did. In the park. But I think he was aiming at Skipper. I had him out for an airing. And you know the finals in the show are tonight—"

"Who shot at you?"

"I don't know. I couldn't see, there was shrubbery. I ran to the avenue, dragging Skipper, and got a taxi. I think somebody is trying to keep Skipper out of the show."

"Call the police—"

"What could I tell them?" she asked reasonably. "Richard, will you come to the show and—well, keep an eye on things? I'll leave a ticket at the box office for you."

There had been a slight coolness between us, owing to the Dog Show and to Jean's kind but firm observations that my own dog, Butch, a Kerry Blue terrier, was not likely ever to take any ribbons.

"You can get somebody else to fault him," she had said mysteriously; but in her opinion Butch's legs were too much or too little like stove pipes and his coat was too black or too blue—in short, he was not a show dog. Jean confidently expected that Skipper, the Kerry Blue she had trained, would walk away with Best in Show.

Right now I swallowed my pride and said I would be there. Jean hung up, and I finished my round of patients as hurriedly as I could and drove home.

Jean was not the type to get the wind up over nothing. On the other hand, a murderous attack on Jean—or on Skipper—seemed very unlikely.

Dogs had brought us together and had very nearly separated us. She had come to me as a patient following a battle between one of the dogs she was training and a beloved old cat; as sometimes happens with a peacemaker, Jean had received the only wounds. Perhaps I prolonged the treatment; in any event we began to see each other frequently. Her father had died when she was a child and had left Jean and her mother with little money. Jean's only talent, she told me, was a kind of understanding and love for cats, dogs, and all small creatures. As she grew older, this talent turned into a profession: she and her mother started a small kennel at their country cottage. They prospered moderately at first, and more noticeably after Jean had undertaken the training of dogs, as well as their handling in various dog shows. She had the infinite patience required and Skipper was the first dog she had trained and steered successfully through the requisite shows and ribbons to what promised to be a peak of his, and Jean's, career. If he won Best in Show tonight it would be a very bright feather in Jean's little professional cap, for the Heather Dog Show was one of the big, important shows of the year.

Skipper, I knew, belonged to a Mrs. Florrie Carrister who lived in the country near Jean and was in affluent circumstances; she was divorced from her husband Reginald Carrister, a stockbroker in the city, who had inherited a considerable fortune. Beyond that—and the fact that Jean considered Skipper a far finer dog than my own Butch—I knew nothing of Skipper, and certainly nothing that could account for anyone taking a pot shot at Jean—or at Skipper. While I could believe that rivalries in a dog show do become fervent, still I did not believe that any rival dog owner would go to such lengths.

Arriving at my apartment I told Suki, who cooks, valets, and answers the telephone for me, where I was going, patted Butch consolingly, told him he was better than any dog at the show, and departed again, this time for the Armory where the dog show was being held.

The whole vicinity of the Armory was a bedlam—taxis arriving, taxis departing, the flash of photographers' bulbs as jeweled and furred ladies and their escorts (or a dog, groomed to the last hair and led along as carefully as if it were the Bank of England on a leash) passed through the foyer. My ticket was waiting for me at the box office and I entered the Armory which I found jammed, confirming my suspicion that all the world loves a dog.

I bought a program. An usher directed me and I went upstairs and came out in a box. It was an end box, a choice one, and sparsely occupied. Two women sat in the front row talking with remarkable volubility and watching some dogs marching sedately around the ring; a man sat in the front row too but at the other end of the box, next to the wall, and leaned intently over the railing.

One of the women in the front row turned, saw me, broke off her flood of talk, and spoke to me. "Dr. Marly? I'm Mrs. Carrister. Jean asked me to leave a ticket for you." She was a large woman, with heavy shoulders that slumped down shapelessly in her seat. The woman in the aisle seat turned and she introduced us. "Miss Runcewell—Dr. Marly. You know—Jean's friend." Mrs. Carrister turned back to me. "I bought Skipper from Miss Runcewell's kennels when he was only six weeks old."

Miss Runcewell, very doggy in a tweed suit and leather hat and gloves, looked modest and Mrs. Carrister glanced back to the ring. "Oh, there's Jean!"

I sat down two rows behind them and watched Jean. She was worth watching—tall and slim and pretty with her short dark hair and level blue eyes; she was wearing a blue skirt, a neatly tailored white coat, and a red scarf, and was putting a lovely blue merle Collie through his paces deftly and precisely. But I didn't see how I was going to keep an eye on things as Jean had so confidently asked me to do. There was too much and at the same time too little to keep an eye on.

So I shifted to the dogs entering the ring and going through their prescribed routine, and decided that in the full view of so many thousands of people nothing in the way of violence was likely to happen. The two women ahead of me talked steadily—indeed, Mrs. Carrister never stopped. The man at the end of the box also watched the dogs. After the second event Miss Runcewell left the box and came back with two orange drinks, one of which she gave to Mrs. Carrister. And just before the next event a man came down the steps, took a seat in the row below and in front of me, and touched Mrs. Carrister on the shoulder. "Hello, Florrie," he said amiably.

He was handsome, as she certainly was not, in his mid-forties, and very elegantly turned out. She turned and said, "Oh, Reginald." Miss Runcewell turned and said how-do-you-do and Mrs. Carrister introduced me. "This is Dr. Marly—my former husband, Mr. Carrister."

We nodded. Mrs. Carrister said, "The Field Trials are coming up. Everything is right on time tonight because the show is on television." She turned absorbedly back to watch the ring and resume the steady talk to which Miss Runcewell contributed only rarely. Mr. Carrister folded his coat over his knees and I felt a twinge of uneasiness. Field Trials—or as the program more accurately put it, Gun Dogs in Action—that meant guns, didn't it?

Jean, however, would not be showing in the Field Trials. And, really, nothing could happen. Corn shocks and brush began to move into the ring. It was like Birnam Wood moving upon high Dunsinane Hill except that the corn shocks and brush were mounted on wood and carried by attendants who placed them at strategic intervals over the green ground-cloth. A brace of setters turned up, straining at a leash held by a man in a hunter's red shirt, a gun was fired, and the so-called "Field Trials" began. The gun shot was obviously a blank.

I leaned back and before I knew it was caught up in the color and drama and magnificent performance of the hunting dogs. Even Mrs. Carrister stopped talking and if Mr. Carrister ahead of me moved at all I was not aware of it. It was indeed so stunning a show that nobody in the box said a word when it ended.

The man at the end of the box rose and avoided Mrs. Carrister's bulk between him and the aisle by neatly stepping back over the rows of seats and out of the box. His face seemed suddenly but vaguely familiar to me, yet something about him seemed wrong and unfamiliar. His clothes? But he wore an ordinary dark coat and hat. He vanished at once, attendants appeared and cleared the ring, and I decided I must have seen him sometime, at the hospital.

The show went smoothly on and all at once I became aware of a kind of tension in the air. Mrs. Carrister seemed to have slumped down even more absorbedly in her seat, Miss Runcewell sat upright even more rigidly, and Mr. Carrister said over his shoulder, "It's coming up now. The Best in Show."

My own pulse quickened. I leaned forward to watch the dogs enter the ring which they shortly did, stepping very proudly, every one of them, and then Jean entered with Skipper. I had to admit that he was a beautiful dog, moving with incredible grace and ease, his square muzzle lifted so he could watch Jean for commands. Mr. Carrister turned briefly to me again. "It's amazing what Jean has done with that dog. A Kerry Blue is not easy to train—unless you use a two-by-four."

"You are quite mistaken," I said. "My own Kerry Blue understands everything."

He gave me an indulgent smile. "Look at Skipper stand like that! What he really wants to do is take on the lot of them and have a rousing good fight."

It is true there was a kind of quivering intensity about the Kerry Blue. It is also true that a magnificent Doberman was eyeing a Chesapeake next to him in a deeply brooding manner. Jean leaned over to make some invisible adjustment to the Kerry Blue's whiskers—and did not so much as count her fingers afterward which, in view of Skipper's extremely adequate teeth, astounded me—and the judging began with a long, slow parade around the ring. It was about then that I became aware of a curious mass murmur rising in the Armory. And then I saw it.

Now I am reliably informed that this cannot happen at any dog show; I can only say that it did happen. Another Kerry Blue, unattended by a handler, had mysteriously joined the parade and was marching jauntily along. He was perhaps darker than Skipper, perhaps not as stylish and certainly a little shaggy, but full of *joie de vivre*. I rose in sudden panic. It was my own dog—Butch!

Did he really understand everything? Was he determined to enter the show and compete with Skipper? In that dazed second it seemed possible. But then he found Jean and leaped on her with glee. Skipper rightly resented this and leaped on Butch, a liberty not wisely taken. Butch has a generous nature—until he is annoyed. In the fraction of a second wild contagion blazed around the ring. I had a flashing vision of the Doberman's handler, who imprudently clung to the Doberman's leash, being dragged across the floor. The Armory rose like a tidal wave and roared. Handlers and judges ran and shouted, whistles blew, some cops came at the double from the main entrance under the correct impression that a riot had broken out, Miss Runcewell jumped up and made for the stairs, and I ran after her.

She knew the way, so she had the best of it through passages that echoed with a truly Gargantuan dog fight to the runway that led to the ring. It was a photo finish, however, for I was frightened. While Butch is remarkably intelligent he could not have induced a taxi driver to bring him to the Armory. And his entrance at that time was not an accident. Once at the runway Miss Runcewell dove into the ring.

I was blocked by a frenzied attendant who was wielding a broom over a Coonhound's back with no perceptible effect. I felt a sharp nip on my ankle, detached a tiny pug who was merely a victim of the contagion and desisted quite amiably, and was seized by Suki, in a dashing Homburg. He also had a walking stick and a wild gleam in his eyes. "I only did what you told me to do! Somebody phoned and said you wanted me to bring Butch to this runway, at exactly this time, and just let him off the leash and—ahhh—" Then Suki dashed into the fray himself, his Oriental calm completely deserting him. His hat flew off, and with his walking stick he flailed at every moving object around him including one of the judges who forgot himself and flailed back—striking, as it happened, one of the handlers who absently struck back also, but instead got a policeman squarely on the chin. This second chain reaction might have gone on and on had not the policeman collared me but then released me with a sharp cry and turned to disengage himself from a large and determined Chow.

Suddenly, magically, people and dogs began to sort themselves out. I do not say that order was instantly restored but it is a fact that judges and handlers of dogs are made of stern stuff. Dogs began to be pulled out of the melee; a doctor and some girls in Red Cross uniform set up a hasty emergency table at the edge of the ring. Their first customer was the policeman who had collared me and he had some difficulty rolling up his trouser leg but valiantly refused to remove his trousers.

I emerged at what was still the focus of a certain amount of activity just as Suki, Jean, Miss Runcewell, and a number of other people succeeded in separating Butch and Skipper. The dogs, surprisingly, took a long look at each other and while I cannot say they exchanged a mutual wink they did look all at once mightily pleased with themselves. Jean's cheeks were pink but she gave me a reassuring wave. Somebody shouted, "Get that dog out of here," and Suki and I complied—although with some difficulty—since Butch obviously wished to remain. However, we finally got him to the runway, put his leash on him, and I told Suki to take him home. Butch gave me a deeply reproachful look but disappeared in Suki's wake and by that time—incredibly!—every dog in the ring was back at his place and looking extremely and mysteriously smug.

A loudspeaker announced in shocked tones that the judging would be resumed, and I made for Mrs. Carrister's box. Once there I paused, panted, and looked around. Little had changed in the box. Miss Runcewell was perched, also panting, on the arm of a seat in the last row. Mr. Carrister was standing, looking down at the ring. Mrs. Carrister was slumped even further down in the first row. The fourth occupant of the box had not returned. The Armory still seethed with a sort of uninhibited joy, but suddenly became quiet as the judging began once more. Jean looked up to find me and I waved encouragement—and then saw her eyes travel downward.

I moved without knowing it. Jean was still staring, her face white and fixed, when I reached Mrs. Carrister's side and saw what Jean had observed from the ring. Mrs. Carrister was still slumped down—too far down.

She was dead.

Suddenly Mr. Carrister and Miss Runcewell were beside me. We all saw the dreadful blotch of wet redness on Mrs. Carrister's white blouse, under her suit jacket. And in a moment I knew that there was nothing I could do for her. I sent Carrister for the police. Mainly, just then, I was afraid of starting a mass panic. I remember telling Miss Runcewell to shut up and that she gulped and did so. I was dimly aware that the judging was proceeding; I had a glimpse of Jean, white but controlled, taking Skipper through his paces. Then a group of policemen arrived and made a blue wall around the box.

One of them said the lady had been stabbed. They tried to find the knife and couldn't, as applause suddenly roared through the Armory, flashbulbs popped, and there was Jean taking the trophy. So Skipper had won Best in Show, Mrs. Carrister had been murdered—and I knew who had murdered her.

But I didn't know how to prove it.

Some time later the situation remained much the same and Jean and I were permitted to gather up Skipper, who was yawning almost as cavernously as the by then empty Armory, and we took a taxi to my apartment. Jean thought it was all over and told me I was wonderful—which was very nice except that the investigation had barely begun and I knew it. The police were still casting about with antennae in the hope of picking up a lead. And the police have remarkably sensitive antennae.

The knife had not been found and it was the considered opinion of a police matron who had retired briefly with Jean and Miss Runcewell, and of the sergeant who had searched me and Mr. Carrister, that none of us had it. There was some muttered talk about the angle of the knife wound from which I gathered that anyone in the box could have killed Mrs. Carrister.

Nevertheless, a few facts did emerge. No one knew, or admitted knowing, the identity of the fourth occupant of the box and all I could say was that his face had seemed familiar to me, but not his clothing—which quite comprehensibly drew skeptical looks from the police.

Mr. Carrister protested that he was on good terms with his former wife, denied killing her, but admitted frankly that he paid her an extremely large alimony. He admitted with equal frankness that he—and only he—had not left the box at any time.

Jean's story of having been shot at in the park elicited the facts that both Miss Runcewell and Mr. Carrister owned guns and that neither of them had an alibi for the time when Jean had given Skipper his run in the park—but then neither of them had a conceivable motive for taking a pot shot at Jean, or at Skipper.

I brought up the problem of Butch's little frolic in the ring and the mysterious telephone call that had led to it, but the lieutenant in charge merely gave me a long look and said something about practical jokes and that young people would be young people. Since I could not possibly prove anything at all, I repressed a desire to tell him that doctors who wish to rise in their profession do not make a hobby of provoking dog fights. It was shortly after that Jean and I were permitted—I do not say asked—to leave.

Suki had heard the news over the radio and was waiting for us, with hot milk and sandwiches for Jean and a highball which he slid into my thankful hand. There was a moment of tension when the two dogs met but now, strangely enough, they seemed to regard each other as old and tried friends. Suki's fuller report of the telephone message was not illuminating. He could not be sure whether it was a woman, or a man imitating a woman's voice. "But orders are orders, Doctor," he said. "I took Butch to the side-street entrance and then to the runway, at exactly eleven o'clock as I was told to do, and just—well, let him off the leash. Nobody stopped me. When Butch saw all those dogs—" He shrugged fatalistically.

I reflected that anyone who had a program for the show knew that the final event was scheduled for eleven—which would include some thousands of people. I did not know what to do and Jean's eyes were clearly expecting something in the nature of a full-fledged miracle. So I told Suki to get my revolver.

I felt it was rather impressive; Jean's eyes widened. But Suki said with insufferable calm that he thought I might require it and pulled it from his pocket. "Load it," I said, trying to regain lost ground.

"Oh, I've already done that, Doctor," and he put the revolver on the desk beside me.

But Jean's eyes still demanded action of some sort and indeed a few questions seemed indicated. I said, "Jean, did Mrs. Carrister ever talk of her husband?"

"Oh, yes. She talked about everything really. She talked all the time. I got so I didn't really listen. But honestly, there wasn't a thing that could be—evidence. She was on good terms with him. And with Miss Runcewell, too. They drove up to my kennels often to see how Skipper was shaping up. Mrs. Carrister had her heart set on Skipper winning. She was going to start a kennel of her own, if he won."

"Mrs. Carrister? Did her husband or Miss Runcewell know of this?"

"I don't know about her husband. But she often spoke of it to Miss Runcewell. You see, if Skipper won the big championship, he'd be—he is—a very valuable dog. The fees as sire alone would be considerable."

"So she would then be a rival—at least, a competitor—of Miss Runcewell's."

"Oh, Miss Runcewell didn't mind. I heard her say something about Mrs. Carrister taking over her kennels. So I think she intends to go out of business. I suppose she was going to sell out to Mrs. Carrister."

After a moment I said, "Did they ever ask questions about—say, me? Or Butch?"

"Oh, yes. They asked all sorts of questions. I told them about Butch and—well, that he isn't a show dog. But he is sweet." Butch heard his name and put his great head on Jean's knee with infuriating complacence. Butch is many things—but he is not sweet.

The telephone rang and I picked it up. "Doctor," said a voice with a heavy French accent. "This is Henri."

"Henri," I said, and light broke upon me. "Henri! You were in the box tonight!"

A flood of English and French burst upon my ear. "My heart, she is not so good. *Le docteur* say no excitement. *Il faut que je parts toute de suite—*"

"Why did you part—I mean, leave?"

He told me at some length. "Thank you," I said at last. "No, I'm sure the police will understand. Give me your telephone number."

He did and I hung up. Jean's eyes were round with questions. I said, "That was Henri. He is headwaiter at—" and I named a famous restaurant downtown. "Mrs. Carrister gave him a ticket to her box for the show tonight. He left after the Field Trials."

I went to my bedroom for my book of special telephone numbers. It seemed to me that there was now enough evidence on which to proceed, so I started to dial the number of a former patient of mine who is a high official in the police department when—if I may speak frankly—all hell broke loose in the front hall.

I felt for my gun, remembered that it was still on my desk, and ran for the hall amid an ear-splitting tumult of barks. Mr. Carrister was just disappearing into my study, Suki and Jean were tugging at Butch, and Miss Runcewell was efficiently scooping up Skipper's leash. Since the dogs were merely in high spirits and meant nothing really serious in the way of mayhem, we soon assembled in the study where we found Mr. Carrister crouching on top of my desk looking extremely indignant.

Miss Runcewell said, "I was worried about you, Jean. You were not at your hotel, so we thought you might be here," and she held a firm grip on Skipper's leash.

Mr. Carrister eyed Butch coldly and said, "I'll put it to you frankly, Doctor. You were in the box tonight. If you have any idea at all about the murder I want to know what it is."

"Why, certainly," I said. "I'll call the police at once and ask them to make the arrest."

His eyes bulged, Jean gave me an admiring glance, and I picked up the telephone and dialed.

"Hello—" my official friend said sleepily.

"This is Doctor Marly. You may send the police to my house to arrest the person who murdered Mrs. Carrister. . . . Yes, I have proof."

Something moved behind me. The dogs burst out in full cry, I seized my gun, and my friend on the phone cried out, "Where's the dog fight?"

"Hurry," I shouted and dropped the telephone but unfortunately dropped my gun at the same time.

Miss Runcewell was already at the front door. So it was the dogs that backed Miss Runcewell into the coat closet, assisted in a hurly-burly way by the rest of us. Suki then neatly locked the door of the closet. Mr. Carrister glanced at Butch, took to the top of the desk again, and said, "Do you mean *she* murdered Florrie? But why?"

"Because you were going to be in the box tonight and Miss Runcewell knew it. She also knew that you had an excellent reason for killing your wife."

Mr. Carrister said, "Huh?"

"It was a pattern of diversionary tactics," I explained. "Your wife appears to have been an exceedingly talkative woman." Carrister nodded unhappily. "I feel sure that Miss Runcewell was told of your expected presence in the box. Certainly at some time she was told of me and my dog. She shot at Jean—not to hurt Jean or Skipper—but merely to induce Jean to ask me to come to the Armory tonight. Then later, on the excuse of getting orange drinks, she left the box and phoned Suki, telling him to bring my dog to the Armory—"

"But he's the dog that started the fight!"

"That was exactly Miss Runcewell's intention. The police would believe that Mrs. Carrister was murdered while everyone's attention was diverted by the—er—confusion attending Butch's entrance in the ring. She saw to it that she was well away from the box during that time. You remained, as she hoped, in the box and consequently became a choice suspect. But your wife was actually murdered during the Field Trials. That's why the police could not find the knife. It was tossed down into the nearest corn shock and carried off when the attendants cleared the ring."

"But how do you know that?"

"Henri—a friend of mine—was in the box. He left after the Field Trials, stepping over the seats behind him rather than disturb Mrs. Carrister to get to the aisle. As you know, we were in an end box. He told me a short time ago that he saw that knife flung down into the corn shock."

"But *why* did she kill my wife?" said Mr. Carrister.

There was clearly only one explanation. I said, "I think you'll find that Mrs. Carrister has loaned Miss Runcewell enough money to keep her kennels going. Possibly the understanding was supposed to be a friendly one and Miss Runcewell did not, in writing, use her kennels as collateral. But Mrs. Carrister was intending to take over Miss Runcewell's kennels and means of livelihood—and Miss Runcewell knew that. She kept up a pretense of friendliness, until the time came when Mrs. Carrister decided to act. Then Miss Runcewell acted first."

Jean linked her arm in mine. "But, Richard, I know that you knew who killed her even *before* Henri phoned! How did you know?"

"Oh," I said. "That. Well—it was during the Field Trials that *both women stopped talking*—Mrs. Carrister for an obvious reason, Miss Runcewell because she knew Mrs. Carrister was dead."

That night Mr. Carrister, handsomely in one way but regrettably in another, presented Skipper to Jean.

After he had gone Jean looked thoughtfully at the two dogs. "They do seem friendly," she said.

Friendly, yes. But two Kerry Blues in the same household? "Butch," I said finally, "may not be a show dog but—"

"But he's your dog," Jean smiled, "and he *is* sweet."

GARM: A HOSTAGE
(1909)
Rudyard Kipling

In 1907, Rudyard Kipling (1865–1936), while barely in his forties, became the first English writer to win the Nobel Prize for literature. Kipling wrote extensively about the countries that formed part of the former British Empire. His best known books are today viewed as classics: *The Jungle Books* (1894–1895), *Captains Courageous* (1897), and *Kim* (1901). The story below is vintage Kipling; it takes place in India, known then as the "Jewel in the Crown," and involves a fabulous bulldog who longs for his master, a British soldier.

One night, a very long time ago, I drove to an Indian military encampment called Mian Mir to see amateur theatricals. At the back of the Infantry barracks a soldier, his cap over one eye, rushed in front of the horses and shouted that he was a dangerous highway robber. As a matter of fact, he was a friend of mine, so I told him to go home before any one caught him; but he fell under the pole, and I heard voices of a military guard in search of some one.

The driver and I coaxed him into the carriage, drove home swiftly, undressed him and put him to bed, where he waked next morning with a sore headache, very much ashamed. When his uniform was cleaned and dried, and he had been shaved and washed and made neat, I drove him back to barracks with his arm in a fine white sling, and reported that I had accidentally run over him. I did not tell this story to my friend's sergeant, who was a hostile and unbelieving person, but to his lieutenant, who did not know us quite so well.

Three days later my friend came to call, and at his heels slobbered and fawned one of the finest bull-terriers—of the old-fashioned breed, two parts bull and one terrier—that I had ever set eyes on. He was pure white, with a fawn-colored saddle just behind his neck, and a fawn diamond at the root of his thin whippy tail. I had admired him distantly for more than a year; and Vixen, my own fox-terrier, knew him too, but did not approve.

" 'E's for you," said my friend; but he did not look as though he liked parting with him.

"Nonsense! That dog's worth more than most men, Stanley," I said.

" 'E's that and more. 'Tention!"

The dog rose on his hind legs, and stood upright for a full minute.

"Eyes right!"

He sat on his haunches and turned his head sharp to the right. At a sign he rose and barked twice. Then he shook hands with his right paw and bounded lightly to my shoulder. Here he made himself into a necktie, limp and lifeless, hanging down on either side of my neck. I was told to pick him up and throw him in the air. He fell with a howl and held up one leg.

"Part 'o the trick," said his owner. "You're going to die now. Dig yourself your little grave an' shut your little eye."

Still limping, the dog hobbled to the garden edge, dug a hole and lay down in it. When told that he was cured, he jumped out, wagging his tail, and whining for applause. He was put through half a dozen other tricks, such as showing how he would hold a man safe (I was that man, and he sat down before me, his teeth bared, ready to spring), and how he would stop eating at the word of command. I had no more than finished praising him when my friend made a gesture that stopped the dog as though he had been shot, took a piece of blue-ruled canteen-paper from his helmet, handed it to me and ran away, while the dog looked after him and howled. I read:

Sir—I give you the dog because of what you got me out of. He is the best I know, for I made him myself, and he is as good as a man. Please do not give him too much to eat, and please do not give him back to me, for I'm not going to take him, if you will keep him. So please do not try to give him back any more. I have kept his name back, so you can call him anything and he will answer, but please do not give him back. He can kill a man as easy as anything, but please do not give him too much meat. He knows more than a man.

Vixen sympathetically joined her shrill little yap to the bull-terrier's despairing cry, and I was annoyed, for I knew that a man who cares for dogs is one thing, but a man who loves one dog is quite another. Dogs are at the best no more than verminous vagrants, self-scratchers, foul feeders, and unclean by the law of Moses and Mohammed; but a dog with whom one lives alone for at least six months in the year; a free thing, tied to you so strictly by love that without you he will not stir or exercise; a patient, temperate, humorous, wise soul, who knows your moods before you know them yourself, is not a dog under any ruling.

I had Vixen, who was all my dog to me; and I felt what my friend must have felt, at tearing out his heart in this style and leaving it in my garden.

However, the dog understood clearly enough that I was his master, and did not follow the soldier. As soon as he drew breath I made much of him, and Vixen, yelling with jealousy, flew at him. Had she been of his own sex, he might have cheered himself with a fight, but he only looked worriedly when she nipped his deep iron sides, laid his heavy head on my knee, and howled anew. I meant to dine at the Club that night, but as darkness drew in, and the dog snuffed through the empty house like a child trying to recover from a fit of sobbing, I felt that I could not leave him to suffer his first evening alone. So we fed at home, Vixen on one side, and the stranger-dog on the other; she watching his every mouthful, and saying explicitly what she thought of his table manners, which were much better than hers.

It was Vixen's custom, till the weather grew hot, to sleep in my bed, her head on the pillow like a Christian; and when morning came I would always find that the little thing had braced her feet against the wall and pushed me to the very edge of the cot. This night she hurried to bed purposefully, every hair up, one eye on the stranger, who had dropped on a mat in a helpless, hopeless sort of way, all four feet spread out, sighing heavily. She settled her head on the pillow several times, to show her little airs and graces, and struck up her usual whiney sing-song before slumber. The stranger-dog softly edged towards me. I put out my hand and he licked it. Instantly my wrist was between Vixen's teeth, and her warning *aaarh!* said as plainly as speech, that if I took any further notice of the stranger she would bite.

I caught her behind the fat neck with my left hand, shook her severely, and said:

"Vixen, if you do that again you'll be put into the veranda. Now, remember!"

She understood perfectly, but the minute I released her she mouthed my right wrist once more, and waited with her ears back and all her body flattened, ready to bite. The big dog's tail thumped the floor in a humble and peace-making way.

I grabbed Vixen a second time, lifted her out of bed like a rabbit (she hated that and yelled), and, as I had promised, set her out in the veranda with the bats and the moonlight. At this she howled. Then she used coarse language—not to me, but to the bull-terrier—till she coughed with exhaustion. Then she ran around the house trying every door. Then she went off to the stables and barked as though some one were stealing the horses, which was an old trick of hers. Last she returned, and her snuffing yelp said, "I'll be good! Let me in and I'll be good!"

She was admitted and flew to her pillow. When she was quieted I whispered to the other dog, "You can lie on the foot of the bed." The bull jumped up at once, and though I felt Vixen quiver with rage, she knew better than to protest. So we slept till the morning, and they had early breakfast with me, bite for bite, till the horse came round and we went for a ride. I don't think the bull had ever followed a horse before. He was wild with excitement, and Vixen, as usual, squealed and scuttered and scooted, and took charge of the procession.

There was one corner of a village near by, which we generally pass with caution, because all the yellow pariah-dogs of the place gathered about it. They were half-wild, starving beasts, and though utter cowards, yet where nine or ten of them get together they will mob and kill and eat an English dog. I kept a whip with a long lash for them. That morning they attacked Vixen, who, perhaps of design, had moved from beyond my horse's shadow.

The bull was ploughing along in the dust, fifty yards behind, rolling in his run, and smiling as bull terriers will. I heard Vixen squeal; half a dozen of the curs closed in on her; a white streak came up behind me; a cloud of dust rose near Vixen, and, when it cleared, I saw one tall pariah with his back broken, and the bull wrenching another to earth. Vixen retreated to the protection of my whip, and the bull padded back smiling more than ever, covered with the blood of his enemies. That decided me to call him "Garm of the Bloody Breast," who was a great person in his time, or "Garm" for short; so, leaning forward, I told him what his temporary name would be. He looked up while I repeated it, and then raced away. I shouted "Garm!" He stopped, raced back, and came up to ask my will.

Then I saw that my soldier friend was right, and that that dog knew and was worth more than a man. At the end of the ridge I gave an order which Vixen knew and hated: "Go away and get washed!" I said. Garm understood some part of it, and Vixen interpreted the rest, and the two trotted off together soberly. When I went to the back veranda Vixen had been washed snowy-white, and was very proud of herself, but the dog-boy would not touch Garm on any account unless I stood by. So I waited while he was being scrubbed, and Garm, with the soap creaming on the top of his broad head, looked at me to make sure that this was what I expected him to endure. He knew perfectly that the dog-boy was only obeying orders.

"Another time," I said to the dog-boy, "you will wash the great dog with Vixen when I send them home."

"Does *he* know?" said the dog-boy, who understood the ways of dogs.

"Garm," I said, "another time you will be washed with Vixen."

I knew that Garm understood. Indeed, next washing-day, when Vixen as usual fled under my bed, Garm stared at the doubtful dog-boy in the veranda, stalked to the place where he had been washed last time, and stood rigid in the tub.

But the long days in my office tried him sorely. We three would drive off in the morning at half-past eight and come home at six or later. Vixen, knowing the routine of it, went to sleep under my table; but the confinement ate into Garm's soul. He generally sat on the veranda looking out on the Mall; and well I knew what he expected.

Sometimes a company of soldiers would move along on their way to the Fort, and Garm rolled forth to inspect them; or an officer in uniform entered into the office, and it was pitiful to see poor Garm's welcome to the cloth—not the man. He would leap at him, and sniff and bark joyously, then run to the door and back again. One afternoon I heard him bay with a full throat—a thing I had never heard before—and he disappeared. When I drove into my garden at the end of the day a soldier in white uniform scrambled over the wall at the far end, and the Garm that met me was a joyous dog. This happened twice or thrice a week for a month.

I pretended not to notice, but Garm knew and Vixen knew. He would glide homewards from the office about four o'clock, as though he were only going to look at the scenery, and this he did so quietly that but for Vixen I should not have noticed him. The jealous little dog under the table would give a sniff and a snort, just loud enough to call my attention to the flight. Garm might go out forty times in the day and Vixen would never stir, but when he slunk off to see his true master in my garden she told me in her own tongue. That was the one sign she made to prove that Garm did not altogether belong to the family. They were the best of friends at all times, *but*, Vixen explained that I was never to forget Garm did not love me as she loved me.

I never expected it. The dog was not my dog—could never be my dog—and I knew he was as miserable as his master who tramped eight miles a day to see him. So it seemed to me that the sooner the two were reunited the better for all. One afternoon I sent Vixen home alone in the dog-cart (Garm had gone before), and rode over to cantonments to find another friend of mine, who was an Irish soldier and a great friend of the dog's master.

I explained the whole case, and wound up with:

"And now Stanley's in my garden crying over his dog. Why doesn't he take him back? They're both unhappy."

"Unhappy! There's no sense in the little man any more. But 'tis his fit."

"What *is* his fit? He travels fifty miles a week to see the brute, and he pretends not to notice me when he sees me on the road; and I'm as unhappy as he is. Make him take the dog back."

"It's his penance he's set himself. I told him by way of a joke, afther you'd run over him so convenient that night, whin he was drunk—I said if he was a Catholic he'd do penance. Off he went wid that fit in his little head *an'* a dose of fever, an' nothin' would suit but givin' you the dog as a hostage."

"Hostage for what? I don't want hostages from Stanley."

"For his good behaviour? He's keepin' straight now, the way it's no pleasure to associate wid him."

"Has he taken the pledge?"

"If 'twas only that I need not care. Ye can take the pledge for three months on an' off. He sez he'll never see the dog again, an' *so* mark you, he'll keep straight for evermore. Ye know his fits? Well, this is wan of them. How's the dog takin' it?"

"Like a man. He's the best dog in India. Can't you make Stanley take him back?"

"I can do no more than I have done. But ye know his fits. He's just doin' his penance. What will he do when he goes to the Hills? The docthor's put him on the list."

It is the custom in India to send a certain number of invalids from each regiment up to stations in the Himalayas for the hot weather; and though the men ought to enjoy the cool and the comfort, they miss the society of the barracks down below, and do their best to come back or to avoid going. I felt that this move would bring matters to a head, so I left Terrence hopefully, though he called after me:

"He won't take the dog, sorr. You can lay your month's pay on that. Ye know his fits."

I never pretended to understand Private Ortheris; and so I did the next best thing—I left him alone.

That summer the invalids of the regiment to which my friend belonged were ordered off to the Hills early, because the doctors thought marching in the cool of the day would do them good. Their route lay south to a place called Umballa, a hundred and twenty miles or more. Then they would turn eats and march up into the Hills to Kasauli or Dugshai or Subathoo. I dined with the officers the night before they left—they were marching at five in the morning. It was midnight when I drove into my garden, and surprised a white figure flying over the wall.

"That man," said my butler, "has been here since nine, making talk to the dog. He is quite mad. I did not tell him to go away because he has been here many times before, and because the dog-boy told me that if I told him to go away, that great dog would immediately slay me. He did not wish to speak to the Protector of the Poor, and he did not ask for anything to eat or drink."

"Kadir Buksh," said I, "that was well done, for the dog would surely have killed thee. But I do not think the white soldier will come any more."

Garm slept ill that night and whimpered in his dreams. Once he sprang up with a clear, ringing bark, and I heard him wag his tail till it waked him and the bark died out in a howl. He had dreamed he was with his master again, and I nearly cried. It was all Stanley's silly fault.

The first halt which the detachment of invalids made was some miles from their barracks, on the Amritsar road, and ten miles distant from my house. By a mere chance one of the officers drove back for another good dinner at the Club (cooking on the line of march is always bad), and there we met. He was a particular friend of mine, and I knew that he knew how to love a dog properly. His pet was a big retriever who was going up to the Hills for his health, and, though it was still April, the round, brown brute puffed and panted in the Club veranda as though he would burst.

"It's amazing," said the officer, "what excuses these invalids of mine make to get back to barracks. There's a man in my company now asked me for leave to go back to cantonments to pay a debt he'd forgotten. I was so taken by the idea I let him go, and he jingled off in an *ekka* as pleased as Punch. Ten miles to pay a debt! Wonder what it was really?"

"If you'll drive me home I think I can show you," I said.

So he went over to my house in his dog-cart with the retriever; and on the way I told him the story of Garm.

"I was wondering where that brute had gone to. He's the best dog in the regiment," said my friend. "I offered the little fellow twenty rupees for him a month ago. But he's a hostage, you say, for Stanley's good conduct. Stanley's one of the best men I have—when he chooses."

"That's the reason why," I said. "A second-rate man wouldn't have taken things to heart as he has done."

We drove in quietly at the far end of the garden, and crept round the house. There was a place close to the wall all grown about with tamarisk trees, where I knew Garm kept his bones. Even Vixen was not allowed to sit near it. In the full Indian moonlight I could see a white uniform bending over the dog.

"Good-bye, old man," we could not help hearing Stanley's voice. "For 'Eving's sake don't get bit and go mad by any measley pi-dog. But you can look after yourself, old man. *You* don't get drunk an' run about 'ittin' your friends. You takes your bones an' eats your biscuit, an' kills your enemy like a gentleman. I'm goin' away—don't 'owl—I'm goin' off to Kasauli, where I won't see you no more."

I could hear him holding Garm's nose as the dog drew it up to the stars.

"You'll stay here an' be'ave, an'—an' I'll go away an' try to be'ave, an' I don't know 'ow to leave you. I don't think—"

"I think this is damn silly," said the officer, patting his foolish fubsy old retriever. He called to the private who leaped to his feet, marched forward, and saluted.

"You here?" said the officer, turning away his head.

"Yes, sir, but I'm just goin' back."

"I shall be leaving here at eleven in my cart. You come with me. I can't have sick men running about all over the place. Report yourself at eleven, *here.*"

We did not say much when we went indoors, but the officer muttered and pulled his retriever's ears.

He was a disgraceful, overfed doormat of a dog; and when he waddled off to my cookhouse to be fed, I had a brilliant idea.

At eleven o'clock that officer's dog was nowhere to be found, and you never heard such a fuss as his owner made. He called and shouted and grew angry, and hunted through my garden for half an hour.

Then I said:

"He's sure to turn up in the morning. Send a man in by rail, and I'll find the beast and return him."

"Beast?" said the officer. "I value that dog considerably more than I value any man I know. It's all very fine for you to talk—your dog's here."

So she was—under my feet—and, had she been missing, food and wages would have stopped in my house till her return. But some people grow fond of dogs not worth a cut of the whip. My friend had to drive away at last with Stanley in the back seat; and then the dog-boy said to me:

"What kind of animal is Bullen Sahib's dog? Look at him!"

I went to the boy's hut, and the fat old reprobate was lying on a mat carefully chained up. He must have heard his master calling for twenty minutes, but had not even attempted to join him.

"He has no face," said the dog-boy scornfully. "He is a *punniar-kooter* [a spaniel]. He never tried to get that cloth off his jaws when his master called. Now Vixen-baba would have jumped through the window, and that Great Dog would have slain me with his muzzled mouth. It is true that there are many kinds of dogs."

Next evening who should turn up but Stanley. The officer had sent him back fourteen miles by rail with a note begging me to return the retriever if I had found him, and, if I had not, to offer huge rewards. The last train to camp left at half-past ten, and Stanley stayed till ten talking to Garm. I argued and entreated, and even threatened to shoot the bull-terrier, but the little man was firm as a rock, though I gave him a good dinner and talked to him most severely. Garm knew as well as I that this was the last time he could hope to see his man, and followed Stanley like a shadow. The retriever said nothing, but licked his lips after his meal and waddled off without so much as saying "Thank you" to the disgusted dog-boy.

So that last meeting was over, and I felt as wretched as Garm, who moaned in his sleep all night. When we went to the office he found a place under the table close to Vixen, and dropped flat till it was time to go home. There was no more running out into the verandas, no slinking away for stolen talks with Stanley. As the weather grew warmer the dogs were forbidden to run beside the cart, but sat at my side on the seat. Vixen with her head under the crook of my left elbow, and Garm hugging the left handrail.

Here Vixen was ever in great form. She had to attend to all the moving traffic, such as bullock-carts that blocked the way, and camels, and led ponies; as well as to keep up her dignity when she passed low friends running in the dust. She never yapped for yapping's sake, but her shrill, high bark was known all along the Mall, and other men's terriers ki-yied in reply, and bullock-drivers looked over their shoulders and gave us the road with a grin.

But Garm cared for none of these things. His big eyes were on the horizon and his terrible mouth was shut. There was another dog in the office who belonged to my chief. We called him "Bob the Librarian," because he always imagined vain rats behind the bookshelves, and in hunting for them would drag out half the old newspaper-files. Bob was a well-meaning idiot, but Garm did not encourage him. He would slide his head round the door panting, "Rats! Come along, Garm!" and Garm would shift one forepaw over the other, and curl himself round, leaving Bob to whine at a most uninterested back. The office was nearly as cheerful as a tomb in those days.

Once, and only once, did I see Garm at all contented with his surroundings. He had gone for an unauthorized walk with Vixen early one Sunday morning, and a very young and foolish artilleryman (his battery had just moved to that part of the world) tried to steal both. Vixen, of course, knew better than to take food from soldiers, and, besides, she had just finished her breakfast. So she trotted back with a large piece of the mutton that they issue to our troops, laid it down on my veranda, and looked up to see what I thought. I asked her where Garm was, and she ran in front of the house to show me the way.

About a mile up the road we came across our artilleryman sitting very stiffly on the edge of a culvert with a greasy handkerchief on his knees. Garm was in front of him, looking rather pleased. When the man moved leg or hand, Garm bared his teeth in silence. A broken string hung from his collar, and the other half of it lay, all warm, in the artilleryman's still hand. He explained to me, keeping his eye straight in front of him, that he had met this dog (he called him awful names) walking alone, and was going to take him to the Fort to be killed for a masterless pariah.

I said that Garm did not seem to me much of a pariah, but that he had better take him to the Fort if he thought best. He said he did not care to do so. I told him to go to the Fort alone. He said he did not want to go at that hour, but would follow my advice as soon as I had called off the dog. I instructed Garm to take him to the Fort, and Garm marched him solemnly up to the gate, one mile and a half under a hot sun, and I told the quarter-guard what had happened; but the young artilleryman was more angry than was at all necessary when they began to laugh. Several regiments, he was told, had tried to steal Garm in their time.

That month the hot weather shut down in earnest, and the dogs slept in the bathroom on the cool wet bricks where the bath is placed. Every morning, as soon as the man filled my bath, the two jumped in, and every morning the man filled the bath a second time. I said to him that he might as well fill a small tub especially for the dogs. "Nay," said he smiling, "it is not their custom. They would not understand. Besides, the big bath gives them more space."

The punkah-coolies who pull the punkahs day and night came to know Garm intimately. He noticed that when the swaying fan stopped I would call out to the coolie and bid him pull with a long stroke. If the man still slept I would wake him up. He discovered, too, that it was a good thing to lie in the wave of air under the punkah. Maybe Stanley had taught him all about this in barracks. At any rate, when the punkah stopped, Garm would first growl and cock his eye at the rope, and if that did not wake the man—it nearly always did—he would tiptoe forth and talk in the sleeper's ear. Vixen was a clever little dog, but she could never connect the punkah and the coolie; so Garm gave me grateful hours of cool sleep. But he was utterly wretched—as miserable as a human being; and in his misery he clung so close to me that other men noticed it, and were envious. If I moved from one room to another Garm followed; if my pen stopped scratching, Garm's head was thrust into my hand; if I turned, half awake, on the pillow, Garm was up at my side, for he knew that I was his only link with his master, and day and night, and night and day, his eyes asked one question—"When is this going to end?"

Living with the dog as I did, I never noticed that he was more than ordinarily upset by the hot weather, till one day at the Club a man said: "That dog of yours will die in a week or two. He's a shadow." Then I dosed Garm with iron and quinine, which he hated; and I felt very anxious. He lost his appetite, and Vixen was allowed to eat his dinner under his eyes. Even that did not make him swallow, and we held a consultation on him, of the best man-doctor in the place; a lady-doctor, who had cured the sick wives of kings; and the Deputy Inspector-General of the veterinary service of all India. They pronounced upon his symptoms, and I told them his story, and Garm lay on a sofa licking my hand.

"He's dying of a broken heart," said the lady-doctor suddenly.

"'Pon my word," said the Deputy Inspector-General, "I believe Mrs. Macrae is perfectly right—as usual."

The best man-doctor in the place wrote a prescription, and the veterinary Deputy Inspector-General went over it afterwards to be sure that the drugs were in the proper dog-proportions; and that was the first time in his life that our doctor ever allowed his prescriptions to be edited. It was a strong tonic, and it put the dear boy on his feet for a week or two; then he lost flesh again. I asked a man I knew to take him up to the Hills with him when he went, and the man came to the door with his kit packed on the top of the carriage. Garm took in the situation at one red glance. The hair rose along his back; he sat down in front of me, and delivered the most awful growl I have ever heard in the jaws of a dog. I shouted to my friend to get away at once, and as soon as the carriage was out of the garden Garm laid his head on my knee and whined. So I knew his answer, and devoted myself to getting Stanley's address in the Hills.

My turn to go to the cool came late in August. We were allowed thirty days' holiday in a year, if no one fell sick, and we took it as we could be spared. My chief and Bob the Librarian had their holiday first, and when they were gone I made a calendar, as I always did, and hung it up at the head of my cot, tearing off one day at a time till they returned. Vixen had gone up to the Hills with me five times before; and she appreciated the cold and the damp and the beautiful wood fires there as much as I did.

"Garm," I said, "we are going back to Stanley at Kasauli. Kasauli—Stanley; Stanley—Kasauli." And I repeated it twenty times. It was not Kasauli really, but another place. Still I remembered what Stanley had said in my garden on the last night, and I dared not change the name. Then Garm began to tremble; then he barked; and then he leaped up at me, frisking and wagging his tail.

"Not now," I said, holding up my hand. 'When I say 'Go,' we'll go, Garm." I pulled out the little blanket coat and spiked collar that Vixen always wore up in the Hills to protect her against sudden chills and thieving leopards, and I let the two smell them and talk it over. What they said of course I do not know, but it made a new dog of Garm. His eyes were bright; and he barked joyfully when I spoke to him. He ate his food, and he killed his rats for the next three weeks, and when he began to whine I had only to say "Stanley—Kasauli; Kasauli—Stanley," to wake him up. I wish I had thought of it before.

My chief came back, all brown with living in the open air, and very angry at finding it so hot in the Plains. That same afternoon we three and Kadir Buksh began to pack for our month's holiday, Vixen rolling in and out of the bullock-trunk twenty times a minute, and Garm grinning all over and thumping on the floor with his tail. Vixen knew the routine of travelling as well as she knew my office-work. She went to the station, singing songs, on the front seat of the carriage, while Garm sat with me. She hurried into the railway carriage, saw Kadir Buksh make up my bed for the night, got her drink of water, and curled up with her black-patch eye on the tumult of the platform. Garm followed her (the crowd gave him a lane all to himself) and sat down on the pillows with his eyes blazing, and his tail a haze behind him.

We came to Umballa in the hot misty dawn, four or five men, who had been working hard for eleven months, shouting for our dâks—the two-horse travelling carriages that were to take us up to Kalka at the foot of the Hills. It was all new to Garm. He did not understand carriages where you lay at full length on your bedding, but Vixen knew and hopped into her place at once; Garm following. The Kalka road, before the railway was built, was about forty-seven miles long, and the horses were changed every eight miles. Most of them jibbed, and kicked, and plunged, but they had to go, and they went rather better than usual for Garm's deep bay in their rear.

There was a river to be forded, and four bullocks pulled the carriage, and Vixen stuck her head out of the sliding-door and nearly fell into the water while she gave directions. Garm was silent and curious, and rather needed reassuring about Stanley and Kasauli. So we rolled, barking and yelping, into Kalka for lunch, and Garm ate enough for two.

After Kalka the road wound among the Hills, and we took a curricle with half-broken ponies, which were changed every six miles. No one dreamed of a railroad to Simla in those days, for it was seven thousand feet up in the air. The road was more than fifty miles long, and the regulation pace was just as fast as the ponies could go. Here, again, Vixen led Garm from one carriage to the other; jumped into the back seat and shouted. A cool breath from the snows met us about five miles out of Kalka, and she whined for her coat, wisely fearing a chill on the liver. I had had one made for Garm too, and, as we climbed to the fresh breezes, I put it on, and Garm chewed it uncomprehendingly, but I think he was grateful.

"Hi-yi-yi-yi!" sang Vixen as we shot around the curves; "Toot-toot-toot!" went the driver's bugle at the dangerous places, and "Yow! Yow! Yow! Yow!" bayed Garm. Kadir Buksh sat on the front seat and smiled. Even he was glad to get away from the heat of the Plains that stewed in the haze behind us. Now and then we would meet a man we knew going down to his work again, and he would say: "What's it like below?" and I would shout: "Hotter than cinders. What's is like above?" and he would shout back: "Just perfect!" and away we would go.

Suddenly Kadir Buksh said, over his shoulder: "Here is Solon;" and Garm snored where he lay with his head on my knee. Solon is an unpleasant little cantonment, but it has the advantage of being cool and healthy. It is all bare and windy, and one generally stops at a rest-house near by for something to eat. I got out and took both dogs with me, while Kadir Buksh made tea. A soldier told us we should find Stanley "out there," nodding his head towards a bare, bleak hill.

When we climbed to the top we spied that very Stanley, who had given me all this trouble, sitting on a rock with his face in his hands, and his overcoat hanging loose about him. I never saw anything so lonely and dejected in my life as this one little man, crumpled up and thinking, on the great gray hillside.

Here Garm left me.

He departed without a word, and, so far as I could see, without moving his legs. He flew through the air bodily, and I heard the whack of him as he flung himself at Stanley, knocking the little man clean over. They rolled on the ground together, shouting, and yelping, and hugging. I could not see which was dog and which was man, till Stanley got up and whimpered.

He told me that he had been suffering from fever at intervals, and was very weak. He looked all he said, but even while I watched, both man and dog plumped out to their natural sizes, precisely as dried apples swell in water. Garm was on his shoulder, and his breast and feet all at the same time, so that Stanley spoke all through a cloud of Garm—gulping, sobbing, slavering Garm. He did not say anything that I could understand, except that he had fancied he was going to die, but now he was quite well, and that he was not going to give up Garm any more to anybody under the rank of Beelzebub.

Then he said he felt hungry, and thirsty, and happy.

We went down to tea at the rest-house, where Stanley stuffed himself with sardines and raspberry jam, and beer, and cold mutton and pickles, when Garm wasn't climbing over him; and then Vixen and I went on.

Garm saw how it was at once. He said good-bye to me three times, giving me both paws one after another, and leaping on to my shoulder. He further escorted us, singing Hosannas at the top of his voice, a mile down the road. Then he raced back to his own master.

Vixen never opened her mouth, but when the cold twilight came, and we could see the lights of Simla across the hills, she snuffled with her nose at the breast of my ulster. I unbuttoned it, and tucked her inside. Then she gave a contented little sniff, and fell fast asleep, her head on my breast, till we bundled out of Simla, two of the four happiest people in all the world that night.

THE COWARD
(1922)
Albert Payson Terhune

This is the second story in the book by Albert Payson Terhune, the master of the dog story genre. Terhune began writing during his junior year at Columbia University and went on to work for twenty-two years as a writer for the New York *Evening World*. He also raised champion collies at Sunnybank, his estate located about twenty miles from Newark, New Jersey. See if you don't agree that "The Coward" is one of the best dog stories.

It began when Laund was a rangily gawky six-month puppy and when Danny Crae was only seven years old. Danny had claimed the spraddling little fluffball of a collie as his own, on the day the boy's father lifted the two-month-old puppy out of the yard where Laund lived and played and slept and had a wonderful time with his several brothers and sisters.

On that morning Ronald Crae ordained that the brown-and-white baby collie was to become a herder of sheep and a guard of the house and farm. On that morning, seven-year-old Danny announced that Laund was to be his very own dog and help him herd his adored bantams.

Now, Ronald Crae was not given to knuckling under to anyone. But he had a strangely gentle way with him as concerned this crippled son of his. Therefore, instead of the sharp rebuke Danny had a right to expect for putting his own wishes against his sire's, Ronald petted the wan little face and told Danny jokingly that they would share Laund in partnership. Part of the time the puppy should herd the Crae sheep and do other farmwork. Part of the time he should be Danny's playfellow. And so it was arranged.

A year earlier, a fearsome pestilence had scourged America, sending black horror to the hearts of ten million mothers throughout the land and claiming thousands of little children as its victims. Danny Crae had but been brushed lightly by the hem of the pestilence's robe. He did not die, as did so many children in his own township. But he rose from a three-month illness with useless legs that would not move or bear a fraction of his frail weight.

Quickly he learned to make his way around, after a fashion, by means of double crutches. But every doctor declared he must be a hopeless and half-helpless cripple for life.

Small wonder his usually dominant father did not veto any plan of his stricken child's! Small wonder he skimped the hours of herd-training for Laund, in order to leave the puppy free to be the playmate of the sick boy!

In spite of this handicap, young Laund picked up the rudiments and then the finer points of his herding work with an almost bewildering swiftness and accuracy. Ronald Crae was an excellent trainer, to be sure; firm and self-controlled and commonsensible, if a trifle stern with his dogs; and a born dogman. But the bulk of the credit went to the puppy himself. He was one of those not wholly rare collies that pick up their work as though they had known it all before and were remembering rather than learning.

Crae was proud of the little dog. Presently he began to plan entering him sometime in the yearly field trials of the National Collie Association, confident that Laund would be nearer the front than the rear of that stiff competition.

Then, when the puppy was six months old, Crae changed his opinion of the promising youngster—changed it sharply and disgustedly. It happened in this wise:

Of old, Danny had rejoiced to go afield with his father and to watch the rounding up and driving and folding and penning of the farm's sheep. Now that he was able to move only a little way and on slow crutches, the child transferred his attention to a flock of pedigreed bantams which his father had bought him and which were the boy's chief delight.

Like Ronald, he had a way with dumb things. The tame bantams let him handle them at will. They ate from his wizened fingers and lighted on his meagerly narrow and uneven shoulders for food. Then it occurred to him to teach Laund to herd and drive them. Luckily for his plan and for the safety and continued tameness of the little flock of chickens, Laund was as gentle with them as with the youngest of his master's lambs. Gravely and tenderly he would herd them, at Danny's shrill order, avoiding stepping on any of them or frightening them.

It was a pretty sight. Watching it, and Danny's delight in the simple maneuvers, Ronald forgot his own annoyance in having to share a valuable puppy's valuable training-time with his son.

One day Danny and Laund sat side by side on a rock, back of the barnyard, watching the bantams scramble for handfuls of thrown feed. Among the flock was a tiny mother hen with a half dozen downily diminutive chicks. Anxiously she clucked to them as she grabbed morsel after morsel of the feast, and tried to shove the other bantams aside to give place to her babies where the feed was thickest.

As the last of the flung grain was gobbled, the flock dispersed. Most of them drifted to the barnyard. The mother hen and her chicks strayed out toward the truck garden, some fifty feet in front of where the boy and the dog were sitting.

Of a sudden the tiny mother crouched, with a raucously crooning cry to her children, spreading her wings for them to hide under. As they ran to her, a dark shadow swept the sunlit earth. Down from nowhere a huge henhawk shot, like a brown feathery cannon ball; diving at the baby bantams and at their frightened dam.

"Laund!" squealed Danny, pointing to the chicks.

The six-month puppy leaped to them. He had no idea why he was sent thither or what he was supposed to do. He did not see the swooping hawk. Never had he even seen a hawk before, though hawks were plentiful enough in that mountain region. But he noted the flustered excitement of the hen and the scurrying of the golden mites toward her and the alarm in Danny's loved voice. Wherefore he bounded alertly into the arena—to do he knew not what.

As a matter of fact, there was nothing for him to do. As he reached the hen, something dark and terrible clove its way downward, so close to him that the air of it fanned his ruff.

A chick was seized and the hawk beat its way upward.

Instinctively, Laund sprang at the bird, before its mighty pinions could lift it clear of the earth. He leaped upon it right valorously and dug his half-developed teeth into its shoulder.

Then, all the skies seemed to be falling, and smiting Laund as they fell.

A handful of feathers came away in his mouth; as the hawk dropped the mangled chick and wheeled about on the half-grown puppy that had pinched its shoulder.

The drivingly powerful wings lambasted him with fearful force and precision, knocking him off his feet, beating the breath out of him, half-blinding him. The hooked beak rove a knife-gash along his side. The talons sank momentarily, but deep, into the tender flesh of his underbody.

It was not a fight. It was a massacre. Laund had not time to collect his faculties nor even to note clearly what manner of monster this was. All he knew was that a creature had swept down from the sky, preceded by a blotty black shadow, and was wellnigh murdering him.

In a second it was over. Even as Danny yelled to the bird and as he gathered his crutches under him to struggle to his feet, the giant hawk had lurched away from the screeching and rolling puppy; had snatched up the dead chick, and was beating its way skyward.

That was all. On the recently placid sunlit sward, below, a frantically squawking hen ran to and fro amid five piping and scurrying chicks; and a brown collie wallowed about, waking the echoes with his terror yelps.

In all his six months of life Laund had known no cruelty, no pain, no ill-treatment. He had learned to herd sheep, as a pastime to himself. He had not dreamed there could be agony and danger in the fulfilling of any of his farm duties.

Now, while still he was scarcely more than a baby—while his milk teeth were still shedding—before his collie character could knit to courage and tense fortitude—he had been frightened out of his young wits and had been cruelly hurt and battered about; all by this mysterious and shadow-casting monster from the sky.

Through his howling he was peering upward in shuddering dread at the slowly receding giant hawk. Its blackness against the sun, its sinister sweep of pinion, its soaring motion, all stamped themselves indelibly on the puppy's shocked brain. More—the taste of its feathers was in his mouth. Its rank scent was strong in his nostrils. Dogs record impressions by odor even more than by sight. That hawk-reek was never to leave Laund's memory.

The pup's wails, and Danny's, brought the household thither on the run. Laund was soothed and his hurts and bruises were tended, while Danny's own excitement was gently calmed. The doctors had said the little cripple must not be allowed to excite himself, and that any strong emotion was bad for his twisted nerves.

In a few days Laund was well again, his flesh wounds healing with the incredible quickness that goes with the perfect physical condition of a young outdoor collie. Apparently he was none the worse for his experience. Ronald Crae understood dogs well, and he had watched keenly to see if the pup's gay spirit was cowed by his mishandling from the hawk. As he could see no sign of this, he was genuinely relieved. A cowed dog makes a poor sheep-herder and a worse herder of cattle.

Crae did not tell Danny what he had feared. If he had, the child would have given him a less optimistic slant on the case. For more than once Danny saw Laund wince and cower when a low-flying pigeon chanced to winnow just above him on its flight from cote to barnyard.

It was a week later that Laund was driving a bunch of skittish and silly wethers across the road from the home fold to the first sheep-pasture. Outwardly it was a simple job. All that need be done was to get them safely through the fold gate and out into the yard; thence through the yard gate out into the road; thence across the road and in through the home-pasture gate which Ronald Crae was holding open.

It was one of the easiest of Laund's duties. True, there was always an off-chance of the wethers trying to scatter or of one of them bolting down the road instead of into the pasture.

But the young dog had an instinct for this sort of thing. Like the best of his ancestors, he seemed to read the sheep's minds—if indeed sheep are blest or cursed with minds—and to know beforehand in just what direction one or more of them were likely to break formation. Always he was on the spot; ready to turn back the galloping stray and to keep the rest from following the seceder.

Today, he marshaled the milling bunch as snappily and cleanly as ever, herding them across the yard and to the road. On these wethers he wasted none of the gentleness he lavished on heavy ewes or on lambs. This, too, was an ancestral throwback, shared by a thousand other sheep-driving collies.

Into the road debouched the baaing and jostling flock. As ever, they were agog for any chance to get into mischief. Indeed, they were more than usually ready for it. For their ears were assailed by an unwonted sound—a far-off whirring that made them nervous.

Laund heard the sound, too, and was mildly interested in it; though it conveyed no meaning to him. Steadily he sent his wethers out into the road in a gray-white pattering cloud. Through the yard gate he dashed after them, on the heels of the hindmost; keyed up to the snappy task of making them cross the road without the compact bunch disintegrating; and on through the pasture gateway where Crae stood.

As his forefeet touched the edge of the road, a giant black shadow swept the yellow dust in front of him. The whirring waxed louder. Frightened, gripped by an unnamable terror, Laund glanced upward.

Above his head, sharply outlined against the pale blue of the sky, was a hawk a hundred times larger than the one that had assaulted him. Very near it seemed—very near and indescribably terrible.

A state forest ranger, scouting for signs of mountain fires, glanced down from his airplane at the pastoral scene below him—the pretty farmstead, the flock of sheep crossing the road, the alert brown collie dog marshaling them. Then the aeronaut was treated to another and more interesting sight.

Even as he looked, the faithful dog ceased from his task of sheep-driving. Ki-yi-ing in piercing loudness, and with furry tail clamped between his hindlegs and with stomach to earth, the dog deserted his post of duty and fled madly toward the refuge of the open kitchen door.

Infected by his screaming terror, the sheep scattered up and down the road, scampering at top speed in both directions and dashing anywhere except in through the gateway where Ronald Crae danced up and down in profane fury.

The plane whirred on into the distance, its amused pilot ignorant that he was the cause of the spectacular panic or that a fool puppy had mistaken his machine for a punitive henhawk.

After a long and angry search, Laund was found far under Danny's bed, huddled with his nose in a dusty corner and trembling all over.

"That settles it!" stormed Crae. "He's worthless. He's a cur—a mutt. He's yellow to the core. If it wasn't that Danny loves him so I'd waste an ounce of buckshot on him, here and now. It's the only way to treat a collie that is such an arrant coward. He—"

"But, dear," protested his wife, while Danny sobbed in mingled grief over his collie chum's disgrace and in shame that Laund should have proved so pusillanimous, "you said yourself that he is the best sheep dog for his age you've ever trained. Just because he ran away the first time he saw an airship it's no sign he won't be valuable to you in farm work. He—"

"'No sign,' hey?" he growled. "Suppose he is working a bunch of sheep near a precipice or over a bridge that hasn't a solid side rail—suppose an airship happens to sail over him, or a hawk? There's plenty of both hereabouts, these days. What is due to happen? Or if he is on herd duty in the upper pasture and a hawk or an airship sends him scuttling to cover, a mile away, what's to prevent anyone from stealing a sheep or two? Or what's to prevent stray dogs from raiding them? Besides, a dog that is a coward is no dog to have around us. He's yellow. He's worthless. If it wasn't for Danny—"

He saw his son trying to fight back the tears and slipping a wasted little arm around the cowering Laund. With a grunt, Ronald broke off in his tirade and stamped away.

More than a month passed before he would so much as look at the wistfully friendly puppy again or let him handle the sheep.

With all a collie's high sensitiveness, Laund realized he was in disgrace. He knew it had something to do with his panic flight from the airship. To the depths of him he was ashamed. But to save his life he could not conquer that awful terror for soaring birds. It had become a part of him.

Wherefore, he turned unhappily to Danny for comfort, even though his instinct told him the boy no longer felt for him the admiring chumship of old days. Laund, Danny, Ronald—all, according to their natures—were wretched, in their own ways, because of the collie's shameful behavior.

Yet, even black disgrace wears its own sharpest edge dull, in time. Laund was the only dog left on the farm. He was imperatively needful for the herding. He was Danny's only chum, and a chum was imperatively needful to Danny. Thus, bit by bit, Laund slipped back into his former dual position of herder and pal, even though Ronald had lost all faith in his courage in emergency.

A bit of this faith was revived when Laund was about fourteen months old. He was driving a score of ewes and spindly-legged baby lambs home to the fold from the lush South Mowing. There was a world of difference in his method of handling them from his whirlwind tactics with a bunch of wethers.

Slowly and with infinite pains he eased them along the short stretch of road between the pasture and the farmstead, keeping the frisky lambs from galloping from their fellows by interposing his shaggy body between them and their way to escape, and softly edging them back to their mothers. The ewes he kept in formation by pushing his head gently against their flanks as they sought to stray or to lag.

Even Ronald Crae gave grudging approval to strong young Laund coaxing his willful charges to their destination. Try as he would, the man could find nothing to criticize in the collie's work.

"There's not a dog that can hold a candle to him, in any line of shepherding," muttered Crae to himself as he plodded far behind the woolly band. "If he hadn't the heart of a rabbit there'd be every chance for him to clean up the Grand Prize at the National Collie Association Field trials, next month. But I was a fool to enter him for them, I suppose. A dog that'll turn tail and run to hide under a bed when he sees an airship or a hawk will never have the nerve to go through those stiff tests. He—"

Crae stopped short in his maundering thoughts. Laund had just slipped to the rear of the flock to cajole a tired ewe into rejoining the others. At the same moment a scatter-wit lambkin in the front rank gamboled far forward from the bunch.

A huge and hairy stray mongrel lurched out of a clump of wayside undergrowth and seized the stray lamb. Crae saw, and with a shout he ran forward.

But he was far to the rear. The narrow by-road was choked full of ewes and lambs, through which he must work his slow way before he could get to the impending slaughter.

Laund seemed to have heard or scented the mongrel before the latter was fairly free from the bushes. For he shot through the huddle of sheep like a flung spear, seeming to swerve not an inch to right or to left, yet forbearing to jostle one of the dams or their babies.

By the time the mongrel's teeth sought their hold on the panicky lamb, something flashed out of the ruck of the flock and whizzed at him with express-train speed.

Before the mongrel's ravening jaws could close on the woolly throat, young Laund's body had smitten the marauder full in the shoulder, rolling him over in the dust.

For a moment the two battling dogs rolled and revolved and spun on the ground, in a mad tangle that set the yellow dust to flying and scared the sheep into a baaing clump in midroad.

Then the two warriors were on their feet again, rearing, tearing, rending at each other's throats, their snarling voices filling the still afternoon air with horrific din.

The mongrel was almost a third larger than the slender young collie. By sheer weight he bore Laund to earth, snatching avidly at the collie's throat.

But a collie down is not a collie beaten. Catlike, Laund tucked all four feet under him as he fell. Dodging the throat lunge he leaped up with the resilience of a rubber ball. As he arose, his curved eyetooth scored a razor-gash in the mongrel's underbody and side.

Roaring with rage and pain, the mongrel reared to fling himself on his smaller opponent and to bear him down again by sheer weight. But seldom is a fighting collie caught twice in the same trap.

Downward the mongrel hurled himself. But his adversary was no longer there. Diving under and beyond the larger dog, Laund slashed a second time; cutting to the very bone. Again he and his foe were face to face, foot to foot, tearing and slashing; the collie's speed enabling him to flash in and out and administer thrice as much punishment as he received.

The mongrel gained a grip on the side of Laund's throat. Laund wrenched free, leaving skin and hair in the other's jaws, and dived under again. This time he caught a grip dear to his wolf-ancestors. His gleaming teeth seized the side of the mongrel's lower left hindleg.

With a screech the giant dog crashed to the road; hamstrung, helpless. There he lay until Crae's hired man came running up, rifle in hand, and put the brute out of his pain with a bullet through the skull.

For a mere second, Laund stood panting above his fallen enemy. Then seeing the mongrel had no more potentialities for harming the flock, the collie darted among the fast-scattering ewes and lambs, rounding them up and soothing them.

In his brief battle he had fought like a maddened wild beast. Yet now he was once more the lovingly gentle and wise sheep-herder, easing and quieting the scared flock as a mother might calm her frightened child.

"Laund!" cried Ronald Crae, delightedly, catching the collie's bleeding head between his calloused hands in a gesture of rough affection. "I was dead wrong. You're as game a dog as ever breathed. It's up to me to apologize for calling you a coward. That cur was as big and husky as a yearling. But you never flinched for a second. You sailed in and licked him. You're *true* game, Laund!"

The panting and bleeding collie wagged his plumed tail ecstatically at the praise and the rare caress. He wiggled and whimpered with joy. Then, of a sudden, he cowered to earth, peering skyward.

Far above flew the forest-ranger's airplane, on the way back from a day's fire-scouting among the hills. With the shrill ki-yi of a kicked puppy, Laund clapped his tail between his legs and bolted for the house. Nor could Crae's fiercest shouts check his flight. He did not halt until he had plunged far under Danny's bed and tucked his nose into the dim corner of the little bedroom.

"Half of that dog ought to have a hero medal!" raged Crae, to his wife, as he stamped into the kitchen after he and the hired man had collected the scattered sheep and folded them. "Half of him ought to have a hero medal. And the other half of him ought to be shot, for the rottenest coward I ever set eyes on. His pluck saved me a lamb, this afternoon, but his cowardice knocks out any chance of his winning the field trials, next month."

"But why? If—"

"The trials are held at the fair grounds—the second day of the Fair. There's dead sure to be a dozen airships buzzing around the field, all day. There always are. The first one of them Laund sees, he'll drop his work and he'll streak for home, yowling at every jump. I'm due to be laughed out of my boots by the crowd, if I take him there. Yet there isn't another dog in the state that can touch him as a sheep-worker. Rank bad luck, isn't it?"

So it was that Laund's return to favor and to respect was pitifully brief. True, his victory prevented the Craes from continuing to regard him as an out-and-out coward. But the repetition of his flight from the airship all but blotted out the prestige of his fighting prowess.

The sensitive young dog felt the atmosphere of qualified disapproval which surrounded him, and he moped sadly. He knew he had done valiantly in tackling the formidable sheep-killer that had menaced his woolly charges. But he knew, too, that he was in disgrace again for yielding to that unconquerable fear which possessed him at sight of anything soaring in the air above his head.

He lay moping on the shady back porch of the farmhouse one hot morning, some days later. He was unhappy, and the heat made him drowsy. But with one half-shut eye he watched Danny limping painfully to the bantam-yard and opening its gate to let his feathered pets out for a run in the grass.

Laund loved Danny as he loved nothing and nobody else. He was the crippled child's worshiping slave, giving to the boy the strangely protective adoration which the best type of collie reserves for the helpless. As a rule he was Danny's devoted shadow at every step the fragile little fellow took. But at breakfast this morning Crae had delivered another tirade on Laund's cowardice, having seen the collie flinch and tremble when a pigeon flew above him in the barnyard. Danny had seen the same thing himself, more than once. But now that his father had seen and condemned it, the child felt a momentary disgust for the cringing dog. Wherefore, when the little fellow had come limping out on the porch between his awkward crutches and Laund had sprung up to follow him, Danny had bidden him crossly to stay where he was. With a sigh the dog had stretched himself out on the porch again, watching the child's slow progress across the yard to the bantam-pen.

Danny swung wide the pen door. Out trooped the bantams, willingly following him as he led them to the grassplot. Supporting his weight on one of the two crutches—without which he could neither walk nor stand—he took a handful of crumbs from his pocket and tossed them into the grass for his pets to scramble for.

Laund was not the scene's only watcher. High in the hot blue sky hung two circling specks. From the earth they were almost invisible. But to their keen sight Danny and his scuttling chickens were as visible as they were to Laund himself.

The huge henhawk and his mate were gaunt from long-continued foraging for their nestlings. Now that the brood was fledged and able to fend for itself, they had time to remember their own unappeased hunger.

For weeks they had eaten barely enough to keep themselves alive. All the rest of their plunder had been carried to a mammoth nest of brown sticks and twigs, high in the top of a mountain-side pine tree; there to be fought over and gobbled by two half-naked, wholly rapacious baby hawks.

Today the two mates were free at last to forage for themselves. But food was scarce. The wild things of woods and meadows had grown wary, through the weeks of predatory hunt for them. Most farmers were keeping their chickens in wire-topped yards. The half-famished pair of hawks had scoured the heavens since dawn in quest of a meal, at every hour growing more ragingly famished.

Now, far below them, they saw the bevy of fat bantams at play in the grass, a full hundred yards from the nearest house. True, a crippled and twisted child stood near them, supported by crutches. But by some odd instinct the half-starved birds seemed to know he was not formidable or in any way to be feared.

No other human was in sight. Here, unprotected, was a feast of fat fowls. Thrice the hawks circled. Then, by tacit consent, they "stooped." Down through the windless air they clove their way at a speed of something like ninety miles an hour.

One of the bantams lifted its head and gave forth a warning "chir-r-r!" to its fellows. Instantly, the brood scattered, with flapping wings and fast-twinkling yellow legs.

Danny stared in amazement. Then something blackish and huge swept down upon the nearest hen and gripped it. In the same fraction of time the second hawk smote the swaggering little rooster of the flock.

The rooster had turned and bolted to Danny for protection. Almost between the child's helpless feet he crouched. Here it was that the hawk struck him.

Immediately, Danny understood. His beloved flock was raided by hawks. In fury, he swung aloft one of his crutches; and he brought it down with all his puny strength in the direction of the big hawk as it started aloft with the squawking rooster in its talons.

Now, even in a weak grasp, a clubbed and swung crutch is a dangerous weapon. More than one strong man—as police records will show—has been killed by a well-struck blow on the head from such a bludgeon.

Danny smote not only with all his fragile force, but with the added strength of anger. He gripped the crutch by its rubber point and swung it with all his weight as well as with his weak muscular power. The blow was aimed in the general direction of the hawk, as the bird left ground. The hawk's upward spring added to the crutch's momentum. The sharp corner of the armpit cross-piece happened to come in swashing contact with the bird's skull.

The impact of the stroke knocked the crutch out of Danny's hand and upset the child's own equilibrium. To the grass he sprawled, the other crutch falling far out of his reach. There he lay, struggling vainly to rise. One clutching little hand closed on the pinions of the hawk.

The bird had been smitten senseless by the whack of the crutch-point against the skull. Though the force had not been great enough to smash the skull or break the neck, yet it had knocked the hawk unconscious for a moment or so. The giant brown bird lay supine, with outstretched wings. Right valorously did the prostrate child seize upon the nearest of these wings.

As he had seen the first hawk strike, Danny had cried aloud in startled defiance at the preying bird. The cry had not reached his mother, working indoors, or the men who were unloading a wagon of hay into the loft on the far side of the barn. But it had assailed the ears of Laund, even as the collie was shrinking back into the kitchen at the far sound of those dreaded rushing wings.

For the barest fraction of an instant Laund crouched, hesitant. Then again came Danny's involuntary cry and the soft thud of his falling body on the grass. Laund hesitated no longer.

The second hawk was mounting in air, carrying its prey toward the safety of the mountain forests; there to be devoured at leisure. But, looking down, it saw its mate stretched senseless on the ground, the crippled child grasping its wing.

Through the courage of devotion or through contempt for so puny an adversary, the hawk dropped its luscious burden and flew at the struggling Danny.

Again Laund hesitated, though this time only in spirit; for his lithely mighty body was in hurricane motion as he sped to Danny's aid. His heart flinched at sight and sound of those swishing great wings, at the rank scent, and at the ferocious menace of beak and claw. Almost ungovernable was his terror at the stark nearness of these flying scourges, the only things in all the world that he feared to the point of insane panic.

Tremendous was the urge of that mortal terror. But tenfold more urgent upon him was the peril to Danny whom he worshiped.

The child lay, still grasping the wing of the hawk he had so luckily stunned. With his other hand he was preparing to strike the hawk's onrushing mate. The infuriated bird was hurling itself full at Danny's defenseless face; heedless of the ridiculously useless barrier of his outthrust fist. The stunned hawk began to quiver and twist, as consciousness seeped back into its jarred brain.

This was what Laund saw. This was what Laund understood. And the understanding of his little master's hideous danger slew the fear that hitherto had been his most unconquerable impulse.

Straight at the cripple's face flew the hawk. The curved beak and the rending talons were not six inches from Danny's eyes when something big and furry tore past, vaulting the prostrate child and the stunned bird beside him.

With all the speed and skill of his wolf ancestors Laund drove his curved white tusks into the breast of the charging hawk.

Deep clove his eyeteeth, through the armor of feathers, and through the tough breast bone. They ground their way with silent intensity toward a meeting, in the very vitals of the hawk.

The bird bombarded him with its powerful wings, banging him deafeningly and agonizingly about the head and shoulders; hammering his sensitive ears. The curved talons tore at his white chest, ripping deep and viciously. The crooked beak struck for his eyes, again and again, in lightning strokes. Failing to reach them, it slashed the silken top of his head, wellnigh severing one of his furry little tulip ears.

Laund was oblivious to the fivefold punishment; the very hint of which had hitherto been enough to send him ki-yi-ing under Danny's bed. He was not fighting now for himself, but for the child who was at once his ward and his deity.

On himself he was taking the torture that otherwise must have been inflicted on Danny. For perhaps the millionth time in the history of mankind and of dog, the Scriptural adage was fulfilled; and perfect love was casting out fear.

Then, of a sudden, the punishment ceased. The hawk quivered all over and collapsed inert between Laund's jaws. One of the mightily grinding eyeteeth had pierced its heart.

Laund dropped the carrion carcass; backing away and blinking, as his head buzzed with the bastinade of wing-blows it had sustained and the pain of the beak stabs.

But there was no time to get his breath and his bearings. The second hawk had come back to consciousness with a startling and raging suddenness. Finding its wing grasped by a human hand, it was turning fiercely upon the child.

Laund flung himself on the hawk from behind. He attacked just soon enough to deflect the beak from its aim at the boy's eyes and the talons from the boy's puny throat.

His snapping jaws aimed for the hawk's neck, to break it. They missed their mark by less than an inch; tearing out a thick tuft of feathers instead. His white forefeet were planted on the hawk's tail as he struck for the neck.

The bird's charge at Danny was balked, but the hawk itself was not injured. It whirled about on the dog, pecking for the eyes and lambasting his hurt head with its fistlike pinions.

Heedless of the menace, Laund drove in at the furious creature, striking again for the breast. For a few seconds, the pair were one scrambling, flapping, snarling, and tumbling mass.

Away from Danny they rolled and staggered in their mad scrimmage. Then Laund ceased to thrash about. He braced himself and stood still. He had found the breasthold he sought.

For another few moments the climax of the earlier battle was reenacted. To Danny it seemed as if the bird were beating and ripping his dear pal to death.

Beside himself with wild desire to rescue Laund, and ashamed of his own contempt for the dog's supposed cowardice, Danny writhed to his feet and staggered toward the battling pair, his fists aloft in gallant effort to tear the hawk in two.

Then, as before, came that sudden cessation of wing-beating. The bird quivered spasmodically. Laund let the dead hawk drop from his jaws as he had let drop its mate. Staggering drunkenly up to Danny, he tried to lick the child's tear-spattered face.

From the house and from the barn came the multiple thud of running feet. Mrs. Crae and the men were bearing down upon the scene. They saw a bleeding and reeling dog walking toward them beside a weeping and reeling little boy. From the onlookers went up a wordless and gabbling shout of astonishment.

Danny was walking! Without his crutches he was walking; he who had not taken a step by himself since the day he was stricken with the illness that crippled him; he whose parents had been told by the doctors that he could never hope to walk or even to stand up without his crutches!

Yes, he was one of the several hundred children—victims of the same disease and of other nerve-paralysis disorders—who regained the long-lost power over their limbs and muscles through great shock and supreme effort. But that made the miracle seem none the less a miracle to the Craes and to the former cripple himself.

In the midst of the annual field trials of the National Collie Association, the next month, a gigantic and noisy airplane whirred low over the field where the dogs were at work.

If Laund heard or saw it, he gave it no heed. He went unerringly and calmly and snappily ahead with his tests—until he won the Grand Prize.

He saw no reason to feel scared or even interested when the airship cast its winged shadow across him. A few weeks earlier he had fought and conquered two of those same flappy things. He had proved to himself, forever, that there was nothing about them to be afraid of.

PUPPY

(2001)

Richard Ford

What would you do if someone left a puppy on your doorstep? That is the dilemma of an upscale couple in New Orleans who are trying to do the right thing for themselves as well as the dog. The story is by Richard Ford, one of the best contemporary writers and winner of both the Pulitzer Prize and the PEN/Faulkner Prize in 1996. First published in *The Southern Review*, "Puppy" was also anthologized in *The Best American Short Stories 2002*. Ford's other novels and story collections include *A Piece of My Heart* (1976), *Rock Springs: Stories* (1987), *Independence Day* (1995), *Women with Men* (1997), and *A Multitude of Sins* (2002).

E arly this past spring someone left a puppy inside the back gate of our
house, and then never came back to get it. This happened at a time
when I was traveling up and back to St. Louis each week, and my wife was
intensely involved in the AIDS marathon, which occurs, ironically enough,
around tax time in New Orleans and is usually the occasion for a lot of
uncomfortable, conflicted spirits, which inevitably get resolved, of course,
by good will and dedication.

To begin in this way is only to say that our house is often empty much of
the day, which allowed whoever left the puppy to do so. We live on a corner in
the fashionable historical district. Our house is large and old and conspicu-
ous—typical of the French Quarter—and the garden gate is a distance from
the back door, blocked from it by thick ligustrums. So to set a puppy down
over the iron grating and slip away unnoticed wouldn't be hard, and I imagine was not.

"It was those kids," my wife said, folding her arms. She was standing
with me inside the French doors, staring out at the puppy, which was seated
on the brick pavement looking at us with what seemed like insolent curiosity. It was small and had slick, short coarse hair and was mostly white, with a
few triangular black side-patches. Its tail stuck alertly up when it was standing, making it look as though it might've had pointer blood back in its past.
For no particular reason, I gauged it to be three months old, though its legs
were long and its white feet larger than you would expect. "It's those ones
in the neighborhood wearing all the black," Sallie said. "Whatever you call
them. All penetrated everywhere and ridiculous, living in doorways. They
always have a dog on a rope." She tapped one of the square panes with her
fingernail to attract the puppy's attention. It had begun diligently scratch-

ing its ear, but stopped and fixed its dark little eyes on the door. It had dragged a red plastic dust broom from under the outside back stairs, and this was lying in the middle of the garden. "We have to get rid of it," Sallie said. "The poor thing. Those shitty kids just got tired of it. So they abandon it with us."

"I'll try to place it," I said. I had been home from St. Louis all of five minutes and had barely set my suitcase inside the front hall.

"Place it?" Sallie's arms were folded. "Place it where? How?"

"I'll put up some signs around," I said, and touched her shoulder. "Somebody in the neighborhood might've lost it. Or else someone found it and left it here so it wouldn't get run over. Somebody'll come looking."

The puppy barked then. Something (who knows what) had frightened it. Suddenly it was on its feet barking loudly and menacingly at the door we were standing behind, as though it had sensed we were intending something and resented that. Then just as abruptly it stopped and, without taking its dark little eyes off us, squatted puppy-style and pissed on the bricks.

"That's its other trick," Sallie said. The puppy finished and delicately sniffed at its urine, then gave it a sampling lick. "What it doesn't pee on it jumps on and scratches and barks at. When I found it this morning, it barked at me, then it jumped on me and peed on my ankle and scratched my leg. I was only trying to pet it and be nice." She shook her head.

"It was probably afraid," I said, admiring the puppy's staunch little bearing, its sharply pointed ears and simple, uncomplicated pointer's coloration. Solid white, solid black. It was a boy dog.

"Don't get attached to it, Bobby," Sallie said. "We have to take it to the pound."

My wife is from Wetumpka, Alabama. Her family were ambitious, melancholy Lutheran Swedes who somehow made it to the South because her great-grandfather had accidentally invented a lint shield for the ginning process that ended up saving people millions. In one generation the Holmbergs from Lund went from being dejected, stigmatized immigrants to being moneyed gentry with snooty Republican attitudes and a strong sense of entitlement. In Wetumpka there was a dog pound, and stray dogs were always feared for carrying mange and exotic fevers. I've been there; I know this. A dogcatcher prowled around with a ventilated, louver-sided truck and big catch net. When an unaffiliated dog came sniffing around anybody's hydrangeas, a call was made and off it went forever.

"There aren't dog pounds anymore," I said.

"I meant the shelter," Sallie said privately. "The SPCA—where they're nice to them."

"I'd like to try the other way first. I'll make a sign."

"But aren't you leaving again tomorrow?"

"Just for two days," I said. "I'll be back."

Sallie tapped her toe, a sign that something had made her unsettled. "Let's not let drag this out." The puppy began trotting off toward the back of the garden and disappeared behind one of the big brick planters of pittosporum. "The longer we keep it, the harder it'll be to give it up. And that *is* what'll happen. We'll have to get rid of it eventually."

"We'll see."

"When the times comes, I'll let *you* take it to the pound," she said.

I smiled apologetically. "That's fine. If the time comes, then I will."

We ended it there.

⌐⊷

I am a longtime practitioner before the federal appeals courts, arguing mostly large, complicated negligence cases in which the appellant is a hotel or a restaurant chain engaged in interstate commerce, which has been successfully sued by an employee or a victim of what is often some terrible mishap. Mostly I win my cases. Sallie is also a lawyer, but did not like the practice. She works as a resource specialist, which means fundraising, for by and large progressive causes: the homeless, women at risk in the home, children at risk in the home, nutrition issues, et cetera. It is a far cry from the rich, *arriviste*-establishment views of her family in Alabama. I am from Vicksburg, Mississippi, from a very ordinary although solid suburban upbringing. My father was an insurance-company attorney. Sallie and I met in law school at Yale, in the seventies. We have always thought of ourselves as lucky in life, and yet in no way extraordinary in our goals or accomplishments. We are simply southerners from sturdy, supportive families who had the good fortune to get educated well and who came back more or less to home, ready to fit in. Somebody has to act on that basic human impulse, we thought, or else there's no solid foundation of livable life.

One day after the old millennium's end and the new one's beginning, Sallie said to me—this was at lunch at Le Périgord on Esplanade, our favorite place—"Do you happen to remember"—she'd been thinking about it—"that first little watercolor we bought, in Old Saybrook? The tilted sailboat sail you could barely recognize in all the white sky. At that little shop near the bridge?" Of course I remembered it. It's in my law office in Place St. Charles, a cherished relic of youth.

"What about it?" We were at a table in the shaded garden of the restaurant, where it smelled sweet from some kind of heliotrope. Tiny wild parrots were fluttering up in the live-oak foliage and chittering away. We were eating a cold crab soup.

"Well," she said. Sallie has pale, almost animal-blue eyes and translucently caramel northern European skin. She has kept away from the sun for years. Her hair is cut roughly and parted in the middle, like some Bergman character from the sixties. She is forty-seven and extremely beautiful. "It's completely trivial," she went on, "but how did we ever know back then that we had any taste? I don't really even care about it, you know that. You have much better taste than I do in most things. But why were we sure we wouldn't choose that little painting and then have it be horrible? Explain that to me.

And what if our friends had seen it and laughed about us behind our backs? Do you ever think that way?"

"No," I said, my spoon above my soup, "I don't."

"You mean it isn't interesting? Or eventually we'd have figured out better taste all by ourselves?"

"Something like both," I said. "It doesn't matter. Our taste is fine and would've been fine. I still have that little boat in my office. People pass through and admire it all the time."

She smiled in an inwardly pleased way. "Our friends aren't the point, of course. If we'd liked sad-clown paintings or put antimacassars on our furniture, I wonder if we'd have a different, *worse* life now," she said. She stared down at her lined-up knife and spoons. "It just intrigues me. Life's so fragile in the way we experience it."

"What's the point?" I had to return to work soon. We have few friends now in any case. It's natural.

She furrowed her brow and scratched the back of her head, using her index finger. "It's about how altering one small part changes everything."

"One star strays out of line and suddenly there's no Big Dipper?" I said. "I don't really think you mean that. I don't really think you're getting anxious just because things might have gone differently in your life." I will admit this amused me.

"That's a very frivolous way to see it." She looked down at her own untried soup and touched its surface with the rim of her spoon. "But yes, that's what I mean."

"But it isn't true," I said, and wiped my mouth. "It'd still be the thing it is. The Big Dipper or whatever you cared about. You'd just ignore the star that falls and concentrate on the ones that fit. Our life would've been exactly the same, despite bad art."

"You're the lawyer, aren't you?" This was condescending, but I don't think she meant it to be. "You just ignore what doesn't fit. But it wouldn't be the same, I'm sure of that."

"No," I said. "It wouldn't have been exactly the same. But almost."

"There's only one Big Dipper," she said, and began to laugh.

"That we know of, and so far. True."

This exchange I give only to illustrate what we're like together—what seems important and what doesn't. And how we can let potentially difficult matters go singing off into oblivion.

The afternoon the puppy appeared, I sat down at the leathertop desk in our dining room where I normally pay the bills and diligently wrote out one of the hand-lettered signs you see posted on laundromat announcement boards and stapled to telephone poles alongside advertisements for new massage therapies, gay health issues, and local rock concerts. PUPPY, my sign said in black Magic Marker, and after that the usual data, with my office phone number and the date (March 23). This sheet I Xeroxed twenty-five times on Sallie's copier. Then I found the stapler she used for putting up the AIDS marathon posters, went upstairs and got out an old braided leather belt from my closet, and went down to the garden to take the puppy with me. It seemed good to bring him along while I stapled up the posters about him. Someone could recognize him, or just take a look at him and see he was available and attractive and claim him on the spot. Such things happen, at least in theory.

When I found him he was asleep behind the ligustrums in the far corner. He had worked and scratched and torn down into the bricky brown dirt and made himself a loll deep enough that half of his little body was out of sight below ground level. He had also broken down several ligustrum branches and stripped the leaves and chewed the ends until the bush was wrecked.

When he sensed me coming forward, he flattened out in his hole and growled his little puppy growl. Then he abruptly sat up in the dirt and aggressively barked at me in a way that—had it been a big dog—would've alarmed me and made me stand back.

"Puppy?" I said, meaning to sound sympathetic. "Come out." I was still wearing my suit pants and white shirt and tie—the clothes I wear in court. The puppy kept growling and then barking at me, inching back behind the wrecked ligustrum until he was in the shadows against the brick wall that separates us from the street. "Puppy?" I said again in a patient, cajoling way, leaning in among the thick green leaves. I'd made a loop out of my belt, and I reached forward and slipped it over his head. But he backed up farther when he felt the weight of the buckle, and unexpectedly began to yelp—a yelp that was like a human shout. And then he turned and began to claw up the bricks, scratching and springing, his paws scraping and his ugly little tail jerking, at the same time letting go his bladder until the bricks were stained with hot, terrified urine.

Which, of course, made me lose heart, since it seemed cruel to force this on him even for his own good. Whoever had owned him had evidently not been kind. He had no trust of humans, even though he needed us. To take him out in the street would only terrify him worse, and discourage anyone from taking him home and giving him a better life. Better to stay, I decided. In our garden he was safe and could have a few hours' peace to himself.

I reached and tried to take the belt loop off, but when I did he bared his teeth and snapped and nearly caught the end of my thumb with his little white incisor. I decided just to forget the whole effort and go about putting up my signs alone.

I stapled up all the signs in no time—at the laundromat on Barracks Street, in the gay deli, outside the French patisserie, inside the coffee shop and the adult news on Decatur. I caught all the telephone poles in a four-block area. On several of the poles and all the message boards I saw that others had lost pets too, mostly cats. *Hiroki's lost. We're utterly disconsolate. Can you help? Call Jamie or Hiram at . . .* Or, *We miss our Mittens. Please call us or give her a good home. Please!* In every instance as I made the rounds I stood a moment and read the other notices to see if anyone had reported a lost puppy. But (and I was surprised) no one had.

On a short, disreputable block across from the French Market, a section that includes a seedy commercial strip (sex shops, T-shirt emporiums, and a slice-of-pizza outlet), I saw a group of the young people Sallie had accused of abandoning our puppy. They were, as she'd remembered, sitting in an empty store's doorway, dressed in heavy, ragged black clothes and thick-soled boots with various chains attached and studded wristlets, all of them—two boys and two girls—pierced, and tattooed with Maltese crosses and dripping knife blades and swastikas, all dirty and utterly pointless but abundantly surly and apparently willing to be violent. These young people had a small black dog tied with a white cotton cord to one of the boys' heavy boots. They were drinking beer and smoking but otherwise just sitting, not even talking, simply looking malignantly at the street or at nothing in particular.

I felt there was little to fear, so I stopped in front of them and asked if they or anyone they knew had lost a white-and-black puppy with simple markings in the last day, because I'd found one. The boy who seemed to be the oldest and was large and unshaven, with brightly dyed purple-and-green hair cut into a flattop—the one who had the dog leashed to his boot—this boy looked up at me without obvious expression. He turned then to one of the immensely dirty-looking, fleshy, pale-skinned girls crouched farther back in the grimy door stoop, smoking—this girl had a crude cross tattooed into her forehead like Charles Manson is supposed to have—and asked, "Have you lost a little white-and-black puppy with simple markings, Samantha? I don't think so. Have you? I don't remember you having one today." The boy had an unexpectedly youthful-sounding, nasally midwestern accent, the kind I'd been hearing in St. Louis that week, although it had been high-priced attorneys who were speaking it. I know little enough about young people, but it occurred to me that this boy was possibly one of these lawyers' children, someone whose likeness you'd see on a milk carton or a Web site devoted to runaways.

"Ah, no," the girl said, then suddenly spewed out laughter.

The big, purple-haired boy looked up at me and produced a disdainful smile. His eyes were the darkest, steeliest blue, impenetrable and intelligent.

"What are you doing sitting here?" I wanted to say to him. "I know you left your dog at my house. You should take it back. You should all go home now."

"I'm sorry, sir," the boy said, mocking me. "but I don't believe we'll be able to help you in your important search." He smirked at his three friends.

I started to go. Then I stopped and handed him a paper sign and said, "Well, if you hear about a puppy missing anywhere."

He said something as he took it. I don't know what it was, or what he did with the sign when I was gone, because I didn't look back.

That evening Sallie came home exhausted. We sat at the dining room table and drank a glass of wine. I told her I'd put my signs all around, and she said she'd seen one and it looked fine. Then for a while she cried quietly because of disturbing things she'd seen and heard at the AIDS hospice that afternoon, and because of various attitudes—typical New Orleans attitudes, she thought—voiced by some of the marathon organizers, which seemed callous and constituted right things done for wrong reasons, all of which made the world seem—to her, at least—an evil place. I have sometimes thought she might've been happier if we had chosen to have children or, failing that, if we'd settled someplace other than New Orleans, someplace less parochial and exclusive, a city like St. Louis, in the wide Middle West—where you can be less personally involved in things but still be useful. New Orleans is a small town in so many ways. And we are not from here.

I didn't mention what the puppy had done to the ligustrums, or the kids I'd confronted at the French Market, or her description of them having been absolutely correct. Instead I talked about my work on the Brownlow-Maisonette appeal, and about what good colleagues all the St. Louis attorneys had turned out to be, how much they'd made me feel at home in their understated, low-key offices and how this relationship would bear important fruit in our presentation before the Eighth Circuit. I talked some about the definition of negligence as it is applied to common carriers, and about the unexpected latter-day reshapings of general tort-law paradigms in the years since the Nixon appointments. And then Sallie said she wanted to take a nap before dinner and went upstairs, obviously discouraged from her day and from crying.

Sallie suffers, and has as long as I've know her, from what she calls her war dreams—violent, careering, antic, destructive Technicolor nightmares without plots or coherent scenarios, just sudden drop-offs into deepest sleep accompanied by images of dismembered bodies flying around and explosions and brilliant flashes and soldiers of unknown armies being hurtled through trap doors and hanged or thrust out through bomb bays into empty, screaming space. These are terrible things I don't even like to hear about and that would scare the wits out of anyone. She usually awakes from these dreams slightly worn down, but not especially spiritually disturbed. And for this reason I believe her to be constitutionally very strong. Once I convinced her to go lie down on Dr. Merle Mackey's well-known couch for a few weeks and let him try to get to the bottom of all the mayhem. Which she willingly did. Though after a month and a half Merle told her—and told me privately at the tennis club—that Sallie was as mentally and morally sturdy as a racehorse, and that some things occurred for no demonstrable reason, no matter how Dr. Freud had viewed it. In Sallie's case, her dreams (which have always been intermittent) were just the baroque background music of how she resides on the earth and didn't represent, as far as he could observe, repressed memories of parental abuse or some kind of private disaster she didn't want to confront in daylight. "Weirdness is part of the human condition, Bob," Merle said. "It's thriving all around us. You've probably got some taint of it. Aren't you from up in Mississippi?" "I am," I said. "Then I wouldn't want to get *you* on my couch. We might be there forever." Merle smirked like somebody's presumptuous butler. "No, we don't need to go into that," I said. "No, sir," Merle said, "we really don't." Then he pulled a big smile, and that was the end of it.

After Sallie was asleep I stood at the French doors again. It was nearly dark, and the tiny white lights she had strung up like holiday decorations in the cherry laurel had come on by their timer and delivered the garden into an almost Christmasy lumination and loveliness. Dusk can be a magical time in the French Quarter—the sky so bright blue, the streets lush and shadowy. The puppy had come back to the middle of the garden and lay with his sharp little snout settled on his spotted front paws. I couldn't see his little feral eyes, but I knew they were trained on me, where I stood watching him, with the yellow chandelier light behind me. He still wore my woven leather belt looped to his neck like a leash. He seemed as peaceful and as heedless as he was likely ever to be. I had set out some Vienna sausages in a plastic saucer, and beside it a red plastic mixing bowl full of water—both where I knew he'd find them. I assumed he had eaten and drifted off to sleep before emerging, now that it was evening, to remind me he was still here, and possibly to express a growing sense of ease with his new surroundings. I was tempted to think what a strange, unpredictable experience it was to be him, so new to life and without essential defenses, and in command of little. But I stopped this thought for obvious reasons. And I realized, as I stood there, that my feelings about the puppy had already become slightly altered. Perhaps it was Sallie's Swedish tough-mindedness influencing me; or perhaps it was the puppy's seemingly untamable nature; or possibly it was all those other signs on all the other message boards and stapled to telephone poles, signs that seemed to state in a cheerful but hopeless way that fate was ineluctable, and character, personality, will, even untamable nature were only its accidental byproducts. I looked out at the little, low, diminishing white shadow motionless against the darkening bricks, and I thought: All right, yes, this is where you are now, and this is what I'm doing to help you. In all likelihood it doesn't really matter if someone calls, or if someone comes and takes you home and you live a long and happy life. What matters is simply a choice we make, a choice governed by time and opportunity and how well we persuade ourselves to go on until some other powerful force overtakes us. (We always hope it will be a positive and whole-some force, though it may not be.) No doubt this is another view one comes to accept as a lawyer—particularly one who enters events late in the process, as I do. I was, however, glad Sallie wasn't there to know about these thoughts, since it would only have made her think the world was a heartless place, which it really is not.

The next morning I was on the TWA flight back to St. Louis. Though later the evening before, someone had called to ask if the lost puppy I'd advertised had been inoculated for various dangerous diseases. I had to admit I had no idea, since it wore no collar. It *seemed* healthy enough, I told the person. (The sudden barking spasms and the spontaneous peeing didn't seem important.) The caller was clearly an elderly black woman—she spoke with a deep Creole accent and referred to me once or twice as "baby," but otherwise she didn't identify herself. She did say, however, that the puppy would be more likely to attract a family if it had its shots and had been certified healthy by a veterinar-ian. Then she told me about a private agency uptown that specialized in find-ing homes for dogs with elderly and shut-in persons, and I dutifully wrote down the agency's name—"Pet Pals." In our overly lengthy talk she went on to say that the gesture of having the puppy examined and inoculated with a rabies shot would testify to the good will required to care for the animal and increase its likelihood of being deemed suitable. After a while I came to think this old lady was probably completely loony and kept herself busy dialing numbers she saw on signs at the laundromat and yakking for hours about lost kittens, macramé classes, and Suzuki piano lessons, things she wouldn't remember the next day. Probably she was one of our neighbors, though there aren't that many black ladies in the French Quarter anymore. Still, I told her I'd look into her suggestion and appreciated her thoughtfulness. When I innocently asked her name, she uttered a surprising profanity and hung up.

"I'll do it," Sallie said the next morning as I was putting fresh shirts into my two-suiter, making ready for the airport and the flight back to St. Louis. "I have some time today. I can't let all this marathon anxiety take over my life." She was watching out the upstairs window down to the garden again. I'm not sure what I'd intended to happen to the puppy. I suppose I hoped he'd be claimed by someone. Yet he was still in the garden. We hadn't discussed a plan of action, though I had mentioned the Pet Pal agency.

"Poor little pitiful," Sallie said in a voice of dread. She took a seat on the bed beside my suitcase, let her hands droop between her knees, and stared at the floor. "I went out there and tried to play with it this morning, I want you to know this," she said. "It was while you were in the shower. But it doesn't know *how* to play. It just barked and peed and then snapped at me in a pretty hateful way. I guess it was probably funny to whoever had him that he acts that way. It's a crime, really." She seemed sad about it. I thought of the sinister blue-eyed, black-coated boy crouched in the fetid doorway across from the

French Market with his new little dog and his three acolytes. They seemed like residents of one of Sallie's war dreams.

"The Pet Pal people will probably fix things right up," I said, tying my tie at the bathroom mirror. It was unseasonable chilly in St. Louis, and I had on my wool suit, though in New Orleans it was already summery.

"If they *don't* fix things up, and if no one calls," Sallie said gravely, "then you have to take him to the shelter when you come back. Can we agree about that? I saw what he did to the plants. They can be replaced. But he's really not our problem." She turned and looked at me on the opposite side of our bed, whereon her long-departed Swedish grandmother had spent her first marriage night long ago. The expression on Sallie's round face was somber but decidedly settled. She was willing to try to care about the puppy because I was going away and she knew it would make me feel better if she tried. It is an admirable human trait, and undoubtedly how most good deeds occur—because you have the occasion, and there's no overpowering reason to do something else. But I was aware she didn't really care what happened to the puppy.

"That's exactly fine," I said, and smiled at her. "I'm hoping for a good outcome. I'm grateful to you for taking him."

"Do you remember when we went to Robert Frost's cabin?" Sallie said.

"Yes, I do." And surely I did.

"Well, when you come back from Missouri, I'd like us to go to Robert Frost's cabin again." She smiled at me shyly.

"I think I can do that," I said, closing my suitcase. "Sounds great."

Sallie bent sideways toward me and extended her smooth, perfect face to be kissed as I went past the bed with my baggage. "We don't want to abandon that," she said.

"We never will," I answered, leaning to kiss her on the mouth. And then I heard the honk of my cab at the front of the house.

Robert Frost's cabin is a great story about Sallie and me. The spring of our first year in New Haven, we began reading Frost's poems aloud to each other, as antidotes to the grueling hours of reading cases on replevin and the rule against perpetuities and theories of intent and negligence—the usual shackles law students wear at exam time. I remember only a little of the poems now, twenty-six years later. "Better to go down dignified / With boughten friendship at your side / Than none at all. Provide, provide!" We thought we knew what Frost was getting at: that you make your way in the world and life—all the way to the end—as best you can. And so at the close of the school year, when it turned warm and our classes were over, we got in the old Chrysler Windsor my father had given me and drove up to where we'd read Frost had had his mountainside cabin in Vermont. The state had supposedly preserved it as a shrine, though you had to walk far back through the mosquito-y woods and off a winding logger's road to find it. We wanted to sit on Frost's front porch in some rustic chair he'd sat in, and read more poems aloud to each other. Being young southerners educated in the North, we felt Frost represented a kind of old-fashioned but indisputably authentic Americanism, vital exposure we'd grown up exiled from because of race troubles and because of absurd preoccupations about the South itself, practiced by people who should know better. Yet we'd always longed for that important exposure, and felt it represented rectitude-in-practice, self-evident wisdom, and a sense of fairness expressed by an unpretentious bent for the arts. (I've since heard Frost was nothing like that, but was mean and stingy and hated better than he loved.)

When Sallie and I arrived at the little log cabin in the spring woods, it was locked up tight, with no one around. In fact it seemed to us like no one ever came there, though the state's signs seemed to indicate this was the right place. Sallie went around the cabin looking in the windows until she found one that wasn't locked. And when she told me about it, I said we should crawl in and nose around and read the poem we wanted to read and let whoever came tell us to leave.

But once we got inside, it was much colder than outside, as if the winter and something of Frost's true spirit had been captured and preserved by the log and mortar. Before long we had stopped our reading—after doing "Design" and "Mending Wall" and "Death of the Hired Man" in front of the cold fireplace. And partly for warmth we decided to make love in Frost's old bed, which was made up as he might've left it years before. (Later it occurred to us that possibly nothing had ever happened in the cabin, and maybe we'd even broken into the wrong cabin and made love in someone else's bed.)

But that's the story. That was what Sallie meant by a visit to Robert Frost's cabin—an invitation to me, upon my return, to make love to her, an act that the events of life and years sometimes can overpower and leave unattended. In a moment of panic, when we thought we heard voices out on the trail, we jumped into our clothes and by accident left our Frost book on the cold cabin floor. No one, of course, ever turned up.

That night I spoke to Sallie from St. Louis, at the end of a full day of vigorous preparations with the Missouri lawyers (whose clients were reasonably afraid of being put out of business by a $250 million class-action judgment). She, however, had nothing but unhappy news to impart. Some homeowners were trying to enjoin the entire AIDS marathon because of a routing change that went too near their well-to-do Audubon Place neighborhood. Plus one of the original organizers was now on the verge of death (not unexpected). She talked more about good-deeds-done-for-wrong-reasons among her hospice associates, and also about some plainly bad deeds committed by other rich people who didn't like the marathon and wanted AIDS to go away. Plus nothing had gone right with our plans for placing the puppy into Pet Pals.

"We went to get its shots," Sallie said sadly. "And it acted perfectly fine when the vet had it on the table. But when I drove it out to Pet Pals on Prytania, the woman—Mrs. Myers, her name was—opened the little wire gate on the cage I'd bought, just to see him. And he jumped at her and snapped at her and started barking. He just barked and barked. And this Mrs. Myers looked horrified and said, 'Why, whatever in the world's wrong with it?' 'It's afraid,' I said to her. 'It's just a puppy. Someone's abandoned it. It doesn't understand anything. Haven't you ever had that happen to you?' 'Of course not,' she said, 'and we can't take an *abandoned* puppy anyway.' She was looking at me as though I was trying to steal something from her. 'Isn't that what you do here?' I said. And I'm sure I raised my voice to her."

"I don't blame you a bit," I said from wintry St. Louis. "I'd have raised my voice."

"I said to her, 'What are you here for? If this puppy wasn't abandoned, why would *I* be here? I wouldn't, would I?'

" 'Well, you have to understand we really try to place the more mature dogs whose owners for some reason can't keep them, or are being transferred.' Oh God, I hated her, Bobby. She was one of these wide-ass Junior League bitches who'd gotten bored with flower arranging and playing canasta at the Boston Club. I wanted just to dump the dog right out in the shop and leave, or take a swing at her. I said, 'Do you mean you won't take him?' The puppy was in its cage and was being completely quiet and nice. 'No, I'm sorry, it's untamed,' this dowdy, stupid woman said. 'Untamed!' I said. 'It's an abandoned puppy, for fuck's sake.'

"She just looked at me then as if I'd suddenly produced a bomb and was jumping all around. 'Maybe you'd better leave now,' she said. I'd probably been in the shop all of two minutes, and here she was ordering me out. I said, 'What's wrong with you?' I *know* I shouted then. I was so frustrated. 'You're not a pet pal at all,' I shouted. 'You're an enemy of pets.'"

"You just got mad," I said, happy not to have been there.

"Of course I did," Sallie said. "I let myself get mad because I wanted to scare this hideous woman. I wanted her to see how stupid she was and how much I hated her. She did look around at the phone as if she was thinking about calling 911. Someone I know came in then. Mrs. Hensley from the Art League. So I just left."

"That's all good," I said. "I don't blame you for any of it."

"No. Neither do I." Sallie took a breath and let it out forcefully into the receiver. "We have to get rid of it, though. Now." She was silent a moment, then she began. "I tried to walk it around the neighborhood using the belt you gave it. But it doesn't know how to be walked. It just struggles and cries, then barks at everyone. And if you try to pet it, it pees. I saw some of those kids in black sitting on the curb. They looked at me like I was a fool, and one of the girls made a little kissing noise with her lips, and said something sweet, and the puppy just sat down on the sidewalk and stared at her. I said, 'Is this your dog?' There were four of them, and they all looked at each other and smiled. I know it was theirs. They had another dog with them, a black one. We just have to take him to the pound, though, as soon as you come back tomorrow. I'm looking at him now, out in the garden. He just sits and stares like some Hitchcock movie."

"We'll take him," I said. "I don't suppose anybody's called."

"No. And I saw someone putting up new signs and taking yours down. I didn't say anything. I've had enough with Jerry DeFranco about to die, and our injunction."

"Too bad," I said, because that was how I felt—that it was too bad no one would come along and out of the goodness of his heart take the puppy in.

"Do you think someone left it as a message?" Sallie said. Her voice sounded strange. I pictured her in the kitchen, with a cup of tea just brewed in front of her on the Mexican tile counter. It's good she set the law aside. She becomes involved in ways that are far too emotional. Distance is essential.

"What kind of message?" I asked.

"I don't know," she said. Oddly enough, it was starting to snow in St. Louis, small dry flakes backed—from my hotel window—by an empty, amber-lit cityscape and just the top curve of the great silver arch. It is a nice cordial city, though not distinguished in any way. "I can't figure out if someone thought we were the right people to care for a puppy, or were making a statement showing their contempt."

"Neither," I said. "I'd say it was random. Our gate was available. That's all."

"Does that bother you?"

"Does what?"

"Randomness."

"No," I said. "I find it consoling. It frees the mind."

"Nothing seems random to me," Sallie said. "Everything seems to reveal some plan."

"Tomorrow we'll work this all out," I said. "We'll take the dog, and then everything'll be better."

"For us, you mean? Is something wrong with us? I just have this bad feeling tonight."

"No," I said. "Nothing's wrong with us. But it *is* us we're interested in here. Good night, now, sweetheart."

"Good night, Bobby," Sallie said in a resigned voice, and we hung up.

That night in the Mayfair Hotel, with the window shades open to the early-spring snow and orange-lit darkness, I experienced my own strange dream. In my dream I'd gone on a duck-hunting trip into the marsh that surrounds our city. It was winter and early morning, and someone had taken me out to a duck blind before it was light. These are things I still do, as a matter of fact. But when I was set out in the blind with my shotgun, I found that beside me on the wooden bench was one of my law partners, seated with his shotgun between his knees and wearing strange red canvas hunting clothes—something you'd never wear in a duck blind. And he had the puppy with him, the same one that was then in our back garden awaiting whatever its fate would be. And my partner was with a woman, who either was or looked very much like the actress Liv Ullmann. The man was Paul Thompson, a man I (outside my dream) have good reason to believe once had an affair with Sallie, an affair that almost caused us to split apart without our even ever discussing it, except that Paul, who was older than I am and big and rugged, suddenly died—actually in a duck blind, of a terrible heart attack. It is a thing that can happen in the excitement of shooting.

In my dream Paul Thompson spoke to me and said, "How's Sallie, Bobby?" I said, "Well, she's fine, Paul, thanks," because we were pretending he and Sallie didn't have the affair I'd employed a private detective to authenticate—and almost did completely authenticate. The Liv Ullmann woman said nothing, just sat against the wooden sides of the blind seeming sad, with long straight blond hair. The little white-and-black puppy sat on the duckboard flooring and stared at me. "Life's very fragile in the way we experience it, Bobby," Paul Thompson, or his ghost, said to me. "Yes, it is," I said. I assumed he was referring to what he'd been doing with Sallie. (There had been some suspicious photos, though to be honest, I don't think Paul really cared about Sallie. Just did it because he could.) The puppy, meanwhile, kept staring at me. Then the Liv Ullmann woman herself smiled in an ironic way.

"Speaking about the truth tends to annihilate truth, doesn't it?" Paul Thompson said to me.

"Yes," I answered. "I'm certain you're right." And then for a sudden instant it seemed like it had been the puppy who'd spoken Paul's words. I could see his little mouth moving after the words were already spoken. Then the dreams faded and became a different dream, which involved the millennium fireworks display from New Year's Eve, and didn't stay in my mind like the Paul Thompson dream did, and does even to this day.

I make no more of this dream than I make of Sallie's dreams, though I'm sure Merle Mackey would have plenty to say about it.

When I arrived back in the city the next afternoon, Sallie met me at the airport, driving her red Wagoneer. "I've got it in the car," she said as we walked to the parking structure. I realized she meant the puppy. "I want to take it to the shelter before we go home. It'll be easier." She seemed as though she'd been agitated but wasn't agitated now. She had dressed herself in aqua walking shorts and a loose pink blouse that showed her pretty shoulders.

"Did anyone call?" I asked. She was walking faster than I was, since I was carrying my suitcase and a box of brief materials. I'd suffered a morning of tough legal work in a cold, unfamiliar city and was worn out and hot. I'd have liked a vodka martini instead of a trip to the animal shelter.

"I called Kirsten and asked if she knew anyone who'd take the poor little thing," Sallie said. Kirsten is her sister, and lives in Andalusia, Alabama, where she owns a flower shop with her husband, who's a lawyer for a big cotton consortium. I'm not fond of either of them, mostly because of their simpleminded politics, which includes support for the Confederate flag, prayer in the public schools, and the abolition of affirmative action—all causes I have been outspoken about. Sallie, however, can sometimes forget she went to Mount Holyoke and Yale and step back into being a pretty, chatty southern girl when she gets together with her sister and her cousins. "She said she probably *did* know someone," Sallie went on, "so I said I'd arrange to have the puppy driven right to her doorstep. Today. This afternoon. But then she said it seemed like too much trouble. I told her it *wouldn't* be any trouble for *her* at all, that *I'd* do it or arrange it to be done. Then she said she'd call me back, and didn't. Which is typical of my whole family's sense of responsibility."

"Maybe we should call her back," I said as we reached the car. We had a phone in the Wagoneer. I wasn't looking forward to visiting the SPCA.

"She's forgotten about it already," Sallie said. "She'd just get wound up."

When I looked through the back window of Sallie's Jeep, the puppy's little wire cage was sitting in the luggage space. I could see his white head, facing back, in the direction it had come from. What could it have been thinking?

"The vet said it's going to be a really big dog. Big feet tell you that."

Sallie was getting in the car. I put my suitcase in the back seat so as to not alarm the puppy. Twice it barked its desperate little high-pitched puppy bark. Possible it knew me. Though I realized it would never have been an easy puppy to get attached to. My father had a neat habit of reversing propositions he was handed as a way of assessing them. If a subject seemed to have one obvious outcome, he'd imagine the reverse of it; if a business deal had an obvious beneficiary, he'd ask who benefited but didn't seem to. Needless to say, these are valuable skills lawyers use. But I found myself thinking—except I didn't say it to Sallie—that though we may have thought we were doing the puppy a favor by trying to find it a home, we were really doing ourselves a favor by presenting ourselves to be the kind of supposedly decent people who do that *sort* of thing. I am, for instance, a person who stops to move turtles off busy interstates, or picks up butterflies in shopping-mall parking lots and puts them into the bushes to give them a fairer chance at survival. I know these are pointless acts of pointless generosity. Yet there isn't a time when I do it that I don't get back in the car thinking more kindly about myself. (Later I often work around to thinking of myself as a fraud, too.) But the alternative is to leave the butterfly where it lies expiring, or to let the big turtle meet annihilation on the way to the pond, and in doing these things let myself in for the indictment of cruelty or the sense of loss that would follow. Possibly, anyone would argue, these issues are too small to think about seriously, since whether you perform these acts or don't perform them, you always forget about them in about five minutes.

Except for weary conversation about my morning at Ruger, Todd, Jennings, and Sallie's rerouting victory with the AIDS race, which was set for Saturday, we didn't say much as we drove to the SPCA. Sallie had obviously researched the address, because she got off the interstate at an exit I'd never used and that immediately brought us down onto a wide boulevard with old cars parked on the neutral ground and paper trash cluttering the curbs down one long side of some brown-brick housing projects where black people were outside on their stoops and wandering around the street in haphazard fashion. There were a few dingy-looking barbecue and gumbo cafés, and two tire-repair shops where work was taking place out in the street. A tiny black man standing on a peach crate was performing haircuts in a dinette chair set up on the sidewalk, his customer wrapped in newspaper, and some older men had stationed a card table on the grassy median and were playing in the sunlight. There were no white people anywhere. It was a part of town, in fact, where most white people would've been afraid to go. Yet it was not a bad section, and the Negroes who lived there no doubt looked on this world as something other than a hopeless place.

Sallie took a wrong turn off the boulevard and onto a rundown residential street of pastel shotgun houses where black youths in baggy trousers and big black sneakers were playing basketball without a goal. The boys watched us drive past but said nothing. "I've gotten us off wrong here," she said in a distracted, hesitant voice. She is not comfortable around black people when she is the only white—which is a residue of her privileged Alabama upbringing, where everything and everybody belonged to a proper place and needed to stay there.

She slowed at the next corner and looked both ways down a similar small street of shotgun houses. More black people were out washing their cars or waiting at bus stops in the sun. I noticed this to be Creve Coeur Street, which was where the *Times-Picayune* said an unusual number of murders occurred each year. All that happened at night, of course, and involved black people killing other black people for drug money. It was now 4:45 in the afternoon, and I felt perfectly safe.

The puppy barked again in his cage, a soft, anticipatory bark, then Sallie drove us a block farther and spotted the street she'd been looking for—Rousseau Street. The residential buildings stopped there, and old, dilapidated two- and one-story industrial uses began: an offshore pipe manufactory, a frozen seafood company, a shut-down recycling center where people had gone on leaving their garbage in plastic bags. There was also a small, windowless cube of a building that housed a medical clinic for visiting sailors off foreign ships. I recognized it because our firm had once represented the owners in a personal-injury suit, and I remembered grainy photos of the building and my thinking that I'd never need to see it up close.

Near the end of this block was the SPCA, which occupied a long, glum, red-brick warehouse-looking building with a small red sign by the street and a tiny gravel parking lot. One might've thought the proprietors didn't want its presence too easily detected.

The SPCA's entrance was nothing but a single windowless metal door at one end of the building. There were no shrubberies, no disabled slots, no directional signs leading in, just this low, ominous, flat-roofed building with long factory clerestories facing the lot and the seafood company. An older wooden shed was attached on the back. And a small sign I hadn't seen because it was fastened too low on the building said: YOU MUST HAVE A LEASH. ALL ANIMALS MUST BE RESTRAINED. CLEAN UP AFTER YOUR ANIMAL. IF YOUR DOG BITES A STAFF MEMBER <u>YOU</u> ARE RESPONSIBLE. THANKS MUCH.

"Why don't you take him in his cage," Sallie said, nosing up to the building, becoming very efficient. "I'll go in and start the paperwork. I already called them." She didn't look my way.

"That's fine," I said.

When we got out I was surprised again at how warm it was, and how close and dense the air felt. Summer seemed to have arrived during the day I was gone, which is not untypical of New Orleans. I smelled an entirely expectable animal gaminess combined with a fish smell and something metallic that felt hot and slightly burning in my nose. And the instant I was out into the warm, motionless air I could hear barking inside the building. I assumed the barking was triggered by the sound of a car arriving. Dogs trained themselves to the hopeful sound of motors.

Across the street from the SPCA were other shotgun houses I hadn't noticed. Elderly black people were sitting in metal lawn chairs on their little porches, observing me getting myself organized. It would be a difficult place to live, I thought, and quite a lot to get used to with the noise and the procession of animals coming and going.

Sallie disappeared through the unfriendly little door, and I opened the back of the Wagoneer and hauled out the puppy in his cage. He stumbled to one side when I took a grip on the wire rungs, then barked several agitated, heartfelt barks and began clawing at the wires and my fingers, giving me a good scratch on the knuckles that almost caused me to drop the whole contraption. The cage, even with him in it, was very light, though my face was so close I could smell his urine. "You be still in there," I said.

For some reason, and with the cage in my grasp, I looked around at the colored people across the street, silently watching me. I had nothing in mind to say to them. They were sympathetic, I felt sure, to what was going on and thought it was better than cruelty. I had started to sweat because I was wearing my business suit. I awkwardly waved a hand toward them, but of course no one responded.

When I had maneuvered the cage close to the metal door, I for some reason looked to the left and saw down the grimy alley between the SPCA and the sailors' clinic to where a round steel canister was attached to the SPCA building by large corrugated aluminum pipes, all of it black and new-looking. This, I felt certain, was a device for disposing of animal remains, though

I didn't know how. Probably some incinerating invention that didn't have an outlet valve or a stack—something very efficient. It was an extremely sinister thing to see and reminded me of what we all heard years ago about terrible vacuum chambers and gassed compartments for dispatching unwanted animals. Probably they weren't even true stories. Now, of course, it's just an injection. They go to sleep, feeling certain they'll wake up.

Inside the SPCA it was instantly cool, and Sallie had almost everything done. The barking I'd heard outside had not ceased, but the gamy smell was replaced by a loud disinfectant odor that was everywhere. The reception area was a cubicle with a couple of metal desks and fluorescent tubes in the high ceiling, and a calendar on the wall showing a golden retriever standing in a wheat field with a dead pheasant in its mouth. Two high school-age girls manned the desks, and one was helping Sallie fill out her documents. These girls undoubtedly loved animals and worked after school and had aspirations to be vets. A sign on the wall behind the desks said PLACING PUPPIES IS OUR FIRST PRIORITY. This was here, I thought, to make people like me feel better about abandoning dogs. To make forgetting easier.

Sallie was leaning over one of the desks, filling out a thick green document, and looked around to see me just as an older, stern-faced woman in a white lab coat and black rubber boots entered from a side door. Her small face and both her hands had a puffy but also a leathery texture that southern women's skin often takes on—too much sun and alcohol, too many cigarettes. Her hair was dense and dull reddish brown and heavy around her face, making her head seem smaller than it was. This woman, however, was extremely friendly and smiled easily, though I knew just from her features and what she was wearing that she was not a veterinarian.

I stood holding the cage until one of the high school girls came around her desk and looked in it and said the puppy was cute. It barked so that the cage shook in my grip. "What's his name?" she said, and smiled in a dreamy way. She was a heavyset girl, very pale, with a lazy left eye. Her fingernails were painted bright orange and looked unkempt.

"We haven't named him," I said, the cage starting to feel unwieldy.

"We'll name him," she said, pushing her fingers through the wires. The puppy pawed at her, then licked her fingertips, then made little crying sounds when she removed her finger.

"They place sixty-five percent of their referrals," Sallie said over the forms she was filling out.

"Too bad it id'n a holiday," the woman in the lab coat said in a husky voice, watching Sallie finish. She spoke like somebody from across the Atchafalaya, somebody who had once spoken French. "Dis place be a ghost town by Christmas, you know?"

The helper girl who'd played with the puppy walked out through the door that opened onto a long concrete corridor full of shadowy, metal-fenced cages. Dogs immediately began barking again, and the foul animal odor entered the room almost shockingly. An odd place to seek employment, I thought.

"How long do you keep them?" I said, and set the puppy's cage on the concrete floor. Dogs were barking beyond the door, one big-sounding dog in particular, though I couldn't see it. A big yellow tiger-striped cat that apparently had free rein in the office walked across the desktop where Sallie was going on writing and rubbed against her arm, and made her frown.

"Five days," the puffy-faced Cajun woman said, and smiled in what seemed like an amused way. "We try to place 'em. People be in here all the time, lookin'. Puppies go fast 'less they something wrong with them." Her eyes found the cage on the floor. She smiled at the puppy as if it could understand her. "You cute," she said, then made a dry kissing noise.

"What usually disqualifies them?" I said, and Sallie looked around at me.

"Too aggressive," the woman said, staring approvingly in at the puppy. "If it can't be housebroke, then they'll bring 'em back to us. Which isn't good."

"Maybe they're just scared," I said.

"Some are. Then some are just little naturals. They go in one hour." She leaned over, hands on her lab-coat knees, and looked in at our puppy.

"How 'bout you," she said. "You a little natural? Or are you a little scamp? I b'lieve I see a scamp in here." The puppy sat on the wire flooring and stared at her indifferently, just as he had stared at me. I thought he would bark, but he didn't.

"That's all," Sallie said, and turned to me and attempted a hospitable look. She put her pen in her purse. She was thinking I might be changing my mind, but I wasn't.

"Then that's all you need. We'll take over," the supervisor woman said.

"What's the fee?" I asked.

"Id'n no fee," the woman said, and smiled. "Remember me in yo' will." She squatted in front of the cage as if she was going to open it. "Puppy, puppy," she said, then put both hands around the sides of the cage and stood up, holding it with ease. She made a little grunting sound, but she was much stronger than I would've thought. Just then another blond helper girl, this one with a metal brace on her left leg, came humping through the kennels door, and the supervisor just walked right past her, holding the cage, while the dogs down the long, dark corridor started barking ecstatically.

"We're donating the cage," Sallie said. She wanted out of the building, and I did, too. I stood another moment and watched as the woman in the lab coat disappeared along the row of pens, carrying our puppy. Then the green metal door closed, and that was all there was to the whole thing. Nothing very ceremonial.

＆

On our drive back downtown we were both, naturally enough, sunk into a kind of woolly, disheartened silence. From up on the interstate, the spectacle of modern, southern city life and ambitious new construction where once had been a low, genteel old river city seemed particularly gruesome and unpromising and probably seemed the same to Sallie. To me, who labored in one of the tall metal-and-glass enormities—I could actually see my office windows in Place St. Charles, small, undistinguished rectangles shining high up among countless others—it felt alien to history and to my own temperament. Behind these square mirrored windows, human beings were writing and discussing and preparing cases, and on other floors were performing biopsies, CAT scans, drilling out cavities, delivering news both welcome and unwelcome to all sorts of other expectants—clients, patients, partners, spouses, children. People were in fact there waiting for *me* to arrive that very afternoon, anticipating news of the Brownlow-Maisonette case—where *were* things, how were our prospects developing, what was my overall *take* on matters, and what were our hopes for a settlement (most of my "take" wouldn't be all that promising). In no time I'd be entering their joyless company and would've forgotten about myself here on the highway, peering out in near despair because of the fate of an insignificant little dog. Frankly, it made me feel pretty silly.

Sallie suddenly said, as though she'd been composing something while I was musing away balefully, "Do you remember after New Year's that day we sat and talked about one thing changing and making everything else different?"

"The Big Dipper," I said as we came to our familiar exit, which quickly led down and away through a different poor section of darktown that abuts our gentrified street. Everything had begun to seem more manageable as we neared home.

"That's right," Sallie said, as though the words *Big Dipper* reproached her. "But you know, and you'll think this is crazy. It *is*, maybe. But last night when I was in bed, I began thinking about that poor little puppy as an ill force that put everything in our life at a terrible risk. And we were in danger in some way. It scared me. I didn't want that."

I looked over at Sallie and saw a crystal tear escape her eye and slip down her soft, rounded pretty cheek.

"Sweetheart," I said, and found her hand on the steering wheel. "It's quite all right. You put yourself through a lot. And I've been gone. You just need me around to do more. There's nothing to be scared about."

"I suppose," Sallie said resolutely.

"And if things are not exactly right now," I said, "they soon will be. You'll take on the world again the way you always do. We'll all be the better for it."

"I know," she said. "I'm sorry about the puppy."

"Me too," I said. "But we did the right thing. Probably he'll be fine."

"And I'm sorry things threaten me," Sallie said. "I don't think they should, then they do."

"Things threaten all of us," I said. "Nobody gets away unmarked." That is what I thought about all of that then. We were in sight of our house. I didn't really want to talk about these subjects anymore.

"Do you love me?" Sallie said, quite unexpectedly.

"Oh yes," I said. "I do. I love you very much." And that was all we said.

A week ago, in one of those amusing fillers used to justify column space in one of the trial lawyers' journals I look at just for laughs, I read two things that truly interested me. These are always chosen for their wry comment on the law, and are frequently hilarious and true. The first one I read said, "Scientists predict that in five thousand years the earth will be drawn into the sun." It then went on to say something like "so it's not too early to raise your malpractice insurance," or some such cornball thing as that. But I will admit to being made oddly uncomfortable by this news about the earth—as if I had something important to lose in the inevitability of its far-off demise. I can't now say what that something might be. None of us can think about five thousand years from now. And I'd have believed none of us could *feel* anything

421

about it either, except in ways that are vaguely religious. Only I did, and I am far from being a religious man. What I felt was very much like the sensation described by the old saying "Someone just walked on your grave." Someone, so it seemed, had walked on my grave five thousand years from now, and it didn't feel very good. I was sorry to have to think about it.

The other squib I found near the back of the magazine, behind the Legal Market Place, and it said that astronomers had discovered the oldest known star, which they believed to be fifty million light-years away, and they had named it the Millennium Star for obvious reasons, though the actual millennium had gone by with hardly any change in things that I'd noticed. When asked to describe the chemical makeup of this Millennium Star—which of course couldn't even be seen—the scientist who discovered it said, "Oh, gee, I don't know. It's impossible to reach that far back in time." And I thought— sitting in my office with documents of the Brownlow-Maisonette case spread all around me and the hot New Orleans sun beaming into the window I'd seen from my car when Sallie and I were driving back from delivering the puppy to its fate—I thought, "*Time*? Why does he say *time*, when what he means is space?" My feeling then was very much like the feeling from before, when I'd read about the earth hurtling into the sun—a feeling that so much goes on everywhere all through time, and we know only a laughably insignificant fraction about any of it.

The days that followed our visit to the SPCA were eventful days. Sallie's colleague Jerry DeFranco did, of course, die. And though he had AIDS, he died by his own dispirited hand, in his little garret apartment on Kerlerec Street, late at night before the marathon, in order, I suppose, that his life and its end be viewed as a triumph of will over pitiless circumstance.

On another front, the Brownlow appellants decided very suddenly and unexpectedly to settle our case rather than face years of extremely high lawyers' fees and of course the possibility (though not a good one) of enduring a crippling loss. I had hoped for this, and look at it as a victory.

Elsewhere, the marathon went off as planned, and along the route Sallie had wanted. I unfortunately was in St. Louis and missed it. A massacre occurred, the same afternoon, at a fast-food restaurant not far from the SPCA, and someone we knew—a black lawyer—was killed. And during this period I began receiving preliminary feelers about a federal judgeship I'm sure I'll never get. These things are always bandied about for months and years, all sorts of persons are put on notice to be ready when the moment comes, and then the wrong one is chosen for completely wrong reasons, after which it becomes clear that nothing was ever in doubt. The law is an odd calling. And New Orleans a unique place. In any case, I'm far too moderate for the present company running things.

Several people did eventually call about the puppy, having seen my signs, and I directed them all to the animal shelter. I went around a time or two and checked the signs, and several were still up along with the AIDS marathon flyers, which made me satisfied, but not very satisfied.

Each morning I sat in bed and thought about the puppy, waiting for someone to come down the list of cages and see him there alone and staring, and take him away. For some reason, in my imaginings, no one ever chose him—not an autistic child, nor a lonely, discouraged older person, a recent widow, a young family with roughhousing kids. None of these. In all the ways I tried to imagine it, he stayed there.

Sallie did not bring the subject up again, although her sister called on Tuesday and said she knew someone named Hester in Andalusia who'd take the puppy; then the two of them quarreled so bitterly that I had to come on the phone and put it settled.

On some afternoons, as the provisional five waiting days ticked by, I would think about the puppy and feel utterly treacherous for having delivered him to the shelter. Other times I'd feel that we'd given him a better chance than he'd have otherwise had, either on the street alone or with his previous owners. I certainly never thought of him as an ill force to be dispelled, or a threat to anything important. To me life's not that fragile. He was, if anything, just a casualty of the limits we all place on our sympathy and our capacity for the ambiguous in life. Though Sallie might've been right—that the puppy had been a message left for us to ponder: something someone thought about us, something someone felt we needed to know. Who or what or in what way that might've been true, I can't quite imagine. Though we are all, of course, implicated in the lives of others, whether we precisely know how or don't.

On Thursday night, before the puppy's final day in the shelter, I had another strange dream. Dreams always mean something obvious, and so I try as much as I can not to remember mine. But for some reason this time I did, and what I dreamed was again about my old departed law partner, Paul Thompson, and his nice wife, Judy, a pretty, buxom blond woman who'd studied opera and sung the coloratura parts in several municipal productions. In my dream Judy Thompson was haranguing Paul about some list of women's names she'd found, women Paul had been involved with, even in love with. She was telling him he was an awful man who had broken her heart, and that she was leaving him (which did actually happen). And on her list— which I could suddenly, as though through a fog, see—was Sallie's name. And when I saw it there, my heart started pounding, pounding, pounding, until I sat right up in bed in the dark and said out loud, "Did you know your name's on that goddamned list?" Outside, on our street, I could hear someone playing a trumpet, a very slow and soulful version of "Nearer Walk with Thee." And Sallie was there beside me, deep asleep. I of course knew she'd done it, deserved to be on the list, and that probably there *was* such a list, given the kind of reckless man Paul Thompson was. As I said, I had never spoken to Sallie about this subject and had, until then, believed I'd gone beyond the entire business. Though I have to suppose now I was wrong.

This dream stayed my mind the next day, and the next night I had it again. And because the dream preoccupied my thinking, it wasn't until Saturday after lunch, when I had sat down to take a nap in a chair in the living room, that I realized I'd forgotten about the puppy the day before, and that all during Friday many hours had passed, and by the end of them the puppy must've reached its destination, wherever it was to be. I was surprised to have neglected to think about it at the crucial moment, having thought of it so much before then. And I was sorry to have to realize that I had finally not cared as much about it as I'd thought.

PERMISSIONS ACKNOWLEDGMENTS

Grateful acknowledgment is extended to the following authors, publications, and agents.

Albert Payson Terhune, "Biscuit," from *The Way of a Dog*, 1932.

Madison Smartt Bell, "Black and Tan," from *Barking Man and Other Stories*, 1990, and originally published in the *Atlantic Monthly*. Used by permission of the author.

Booth Tarkington, "Blue Milk." First published in *Saturday Evening Post* in 1934. Copyright © 1934 by Booth Tarkington. Reprinted by permission of Brandt & Hochman Literary Agents, Inc.

Eric Knight, "Lassie Come Home," Copyright © 1938 by Curtis Publishing Company.

Arthur Miller, "Bulldog," Copyright © 2001 by Arthur Miller, from PRESENCE by Arthur Miller. Used by permission of Viking Penguin, a division of Penguin Group (USA) Inc.

P. G. Wodehouse, "The Mixer," from *The Man with Two Left Feet*. Copyright © 1917.

E. S. Goldman, "Dog People," originally published in the *Atlantic Monthly*, August 1988. Used by permission of the author.